LOVE DIES TWICE

Pam Nilsen Mysteries

Murder in the Collective

Sisters of the Road

The Dog-Collar Murders

Cassandra Reilly Mysteries

Gaudí Afternoon

Trouble in Transylvania

The Death of a Much-Travelled Woman

The Case of the Orphaned Bassoonists

Not the Real Jupiter

LOVE DIES TWICE

A Cassandra Reilly Mystery

BARBARA WILSON

CEDAR STREET EDITIONS

Love Dies Twice
Copyright © 2022 by Barbara Sjoholm

Cover Design: Ann McMan/TreeHouse Studio
Text Design: Raymond Luczak

ISBN: 978-0-9883567-8-8 (print)
ISBN: 978-0-9883567-9-5 (e-book)

Library of Congress Control Number: 2022900075

For Betsy

"There are among us women whom we have no idea what to call, ordinary women or nuns, because they live neither in the world nor out of it."
—Gilbert of Tournai, 1274

The Beatrys Mysteries by Stella Terwicker

PART ONE

1.

On my own I would never have decided, especially on a filthy wet afternoon in early February, to take the train to Southeast London and to dash through the rain to a college lecture hall to hear a topic like "Stella Terwicker and the Medieval Mystery."

A month or so before, at a holiday party, I'd run into Avery Armstrong, a literary agent, and we'd agreed that it had been far too long since we'd lunched and caught up properly. With a glass of champagne in her hand, she'd asked me if I was translating any authors she should know about.

We made a lunch date for late January, and I'd looked forward to it, since Avery always chose a good restaurant and she always treated. At the last minute she canceled but proposed Thursday, February 10. She hinted on the phone that she could use my help with a literary problem, which I naturally took as an opening to bring along several books I was interested in translating from Spanish for the English market. Certainly, I could help, but in exchange I'd encourage her to hear a few pitches.

Years ago, Avery and I had worked together to place a literary manuscript by a young Spanish author with a British publisher. Her novel had bad reviews and didn't sell. Since then, from time to time, I'd tried to interest Avery in other Spanish or South American writers. She generally took a pass on my projects, with the reminder that her business, unlike mine, was not a charitable trust. She had an assistant and an office to maintain, and the authors she took on had to be moderately to wildly successful for her to remain solvent.

"Whereas your protégés, Cassandra, always seem to be down on their luck. Except for Gloria de los Angeles and Rosa Cardenes. You're lucky Rosa is so prolific. A mystery every two years like clockwork. What are we up to now?" Avery twisted the last strands of her linguini and delicately slurped them up, before putting down the fork. The trattoria in Camden Town was near her office.

"I just finished proofing number twelve, *Madrid in Widow's Weeds*," I said, "Meanwhile I have some promising titles you might be interested in." Two were literary novels and the third a mystery. As I pulled them out of my bag and set them on the table, her eyes took on the familiar polite gaze of *if I must*.

As always, I marveled at how well Avery had come to fill the role of prosperous literary agent over the years. Like me she was an American from the Midwest and like me she'd knocked around a bit in Europe before settling down in London. But Avery had the advantage of an Oxford degree and had gone into publishing in her twenties. After a half a dozen years of smart acquisitions, she'd progressed to senior editor. Then, foreseeing a publishing merger, she left to start her own literary agency and did well. She was hard-headed about contracts and agreements, had an eye for the main chance, and could keep a secret, even though she was also a diplomatic gossip.

Although we were both in our sixties, she mid and me late, she looked much younger. Spa visits, the gym, and probably light cosmetic surgery. She understood make-up and whatever went under make-up that smoothed out wrinkles and made skin glow softly with color. She was well-dressed, only giving a hint in her jackets, expensive jeans, and Oxford shirts with a button or two undone that she wasn't averse to an edgier queer identity. Her hair was her glory; she and her hairdresser had figured out a way to keep it looking short but layered in a blond rocker tangle. She'd had a number of girlfriends, but I was never one of them. I might have been interested once, but she'd told me she didn't go for Michiganders. And that was that.

As she drank a second glass of wine, I made my case for why two slender Ferrante-type novels set in Bilbao and Salamanca, one about a childhood friendship and another about a marriage on the rocks, would be easy sells to a top publisher in the UK. But Avery looked unimpressed when I told her that neither book had won any awards and their authors weren't translated "as yet" into any other languages. Her eyes went instead to the more lurid red cover of the mystery by Lola Fuentes.

"Lola Fuentes, her name sounds familiar. What's her story?"

I explained that this novel, *Verónica,* was the author's third thriller, featuring a female former matador who had been severely gored and had to take up private detection. Most of the novel took place in and around the Plaza del Toros in Seville.

"Lola, Lola, Lola," said Avery pensively. "I think you might have talked up her first novel to me a few years ago. Why isn't she already translated and published if she's so good?"

The usual agent response. They wanted a new face, but they also wanted a sure thing.

"And then there's the bullfighting," she added. "British readers don't have the stomach for it."

She finished her wine and gave a polite shake of her head. "Sorry to disappoint, Cassandra, but I think I'll pass." She paused an instant to show sympathy, as I put the books back in my bag.

"So, you're still managing?" she said. "I know it's not easy to make a living as a translator."

"Oh, I don't need much," I said, for I don't like sympathy, even when it's well-meant. I had something Avery didn't and that was freedom. "I always have plenty of work. I'm taking a business trip to Barcelona in a couple of days. One of the wonderful things about translation is it's so portable."

"I envy you there!" she said, but she didn't look particularly envious, sleek and successful as she was.

"So, what was it you needed my help with?" I asked. "The literary problem you mentioned. Is it something to do with translation?"

"Oh no, nothing like that." She looked at her watch and suddenly waved for the check. "I'll explain it on the way. We'll have to hurry if we're going to make the lecture. We'll hop a cab to King's Cross and change at London Bridge for New Cross. The talk's at four. Sorry there's no time to linger over coffee, but I think they're offering something there at the college. Fiona said shortbread."

"What talk?"

"I thought I told you on the phone. Fiona Craig's talk. About her biography of Stella Terwicker. Come along!"

It was drenching outside but we managed to catch a taxi and were soon hustling through corridors at King's Cross, passing equally damp strangers.

On the tube I asked her why she needed to attend a lecture far from her usual haunts in Central London, and why she required my presence.

"Well, it's a bit knotty," she said. With Avery that sometimes signaled a delicious bit of gay literary scandal. Then I realized she hadn't said "naughty."

"It's Fiona Craig who asked me to come. Fiona is one of my

authors," she went in. "You know I represented Stella Terwicker and her historical mysteries for years, and so it was natural to help Fiona with correspondence and rights issues connected with her biography. You probably remember that Stella died around ten years ago. She was only fifty-one, though she'd had Chronic Fatigue Syndrome for years. I didn't know Fiona well before Stella's death, just that she was related to Stella."

She lowered her voice. "Fiona was married to Stella's older brother, Stan. He inherited the estate, but then *he* died a few years after Stella, so it all went to Fiona. She's the executor. Retired lecturer in medieval history, up north. A few years ago she decided to write this biography. Aside from being sisters-in-law, they'd studied together in York. Fiona had always been Stella's go-to on the Middle Ages. Hence the biography. It's doing very well. Readers still adore the Beatrys series, both the books and the television series. Anything with nuns, really. Though they're not really nun-nuns, as you know. Beguines. But basically the same thing except they had more freedom."

"Is Fiona giving you difficulties?" I'd not actually read any of Stella Terwicker's historical mysteries nor had I ever watched the television series back when it first came out. After a rigorous eight years in childhood among real nun-nuns at St. Monica's in Kalamazoo, I didn't share the media enthusiasm for women in habits.

"No, it's not Fiona. It's someone else, someone who's writing a memoir of life in the women's movement in the eighties and nineties, someone who has a problem with a few things in Fiona's biography. Nothing important, of course. But Fiona's afraid that this woman— whom I think you might know—could be at the lecture and cause a disturbance."

"Now I *am* intrigued," I said, as we alighted at London Bridge and made our way to the platform where the Southern trains departed. "You know I'm always curious about people I might know who turn out to be stalkers."

"Yvonne Henley."

"Vonn? But that's crazy. I can't imagine her menacing a retired medievalist. Vonn was," I struggled to recall, "in publishing, wasn't she? A member of a publishing collective that only published lesbians. That was years ago."

"I only know what Fiona has told me," said Avery. "She feels threatened."

"So we're going to a lecture to provide physical protection? Sorry, I forgot my sword and shield."

"I have to take this seriously," said Avery. "But don't worry about Vonn. I can manage her. Just keep her away from Fiona."

"Why me?"

"It's not everyone I could call on for such a delicate operation," Avery said smoothly.

"Something you're not telling me? Let me guess. Vonn wants you to represent her memoir? You're planning to pass, of course. But where does Fiona come in? Has Vonn written something about Stella?"

"See? I love how your mind works, Cassandra. You're naturally suspicious, so no wonder you're a brilliant translator of detective fiction."

The train to East Croydon came in with a rush, but I hesitated. "I don't know, Avery. Thanks for lunch and everything and lovely to see you, but I'm not sure I'm in the mood for the Middle Ages."

Avery looked uncharacteristically anxious. She grabbed my elbow and piloted me into the carriage. "I didn't really give you half a chance with the crime author from Seville. It just might be that I could do something with Lola Fuentes. There was Dick Francis's jockey and the racecourses, so why not bullrings and an emotionally conflicted ex-matador? A two-book deal maybe—and if the PETA people object, the right publisher may very well profit from the controversy. Candleford is out, of course, and some of the larger houses. But there's a scrappy newcomer doing thrillers, SNP, what do you think? Short and Pryce, after the two owners. They don't shy away from ruffling feathers."

Avery had me in a firm grip. She was surprisingly strong. It must be all that weightlifting at her private gym. I shook her off eventually and sat down, but the opportunity to sell Lola's books in England was too good to pass up. Lola was not a retired, wounded matador, but a single mother with a useless degree in geography.

As Avery said, a typical protégé of mine.

2.

Anyone less likely than Dr. Fiona Craig to create a stir was hard to imagine. She stood behind a wooden podium as a sedate academic, her slight Yorkshire accent still audible under the crisp, slightly pedantic delivery. She was used to lecturing to students so that they could take notes or absorb the full import of her words. No PowerPoint slides for her, much less videos with animations and a soundtrack. No moving around the room with a small head mike, no engaging in jokes or questions with her audience. Just a few note cards and a minimum of gestures with the index finger of the right hand when a single point needed stressing.

The audience was a mix of pensioners, the flexibly employed, and college students. The majority were women in raincoats or with umbrellas that dripped depressingly on the linoleum floor. If it weren't for the fact that a couple of them had inventive hair colors, you might imagine yourself at Shrewsbury College, Oxford, with some of Dorothy L. Sayers's female scholars. The room itself had echoes of British austerity either from the thirties or the Thatcher era. It was chilly and uncomfortable, with a mix of battered wooden and uncomfortably molded plastic chairs, and single-pane windows against which the raindrops splashed on this dreary afternoon.

Fiona herself wore a coffee-colored wool skirt with tights to match, and a toasty brown cardigan. A scarf in autumnal colors. Shoulders back, neck a little stiff when she very occasionally turned her head to the side door, which was open. The chin-length bob was tinted dark chestnut, unbecoming to the pale winter skin of a sixty-year-old woman. But if the face was ivory and the thin lips only slightly reddened, the brown eyes still snapped with intellectual vigor.

Hearing her introduced by a college lecturer as "one of our most respected British medievalists and now an authoritative biographer" made my heart sink at first, but in fact Dr. Craig was not a dull speaker.

The fifty-minute lecture began with Stella Terwicker's decision to set the mystery novels and the TV series in thirteenth-century Flanders, at the celebrated Beguinage of the Vineyard, or *Begijnhof Ten Wijngaerde,* in Bruges. It then moved into an exploration of how Fiona worked with Stella over the years to make sure all the medieval references were correct in both the books and the filmed episodes.

We were skillfully drawn into the story of how Fiona and Stella met and bonded, as first-year students in the same department at the University of York. Fiona was from a small town in Yorkshire, already committed to an academic career in medieval history. Stella came from the south of England and was reading Old French and Latin. The spring of their third year, just before they graduated, the two of them decided to visit Belgium, specifically Bruges, to see the museums.

"We set off by train and ferry—Eurostar didn't exist then, it was the late seventies—and rented bikes in Bruges. We soon found ourselves in the quiet environs of the beguinage, by one of the canals. The buildings there, as you may know, are not the originals from the late thirteenth century when the beguinage was founded but are instead largely from the eighteenth century. Nor are there still beguines there. The last one died in 1927, and the community is now a convent run by Benedictine nuns. But the building was still organized around a central meadow with trees and a profusion of daffodils in the spring."

She smiled warmly at us. "Have any of you ever been to Bruges?" A dozen hands went up, and someone called out, "On a *Beatrys* tour!"

"Ah," said Fiona, smiling broadly, "then you know how exceptionally beautiful the city is, and how remarkable that it still stands, with many of the older buildings from the days when Bruges had 50,000 people. When it was a thriving wool town, crisscrossed by canals, with ships coming and going daily, a religious center with many churches, convents, and of course the beguinage, a working haven for women who wanted to live independently but also together in groups, as weavers and lace-makers, as nurses and teachers, and as wealthy merchants and even bankers. As many of you know, from the books and the television series, the women formed a lay order, that is, they didn't take binding vows, meaning that they could come and go."

She paused and smiled at us. "Our visit later found expression in the story of Beatrys Hartog, who came to the beguinage in Bruges as a sixteen-year-old escaping an arranged marriage, and who thrived as a weaver. You can imagine," added Fiona, "how interesting, as young women who were just being exposed to the idealistic goals of the Women's Liberation Movement, Stella and I found this idea of an independent women's community dating back some seven hundred years."

To my ears this sounded a bit stodgy. I wanted to protest to an indifferent-looking young woman a few seats away that life back then had been more than about idealistic goals. My own "exposure" to the women's movement of the time had involved much more shouting in the streets and sex in the bedrooms.

"Not that these beguines had full control over their lives," Fiona went on more gravely. "They were under the spiritual direction of a male priest as well as a Council of Elders in the beguinages, headed by a Magistra. They also were supported by Margaret II, the Countess of Flanders, who established the beguinage in Bruges in 1245. You might recall that Judi Dench had a recurring role as Countess Margaret in the series."

Oh yes, they remembered. And a sigh ran through the audience. Wonderful Judi, sweeping in with a large entourage to majestically settle disputes.

"Countess Margaret was a great supporter of the arts and that was reflected in the books and the television series. Some beguinages were well known for their illuminated manuscripts and more than a few had choirs who sang music composed by the beguines themselves. You may remember the mystery titled *Illuminated by Death,* which had a plot focused on a small group of beguines working with manuscripts. Or *Schola for Murder,* with its choir of beguines, and the rivalry between two women composers."

Fiona Craig spoke for a while longer about the different mysteries, and how Stella came to rely on her to do the research for some of her ideas, eventually hiring her as a consultant on the television series. "For instance, she wanted very much to have a character who was a property-owner, so I went looking in libraries and archives for deeds, wills, and other documents that would show that some of the beguines were very wealthy indeed. I also helped research the kinds of herbal medicines, potions, and poisons that would have been frequent in those days. The perspective was always feminist, when we wrote, when Stella wrote about forced marriage, prostitution, rape, and violence against women. There were so many subjects to touch upon and we wanted to be as accurate as possible. We had enough material for ten more books, and it's always been annoying that the series wasn't renewed after the second season. But of course," she paused and collected herself, "that's television."

I caught a glimpse of something less controlled and surprisingly resentful in her expression, and then it was gone. Fiona then reached down to the shelf inside the podium and brought out a copy of *Stella Terwicker: A Medieval Life.*

"Some of what I've said, about Stella's early inspiration and the beguinages comes from the first chapters of the biography. Later, I discuss her growing fame as a mystery writer and the experience of making the television series." Discreetly, she waved in the direction of the side door, next to which was a table with a pile of hardcovers. Since the lecture had begun, a young woman and several plates of biscuits had appeared.

"There will be tea afterwards, and Yorkshire shortbread, both plain and with chocolate, and I'll be glad to chat and sign books," she said. "But first, are there any questions?"

There were a few scholarly questions about sources, then someone asked whether Fiona had really met Judi Dench ("Yes, and she's just as lovely as you'd expect, very kind and amusing."). Another person wanted to know how she could find a publisher or agent for a historical mystery she'd written, set in France in the fourteenth century. It had no beguinages, but it did have compelling plot about an abbess who discovered a body on the grounds of the convent. This plot was recounted at some length.

I felt Avery tense up beside me. She whispered, "Please don't let Fiona mention that there's an agent here in the room."

From time to time I'd been aware of Avery next to me in the uncomfortable plastic chairs. She looked out of place here, much better-dressed than the rest of the audience, with her blonde hair and pleasingly bronzed face and neck, suggesting warmer climes and more money. Like Fiona, and for the same reason, she too had had occasion to glance at the side door, on the alert for the possible disruptive arrival of Vonn. When Fiona said that publishing was a hard nut to crack but if you believed in yourself, you should just keep trying, Avery nodded approvingly and relaxed.

The lecturer who'd introduced Fiona stepped up to bring things to a close, with the suggestion that books were for sale and Fiona could answer further questions over tea.

Avery turned to me, "We'll just have a quick cup to be polite, shall we, and then be on our way? There's a pub nearby and I'll buy you a drink. I could use a large gin myself. Sorry to have dragged you all the way over here for this, Cassandra. I was expecting some sort of confrontation that I'd have to defuse. So thank God..."

But halfway out of her chair she stiffened, groaned, and sat back down. "Spoke too soon."

I cast an eye at the table where Vonn, leather jacketed as in the old days, bike helmet swinging from one elbow, was loading a napkin with Yorkshire shortbread. She looked up and seemed pleased enough to see Avery, which was reassuring. For Vonn had been a pugnacious woman, apt to jump on the attack immediately.

"Might you go up to Fiona and keep her busy for a minute, ask a question or something? I'll get Vonn back out into the corridor and talk to her, see what she's up to."

I nodded and headed to the podium, where Fiona was chatting with a student and the lecturer who'd introduced her. She stood, deliberately or not, with her back to the refreshment table and the door beside it. I glanced over and saw Avery and Vonn, now face to face. Vonn had always been rather athletic and wiry. While she was still wiry—she had obviously cycled here—she looked more like a half-drowned mutt, hungrily gnawing a piece of shortbread as if it were her evening meal. Her hair was gray and longer than I remembered; it hung in strands around her aggressive jaw and prominent forehead. She had crumbs on her lower lip from the shortbread. It was hard to see in her the swaggering dyke of the old days, who loved to turn up at meetings and cause a ruckus with provocative questions.

Although I'd never been a friend of Vonn's, I recalled her well from various women's conferences and international feminist bookfairs of the eighties and nineties. She was the founder and mainstay of the publishing collective, Brize, meaning "gadfly" in Greek. The Goddess Hera sent such a gadfly, the size of a sparrow, with a stinger the length of a knife, after another goddess, Io, to torment her. It was the mission of Brize not just to torment the patriarchy, but to sting other women's organizations that the group deemed insufficiently radical. Brize was proudly under-funded and egalitarian. They had no board of directors, no publishing director, no top editors, no office underlings. The collective of six to ten women did all jobs, so that everyone had a chance to make decisions and learn the publishing business.

In theory and often in practice this resulted in a far more diverse and open publishing style, but it also resulted in some difficulties getting manuscripts through the editorial and production pipeline. In short, they published very little and were known for their long meetings that ended in tears and with one or more collective members leaving through the revolving door.

Fiona was now talking to an older woman fan of Stella's mysteries. They widened their circle to include me. After a few general questions about which episodes Fiona had worked on and which were favorites ("Almost all of them, but especially some in the second series, when we got our feet under us."), she was asked whether she herself had published any books or articles on the beguines during her career. I thought she seemed slightly defensive, or perhaps she was just anxious. She glanced at the lecturer and then at the table, where a queue had formed. There was no sign of Vonn and Avery, and Fiona might be wondering what had happened to them.

"No, I wanted to, but I simply never had time," she said. "I'd written my dissertation on medieval women writers and composers, but lecturing took much of my time and then there was doing research for Stella. And of course I was increasingly involved in her career as time went on, as a consultant for the television series."

The student seemed disappointed, but the lecturer stepped in diplomatically. "As a full-time professor myself, I know how difficult it is to both write and teach. But the fact that you consulted on your sister-in-law's mysteries really speaks well for how scholarship can contribute to popular literature. I'm a big fan of Stella Terwicker's books—I much prefer them to Ellis Peter's mysteries about Cadfael. Now, I wonder if you'd like to come over to the table and sign a few books?" She began to move off.

"I'll be there in just a moment, Ruth." Fiona Craig nodded to me. Her face was really very pale against the dark-dyed hair. "Did you have a question?"

"I... Yes, I wondered about the subtitle: *A Medieval Life*. Simply curious, as I haven't yet had a chance to read the biography. Why not just *A Life*?"

She nodded. "The subtitle was my suggestion. There was a medieval church tradition of writing about holy men and women's lives. *Vitae,* they were called in Latin. They weren't biographies in the modern sense, full of psychological insight and set against a historical background. They concentrated on a religious search for meaning, so to some extent they were like morality plays. Thinking of Stella's life as a form of *vita* emphasizing the beguinages helped me structure her story."

"Right," I said. "It must be a challenge, what to include and what to leave out. What is too personal or private about the subject, I mean." I was thinking of Vonn's purported objections to the biography. Why would Vonn even bother to read a book like that? Had she known Stella Terwicker?

Fiona gave me a closer look. "You were sitting next to Avery, weren't you? Where's she gone?"

I hesitated. I hadn't meant anything by my comment. I certainly didn't want to bring up Vonn, or to mention that Avery had brought me along in case of trouble. "Not sure. Maybe she's in the loo? Avery told me about the lecture, and we popped over from North London together. I loved the television series. I'd better get over to the table and snap up one of the copies. If I buy a book, will you sign it?"

"Oh, certainly," she said, as we walked over together to the table. To my dismay, the last book had just been sold and the shortbread had vanished as well. Fiona sat down and began signing and answering more questions. I investigated the corridor. No sign of them. I said casually to Fiona, "I'll look in the ladies. Avery has no sense of direction sometimes," and disappeared into the corridor.

I had done my part. And if accompanying Avery here had been pointless, as I suspected, since she had clearly taken Vonn off somewhere to discuss whatever problems they were having, then at least I had learned something about the beguinages of the Middle Ages. The next time I saw Avery, I'd ask her what happened. I was curious, after all, about why Vonn had surfaced again and what this memoir of hers might reveal.

On second thought, maybe I wouldn't ask. I had only done Avery a favor in hopes that she would consider my author Lola Fuentes and her ex-bullfighter detective Rita.

For now, there was nothing to do but head back to New Cross station. Fortunately, the rain had lessened considerably. I texted Avery and looked a few times at my phone over the hour it took me to get from Southeast London up to North Islington. But the only text that came in was from my flatmate Nicky Gibbons, just as I was changing at King's Cross. She said her friend Gayle had come by and they were ordering takeaway curries, and did I want to join them?

Yes, I answered. Yes. Yes.

I recalled that Gayle was a former flame of Vonn's, who might still have remained in contact with her. Maybe Gayle would have some insight of why Avery seemed to think Vonn posed a threat to Fiona.

Meanwhile, I'd stop at the Waterstone's on Islington Green and buy a copy of *Stella Terwicker: A Medieval Life*.

3.

Gayle and Nicky knew each other from the musical world. Nicky, a classical bassoonist who had provided me with a base in London for ages, was now retired from the London Symphony Orchestra, but still traveled for woodwind concerts and continued to instruct a few students—fortunately not in the flat in Islington. As everyone knows, I'm an aficionada of the bassoon repertoire, but only as played by virtuosi like Nicky.

Nicky was a large woman, though less like a woman than a lioness or a German opera tenor: lightly treading, graceful, dominant. Her shoulder-length hair was still thick, curly, and tawny-brown, but she had a slight mustache now and a definite third chin. On stage, she generally wore black velvet, a long dress with a plunging neckline. At home she often donned wide velour trousers and tunics together with draped Indian shawls and red Moroccan slippers, pointed and heel-less. She was wearing that outfit tonight, though with heavy socks, because it was chilly.

To my mind she was a perfect flatmate. She was good-tempered, generous, and had no bad habits except a tendency to clutter. "Recycling" was a word you never associated with Nicky. She didn't much like cleaning or cooking but employed a weekly char and ordered takeaway. She was rather handy about the home though, having learned how to use power tools from her father, who had a shed in an allotment near the family home in a Glasgow suburb. She also knew how to hunt with bow and arrow.

Gayle was about half Nicky's size, a light lyric soprano with a deeper speaking voice. She'd performed in both church settings and secular venues as part of the Renaissance choral ensemble the Tudor Roses. I recalled her with wavy light brown hair once, flowing down her back. Her chocolate-drop eyes had always had a narrow slant, with plump eyelids. Now her hair was cut in feathery white curls, so her pretty ears showed. She was smaller than I remembered, round-faced and elfin. Her smile was still at the ready. Nicky called her Wee Gayle.

Over what was left of the Indian curries, I told them both where I'd been, in Southeast London at Fiona's lecture. Gayle had some acquaintance with Fiona Craig and Stella Terwicker, and more than mere acquaintance with Vonn Henley. I remembered there had been an entanglement, years ago, the kind that was gossiped about and then forgotten. But Gayle refreshed our memories.

She and Vonn got together shortly after Vonn had left the Brize collective and had gone freelance. One of Vonn's jobs was editing the newsletter of a gay and lesbian health organization. Vonn also did copyediting and design for various groups, like the Tudor Roses, who needed help producing printed programs for their concerts and liner notes for their CDs.

"For a certain kind of woman—and I turned out to be one of them—Vonn was catnip," Gayle said.

"Meaning?"

"Inexperienced, romantic young women, like most of us in the Tudor Roses. Vonn was very athletic, I mean, *muscled*. She had a poetic mop of dark hair on top, very short on the sides. Ear studs. She wore a leather vest, sometimes without a shirt underneath. Made your knees weak. The Tudor Roses had met at uni in the music department, and we took ourselves seriously as scholars of Renaissance music as well as singers. At our concerts and in all photographs, we wore flat velvet pancake hats and velvet robes. Some of the members also played period instruments. Vonn was a cat among the pigeons."

"A fox among the swans," said Nicky. "Give yourselves a little credit. How many fell for her?"

"Seven of the ten," said Gayle. "But most were flirtations that went unacted on. Half of the women had boyfriends and one a husband. There were only three of us who were more involved with Vonn. We didn't know it at the time, of course. She approached us separately. The bookkeeper Sara was especially angry about the whole thing. She'd advanced Vonn some money for a copyediting job that Vonn then didn't do, because the director of the choral ensemble, Lu, who was also sleeping with Vonn, found out and fired Vonn. Sara quit too."

She pulled out her phone and found a photograph of the Tudor Roses from thirty or more years ago. There was Gayle in a velvet cap, holding a lute in one hand, her round, sweet face glowing, wavy hair cascading over her shoulders, the eyes squeezed almost shut in a musical trance.

"What a cherub you were," laughed Nicky. "When I know for certain you've always been a cheeky wee devil."

"Yes, you were—are—angelic," I said. Actually she was more like a lady leprechaun than an angel, but I didn't want to offend.

"The gallant Cassandra," she smiled. "You always liked to tease."

"Past tense?" I said, more flirtatiously than I intended, mainly to remind her I wasn't all washed up.

"Well, we're all older now, aren't we?"

Nicky wisely steered us away from this topic.

"What happened to you and Vonn?"

"I was crushed to hear about Lu and Sara obviously, and there were scenes, and then she swore undying love to me only, and we had another month of intense bliss, but it wasn't easy. I found out she had another lover in *addition* to the three of us."

Gayle sighed. "And there was her anger. She wasn't physically violent of course, but she was confrontational. I think it made her feel more alive. And when she wasn't complaining about the misdeeds of all and sundry, she went around miffed about something or somebody. When I knew her, it was often the women she'd worked with at Brize, or other women editors and writers in London. She couldn't get over the fact that she, who had *started* Brize, had been eventually ejected by the others. The grievances got old rather quickly. Still, I adored her. I wasn't prepared for her to just leave me one day. But she did that with everyone, she just couldn't sustain a relationship. As I say, I was crushed, though we stayed friendly. Susan and I got together soon after."

"And how's Susan?" I asked. I'd forgotten about Susan.

"Oh, Susan is long gone, I thought you knew that. Though we were together for ages. I dated other women and then Joan came along. Another seven years with her, not easy ones."

"Joan was the alcoholic," Nicky put in helpfully.

"Oh, right," I said. But I didn't remember Joan well at all. That was a problem with traveling so much. It was hard to remember everyone's girlfriend and ex-girlfriend, especially from the older days when one friend's ex might be another's present squeeze, only to turn into an ex. No, my mind was blank about Joan, but good job Gayle had gotten rid of her. Was she free by chance these days? That could be nice. I'd always had a bit of a soft spot for Gayle.

"You're always on the move, Cassandra!" said Gayle with a mischievous smile. "When I've asked Nicky about you over the years, it's always *Oh, Cassandra's in Santiago for three months* or *She's hanging out in Tokyo learning some Japanese.* I guess that's why you've never settled down with anyone in London."

I didn't think that was the reason, but it was a convenient explanation for many of my friends, and usually for me too, so I just shrugged and turned to Nicky. "And what's your excuse, Nicky?"

"I've settled down with you, my bonnie friend. Don't we have the perfect household? Much more peaceful than some of our married pals, I suspect."

Gayle laughed. "Well, my current cuddle can be a challenge at times, but I find her company very stimulating. Anyway, I was going to show you something on YouTube if I can find it, to do with Stella and the TV series."

Nicky and I waited a moment, and then started talking while Gayle scrolled on the phone. I'd have to find out who the current cuddle was. It's true I was off to Barcelona very shortly, but I'd be back. And Gayle hadn't said "partner" or the dread "wife."

"So why again did you trek over to hear a lecture about Stella Terwicker?" Nicky asked me. "And why again was Vonn there?"

"My friend Avery is Fiona's literary agent, and she was or rather still is the agent for Stella Terwicker's mysteries. As for Vonn being there, I think she and Avery might have had some business to talk about. They left and I stayed to talk briefly to Fiona. I'd found the lecture interesting. It was about how she and Stella, when they were students, discovered medieval women's communities in Flanders, and how eventually that led to the Beatrys series, about some nuns, not nuns exactly, but lay religious women, who lived in these communities."

"Not *some nuns*," said Gayle, and she and Nicky said in unison, "Beguines!"

"You know that Cole Porter tune?" Gayle said, and sang, "Let the love that was once a fire remain an ember... that I only remember when they begin the beguine. That's Ella Fitzgerald with a peppy beat," she added. "Frank Sinatra has a more melancholy version."

"Yes, the *beguines*," I said patiently.

"I watched every episode of *Beatrys*," said Nicky. "I even bought the DVD set. I know it's around here somewhere. Have we not watched this together, Cassandra? I distinctly have a memory of sitting around with you watching something medieval."

"I've never seen the DVDs around, but then I'm not completely sure sometimes what buried treasures are in these cabinets and bookshelves. I have seen *Cadfael*. I think we watched that together. Derek Jacobi in his robe and sandals inside his little hut with the bunches of herbs hanging from the ceiling."

"Well, *Beatrys* was like *Cadfael* but a hundred times better, because it was all women in charge, not a load of friars and sheriffs."

"And women criminals and murderers?"

"Naturally, but also women artists, merchants, nurses, and a sleuth, Beatrys the Weaver. A detective, Cassandra. Like you with your propensity for getting involved in investigations. The more I think about it, the more I'm surprised you were not a fan of *Beatrys*."

"The books, the series, they were everywhere for a while," said Gayle. "Before that, who knew anything about beguines? Suddenly they were all over the Culture and Travel sections of the papers, and there were bus tours advertised to visit the Netherlands and Belgium to see the old beguinages. The beguines were all gone but the buildings remained."

"I do have some memory of everyone going wild about *Beatrys*," I said defensively. "Maybe I was busy or out of the country. But I probably didn't watch it for the same reason I don't watch *Call the Midwife* or *Orange Is the New Black*. Walled institutions full of women sort of give me the creeps. I prefer to see women roaming freely around the world on horseback and camel. Explorers, sea captains, aviators, astronauts— that kind of thing."

"If Nicky can't find her DVDs, I have them to lend." Gayle held up her phone. "But here's the little video clip I wanted to show you. It's from the first season. Stella and the producers had hired a specialist in early music history to advise on music in the series. The beguines developed a tradition in the late thirteenth century of liturgical music. They were taught music and Latin in a *schola* and formed choirs with a choir mistress to sing at masses and festivals, and some of them composed original music too. For this special episode that had to do with the death of a female chorister, our group was asked to dress up as beguines and sing. None of us were the corpse fortunately; that was one of the real actors."

We crowded around Gayle's phone and watched a minute or two of the Tudor Roses singing in polyphony, Gayle in the front.

"It was a highlight of my career," she said. "I think we all hoped that the choir would become a regular part of the series, and that we could piggy-back on its success by releasing a CD of music sung in the beguinages, but that never happened."

"And that's how you got to know Stella Terwicker?" I prodded.

"Yes. Well, I don't know if I could say I really knew her, because we were never on set in Ireland where it was filmed. Our little bit was filmed at St. Albans Cathedral, in the Lady Chapel. But we all had lunch once in London, the choir and Stella and her sister-in-law. And we were invited and paid to sing at a launch party for the second series. I remember Stella as unassuming, fragile looking, but pretty."

"Unassuming?"

"Well, you know what I mean. Friendly, not swanning about or anything because she was famous." She thought back. "She sat on a small sofa with a shawl over her legs. Her brother and sister-in-law sort of kept people from crowding too close and tiring her out. People came over to her one by one. I don't think she had a partner, none I ever heard about. Of course, there was speculation, there always is, that Stella was gay. She'd published her first two mysteries with Aphra, the women's press. The second book had a sort of lesbian theme. That was never in the television series. But I suppose with her illness, the chronic fatigue, she didn't have energy for a relationship."

"Did Vonn know Stella?"

"It's possible. I wouldn't have thought so," said Gayle vaguely. "Stella moved in a different crowd, crime writers and media people."

Nicky had gone to the kitchen, not to tidy—that was something neither of us routinely did until all the dishes were used up—but to get a carton of ice cream and put the kettle on. Gayle said she had to leave soon, she didn't want to be out too late, but she'd stay for tea. The talk turned to old times, and back again to Vonn.

Gayle volunteered that Vonn had had a serious bout with breast cancer but had recovered after surgery. "I hadn't seen her for a while. None of my partners liked Vonn or liked me being in touch with her. I'd heard she'd moved out of London, to Bristol, to get some further treatment and recuperate. It was summer and a friend had suggested we head over to the Ladies' Pond at the Heath. So, there we were sitting on a blanket on the shore, and Vonn pops her head out of the water and then gets out and comes over in her swimsuit. Breasts gone, but otherwise still the same. It was good to see her. This was a couple of years ago. I'm not really in touch with her now."

She sighed. The implication was that the current girlfriend didn't like Vonn either.

I used to swim occasionally in the Ladies' Pond when Nicky and I lived in Hampstead. Nicky never liked the idea of it—well, she liked the idea of ladies, but she disliked wearing a swimsuit in public, though she claimed she was nervous about damaging her professional lungs with swampy bacteria. I enjoyed the cool water and the gossip on a warm summer afternoon. There were regulars though, who swam every morning, every day of the year. Vonn was one of those, according to Gayle.

"Isn't Vida a swimmer too?" Nicky asked Gayle. "The last time I saw her, she bent my ear about the natural world."

"She's into wild swimming," Gayle said. "Rivers, the sea, waterfalls. She finds the Ladies' Pond too tame. She grew up swimming in the Atlantic, on the Galician beaches."

I had been naturally wondering about the girlfriend waiting for her at home. Vida, then. And there could only be one Vida. The long-legged Spaniard with the sweep of black hair. A woman on the edge of my world. Friends took their computers to her repair shop in Stoke Newington. They highly recommended her. They also said to me, "Oh you translate from Spanish. You must have met Vida."

I had met Vida, a long time ago, and I didn't like Vida much.

I had a feeling Gayle knew that.

After Gayle departed to catch a bus to Stoke Newington, Nicky opened a cabinet stuffed with books, magazines, and folders, and began looking for the DVDs of *Beatrys*.

"It's not the easiest thing to start a new relationship when you're in your sixties," Nicky said, into my silence. "I think Gayle is trying."

"I don't think it will last," I said. "Why did Susan and Gayle break up?"

"That was years ago. Susan was really jealous, she kept Gayle in fear of saying hello to another woman, then she herself found another lover and dumped Gayle. Gayle's had two or three girlfriends since then, none of them good for her. Joan was the last, the one with the drinking problem. Gayle stuck by her until Joan started AA, but then Joan decided it would be best to move in with another woman in recovery. These women tend to have problems. Gayle to the rescue. Then, ungrateful sods, they say ta-ta. I don't get the feeling she's madly in love with Vida, but Gayle is one of those women who always has to have someone, and it's usually someone with an outsize personality."

"Gayle probably needs rescuing herself," I said as a joke, but Nicky took me seriously. "Don't even think about it," she said.

4.

It was at the beginning of my second week in Barcelona that I got a message from Nicky that Vonn Henley had died by drowning in one of the ponds on the Heath.

Contrary to expectations, I hadn't been enjoying the best of times in one of my favorite cities. The weather was wet, hardly better than the rain of London, and my living circumstances weren't ideal. Since Ana had finally sold up and moved to the Costa Brava a few years ago, I no longer had the use of her large flat on the Rambla de Catalunya. Other friends were leaving the center of the city as well, complaining of the inflated cost of real estate and the proliferation of tourists. Some rented out rooms in their flats or even the entire flat to these same tourists as Airbnb accommodations. Which meant that now these friends often had no room for me in the city when I came for a two-week business-pleasure trip.

The studio flat I had booked from Airbnb was bigger than a closet, but not by much. I should have paid more attention to the listing, where "hangers" was the main item under "Amenities." It was clean enough, and the furnishings, from the IKEA near the Barcelona airport, closely matched some of what was in my room at Nicky's. But somehow one wants more from an address in the Barri Gòtic. Still, the Neoclassical building did have the original windows, and the fifth floor flat boasted a balcony with an urban view. The lack of an elevator meant I did get a good workout several times a day, and the wi-fi was excellent near the windows.

I had pushed the white dining table over to those windows overlooking the street and most mornings I sat there with my coffee, notebook, and laptop, working on a sample translation from *Verónica*. It troubled me that, when I'd finally heard from Avery, two days into my Barcelona trip, there was no mention of Lola Fuentes and her books. Avery simply wrote:

Cassandra,

I failed you, I know. But I really had to deal with Vonn right there to stop her hounding me about that bloody memoir of hers. I know you understand the delicacy of rejections. At any rate, it's done. So, forgive me, and thanks for going with me the other day and chatting with Fiona. You must admit, beguinages are a brilliant idea. Sometimes I think I'd like nothing better than to just disappear behind the walls of a convent.

We'll have a drink soon—when you come back from Spain. Olé!

Cheers, Avery

The language of the email: "I failed you," "forgive me," and worse of all "the delicacy of rejections," might as well apply to Lola's mystery as to Vonn's memoir. Agents were masters at the arts of refusal. I was fairly sure that Avery had only showed an interest in *Verónica* to make sure I attended the lecture. But why? She couldn't have really thought Vonn would cause a scene or threaten Fiona.

And in fact, it sounded from the email that Fiona had played only the role of decoy. What Avery had probably wanted to do was reject Vonn's memoir in a public space, where she could make a getaway afterwards into the rain-soaked streets around the college. She'd had it all worked out. I was there to keep Fiona distracted. Avery's groan when she saw Vonn by the table was pure theater. She must have been certain Vonn would turn up.

These suspicions did not stop me from continuing with the sample translation. I could always bypass Avery and go directly to some of the publishing houses in London. But the editor I worked with at Candleford, who happily published Rosa Cardenes and other translations of mine, had given a thumbs down to Lola Fuentes and bullfighting in general. It would be better to stick with Avery if possible and hope that SNP— Snake and Possum?— might take a proper look at *Verónica*. Until that happened, I wouldn't call Lola.

In the afternoons I visited familiar publishing houses or literary agencies, often walking through the rain, and trying to rekindle my romance with the city streets where I had often been so at home and so enchanted. It was important to keep up these connections with editors and agents and to trade gossip. I had an in with most of them because of

Rosa Cardenes, and past successes in translating South American writers. In the evenings I saw some of these same editors, as well as my friends. One night a group of us went to the Gran Teatre del Liceu to hear a recital, other evenings we went for drinks and tapas.

I was cheerful enough, but somehow our conversations, instead of being about future plans and projects, as they once had been, became more about the past. All my friends in Barcelona were at least semi-retired. Some had been knocked out of the job market earlier than expected by the economic collapse of 2008. Others had managed to get to sixty-five, pension and savings intact. In offices, in bars, in restaurants, I heard a lot about how Spain had changed, about the EU, and about health issues. Some of the editors I met with during the day were now half my age and, increasingly, when I made reference to authors I admired, it turned out they were dead.

My close friend, Ana, whom I'd been longing to see, wasn't back from Germany yet. She emailed that she was unavoidably stuck in Kassel, overseeing a retrospective of some of her installations. She was the one friend I counted on to provide good news, because her old age was filled with new projects and recognition for a lifetime's work in the fields of architecture and sculpture. She had offered to let me stay in her casita on the coast, but I couldn't make that work with all my appointments, so I remained in the Barri Gòtic and tried to make the best of it.

Into this melancholic mood came Nicky's jolting email, which I received mid-day when I'd slogged back to the flat through puddles with a baguette, tomatoes, and slices of a nutty goat cheese.

Dearest Reilly,

Wanted to let you know that early yesterday morning Vonn was found in one of the ponds on the Heath, not the Ladies' Pond, but nearby. Drowned. The word's just getting out. Shock horror. It was Sunday evening when it seems to have happened, twilight, rainy, no witnesses, a birder found her body near the shore on Monday morning, fully dressed, and one of the lifeguards at the Ladies' Pond could identify her. The police are looking into it, but Gayle told me they think it's suicide. Apparently, Vonn was in a depressive state and on medication. Gayle's taking it hard. A neighbor of Vonn's let her know.

Pouring here. I envy you in sunny Spain. Have some of those cocoa-dusted almonds for me (bring some back?)
Love, Nicky

I wrote back to Nicky right away of course. Neither of us had been friends with Vonn. It must be much harder for Gayle, who had been her lover once and had reconnected more recently. I wondered how Gayle knew Vonn's neighbor. It wouldn't hurt to email Avery either, I decided. It gave me the excuse to remind her about Lola's mystery and tell her I'd have excerpts for her soon. Casually, I added a P.S. *Heard about Vonn. Could it really be suicide? Do you know any more?*

Then I deleted the last question and replaced it with *Did she seem down or depressed when you saw her?* Then I scratched that one too, as bloody clueless, before sending it off.

Of course, Vonn could have been down or depressed after hearing from Avery that she didn't want to represent her memoir. Depressed enough to go out to the Heath in the night, in a rainstorm, and drown herself? If so, there was no reason to add to the guilt Avery might be feeling.

Assuming literary agents ever felt guilt.

The days went on, most of them rainy. Even the bright mosaiced facades and the tiled entryways of buildings seemed dulled by pollution and time. Was this how travel was going to be from now on, merely haunting beloved streets and plazas, staring up into windows of rooms where I'd slept, eaten well, worked, and loved? There was no word from Avery, but Nicky wrote again after a few days, suggesting that all was not well.

The first message had to do with Vonn's flat in a building off the Caledonian Road. Apparently, Gayle and the neighbor, Kristi, had gone into Vonn's flat with the landlord and a police officer, and found things tidy and intact, but the next time Gayle and Kristi went over to begin packing things up, since the landlord wanted it emptied to paint and rent out again, things were slightly more disarranged. The door hadn't been forced, but some of Vonn's things seemed to be missing, her telly and laptop. The police assumed it was an opportunistic burglary, possibly by someone in the building, maybe someone that Vonn might have once given a key to.

A follow-up email from Nicky told me that the word from Gayle, via a journalist who frequented the Ladies' Pond and who got a copy of the police report, was that the postmortem showed death by drowning, with no evidence of foul play. Vonn's GP had identified the body, since she had no family in London, and said she had prescribed some muscle relaxants over the last couple of years for Vonn's back pain. More recently Vonn had been taking an antidepressant. Traces of both drugs were found in her body after death, but it wasn't an overdose. There were no witnesses. Vonn's wallet was with her, nothing obvious had been taken. Gayle maintained it must have been an accident, that Vonn wouldn't have intentionally killed herself. The drugs in her system could cause drowsiness.

There was initially some confusion about to whom the body should be released. There had been a brother once, but he was dead, and a cousin in Australia, who didn't seem willing to do much but pay for her cremation at a funeral home. According to Nicky, Gayle had gotten herself involved in everything and Vida didn't seem that happy about it.

The day before I was scheduled to leave Barcelona, when I was scrambling to organize a couple of last meetings and buy some wine and olives to take back with me to London, I was surprised by another message from Nicky, this time a phone text with no salutation: *Gayle and Vida have split. Suddenly. Gayle needs a place until she gets sorted. All right she stays in your room? I'm off to Copenhagen soon so she can have my room then. Dyke drama! Good to know age does not wither it.*

I texted back, *Of course.* I reminded Nicky that I'd be staying a night in Paris on my way back. *Best to Gayle, and I'm sorry.*

I thought Gayle must be fooling herself by thinking Vonn had drowned by accident. But suicide? The woman I remembered would have scoffed at suicide. But then, I hadn't really known Vonn personally. I thought about Vonn at the lecture, eating shortbread. She hadn't *seemed* depressed, but then you never knew. People could keep up a brave front.

If it hadn't been for the fact that Avery made me go to that lecture and claimed that Vonn was threatening Fiona, I wouldn't have asked a single question about Vonn's death.

That evening I went out for a last dinner with a couple of friends, but I returned early to tidy the flat and pack up the books and manuscripts I'd collected. Some of the titles I'd discussed with editors would be posted to me in London, but there were a few I wanted to look at sooner. Among the books was a hardback I'd dragged from England and hadn't opened yet: *Stella Terwicker: A Medieval Life*.

I flipped through the pages to look at the black-and-white photos and their captions. The earliest picture of Stella was as a baby with her mum in their garden in Sussex, followed by a school photograph on an outing to a cloister somewhere, and then one of Stella as a teen with long, light hair, acne, and heavily made-up eyes. She looked like any other white teenage girl of the seventies, with a vaguely desperate look in her eyes, and a turtleneck pulled up to her chin.

More interesting were two photos of her with Fiona, one in a courtyard at the University of York and one by an arched gate at the beguinage of Louvain, Belgium. I could hardly recognize Fiona as the lecturer with a matronly figure. At nineteen or twenty, she was skinny in face and body. Her chin lifted rebelliously, short dark hair messily trimmed with a flyaway fringe. Fiona was rougher at the edges than Stella, who still had a childlike softness, wore a skirt and embroidered cardigan, and protected herself with a scarf wrapped around her neck and chin. Fiona was in jeans and a white shirt open at the neck, with a jacket. Looking at them, you would have thought that Stella was destined to become a folk singer, not a mystery writer, and you wouldn't have suspected Fiona would ever teach medieval history.

Photos of Fiona were missing from most of the rest of the book. She only turned up at the end, off to the side in a group photograph of Stella on the set of *Beatrys* along with several of the actors in costume. By then Fiona looked heavier and less rebellious, more like one of the crew, wearing a windbreaker and carrying a notebook. Stella, meanwhile, had become frailer, hidden in expensive clothes, coats to warm her, big scarves, protective gloves. Within those clothes, she held herself very differently, fragile in her body.

Finally, there was a photo of Stella the year before she died, seated in a chair with a throw around her knees. Behind her was a framed reproduction of a medieval illuminated page, and in her hands a large book opened to another page of medieval script. I was struck somehow, both by this photograph and many of the earlier ones—they seemed deliberately chosen to echo the title: *A Medieval Life*.

I looked through the index. Fiona Craig was there, and Stan Terwicker, Stella's brother, a professor of environmental science at the University of the Highlands and Islands in Inverness. He only had a few entries connected with their childhood and the last referenced his death, sudden, from a heart attack. Why did I get the feeling he and Fiona weren't terribly close? Actors from the series. Avery on and off through the years, brief mentions only. No entry for Yvonne Henley. A single entry for an editor at Aphra Press, Lucy Aspin, who first acquired *Woven into Murder* in 1987. Perhaps unsurprisingly, beguines and other religious orders took up quite a bit of space in the index, as did the history and politics of Flanders, cities in Belgium, the growth and population of the beguinages, the wool trade, lacemaking, nursing, and prostitution. It struck me that Fiona Craig, who had never published an academic book about beguinages, had taken the opportunity of writing Stella's biography or *vita* to inform the reader about her favorite subject: medieval women.

The index seemed to prove Gayle's comment that Stella and Vonn didn't move in the same crowd. Because Vonn was the last person I'd ever associate with the Middle Ages. She was thoroughly of her time, the hardscrabble years of Thatcher's defunding of gay and lesbian organizations, of AIDS, of marches against Clause 28, which outlawed "the promotion of homosexuality," of women's publishers and bookstores, and of the tedious fights about who was sufficiently lesbian. Those were arguments I remembered well, if only in fits and starts. Whenever I returned to London from my travels abroad in more sexually fluid social circles, I had to re-establish my credentials as a paid-up lesbian feminist.

I flipped through the pages to a few paragraphs in Chapter 4, "Beatrys Emerges," that covered a vague, transitional period in Stella's life after she had left York and moved to London, when she must have been writing the first mystery in the Beatrys series. It was the mid-eighties, but the details were surprisingly thin compared to all Fiona seemed to know about Stella's childhood, and school and college years. The two-week trip to Bruges and the beguinages of Belgium and the Netherlands were given a whole chapter, and there was a lot about the research Stella had done alone and with Fiona, but much of that seemed to happen *after* the first two books were published by Aphra Press in 1988 and 1990. It seemed that Fiona had been missing from Stella's life for a few years, before reappearing to become a valued consultant in the nineties.

Where had Stella lived in London in the eighties and what had she been up to? Fiona wrote only:

Stella took a job in publishing as an editorial assistant and learned the rudiments of how books were acquired, edited, and published, knowledge that would stand her in good stead as she cast around for a character and milieu to make her own. Stella had always been a great mystery reader, especially of the classics like Christie, Allingham, and Marsh, and she especially was drawn to historical mysteries, not surprising of course, given her background in medieval history. She was aware of Edith Pargeter's books about Brother Cadfael, which she began writing in the 1970s under the pen name Ellis Peters.

Instead of more about the London years, Fiona went on to compare Cadfael to Beatrys, and his mid-twelfth-century abbey in Shrewsbury to the late thirteenth-century beguinage in Bruges. After which followed a good deal more about the differences between beguinages and convents, and male and female religious orders in Flanders. Fiona made them all sound extremely pleasant places, with interior fountains, shaded walks through poplars along the rivers and canals, and happy hubs of domestic industry in the orchards among the beehives. Refuges from the often-chaotic world outside, where music and reading were valued, and life was simplified to work and worship.

When I was growing up, a convent always seemed one of the more frightening places you could live. Shut off from the world, immured in sisterhood and not the fun kind, only able to go out to teach in Catholic schools or serve meals to poor people, and then to return home for an evening of spiritual study, crosswords, knitting, and of course, endless praying. I had a great-aunt who'd been a nun for most of her life. When I was a child, we visited her once a year in her convent in a run-down area of Chicago. They were mostly older Irish and Polish nuns in the chilly brick and stone building. My mother said she felt the presence of God strongly in the convent. So did I. He was looking down with a severe squint in his enormous eye, wondering what to make of me.

But what if you could pass easily back and forth through the gates of the beguinage, finding refuge and companionship among women, but getting out for a walk or a horseback ride from time to time, and then returning to a glass of wine in your private house and some choral music in the church? In the options available to women in medieval times, it didn't seem the worst fate.

On the Eurostar from London to Paris two weeks ago, passing through northern France, I'd thought idly that I should go back to Bruges sometime. It was a beautiful little city and one I'd not visited in years. Why shouldn't I alter my return trip slightly now? It was too late to change my early morning train tomorrow morning to Paris and my plan to stay a night in a hotel. But I hadn't yet made the Eurostar reservation to London and could easily change it so that I returned via Brussels.

What was the point, after all, of cultivating a traveler's identity if you always stuck to the itinerary?

5.

I arrived in Bruges around ten in the morning, after a night in Paris. Low-lying fog across Belgium had erased the most obvious signs of modern life, and as I'd looked out the window of the carriage, I found it easy to imagine that behind the fog lay medieval villages and convents, not supermarkets and office buildings. Here and there a church spire was visible, or a farmyard. The heavy mist out the train window gradually streaked into rain as we passed canals and alleys of bare-branched poplars like so many tall gray scrub brushes. The towers of Bruges came into view and then the train smoothly pulled into the station.

The last time I'd been here had been on a sunny summer day more than ten years ago, when a friend and I had been driving through Belgium to Amsterdam, and we'd stopped for lunch. The famous market square with its medieval and Renaissance houses was thick with tourists in baggy shorts and sun visors drinking Belgian beers in the outdoor cafes. But this wet February morning few people were about. I could imagine the hunched figures in black and gray raincoats as monks and beguines moving through the narrow streets, unpaved and muddy in the thirteenth century. I saw what Fiona had described, a wealthy city of religious orders and wool merchants, whose ships at the time could sail right up to the walls of the city from the North Sea.

Ten years ago, my friend and I had drunk some Belgian beer, bought chocolates, and driven on to Holland, without visiting the Memling Museum or even the Frites Museum, dedicated to French fries. I'd seen on my phone that the beguinage was close to the station, and I sloshed off across the ring road into the medieval alleys that twisted through the city over bridges and alongside canals.

Like so many self-contained women's communities it was invisible until you stumbled through its portals, which I finally did, to find myself in an open, grassy space, surrounded by two-story stone buildings where the beguines had lived. These weren't the originals from the thirteenth century. Those had likely been timber and wattle. These had gone up in the eighteenth century, after the communities of beguines had largely died out or been replaced by Benedictines. I had been reading some of Fiona's biography on the train. According to her, in the late seventies when she and Stella first visited some of the remaining beguinages in Bruges, Louvain, and Ghent, few people were very interested in the history of the medieval women's movement or in these old buildings in Flanders. Many of the surviving beguinages had become either convents or housing for the elderly.

"Part of the excitement for me and Stella," Fiona had written, "was the discovery of the silent, enclosed space in the midst of a modern city.

The large beguinage in Bruges, the *Begijnhof Ten Wingaerde*, had never been pulled down, it had never been repurposed as senior or artist housing as happened in some Belgian cities. There was a church, and a small museum in one of the old buildings. We chatted briefly with one of the nuns in the shop, who seemed touched at our enthusiasm. She said that tourists often came to the beguinage, took a few photographs, bought a postcard, and wandered out again.

The nun knew and appreciated the hundreds of years of history here. Although she was Benedictine, she was fascinated by the beguines and their work in the community, their work as musicians and illuminators and poets. We spent hours in the beguinage that day and bought everything in the shop that had to do with its history, mostly small pamphlets in Dutch and French. One of them was *The Seven Ways of Divine Love* by Beatrice of Nazareth, a thirteenth-century Flemish nun and mystic who was educated by beguines. She was the first prose writer of early Dutch. The list of ways of holy loving made a profound impression on both Stella and me, as did the presence of the nun herself. The whole experience in Bruges was formative for us. I would eventually discuss Beatrice of Nazareth in my dissertation on women writers and musicians of the thirteenth century. And Stella would name her medieval detective Beatrys.

Today, a Monday morning, the museum and gift shop were closed, but I went into the church for a dry space to read about Fiona and Stella. The stone walls gave off a chill and the pews weren't much warmer. I remembered that as a tiny girl I'd loved the candles, the waxed scent of wooden pews and railings, the sonorous ring of the bells, the deep mumblings of the Mass. Later, as Latin was retired and as the mumblings of the Mass became actual English words, I was less enchanted. I came to dread most of my Saturday visits to the confessional boxes, having so many small transgressions to admit to. I had refused to go to confession from the time I was fourteen, the last year I'd taken the sacrament.

Religion was another gulf that set me apart from my family. Sinners they had also been, but they had repented regularly. I rarely did.

Of course, over decades as a traveler, I'd been inside many churches to see the art, to listen to concerts, and to get out of the rain, but there was never a time when I didn't feel subtly resistant or guilty, or as though I were trespassing on other people's sincere faith.

When I was a child the only images available to me of religious women were suffering Mary, meek and mild, and the terrifying martyred female saints, who took arrows and brickbats for their faith and had their innards and eyes plucked out. The nuns who taught me up through the eighth grade were their own kind of terrifying. All the same I glimpsed, in their unstudied moments and snatches of conversation, some kind of female friendship, some kind of sisterhood that existed in a world apart from the patriarchal hierarchy of the Roman Catholic Church.

Something different seemed to be going on with the beguines and their communities. Perhaps it was projection on my part, but it was encouraging to imagine their lives here in Bruges. There were so few structures ever built just for women, and most of them were convents. The beguinages hinted at something less immured and more flexible. This female space was still standing, still visited, and still written about with admiration, seven hundred and fifty years after its founding.

I went back outside into the rain and immediately began thinking about a hot lunch with a glass of Belgian beer in some cozy nook. Being who I am, I couldn't help wondering what the beguines did when one of the women caused trouble. Was she given a talking to, made to do more washing with lye soap, or summarily escorted to the gate and booted out? Feminist histories and biographies often celebrated women who didn't submit to patriarchal expectations, or who found creative or subtle ways to subvert them. Such histories didn't always talk about women who didn't submit to anyone's expectations and caused trouble within their own feminist ranks.

That was probably the reason that someone like Stella had a laudatory biography and someone like Vonn had to write her own memoir.

Stella, as Gayle recalled her, was "unassuming," "friendly," and didn't "swan about."

While Vonn was, in collective memory, "argumentative," "angry," and "annoying."

Vonn had been ejected from the Brize collective. It was likely she would have been unwelcome here in Bruges among the devout women who aimed, despite their wish for self-sustaining independence, to live the simple life of the apostles.

After a dish of *moules-frites* in a nearby restaurant, I was back on the train to Brussels to catch the 16:00 Eurostar to London. The light rain hadn't let up all day, and as we left Brussels it became a dreary twilight downpour. I'd put aside *Stella Terwicker* and had turned to my translation of *Verónica,* polishing the excerpts with a word change here and there on the computer, and referring to a handy pocket guide to bullfighting terminology that I'd found in a secondhand bookstore in Barcelona. The word *verónica* itself was easy. It was the basic slow pass the matador made with her large cape at the bull, and it was named for Saint Veronica, said to have wiped Jesus's face with her veil as he passed by on the road to Golgotha. Legend said an image of the face remained on the veil.

There were many more difficult-to-translate terms for what the matador did after the *verónica* or instead of it. The *faro de rodillas*, for instance, in which a daring matador dashed right in front of the bull, dropped to her knees, and then swung the cape over and around her head as the bull charged her. It was this dash in front of an enraged animal that had felled Rita in the bullring and left her with an ugly gash on her thigh.

A bullring, a beguinage. Two enclosed spaces. It was just our luck that as female bullfighters were starting to break into the ranks of toreros and matadors that people were having serious second thoughts about killing bulls. Rita herself had second thoughts these days about the bulls she'd managed to dispatch. She had prided herself on mastering the art of the corrida, but later regretted the bloodshed. That was what drove her into detective work: investigating murder and preventing more violence.

What drove the beguine Beatrys into detective work? A different motive, I guessed. Protecting her sisters and their chosen way of life, righting wrongs within and without the community of a dedicated all-women's space. That was in part what was so appealing to the largely women readers and viewers of the *Beatrys* series. A woman detective who was moral and well-intentioned, sisterly and brave, clever but not proud. Able to sort out misunderstandings between women and defuse murderous impulses.

For certainly women were no angels. And women's space was no guarantee of a conflict-free zone.

In the darkened windows of a train speeding through the wet evening, my mirrored face, cleared of wrinkles, looked years younger. I found myself thinking of another trip to London from Barcelona one summer thirty-five years ago. I'd been on my way to the First International Feminist Book Fair, to be held in an exhibit hall in Convent Garden and in venues around the city. Women's book and magazine publishers and publishers with women's titles had tables and displays all around the hall. Panels, readings, and discussions took place day and night in venues around the city. I remembered Audre Lorde speaking and Adrienne Rich reading. I met and listened to editors and publishers from India, Quebec, and Denmark, and writers from San Francisco, Oslo, Sydney, and Johannesburg.

The public stood in long lines to enter the exhibit hall and it was hard to get a ticket to many of the events. It seemed to me that the book fair went on for weeks, but I suppose it was only over three or four days. After which everyone scattered back to their home countries to reconvene again in two years in Oslo, and then in Barcelona, Amsterdam, Montreal, and Melbourne. I went to four more of the book fairs and helped organize the one in Barcelona, but none of them could ever be as exciting to me as that first one, where I met so many of the friends and lovers of the next decades, as well as some of the editors I'd work with in future.

All the same, even then there were rumbles and splits, accusations and confrontations. About important things and about hurt feelings too.

Brize Publishing Collective had a table, and this is where I first encountered Vonn Henley, who seemed willing enough to sell me a book of poetry and spoke vaguely of how they'd like to publish some works of translation in future. She was in her prime then: strong chin, sly grin, ear studs, leather jacket with a violet pin that said DYKE. Later I heard her arguing with one of the organizers in a corner of the exhibit hall. She was complaining that mainstream publishers had taken too many of the tables leaving the small feminist and lesbian presses like Brize and Womenonly clustered in dusty corners. Womenonly was another small collective: two or three white women, all lesbians. I seem to recall a petition was circulated that resulted in Brize getting a more prominent table near the entrance.

That book fair was also where I saw Vida for the first time. She was moderating a panel of women writers from the Southern Hemisphere. Though she herself was from Galicia and lived in London, she was probably asked because she could provide translation for two women from Argentina and Chile, which she did with swift accuracy. Her own English was almost flawless, though with an accent. She introduced herself as a poet and essayist. She looked about twenty-five. Her manner was correct, but not warm, a northern Spaniard's business-like style. I was taken by her authoritative voice and long mane of dark hair and her very upright bearing. She had beautiful hands and her gestures were easy and yet forceful. She cut people in the audience off if they were rambling in their questions.

Afterwards I went up to her and, in Spanish, said how much I'd enjoyed the discussion, how important it was to hear voices from the Southern Hemisphere, and... She cut me off, just as if I were one of those irritating, too-wordy people in the audience, and said, in English, "You must be from the United States," and then I got an earful on hemispheric imperialism and how we called ourselves Americans and we should call ourselves North Americans. Several others on the panel stared at me in disapproval and I retreated. Useless to say I agreed with them about northern hegemony, and that I too was ambivalent about my (North) American heritage.

From then on, I generally avoided Vida. When I next heard anything about her, personal computers had come on the scene. She took to them right away, worked first selling Amstrads in a shop, and then opened a storefront for PC and Mac sales and repair in Stoke Newington. She was the expert of choice among some of my friends, but I went elsewhere for help.

What a long time ago that all was! I now couldn't imagine life without a laptop and a smart phone. Which reminded me of Nicky's last email.

Vonn's TV and laptop had been taken by someone who had entry to her flat. Was it simple theft to make a few quid, carried out on the quiet by someone in Vonn's building, or was it something more insidious, to do with Vonn's bank account or personal life.? Could it even have anything to do with the memoir she had tried to get Avery to represent? For surely Vonn would have had correspondence and files on the memoir. And if, as Avery suggested, there was some connection between Vonn and Fiona that was possibly upsetting to Fiona, perhaps there were others who might have realized they were in the memoir and who had reason to fear that past or even more recent secrets might come to light in that manuscript.

Could anyone from Vonn's past, for instance from Brize, have broken into her flat on hearing of her death, to take the laptop? More dramatically, could someone have caused her death in order to take her laptop?

I didn't know the particulars of Vonn's ousting from the publishing collective, and I didn't know anyone who'd been on the collective, except one acquaintance who'd lasted a week before walking out in frustration. Gayle would probably know, but I wondered if, since I had some time now on the train and there was wi-fi, I could find out more about Brize.

My curiosity was only partially rewarded. I did find out that the papers, catalogued and uncatalogued, of two other small feminist presses of the same era, Sheila and Womenonly, were housed at the Women's Liberation Movement archives at the London School of Economics, along with back issues of *Spare Rib,* a newspaper of the movement. But there was no mention of Brize and its records at LSE or at another archive in London, the feminist library in Peckham, which seemed to have collected masses of books, periodicals, and ephemera from the Women in Print era.

According to one of the few articles I could find about women's publishing back then, Brize only operated from 1982 to 1986. But otherwise Brize seemed to have existed and disappeared mainly beyond the ken of Wikipedia and other internet sites. I had forgotten it until recently. Brize had published relatively little. I might have one of their poetry anthologies, *Lesbian and Liking It,* in my bookshelf, but I doubted it. When Nicky sold the house in Hampstead and bought the flat in North Islington, I took the opportunity to donate or sell many of my once cherished feminist books. I suppose that others discarded those books too.

Another reason, perhaps, that Vonn's memoir was important—biased as it possibly was. It was a record of a time that was in danger of being quite forgotten. Ironic, since one of the missions of many of the women's presses of that era was to rediscover and republish women's writing from the past century or two that had been out of print for decades.

One search on the internet led to others and soon I was reading the British news—rain and flooding to the West and North—and after that, I dozed, only waking when we came into St. Pancras station.

It was late and I thought I'd better call Nicky, but her phone went to voicemail.

I hoped she remembered that I was coming in tonight and hadn't given my bed away to Gayle.

Nice as that thought was, Gayle was only separated from Vida. And Vida still made me nervous.

6.

It was after eight that evening when I arrived back at the Islington flat. I hoped that I might be able to have a cup of calming tea with Gayle and Nicky before slipping off to my bedroom.

No such luck. The flat was in familiar chaos as Nicky prepared for her trip to Copenhagen tomorrow. She was only going for a week and would mainly be inside rehearsal halls and concert venues. Nevertheless, she'd dragged out a staggering number of coats, hats, scarves, and boots from the big hall closet, as if she were outfitting herself for a polar expedition. Many of these garments lay strewn over the sofa in the living room, though she had put on one of the wool knit hats, red with white reindeer, and a big white bobble, perhaps to get in the mood. With her dark green sateen pajamas, she looked like a moving Christmas tree.

The upside of the chaos was that Nicky had located the *Beatrys* DVDs on a shelf in the hall closet, under a pile of heavy scarves.

In a corner of the sofa, under the warm golden light of a lamp, Gayle was reading a thin booklet that had been tucked into the boxed set. Its cover had a photo of the actor who'd played Beatrys, with a background of the archway into the beguinage of Bruges. Gayle too was in pajamas, flannel, with one of Nicky's big colorful scarves wrapped around her shoulders, and looked well settled in with a cup of tea and a small glass of whiskey. It seemed a long time since Nicky and I had had a visitor stay overnight. Nicky had always preferred to tryst in seaside hotels with room service. And I preferred to have my affairs with women in other countries.

I wanted to say something off the bat about being sorry about Vonn, but Gayle's reddened eyes warned me not to go there, at least quite yet.

"May I join you?"

"Have my drink," she said. "Nicky poured it for me but I'm better off with tea. How was your trip to Barcelona? I can't remember, were you only going to Barcelona?"

I sat down next to her on the sofa, shoving aside a once chic squirrel-fur boa that Nicky had inherited from her old friend and mentor Anna Wulf. I hoped that Nicky was not intending to wear this out of the house. It should have gone to Oxfam years ago, not that they would want to sell it in their store.

I took a sip of the whiskey, and it went down smoothly and warmed me. "I stopped for a night on the way back in Paris. Just to break the journey and have a nice meal."

It seemed unimportant to mention that I'd been reading Fiona's biography and that I'd had the strong desire to return via Bruges just to visit the beguinage and eat a bowl of *moules-frites*.

Instead, I told her about my Airbnb experience in the Barri Gòtic, making a joke of it, and a bit about my meetings with publishers. Gayle smiled once or twice, and her eyes almost disappeared. She had a way of tilting her head to listen that was always flattering. Still, she looked drawn and preoccupied. And why shouldn't she be preoccupied? Her ex-lover Vonn had apparently drowned herself. She had quarreled with her current lover, Vida, seriously enough to leave their home.

Nicky had removed her hat and plunged into an armchair, turning it forest green with her ample presence. "That's enough for tonight. I'll put some of this back in the closet and decide on my final attire for the morra. My flight's not until the afternoon. Tonight, Gayle's sleeping on the sofa, but we'll put her in my room in the morning."

"Oh, the sofa will be fine," said Gayle. "Really, I'm so grateful to you both. I have a lot to sort out, but I hope to find a new place soon. I've put out the word. And if push comes to shove, there's always my sister in Torquay."

I had questions about Vida and what had happened—but now was probably not the time to ask them. How long had they lived together? Had Vida thrown her out? Was this temporary or a final break? Without knowing the circumstances, purely based on my memory of Vida attacking me for being a North American, I was certain Vida must be in the wrong.

"You can stay here for as long as you like," said Nicky. "One of us is usually traveling, and there's always the sofa. You don't want to bury yourself in *Torquay*, Gayle. But let's not worry about that now. Let's watch an episode of *Beatrys* and take our minds off things. It's been years since I've seen this series."

The first disk was already in the DVD player: *Woven into Murder*. The opening credits showed a hooded woman in gray with a covered basket walking through a few streets of a medieval town. She approached and entered a stone entrance with the words *Sauvegarde* carved into its arch.

Following her inside, we saw an open meadow ringed by two-story, timbered houses, with some children running about and women carrying laundry and baskets of wool. The youngish woman slipped off the hood of her gray robe and we saw her head (coiled blonde hair) and her face (resolute, strongly featured). I'd seen this actor more recently on television, sometimes wearing a corset or a copper's stab vest, always looking both sympathetic and authoritative.

The murmur of women's voices in conversation was muted as the soundtrack of a women's choir soared. Next to me I saw Gayle smile. Somewhere in the plainchant she heard her voice.

Woven into Murder had a simple plot line: a dead body of a young man was found in a blood-soaked bundle of raw wool in a warehouse. Beatrys was a weaver at her own loom, living in a house owned by a wealthy beguine, Jeanne, who bought wool from England, and sold the finished product for a profit. Her house abutted a canal. There were flashbacks of how Beatrys came to the beguinage as a sixteen-year-old, running from an upcoming marriage arranged by her noble father. After she did not do well in the laundry, infirmary, or kitchen, she was taken in by the stern but kindly Jeanne and set to spinning and weaving. She proved to have a talent for it.

Beatrys also had a talent for sleuthing, as it turned out in this first episode. The young man stuffed into the bundle of wool was no one anyone admitted knowing. At first Beatrys believed the man might have been Jeanne's lover or even her son. The man had upon him certain papers that suggested he was named Robert, from England. He was in fact a friend of Jeanne's nephew, who had been living in London and acting as her wool-buying agent there. Robert had had to leave London in hurry after a duel that killed a man; he had fled to Bruges to ask Jeanne to protect him. There, in secret, he fell in love with the young beguine servant, Marie, who brought him food. It was Marie's father who stabbed and hid Robert's body. Marie's father then tried to put the blame on Jeanne.

It was up to Beatrys to untangle this, which she did in the time-honored ways of interviewing purported eyewitnesses, sifting through evidence (wool bales), following suspects, and eventually tracking down the killer and confronting him in front of his family. He tried to get away and fell into a canal, only to be rescued and led away to jail by a handsome young sheriff, who looked rather intently at Beatrys. There was more than a hint that in future Beatrys might have to decide whether she wanted to stay in the beguinage or to choose love outside its walls.

About halfway through, Nicky fell asleep in her chair for a while, waking up only at a shouting match between the sheriff and Marie's father near the end. With a groggy wave she staggered off to her own room and closed the door.

Gayle and I watched the video through and exchanged a few words at the end about it being too bad they had to bring in the sheriff at the end. Really, shouldn't the beguines have been able to deal with this murder mystery themselves?

Gayle stood up and began removing some of the scarves and coats from the sofa, which would be her bed tonight. She explained, "In later episodes, as Beatrys takes on more interesting cases and more responsibilities at the beguinage, she often has to decide whether to punish the villain or not. When a woman's the murderer, there's usually a reason—rape, unhappy marriage, jealousy—and sometimes Beatrys keeps the results of investigations quiet. She usually says, 'Her conscience will hurt her more than prison ever could.' Or something about the men perhaps having deserved to die. But the men who murder are usually hanged or at least dragged off by that sheriff. Bit of a double standard, I suppose."

I helped her make up the sofa, tucking sheets into the cushions and finding two pillows and a duvet. Gayle said again she was sorry for putting us to any inconvenience. "Nicky was so lovely when I called. She just said, come right over."

"It's no inconvenience," I said. "I'm happy you felt you could rely on us. You're always welcome. We're often coming and going, so sometimes you'd have an actual bed."

"I think it's a wonderful relationship the two of you have," she looked somber. "Vida is always so possessive. She always says it's important that we have our own friends, and she's kept her friends, but she didn't like it when I showed I was upset by Vonn's death and offered to help with packing up the apartment."

I kept my expression neutral. Indeed, it did seem possessive to worry about a partner's long-ago affair with an ex-girlfriend, especially when said ex was now dead.

Was there a chance that the possessiveness had begun before Vonn drowned?

"It must have been horrible for you," I said. "I mean, Vonn's death. It sounds like you got a call from Vonn's neighbor?"

"Yes, Kristi called me. Kristi remembered me from last year. Her son-in-law has a big van, and I'd hired him to help me move from one friend's cellar to a studio I was subletting. The police were at the flat and Kristi asked me to come over. They wanted to talk to friends of Vonn's. It was the first I knew. I was in shock, but I went over. Vida asked why they would call *me*. I don't know. I hadn't seen much of Vonn after I moved in with Vida last autumn." Gayle straightened the last of the bedding and then sat down on the duvet, as if her legs suddenly wouldn't support her. Her eyes filled with tears.

"The police were still talking to Kristi when I got there. They'd found pills in Vonn's cabinet, the muscle relaxants for her back, but also antidepressants. The vials had the phone number of Vonn's pharmacy and her doctor, who had prescribed them. Kristi had told them Vonn was not well, had had breast cancer, was depressed, had been depressed for at least six months about her health and her financial situation. She wasn't surprised that Vonn drowned herself. 'You could see it coming,' she said.

"I just started sobbing," said Gayle, and now her tears were falling hard at the memory. "I cried the whole time they were interviewing me. The police were truly kind. I said I hadn't seen too much of Vonn lately and that was true. Vida hadn't wanted me to continue my friendship with her after we moved in together. Vonn and I had a coffee before Christmas, and she did seem down, but not unreasonably. It was the holidays, mostly, I thought. In January I talked with her on the phone a couple of times. She seemed fine."

I sat down beside Gayle, tentatively, and took her hands in my mine. They were small and very cold. "Did the police tell you the details?"

"I asked. Because, unlike Kristi, I couldn't believe that she would have committed suicide. I was convinced it was an accident. I still think it must have been accidental. That for some crazy reason she'd gone swimming in the evening. People do that sometimes, even after the Ladies' Pond is closed for the day. A few years ago, a woman photographer who had a heart condition slipped under the water at the Pond without the lifeguards noticing and drowned. I thought maybe the same thing happened to Vonn. Not at the Ladies' Pond, but at the wildlife refuge right near there that's called the Bird Sanctuary Pond."

"Did she have a heart condition?"

"No, but she had severe back pain. Her back would seize up. She started swimming to strengthen her body after the mastectomies. The back pain was long-standing, from working at the computer, but it had gotten worse."

"So you thought her back might have seized up while she was swimming at night?"

"Yes, but then they told me that she was fully dressed, jeans, jumper, even a jacket. They'd know more after the postmortem, they said. I don't know if they ever decided whether there was intent or not, but they wrapped up the case in less than a week and released the body."

"Did they find a note or anything on her?"

"No. I think more than anything they relied on what Kristi said. Kristi wasn't a friend exactly, but she saw Vonn nearly every day, since she lived down the hall. The coppers were respectful, I'll give them that. They asked me about Vonn's personal life, her family, who they should contact. I didn't even know that. I could see that they thought Vonn's life was sad and lonely, an old lesbian living alone, breast cancer survivor, bad back, prescription pain pills, antidepressants, living on a state pension and the odd freelance editing job. She was seventy-three. One of them said to me, 'We see this with older people sometimes, they just don't want to go on.'" Gayle leaned against my chest, in her printed flannel pajamas, and whimpered. "I just couldn't believe she was dead, but I had to believe it."

I shuddered at the picture of the police in Vonn's flat, at their kindness to Gayle, at their assumption that a lesbian in her seventies would be depressed and lonely enough to kill herself. But how did that square with the Vonn I'd glimpsed at the lecture, the scruffy woman in the leather jacket, hungrily eating shortbread, nonchalantly grinning at Avery?

"So that's the end of the investigation, is it?" I said. "Probable suicide. No further inquiry. Case closed?"

"I feel so helpless," she said. "I went back to Vida's after meeting with the police, but I couldn't keep my mind off Vonn. Vida acted strangely, I thought. She asked me if I was still in love with Vonn. She said there was something odd about the whole thing. I almost felt she knew something she wasn't telling me. Two days later Kristi called again and asked if I'd help her clean out the flat."

Gayle pulled away from my damp shirt and wiped her eyes with her hand. "Vida didn't want me to take that on. She said it would just make everything harder for me. She asked if I was hiding something. But I did go over to the flat. That's when Kristi and I discovered that the laptop had gone missing. I feel guilty."

"Guilty?"

"I should have been a better friend to Vonn."

"We all think that when someone we care about dies, especially when it might be suicide. It's not about us, it's about their pain. Of course, sometimes, people are killed by other people. That's a different story."

"Nicky said you've helped in some investigations over the years, even a murder case. I remember you got her off the hook in Venice once."

I smiled thinking about the case of the missing antique bassoon, and said, "That was a long time ago. Anyway, most of the cases I've been involved in, accidentally, mind you, have involved crimes other than murder. Theft, for instance. But I'm the rankest of amateurs." I paused. "You're not suggesting that Vonn's death was murder?"

"No!" Gayle said. "Nobody is saying that. The journalist who swims at the Pond was really clear that the postmortem report says Vonn drowned on her own." Her eyes filled with tears again. "I didn't just go over to Vonn's because I felt guilty for neglecting our friendship, but because I feel responsible for keeping something of her work, her spirit, her best qualities alive. That's what I told Vida. I thought eventually we should have a memorial gathering for Vonn, a small one. For now I want to box up her papers. There are things worth saving for lesbian history. They should go to an archive."

I didn't want to get involved. Nevertheless, I asked if there was anything I could do.

Gayle looked at me gratefully. "Yes, you could come over tomorrow and help a former collective member, Amina, with organizing what's in Vonn's file cabinets. Amina thinks that there's a feminist archive in Bristol that would be interested."

I nodded. "Of course."

"Thanks, Cassandra. Kristi's arranged with her son-in-law to cart some of the furniture away. The police are finished with their work, and after the burglary the landlord changed the locks. He wants it emptied and painted, so he can rent it out again. Unsentimental sod." She made a wry face. "If it were someone else's flat, I'd probably ask if I could rent it myself. I like that neighborhood."

"You got to know it when you were in your relationship with Vonn?"

She didn't answer directly. "My friend Charlotte lived in that building, and *she* was involved with Vonn. I used to visit her, and I'd run into Vonn. A year or so later, when Vonn started writing copy for the Tudor Roses, that was when Vonn and I—and Lu and Sara—started up. I used to spend time at Vonn's place occasionally. Charlotte was long gone by then. Oh God, it's incredible to think about those days when we were all in and out of each other's beds. Impossible to remember those days without *rue*. That's a good word, isn't it? Not used as a noun anymore, and hardly as a verb. It comes from the Old English, *hrēow*. Sorrow."

A Tudor Rose would know that.

I gave her a hug and didn't allow myself to think about the small soft body in the flannel pajamas. Then I went into my room and closed the door. Everything was the same after her two nights here and she'd obviously washed or changed the sheets. But the fragrance of another person lingered a little in the pillow and the duvet.

Gayle's fragrance. Rose and citrus with a deeper note of rue.

7.

Vonn's street off the Caledonian Road north of King's Cross hadn't yet seen the effects of gentrification that had infected other parts of this district. The rows of three-story brick blocks had aluminum windows, and bars over those on the ground floor. There were trees in some nearby streets, but not on Vonn's, just some scraggly, barren bushes planted in gravel in the pocket-sized front gardens. But the rainstorm of last night had blown itself out, and the early March sunshine brightened the shared entry hall of the building. Inside I could see bikes and prams, and some children's crayon drawings on one of the doors, as well as a political poster.

I pushed the buzzer and Gayle let me in, directing me upstairs to the flat. As I approached, I heard a strident voice through the half-opened door: "Wouldn't surprise me one bit if those boys on the third nipped down and took the telly and everything. They're only twelve and thirteen, but they're going the way of their parents. Smoking dope all day, claiming they work at home. Kids have no supervision, don't even go to school half the time. I told the police, but I doubt they did anything, they don't care."

"Hello, Cassandra!" Gayle said and looked relieved to see me, as I came in. "This is Kristi, from a couple of doors down."

Kristi was a sharp-eyed woman with high, arched brows. Her tinted pink hair was pulled back into a thin little ponytail, so her ears, hooped with silver, protruded like milk pitcher handles. A disappointed mouth was outlined on each side by a groove, and these grooves of disillusionment contrasted strongly with the eyebrows, which were merely surprised. She was mid-forties, I guessed, with a figure that, as my mother used to say, only makes trouble for a girl. That is, she had long legs and large breasts under a slightly too small yellow jumper.

"Come to help, have you?" she nodded. "That's good. Little Gayle here can't do it all herself. I'd be working alongside her, but I've got

49

the grandbaby to watch over, haven't I? My daughter had to get back to work and so it's Mum to the rescue. This is the kind of thing family should do, isn't it?"—she gestured to bags and boxes in the flat. "But poor old Vonn, not a relative in the world apparently, except that cousin of hers in Brisbane, and *he's* not coming all the way over to sort things, is he?"

The questions tacked on to Kristi's comments were largely rhetorical, so I just nodded back and said with as much cheerful resolution as I could muster, "Where shall I start, Gayle? The desk, maybe?"

"That'd be lovely, thanks." Gayle was wearing a loose, halter-style apron printed with spoons and forks that made her look like a housewife from the fifties. She added, "It looks worse than it is, but we should be able to get some of this moved out today. The clothes to Oxfam and some of the furniture too. Amina is coming by soon to get things into boxes for the archives."

"Well, I'll be off then," said Kristi. "Neville should be by around three with his van to load things up for the charity stores, whatever you've got ready. He doesn't charge much, but some pub money wouldn't come amiss."

With a wave she was off. "Don't work too hard," she advised.

"Heart of gold," said Gayle, uncertainly. "That is, I think she was genuinely sorry to hear about Vonn. They'd been neighbors for several years, ever since Kristi arrived as an unexpected widow. Her husband died in a motorway crash, turned out he'd never made the insurance payments and had a load of debt. It's Kristi's opinion that Vonn was on the point of death from a new cancer diagnosis. That's what she told the police anyway. Her stories have become more dramatic as the days have gone on."

"Does Kristi look like the kind of person Vonn would confide in?"

"To be honest, she looks like the kind of person Vonn would avoid," said Gayle. "For one thing, those poor boys upstairs. It's pretty clear Kristi used this as an opportunity to accuse them of theft." She made a face. "There really wasn't much here to take of any value. The telly was old, and the radio/boom box was from a million years ago. Vonn was old-fashioned in her technology, she only had a flip phone. It was only recently that she got a new laptop, she told me when I saw her around Christmas. Her printer is still here—probably too bulky and old to knick."

"What happened to the flip phone?" I asked. "I suppose she had it on her when she... went into the pond?"

"I don't know. I guess she would have. The police identified her through her wallet in her pocket. I don't think they dredged the pond." Gayle looked around, "I'm almost sorry whoever burgled the place didn't take some of the furniture and household goods. It's a chore deciding what to do with everything."

It was easy to agree. The flat was a chaos of boxes of books, clothes, utensils, and the sad plastic detritus of modern life. A well-worn futon sofa, ungainly side tables and dressers, some bookshelves, and lamps were piled and pushed into corners. The kitchen table, of painted wood, was buried under saucepans and crockery. There was no separate office, only a largish bedroom where she slept and worked. Besides the double bed, shoved into a corner, there was a sturdy wooden desk, with drawers, a table for the printer, and two black metal filing cabinets. On the walls was a paper calendar and some old posters from the seventies and eighties, including one that demanded: SISTERS: QUESTION EVERY ASPECT OF OUR LIVES. RECOGNISE AND FIGHT AGAINST EVERYDAY OPPRESSION. Her calendar was still on February. Most days were empty.

I walked over to the file cabinets and Gayle followed. "One of them is mostly personal and editorial work. The police looked for a will and didn't find one. It looks like she had modest savings and a reasonable amount of money in her checking account. I suppose the cousin will get it eventually, or the Inland Revenue. The cousin arranged for the cremation. That's already happened. It's a bit weird, but there was nothing we could do. The cousin didn't see any need to fly to London, said the police. Vonn never mentioned family in Australia. I did know her parents had died years ago, but it seems an uncle went out to Australia and married, so Vonn must have been minimally in touch with them. Not enough obviously for them to care she's dead. So, it's up to us, her lesbian friends, to make sure her things are treated decently, and at least some of her papers are preserved."

I felt the chill of mortality land squarely on the back of my neck like a cold, wet towel. Is this what it would all come to? Once-beloved clothes in piles and a filing cabinet drawer of invoices marked "paid"? None of my relatives in Michigan were likely to want to fly to London to see me to the grave. The family members I'd liked best, my older sister and one of my aunts, were long dead now.

Gail had been here on and off for several days, so she must know the feeling very well. She pointed to the taller of the two cabinets. "That's the one with her editorial work, as well as material from the Brize collective days. Amina is going to put it all in shipping boxes and see that it gets to Corinne in Bristol. Amina and Corinne were members of the collective once. There are another few shoe boxes in the closet. I haven't looked in them yet."

She pointed to the second, two-drawer file cabinet, and opened the top drawer slightly. "This is what I'd like you to look through, her business files, see if there's anything worth saving for the archives."

"How will I tell, what's worth saving?" I asked.

"I'm not sure. There's correspondence mixed with the invoices. Maybe some of that should be saved."

I nodded, following Gayle back into the living room. I wondered if her correspondence with Avery would have a folder. Could Vonn have kept a copy of any threatening letters she wrote to Fiona?

"How do you just walk away from your life like that?" Gayle asked. "Knowing other people will paw through your things, make assumptions, judge you and find you pathetic?"

"I don't think Vonn was pathetic," I said, perhaps more firmly than I meant. After all, I hardly knew the woman. "She was a feisty, strong voice in her day. It's just that her day passed."

"It didn't ever really pass, for Vonn," said Gayle, looking at the posters. "Maybe not for any of us. Seriously, wouldn't you rather be twenty-five again and marching in the streets arm-in-arm?"

I couldn't answer that. I didn't live much in the past myself, but in a present world of deadlines and projects that stretched a few years into the future. When I stopped having deadlines, I'd likely be dead.

"Vonn wasn't herself when she died," I tried to reassure Gayle. "You told me yourself, they said she had some medication in her system. So likely Vonn was impaired that night. She might not have intended to drown herself. After all, there's no note. Maybe she had some idea of swimming, and forgot she was dressed."

Gayle nodded, tears welling. I wondered if she always cried this easily, or if her feelings for Vonn were stronger and more persistent than she had let on. The first time she'd told me and Nicky about her youthful affair with Vonn, she'd treated her rejection light-heartedly. But what if, when she and Vonn had reconnected a couple of years ago at the Ladies'

Pond, the spark had returned? How did Vida fit into this picture? Why did Vida find Gayle being upset about Vonn's death suspicious?

We made ourselves some tea in the kitchen and went back out into the living room. The mid-day light came in through the streaked and spotted windows with the blinds pulled up to the top but askew. The drapes had been taken down and lay in faded heaps on the floor nearby.

I said I'd go through the one file cabinet carefully, sorting out the financial records and medical reports and putting them in a stack on the desk and the editorial work in another pile. If I found anything interesting, I'd let Gayle know. What I was really curious about was what happened to the manuscript of her book. I asked Gayle if she'd seen it anywhere in the apartment.

She shook her feathery white curls and sipped the hot tea with milk. Her round, sweet face was blotchy from the tear storm. "No, though I've not searched for it or anything. I think the file cabinet with the Brize folders is mainly old stuff from years ago. It could be there."

"But you're sure there *was* a manuscript?"

"She was working on something to do with Brize and that whole time period. I don't know how far along she was with it. Vonn didn't want to say too much, but she thought people would be shocked by a few things in the book." Gayle paused. "It's always possible she hadn't really written that much. She was more of an editor. She liked to work on other people's manuscripts. She once told me that her ideas only came when she had someone else's words to correct."

"Could it have been on her laptop? Is it possible that anyone took the laptop because they felt threatened?" I was thinking of Fiona, but there could be others. "You said that Vonn suggested there was something shocking in it?"

"Vonn's idea of shocking was probably that someone at Brize was only pretending to be working-class." Gayle sighed. "I really doubt there was anything in the book that would have been a real exposé, or that by now anyone would care."

"If the memoir has to do with Brize and publishing, maybe it's in the file cabinet with other Brize materials."

"Yes, maybe. I can't stop to look now, but Amina can go through it all when she boxes it up. Thanks, Cassandra. Thanks so much for your steadiness. I've been on edge with everything lately." She looked at me with her narrowed brown eyes and tilted her head a little, and I remembered how taken with her elfin looks I'd been once. The feelings weren't all gone, and I didn't think they were gone for Gayle either.

The door buzzed from the street. "Oh, that's probably Amina!" she said.

"What's with the pink-haired bitch in the hallway?" said Amina as she came in. "She gave me the evil eye when she saw me coming upstairs."

Gayle shook her head and did not say anything feeble about "heart of gold," but explained, "Neighbor with a son-in-law who's going to cart off a lot of furniture later today and sell it or donate it. Kristi's the self-appointed security guard."

"Keep her away from me, do me a favor." Amina stared around, "Crickey, there's a lot here." And then to me, "Hiya, I'm Amina, from the old days."

"Cassandra. Also from the old days."

Amina had held up better than I had if she was in her sixties. Pale gold skin, straight white hair, parted on the side and cut asymmetrically to show one ear, a working woman's suit, and low heels. She carried a shoulder bag with a smartphone sticking out of the side pocket, and which vibrated quietly from time to time. Gayle had said Amina was in finance.

"Well, darling," she said to Gayle. "This is a right old mess, Vonn drowned, and you left with all this to handle. I'm glad you called me. I let Corinne know and she's thrilled to take the Brize files. The women's archive in Bristol is just the place for them, she says, and she'll make sure they're tidy and organized before they go to the archive."

"It's really good of you to come over and deal with them," said Gayle. "There's packing material and shipping boxes in the bedroom. I know Vonn would appreciate it."

"Oh, I'm not doing this for Vonn, pet. I'm glad to help, but it's because Brize was, among its many failings, an experiment that brought a lot of women from different backgrounds together. It's for lesbian herstory that I want to help."

Gayle said, "I understand. I want that too."

"Lead me to the remains of the day," Amina said.

"Cassandra can show you," Gayle said. "I'd better keep on with the clothing. I thought I'd give some of it away to friends, but no one wanted anything. I suppose it's too strange to wear the clothes of someone who's just died." She looked at me and held up a pair of short boots in bronze leather. "She has some nice boots, Cassandra."

"She was shorter than me," I said. Inside I shuddered with the memory of Vonn at Fiona's lecture. Those were exactly the boots she'd worn.

8.

"Right," said Amina, taking off her jacket, and rolling up her cuffs, so that several thin gold bracelets and a small watch were visible.

"What's your connection to Vonn?" she asked me, as she opened the first drawer and began flipping through the hanging files with a ringed and polished finger. I was fascinated by her combination of no-nonsense efficiency and elegance. Neither of which I associated with what I knew of the Brize collective.

"Almost none," I admitted. "I know Gayle and she needed some help. I'm supposed to sort through these files and make a stab at deciding what should be recycled and what should be saved. It's mostly her editorial business side, I gather."

"Oh, so you don't know much about Vonn and feminist publishing?"

"Yes and no. I'm a translator. I did cross paths with Vonn, but I mainly saw or rather heard her from afar, with her raised voice. She had a reputation, but you'd know all about that. In those days I was traveling a lot and when I came to London, I was usually scrabbling to meet editors and publishers who could offer real money. Not many women's presses had budgets for translators, certainly not Brize."

As I was speaking, I'd been emptying one of the cabinet drawers, and putting the folders in a pile on the desk. Statements from a bank account that showed regular deposits from the state pension and regular payments for rent and utilities. Her savings amounted to only a few thousand pounds. For now, I set them aside. I was more interested in her editorial correspondence and copies of invoices sent, especially anything that might link her to Fiona or Stella. But I could only find folders dating back five or six years, and most of them were boringly professional. Vonn mainly did copyediting. The last year it appeared she'd done very little freelance work at all.

"American, are you?" Amina kept flipping through the files with her ringed fingers.

"Yes, but I've not lived there since I was about twenty. I go there from time to time for different reasons. It seems a scarier place these days. And yet it's home too, so very much home that I'm surprised each time."

"I've never been to Pakistan without feeling I belong," she laughed a little. "That lasts about a week and then I want to run like the devil. I was born here, my mum and dad moved here to study and stayed. But the older relatives are there, so we had to visit Lahore at least once a year when I was a kid. I wasn't too popular when I came out at seventeen. They didn't exactly disown me in Milton Keynes, but let's say I wasn't welcome at holiday dinners for a very long time. The uncles and aunties weren't supposed to know or we'd all be disgraced."

"It's funny it's always about protecting the relatives," I said. "My Irish-American family was the same. My mum said it was a sin, but she would still love me, especially if I never acted on my feelings and strived to overcome them. But granny must never know. It would kill her."

"Hard burden to carry," Amina cracked a smile. "Murdering a load of relatives through simply saying the word lesbian." She went on to the second drawer, for now merely ascertaining the extent of what was there. "Oh, goodness, this brings back memories," she said. "Meeting notes!"

"How long were you part of the collective?"

"Not so long, six months? I was studying at the LSE and feeling a bit isolated and fed up, and a Black girl I knew took me along to one of Brize's work parties to fix up some hovel or other in Shoreditch as an office space. And wow: lesbians like me, Devi from India, Glo from Jamaica, Corinne, Caribbean-Canadian from Toronto. White girls too, the untidy, short-haired kind like Vonn and one rabid separatist from Dusseldorf. With *no hair* on her head, but a lot under her arms. Frightening, but kind of exciting. I didn't know anything about publishing, but they were thrilled I was studying international finance. They needed a bookkeeper, they said."

She sighed and closed the drawer. "I thought collectives were something from Stalin's time. So I got an education. At first, mind-blowing! No hierarchy, decisions by consensus, everybody gets a say. Class, race, gender arguments and debates. I'd missed out on a lot of that discussion growing up where I did and how I did. I learned. But I also learned you can't say everything you think. The white women really didn't want to hear it."

"Including Vonn?"

"Actually, she sorta kinda did recognize racism, I mean as a structure, not just a personal shortcoming. I think she did have a real vision of inclusion and diversity. Said so, anyway. But, no, lesbianism was her thing, everything through that prism. I remember when she found out Corinne was seeing a man, Vonn hit the roof. How could Corinne sleep with the enemy, act of betrayal and so forth. Corinne, who was committed to the collective, left in tears after that meeting and never came back. Glo went with her, in solidarity, though she was a dyke through and through." Amina moved on to the third drawer. "And I'm embarrassed to admit, I didn't run after Corinne that day, though later we became good friends. I was sort of brainwashed for a bit. I wanted to believe lesbianism was a brave new world, and those who didn't pay the full subscription should be canceled."

By now I had all the files out on the desk and was putting some to the side and others in a box for recycling or for Gayle to look at.

"Oh, golly," said Amina, "Here's a goldmine of trouble. The Triple L project. There's practically a whole drawer about it!"

"Triple L?"

"It was an anthology without a title," said Amina, pulling out some folders and setting them on the mattress, since I'd already laid out Vonn's business files on top of the desk. "Lives of Lesser-Known Lesbians" was the subtitle, but we soon started calling it The Triple L. I was there at the beginning but not at the end. Because it had no end. It was never published. It was too big a project. It was too messy a project. And its main editor, Vonn, was kicked off the collective midway through the process."

I went over to look as Amina continued to pile all the folders from the drawer on the bed. Folders with names like "Willa Cather," "Gertrude and Alice," "Ethel Smythe," and "Lorraine Hansberry," but also with names I'd never heard of.

"The book came out of a brainstorming session," Amina said, sitting down on the bed and opening some of the folders. "We needed to know more about lesbians of the past and tell their stories. A common theme then, right? Lesbian visibility, lesbian herstory. Over about two years, maybe more, it went through various stages and editors and advisers, depending on who was in the collective at the time. Vonn was always one of the editors. Initially the idea was to go back as far as possible in time, to Sappho, but at other times the focus went to the twentieth century, to include a broader number of women. The call would go out, women would be invited to write a few pages about different figures, then the submissions and suggestions would be talked about in special Triple L meetings."

I sat down on the bed for a minute as she made her neat piles. "I think I remember that anthology," I said. "At least I remember a couple of friends of mine who thought they were being invited to contribute and wrote something, and then it was mailed back to them with a brisk form letter, as 'not what we are looking for.'"

"Yeah, the suggestions were all over the place and the criteria kept changing. There were endless discussions about who exactly could be called a lesbian, especially back in the past when lesbians were not recognized as such or didn't identify as lesbian in the way we did in the eighties. What about bisexuals, like Colette or Bessie Smith, or closeted women? Vonn was adamant she didn't want "dilettante lesbians," whatever they were. So Virginia Woolf was out and so was Eleanor Roosevelt. Radclyffe Hall was in, definitely, except she was hardly lesser known. Romaine Brooks and Natalie Barney were in then out. Nobody wanted a book solely about upper-class and middle-class white women writers and artists, but the lives of the lesser-known lesbians weren't very well documented, especially outside Britain. Eventually some of those suggestions became articles for newspapers like *Spare Rib* or even stand-alone novels or nonfiction books. Cross-dressing sailors, society ladies, working girls, suffragettes."

"You say that Vonn was ousted before it was finished. But why didn't the other women in the collective carry it out?"

"Because there wasn't anyone with such a steamroller personality, and probably the fights had exhausted them. Remember, no one was getting paid at Brize. You were supposed to work in exchange for getting experience in publishing or for the greater good. I'd already left before Vonn was voted out. After she was gone, one by one, women left for real jobs. A couple joined Sheila Press, a truly diverse group that actually published books and good ones."

"But Vonn never came back."

"No, it was too bitter a rejection. Or maybe she realized she needed to make a living and it wasn't economically feasible."

"Still, she ended up with all the files of Brize."

"Yes, I hadn't quite realized that," said Amina. "I didn't really think about what happened with Brize after it closed up shop. But Vonn must have cared enough to save everything."

I stared down at the folders from the Triple L anthology, wondering if I should say anything about Vonn's memoir that apparently told stories of feminist publishing in the old days. Did the past members of the Brize collective know Vonn was writing it? Would anyone have wanted to stop the memoir from being published? I didn't have time to read through all this stuff, strangely fascinating though it might be.

"Here's one example I remember," said Amina, handing me a folder with the tab subject *The Lieutenant Nun*. "We ended up discussing this contribution for an *entire* meeting. Basically, the argument was about the definition of lesbianism, particularly in centuries past. The crucial question to ask about pre-twentieth-century lesbians was: Had a woman lived openly with another woman or was she known to have loved women? Obviously, there were going to be some women who had worn male clothing and a few who had taken on a male persona. Vonn seemed okay with that. But then this submission came in about a convent girl from seventeenth-century Spain who escaped the convent right before she took vows. She chopped off her hair and dressed as a man, and eventually went to fight in South America. She romanced various ladies, maybe even got married. I remember that meeting well, because Vonn was outnumbered by those of us who argued that this nun was just the kind of 'Lesser-known Lesbian' we wanted, but Vonn still prevailed. Sometimes she could be reasonable, but often she was totally scorched earth. As a result, lesbians who were too 'male-identified' were expressly to be left out of the anthology."

This story about the Lieutenant Nun rang a bell somehow, but I couldn't place it. As a Spanish translator it seemed like the sort of thing I should know.

"Oh, Corinne's going to be well pleased," Amina said, looking around for the packing materials that Gayle had had delivered, the flattened boxes, the tape, the labels. "She'll get it sorted and annotated. I know she'll do a proper job. She'll have a good laugh too. She'll remember that badass Lieutenant Nun!"

I hated to see the Brize files all going straight into the shipping boxes, but I wasn't sure how to intervene. If Amina didn't tape them up, perhaps I could look through them again after she left. "I wonder if

Vonn's personal correspondence should go to Bristol," I said gesturing to the editorial files on the desk. "I should probably go through them a bit and see what's there, especially if it relates to publishing. If you leave your boxes open, I could just toss them in."

"Righto," she said, working quickly now.

From the other room, I heard the street door buzzer and Gayle on the phone to someone outside. Her voice rose, in some panic. "But I'm not ready," she said. "You're two hours early. Well, then, come up."

I went into the living room to find Gayle near tears.

"It's that bloody son-in-law, Neville. Kristi told me he was coming at three for the furniture and it's barely one thirty. He's got two mates with him, and they're double-parked, so I can't put him off."

"But the furniture's ready to go, isn't it?"

"Yes, I suppose so. But not the desk and bed and cabinets, where you and Amina are working."

"He'll just have to come back then," I said, but as Neville and his large mates barged through the door, I reconsidered. Maybe it would be better to get it over and done with.

Gayle looked at me for help, and I could see she was emotionally exhausted.

"Neville, is it?" I said. "Take the furniture, and there's a bed and desk too, in the bedroom, but we need at least twenty minutes to finish our work there."

I went back to the bedroom, where Amina was busily dumping the contents of the file cabinets into boxes, and I followed her example, hastily piling all the financial records in one box, all the editorial and personal correspondence in another. I cleared the desk and shoved my two boxes in a corner. By the time Neville came to the bedroom, Amina had filled six shipping boxes, and was looking at her phone.

"Sorry," she said. "I've got an appointment at two I must get to. Can I drop you anywhere? I've got my car. I can come back later and finish labeling and taping the boxes for Corinne."

I was tempted to jump into a car with Amina and be carried far away from Caledonian Road and the dusty files and old clothing of a dead woman, but I felt I shouldn't desert Wee Gayle. She was looking more and more worn out by the shouting up and down the stairs about watching corners and by the occasional thump as a wooden object crashed into a wall.

Amina pressed a cool cheek next to mine. "Good to meet you, Cassandra. See you later if you're still here." She walked out past Neville without giving him a glance.

I wished I could follow her. Instead, I hovered in the bedroom as the burly young men, who seemed to have no experience moving furniture except by groaning and punching their fists, before grasping the object in the most illogical place, carted out the mattress and frame, the desk, and file cabinets, whose drawers banged open and shut with a sound like a coffin closing. The bottom drawer still had a single file folder left inside way at the back, that Amina hadn't seen.

I grabbed the folder quickly and set it on the windowsill behind a dusty Venetian blind. "Leave all the boxes," I said. "It's just the furniture and file cabinets you're taking."

You can see how easily lesbian history could vanish. Into the double-parked van of Kristi's son-in-law Neville.

After Neville and his friends had left, and the battered furniture was finally out of the flat and the building, Gayle put the kettle on, and we opened a package of crisps and sat on a couple of throw rugs in the much emptier living room. Even with the drapes in piles on the floor and blinds open, it was exceedingly dreary. The walls were splotched from where pictures had hung and corners that hadn't been dusted in years.

I had somehow expected this day to be more convivial, with old friends of Vonn's coming and going and bringing snacks and wine, but what friends there were had come yesterday, leaving Gayle to do most of the work. Even Amina had been here hardly more than an hour and a half.

"I didn't find anything in Vonn's papers that looked suspicious," I said. "The recent bank statements and bills don't show anything but someone without a lot of extra income. There's no legal paperwork at all, just a passport and birth certificate. I only glanced at the medical records. She seemed to be seeing her doctor a lot over the winter, different blood tests and a couple of prescriptions. Aside from a few notes about depression, there's nothing to indicate she'd had a recurrence of cancer."

"That was probably just Kristi's vivid imagination. I don't honestly think, even if Vonn were really ill, that she'd tell Kristi."

"I'm going to take another look through the personal files, and then you can decide if you're going to recycle."

"Right," said Gayle. "I owe you, Cassandra."

"Oh, don't worry about it," I said. A cup of tea had helped. I'd do what I promised and then leave.

I hadn't seen what Amina was tossing in the shipping boxes. Back in Vonn's old bedroom-office, I flipped briefly through the folders myself. What had seemed promising turned out to be mundane. The Brize collective had documented their meetings extensively with all the jargon of the era about heterosexual privilege and lesbian space.

There was correspondence with would-be authors and authors, some of which, at a glance, looked quite vitriolic. A sample: "After waiting two years to see my poetry book in print, I now get a letter from 'members of the collective' claiming that 'your priorities' have changed and that you are no longer interested in my work. That the poems were acquired by someone who is no longer on the collective. Fuck you, you Brize bitches, whoever you are now!"

Vonn's business correspondence from the other file cabinet was more courteous but not very enlightening. I hesitated to recycle too much since there could still be something I was missing, so I just taped shut the two boxes I'd already filled, and left Amina's for her to do. I wrote a quick note to Amina, thanking her, and asking her if she could give Gayle Corinne's email address for me.

I was about to leave when I recalled that Gayle had mentioned a few shoeboxes in the closet. There were two. One held a hodgepodge of office supplies not used much anymore, a dried-up bottle of the correction fluid Tippex, an envelope knife and hole-puncher, along with a couple of floppy disks and strangely, a fork. The diskettes were the small, hard kind, not floppy at all; one of them was labeled "Editorial Work 1997-2002" and the other "Editorial Correspondence." I wouldn't be able to read them on my laptop but decided to put them in my jeans pocket anyway.

The second shoebox was larger, outdoor-boot size, and I lifted its lid, hoping that there could be something there, like an envelope with a manuscript. It only held some nondescript sex toys that looked like they hadn't been used in quite a few years, and a small red case marked First Aid. I did open that, thinking it could have been a hiding place for drugs or other paraphernalia, but it merely had some over-the-counter allergy pills, Paracetamol, and Band-Aids. I left the box for Gayle to deal with. What could be sadder or braver somehow than an old dyke's sex toys and unused Band-Aids?

I felt tears prick my eyes, and I wiped them away, glancing at the March sky, now overcast, through the grimy Venetian blind. On the window sill I saw the folder I'd snatched from the back of the file cabinet when Neville and his mates were here.

This file wasn't labeled on the tab, but inside were two typed sheets titled "Possible table of contents," with a long list of the names of lesser-known lesbians and the contributors. At the top was a hand-written date, June 8, 1985, and some of the names and/or contributors were also crossed out or added to in blue ink.

I recognized several of the lesbians proposed as subjects. Lesser known they might be but, all these years later, some were no longer completely unknown. Some, in fact, had had their stories filmed, like nineteenth-century English diarist Anne Lister. In these times of gender fluidity, cross-dressing meant little. But what struck me, as I stood there in Vonn's empty bedroom, were two names, both in the contributor column: Stella Terwicker and Vida Carrasco.

Vida's name was attached to "The Lieutenant Nun," though both her name and that of the nun had been scratched out. Stella's proposed contribution, "The Passion of the Saints: Perpetua and Felicity," had been left in the list, with someone's notes in faded blue pen: "fascinating, North Africans, mauled by animals in arena, beheaded, lovers."

This was the first real proof I had that Stella might have been queer. And the first proof that she and Vonn could have known each other before the Beatrys mysteries made Stella famous.

9.

A few days passed. Nicky sent a selfie. Wearing her heavy coat and a knit hat, she stood next to a statue of the Little Mermaid with a shawl of snow. Gayle continued to sleep in Nicky's bedroom and to spend much of the day in Vonn's flat, sorting through household things for Neville to take another day. Gayle didn't mention the shoe box of old sex toys, so maybe those went in a bag to a more discreet rubbish bin somewhere. The boxes of files had been shipped to Corinne in Bristol.

I didn't go back to Vonn's to help Gayle after that first day. In fact, it now struck me as odd that Gayle was devoting so much time to dealing with Vonn's possessions when her own, presumably, were still sitting in Vida's house in Stoke Newington. I imagined it was a form of displaced energy, or even a form of grieving for her own youth and for what she'd had with Vonn. I could see why Gayle felt a certain responsibility to sort through the files and books, but to wash the cupboards and floors? It wasn't as if the landlord was going to give a cleaning deposit back to a dead woman. It took a passing comment from Gayle about "what the landlord is expecting," for me to realize that he was probably paying her for the cleaning. I was pained to see my own blindness here. I knew any number of lesbians who had never saved a penny after years of working for arts groups or political nonprofits. Gayle came from the middle class, but as was the case with many women in history and literature, gentility without marriage equaled straitened circumstances. Maybe she'd saved something, probably not much.

Meanwhile, having seen the contents of Vonn's files, I seemed to be affected by the urge to organize myself. I'd prided myself on traveling light most of my life. I'd once had possessions scattered in several countries, but now almost everything was condensed to this room in the Islington flat, with a few boxes in the storage area of the cellar.

My desk wasn't cluttered with cords. I had a laptop and wireless printer, and I replaced the laptop every two or three years, simply transferring the contents of the hard drive from one new machine to the next, saving the old laptop for a while and then recycling it. My files on projects past and current were in a three-drawer filing cabinet, though I couldn't recall the last time I had gone through the bottom drawer to get rid of things. So for an hour or so one day, during a break in my translation work, I pulled out folders of projects long finished and put them in the recycling bin.

They were as boring as what had been in Vonn's business files, which the archive in Bristol would probably dump as soon as they received them. They'd be interested in Brize, of course.

That reminded me of the table of contents of the anthology of "Lives of Lesser-Known Lesbians," which I'd folded and tucked into my pocket. I hadn't told Gayle I'd kept it but had asked her the day I was at the flat if Vonn and Vida had known each other.

"Probably, a bit," she said. "The way we all know each other or of each other. Our generation anyway."

"But was Vida connected to Brize in some way?" I pushed a bit harder. "As a writer or anything back in the old days?"

"I don't think so," Gayle said, with a slight frown, as if trying to remember. "Vida did write poetry once and tried a bit of translation from Spanish. But that's long ago."

I tucked the list of possible contributions and their authors to the never finished Triple L anthology in my desk, along with the unreadable diskettes. On the internet I looked up the Lieutenant Nun, Catalina de Erauso, born in 1650 in the Basque country and also known at times as Alonso and Antonio. There was far too much to read about her adventures at one sitting, so I bookmarked a few sites instead.

I also searched for Perpetua and Felicity and found that they were women friends who were executed for their Christian faith in first-century North Africa. Today they were considered patrons of same-sex couples looking for Catholic saints to worship. Perpetua was even regarded as a transgender saint because she kept a journal that included dreams, in one of which she was transformed into a man, and not only a man, but a gladiator, who strips off his clothes and enters a Roman arena to do battle.

In real life, Perpetua was a noblewoman, married (though her journal never says much about her husband), and also a nursing mother. Felicity, or Felicitas, her slave, was pregnant at the time the two women were arrested and imprisoned in 703 for their Christian beliefs. They were sentenced to death and killed by wild animals, all the while embracing each other. Their martyrdom made them famous, along with Perpetua's journal, later called *The Passion of Saints Perpetua and Felicitas,* the first known written document by a woman in Christian history. I had no idea what drew Stella's attention to this pair.

For now, my own paying work came first. I had a short autobiographical essay to translate for a Chilean novelist and a longer article by a professor in Salamanca for an academic journal. And then I had the opening chapters of *Verónica* to polish. I decided to do this first, and it went quickly. I sent the excerpt off to Avery with a synopsis and an email that explained I wasn't sure of some of the bullfighting terminology but could rework some of that later.

I'd been persuaded to take this project on by my author Rosa Cardenes who knew Lola from mystery conferences. "Lola needs a break. She has that little girl to raise all on her own." Rosa had brought me so much steady income over the past years that I rarely said no to her requests. But I noticed I felt vaguely resentful the whole time I was working on the *Verónica* excerpt in Barcelona. I was certain Avery would bury the project and pretend, the next time I saw her, to remember very little about it. To my surprise, I got an email from her within two hours of having sent both attachments, which assured me that she'd read the synopsis and excerpts and she'd get it over to SNP very soon. They were expecting it.

I was so pleased by this news that I almost didn't notice the postscript below her signature.

Sad about Vonn. She did seem rather forlorn when we met. I was away in Dublin for some meetings and only heard on my return. Is someone clearing out her flat? I only ask because rentals are hard to come by in Central London, and a friend is looking for a place near Camden, on the affordable side. Do let me know the address and I'll pass it on.

In my gratitude that Avery might have already found a publishing home for Lola Fuentes, I'd almost responded right away to say that, as it happened, Gayle was cleaning Vonn's flat, and it should be available soon. But my fingers paused on the keyboard. Not in surprise that all

Avery cared about was real estate. That was a given, since the rental market was so tight, and personal tips were precious. But somehow the phrasing seemed off, too studiedly casual. She obviously knew that Vonn had lived near Camden, but she didn't seem to know quite where. Had the memoir submission come to her only as an email attachment? And even if it had, wouldn't correspondence between Vonn and Avery carry signature stamps with a physical address?

Was Avery simply playing dumb—or was she fishing to know who had been in the flat after Vonn's death? Or who might be there now, clearing out Vonn's possessions and cleaning? Did she have any reason to want to go through Vonn's things herself, to find out if there was correspondence linked to the literary agency or Avery personally?

For a moment, my mind went further in conjecture. What the hell did she mean, "forlorn"? Vonn did seem a bit wet and shabby that afternoon, but she'd flashed a smile at Avery with familiar bravado. "Forlorn" seemed an odd adjective for someone whom Avery had accused of worrying or intimidating Fiona. Later Avery had tried to walk those words back, but there had to be a story. How serious was the threat and could it affect Avery as well as Fiona? I found myself wondering, had Avery really gone to Dublin? Before Vonn's death, or after? Easy enough to create an alibi somewhere around that time.

I shook off the suspicion as an example of how effortlessly conjecture could became paranoia. Vonn would have had to have had something serious on Avery for Avery to drown her. I had been translating too many mysteries lately, that was the problem. In thrillers every simple human question, one person to another, became a clue to unsavory secrets. Couldn't Avery just ask about a possible rental without me briefly imagining her as a murderer?

I wrote instead in a measured tone to thank Avery and suggested that if she liked the excerpt, that maybe we could arrange a meeting with SNP (Slush and Publish?). I said nothing about the flat, the address, the boxes of files on route to Bristol, or even about Vonn, and she didn't reply except to say, "Sounds fine. I'll check my calendar and get back to you."

Gayle returned that evening with the news that Neville had been by again, this time alone, to take the rest of the things. "I kept out some old photos and a bit of ephemera, some flyers and posters, to scan into my computer. I thought of making a slideshow of Vonn's life, if we hold a memorial." She pointed to her large, bulging daypack, "That's the last of everything, in there. I'll wind up the cleaning tomorrow morning. The decorators are coming at noon to start prepping the walls. I imagine they'll be a bit slapdash, but the landlord's in a hurry. As it turns out, Vonn was a bit behind on her rent, so he's not an ogre."

"Good work," I said. "I suppose people have been inquiring about the flat, prospective tenants? Anyone stopping by?"

"Not quite yet," she said. "But yes, I suppose the landlord will be showing it soon. For now, it's just Kristi popping in two or three times a day. Sometimes it's fine. But she doesn't really do anything useful, she's lonely, just looking for a chance to complain about the building and the landlord or to say, 'poor old Vonn.' Sometimes her company helps though. Today, with all the books gone and the cupboards open and the blinds removed, the flat didn't feel that Vonn ever lived there. It's the Venetian blinds, I suppose. They were always a bit askew, but they were hidden by the drapes. I thought it would be better to take them down, but then the rooms lost all personality." Gayle sighed. "You wouldn't believe it, but it was really quite a cozy place once, the rugs, the posters, the books, the piles of newspapers and journals."

"In the old days, you mean?" I paused. "I had the impression, from what you said the evening we all had curry, that after you and Vonn broke up, you didn't see her much until you ran into her at the Ladies' Pond."

"Well, of course I *saw* her, I mean, even though London's huge, you still run into people all the time. Readings, talks, films, political protests. And Vonn was always glad to see me. She always wanted to know how I was, she was sympathetic about my love life." Gayle had seated herself on a chair in the living room to take off her shoes. "We'd stand on the pavement or have a cuppa in a café and catch up. Once or twice I may have stopped by the flat. Susan was so beastly at times. It was good to have someone to complain to. That's the thing about Vonn," Gayle smiled wryly. "She was such an inveterate grouser that you never felt like a bad person when you bitched about your girlfriend. And when Susan dumped me, Vonn was there to hold my hand."

"You never thought of getting back together with Vonn?"

"No," said Gayle, but she sounded wistful. "Well, I suppose it crossed my mind. But she had other women in her life, I couldn't even keep track of them. No, Vonn was better as a friend. After Susan, I dated for a while. Eventually I was pursued by Joan. Susan was an academic. Joan also taught at the University of London, though in a different department. Susan had a terraced house in Notting Hill, bought when things were a bit rougher around there, and Joan had some family money and a lovely flat she inherited near Regent's Park," she added. "Vonn was different."

"She didn't own a house or a lovely flat."

"She was radical. And I loved that about her. Sometimes I just wanted to see her to remind myself of who I'd been with her. She was my first woman lover, and sexually, well no one has ever made me feel like Vonn did," she said, surprising me with her frankness. "But that's sometimes the way, isn't it? You don't want to make a life with someone like Vonn. But yes, I'd see Vonn sometimes. Very rarely. Susan never knew. Joan never knew."

And Vida? Did she know, or did she suspect that Gayle had never really given up Vonn?

"You didn't see her often," I summarized. "Then she had surgery and she moved out of London, and when you ran into her again at the Pond a couple of years ago, you resumed your friendship."

"Yes, we'd get together at least once a month. Cancer changed her. Vonn hadn't lost her critical ways, but she somehow was more vulnerable. We'd have tea and go for a walk somewhere. But then Vida came along, and that put an end to seeing as much of Vonn. I shouldn't have let it. Vonn needed me, but Vida is a strong personality. I got swept up in her life." She looked dejected, the way she often did when she mentioned Vida. "Vida had had girlfriends too, but she'd never stayed in touch with them. She didn't understand that it can be nice, sometimes, to visit with an old lover. Long after everything is over and there are no sparks left and no pain either, you still have your memories." She looked down at her intertwined fingers.

"The thing about first loves is that something in you dies when it's over. And you never get over it, not properly. In the case of Vonn I lost her twice. First when our affair ended, and now through her death."

I sat there beside her, tempted once again to hold her in my arms and comfort her. She aroused some protective feeling in me that was slightly worrisome.

I changed the subject instead. "What do you think about going out for dinner? You take a nice hot shower, and we can walk down to BabaBoom. I know you like their chargrilled cauliflower. We could watch another episode of *Beatrys* if you want."

"That sounds lovely," Gayle said, getting up again. "And it reminds me, I brought you and Nicky something." She opened her backpack and took out trade paperbacks of Stella Terwicker's Beatrys mysteries, all eight. "Vonn had this nice set."

I thanked her and asked, "But didn't the first two come out from Aphra Press? I suppose the current publisher acquired the rights and did this new edition?"

"Yes, I suppose so. Vonn had most of the books in the earlier editions, and a few are signed by Stella. But they're more beat-up, so I thought you and Nicky would like these. I've taken the other ones."

I couldn't very well say that I would have liked to take a closer look at Vonn's beat-up collection of the earlier editions of the mysteries. Did "signed" mean just Stella's name, or was there a personal inscription to Vonn, and if there was, how personal? But I felt I'd already taken up too much of Gayle's time with my questions, and the poor wee thing needed to eat. I'd ask her later, I decided, but in the end I forgot.

A few more days passed, leaving only a short time before Nicky was scheduled to return from Copenhagen. Although I assured Gayle she'd be welcome with us for as long as she wanted to stay, I could see she was growing more distressed. Her cleaning of Vonn's flat had ended, but she didn't seem to be making much headway with finding a new place of her own. She said she might be able to stay for a while with friends in Clapham who had an extra room. Another possibility was to move out of the city. A couple she knew from the Tudor Roses owned a farm in Kent and had a former goat shed she could fix up. And then there was the relative in Devon, a widowed sister with a big house in Torquay. "That would be my last choice. A goat shed would be preferrable. Even with goats in it."

I felt her pain. Once or twice, Nicky had made noises about leaving Islington for Scotland, and each time that happened I had worried I'd be out of luck finding a place to live that either didn't cost a fortune or that wasn't miles from North London. But at least I was still working and had savings and if all else failed I could travel for a while and stay with friends in various countries.

Gayle and I had this conversation the evening before Nicky was to fly back from Copenhagen, an open bottle of wine on the coffee table before us, some easy lasagna bubbling in the oven, each of us conscious that perhaps it was our last chance to be alone together in a way that might lead to a romantic embrace or a bit more. At least I was conscious of this opportunity. Gayle was maybe too focused on making sure the lasagna didn't burn. Finally, she got it out of the oven, and we carried our plates to the coffee table to eat and drink in comfort side by side on the sofa.

But sadly, the more she drank, Gayle's thoughts seemed less on me and more on Vida. Vida was a fantastic cook, for instance. Gayle could only make things like pasta and scrambled eggs, while Vida did recipes from Spanish cookbooks. All kinds of Galician specialties like a traditional stew with pork shoulder, chorizo, and pig's ears. She had special butchers and fishmongers she patronized. Sometimes they had shrimp in garlic and even octopus. For dessert: almonds and fruit, or flan. I sensed some longing in Gayle's voice. She had been sleeping in Nicky's comfy queen-sized bed, but soon she'd be back on our sofa until she found a new berth. The last day or two, her references to Vida had become more frequent and more positive.

"What I admire about Vida is her energy," Gayle continued. "Sometimes it's overwhelming, but I also find it so inspiring. It's not just her cooking, it's how she lives her life. She's sixty-two but she has the body of a much younger woman. She goes to the gym on Clissold Road every morning, she swims twice a week there, and in the sea and rivers when she can. She practically remodeled the house in Stoke Newington herself. When she moved to the area, she looked for a run-down house to do up, and spent thirty years turning it into a beautiful home with a garden. Yes, she gardens too! I mean, it tires you out just to think about all she does with her life."

I nodded. I felt tired just hearing about it, truth be told. But Gayle went on, a little mocking, a little resentful, but actually full of pride. "And Vida is brilliant with money. She came to the UK as a student to learn English in a business school. She was a *maid* in a Bayswater hotel while she was studying. Now, she not only has the house in Stoke Newington, but she also has other properties, she has investments, she has a nest egg."

"Some people are good with money," I said neutrally, though I did feel envious. "And some of us just live interesting lives. Surely you don't regret your time with the Tudor Roses?"

"No, no," Gayle said, though she didn't look convinced. "It was fine at the time. But it didn't leave me with anything other than some very nice Tudor-style robes and unsold copies of three CDs. I look around at some of the others in the group. Some married men and had kids, they're grannies now. One has a proper job teaching at music college. The friends in Kent have their farm and teach piano privately. I seem to have fallen through the cracks even though I did my best to make a living."

"But you've had work that was creatively satisfying," I reminded her. "At least that's what I tell myself sometimes when I look at my bank balance. I've never been well-off, but I've managed, thanks to friends like Nicky. Having a base in London has made all the difference."

"I guess, when you don't have much money yourself, you look for a woman who has it. That's my situation too. Like you and Nicky."

Was that how she saw my friendship with Nicky? She'd misunderstood me completely.

"No, that's not what I meant." My voice had an unexpectedly defensive note. "I have a successful freelance career, even if it's a bit up and down at times. Some translations pay very well. And I get royalties and other fees from some of the more successful books. I'm not in financial distress. At all. And although this is Nicky's flat, we share expenses. And the most important thing is, I didn't go looking for Nicky. Nicky has been my *friend* for donkey's years. She was lucky enough to inherit Anna Wulf's house, and to sell it for a good sum and buy this place. But we're *friends* first and foremost."

"Don't get so riled, Reilly," Gayle said, moving into a corner of the sofa. Her tone was chilly. "I know you two aren't in a romantic relationship. Forget I said anything. I was just joking about Vida and her money, anyway. I like Vida for a lot of reasons, not just her financial stability. And I have options. There's the goat shed. And my sister's. But I'll probably head off to Clapham tomorrow. Which reminds me, it's probably a good idea to pack up tonight."

In the space of a few minutes, just a few sentences, the closeness we'd developed over the past week was abruptly over.

The next morning, I took my coffee into my room and set to translating with renewed vigor. I was so occupied with my work that I hardly heard Gayle in the flat. It was only when I went out later to the toilet that I realized she was gone, and all her things with her.

There was a note on the kitchen table to me and Nicky, thanking us profusely for our hospitality and kindness. She was off to Clapham and left an address. A second note was paperclipped to the first, just to me, that apologized for drinking too much last night and for possibly offending me. She thanked me for helping her with the boxes in Vonn's flat. She wished me well with my translating work.

I felt like a heel. The poor mite had only been joking, her tongue loosened by a few glasses of wine. I'd overreacted, mostly because I was embarrassed that anyone should imagine I was freeloading off Nicky. Now Wee Gayle was gone, to Clapham, and maybe eventually to Kent or Devon. Maybe back to Vida.

I lost all interest in translating that morning and instead went out for a long walk that ended with buying a lot of groceries for Nicky's return, a bunch of daffodils, and a new bathmat, after which I decided to give Nicky's bedroom a tidying up. Gayle had stripped the bedding and I put it all in the wash, then returned with the vacuum cleaner, a cannister with a hose. As I was pushing the hose with the roller brush under the bed, I encountered some sort of obstacle. It turned out to be a book that Gayle had probably been reading before sleep, a hard copy of Stella's third mystery, *Schola for Murder,* the one about the two rivalrous composers who wrote liturgical music for the beguines to sing. We'd watched this episode a couple of nights ago. It was the one where the Tudor Roses performed, Gayle among them.

I turned off the vacuum and sat down on the mattress to look at the book. First published in hardcover in 1993, its dust jacket was covered with advance quotes from well-known British mystery authors. The author photo showed Stella in a satin blouse, dangling earrings, and hair in an artful updo with tendrils and wisps and decorated with barrettes. She looked a long way from the timid teenager or the ethereal author in the photos used in *Stella Terwicker: A Medieval Life.* Had Avery Amstrong hired a stylist to reshape her image? I recalled that Avery herself had gone through an updo period in the nineties.

On the title page, in tall, narrow handwriting was written: *To my dearest Vonn, with thanks for all your help, your friend Stella.*

What could this possibly mean? What help had Vonn offered Stella—

help with the book or just help in general? And how did "dearest" square with "your friend." However you parsed it, there was obviously a stronger degree of acquaintance than anyone had yet admitted.

I read the book's brief acknowledgments, but while Avery was thanked and "my sister-in-law Fiona Craig, whose knowledge of medieval music proved invaluable," there was no mention of Vonn. I recalled that there had been no mention of Vonn in the index of Fiona's biography either.

Abandoning the vacuum cleaning, I went into my room and looked through the trade paperback set of the Beatrys mysteries. In the uniform reprinted edition, which came out a few years after Stella's death, all acknowledgments had been omitted, so there was no way of telling if Vonn had been thanked in the earlier or later books. The author's bio had been updated and was the same throughout. It mentioned Stella's degree in medieval history, her fascination with the beguines, her awards, the television series, and her death at age fifty-one in 2008.

There are many ways to scrub queer history. An author's bio is sometimes one of them.

Gayle said that Vonn and Stella didn't move in the same crowd. That might have been true later, when Stella was a famous author, but what about when Stella was new to London and just starting her writing career? After all, Stella had submitted an article to Brize's Triple L anthology about Perpetua and Felicity.

Had Gayle not been telling the truth or was she just uninformed? Vonn had had lots of women in her life over the years, friends, colleagues, clients, lovers. Why should Gayle imagine Stella was not one of them? Especially when she signed a book to her "dearest Vonn."

10.

Nicky returned from Copenhagen with a suitcase full of *hygge*. Literally. She'd bought so many colorful hand-knit socks and pewter candleholders that she also had to buy a new bag to carry them. Of course, like most people, she'd seen all the articles on *hygge* a few years ago when it first became a thing. But suddenly, *she got it*. It was about staying home, with a log fire, and a glass of mulled wine, and a good friend nearby, just reading a book by candlelight.

We didn't have the roaring fire with wood we'd cut in the forest, but everything else was to hand, except that wool made my feet itch, and I needed more light to read by than a candle. Otherwise it was fine with me to cozy up in the flat in Islington, order takeaway from Taste of India (though perhaps chicken korma wasn't very *hygge*) and turn on the electric fire. Also, we felt more like talking than reading, not having seen each other in well over a week.

She wanted to know if things had gone all right with Gayle and what had happened to her. "So she went off to Clapham. I thought she'd go back to Vida. Is that definitively over? Or did Vida not want her back?"

"I think she's considering it. Strongly. She didn't want to talk about her at first, and then last night she went off on a paean to Vida's toned body and many accomplishments, from cooking to gardening to investing in real estate. I got the feeling that Gayle missed whatever security she'd had with Vida and in Vida's house."

I didn't mention to Nicky that Gayle had suggested Vida was her meal ticket, just like Nicky was mine. I'd put our chicken korma and saag paneer on my credit card and had resolved to pay more attention to splitting everything equally, just so no one could accuse me of sponging off my best friend. With Nicky here in the living room, lounging in her favorite armchair and ottoman, new wool socks pointing at the electric fire, just like in the photographs demonstrating how to live the good life, Danish style, it seemed beyond ridiculous to think that our friendship, which had stood the test of time for decades, was based on economics. I couldn't help what people thought when they looked at our arrangement.

We were suited, that's all that mattered. She was my *hygge*.

"Did you get the story of why they broke up?" Nicky asked, sipping her wine (not mulled because that was too much work). "Gayle only ever told me it was about Vonn, that Vida was upset Gayle was so upset about Vonn's death."

"That's probably the truth. But I think there could be a reason for Vida's jealousy. Gayle opened up more about having seen Vonn after they broke up. I imagine that they went to bed together, at times when life was difficult with Susan and with Joan. Vonn was a habit Gayle couldn't break and maybe that was true for Vonn as well. I think it's possible that she and Vonn were more serious than Gayle will admit. I'm guessing Vonn could have had a hard time when Gayle got involved with Vida last autumn. The neighbor woman mentioned a couple of times that Vonn had been depressed for around six months. Maybe that depression was caused by Gayle moving in with Vida. Vida's the jealous type and she obviously had some inkling of Gayle's old feelings for Vonn."

"Then why did Gayle move in with Vida if she still had feelings for Vonn?"

"Vonn lived in a one-bedroom flat with her office in her bedroom, same as she had for years. Her income was reduced. I glanced at her invoicing for last year, and it was almost nothing. It's Jane Austen for lesbians. Gayle looked at what Vida had to offer and what Vonn could provide and chose Vida. Vonn crumbled and, despite taking antidepressants, eventually killed herself." I finished my glass and put it down. Was it just me, or was there a smell of burning wool? "That's one hypothesis," I said. "And by the way, I think you should move your feet away from the heater."

Nicky put her feet down and yelped a little. "I'm going to turn this fire off," she said. "After all, we have central heating." She did so, then asked, "You say 'one hypothesis.' Do you have another? Did Vida kill her then, from jealousy?"

"Gayle said that Vida was acting strangely. Seemed to know something Gayle didn't, Gayle said. I guess it's possible that Vida drowned Vonn, I wouldn't put it past her. But there's something else I've been wondering about, a different sort of triangle: Vonn, Stella, Fiona.

Something to do with the past, maybe possibly to do with the Beatrys books. I don't have much to go on, just the fact that Stella inscribed her third mystery to 'my dearest Vonn,' and thanked her for her help. But it's the only thing so far that seems to tie Vonn and Fiona together. And there is some connection because Avery more or less told me so. She said Fiona had felt threatened by Vonn. I assume that Vonn wrote something or other in the memoir that alarmed Avery. And now the laptop is gone, possibly stolen, and there's no print version of the memoir in Vonn's papers."

Nicky looked interested, but not convinced. "So you think Fiona could have killed her?"

"Hard to imagine" I said. "But I can't help wondering... Vonn was taking antidepressants, maybe since last autumn, but aren't these medications supposed to make you less depressed? Vonn obviously was well enough to continue writing her book and to try to get Avery to represent it."

"What are you thinking of doing about all this?" Nicky prompted.

"Me? Nothing. The police seem to think it's a clear case of suicide even though there's no note. I gather from Gayle that the edge of the bird pond was too muddy and messy to get any decent footprints, and there were no witnesses to a struggle or even a conversation. Her phone might have gone into the pond with her if it was in a pocket. I don't know if they've checked her call log, but they must not have seen anything too suspicious, like an arranged meeting with someone that night. The cops have multiple ways of investigating someone's movements and contacts. I'm sure they did everything they were supposed to." My mind went to Gayle's description of the two Met officers she talked to in Vonn's flat after the death. *We see this with older people sometimes, they just don't want to go on.*

"But you don't believe it was suicide, do you?" said Nicky.

"It's just that, I know what the coppers probably saw in Vonn's death. An old woman, an old lesbian with back pain and depression, living alone, not much extra income. They didn't see who Vonn had been most of her life. There's more to this story. The Vida angle. The Fiona and Avery angle. Someone must know more about this."

"And knowing you, you won't let this go until you've found out more."

"I'm just curious," I protested. "I could start with Avery and Fiona.

I'm already working with Avery on the Lola Fuentes translations, so I have an excuse for nosing around a bit. And maybe I can find out more about the memoir through Avery. Or the laptop might turn up, or maybe the memoir. If Vonn had only written a chapter or two, we might have missed it in the Brize papers that were shipped up to Bristol."

"Sometimes I think you're mad with these investigations, but then sometimes it turns out you have a talent for finding out what happened. So I'd say, go for it. And while you're about it, you should read all those mysteries about the beguinages. Maybe there are some clues there. Stella, after all, was kind of a mysterious person, wasn't she? And she died young. Maybe she was slowly poisoned?"

"Don't joke, Gibbons. Everyone knew she was ill, she had chronic fatigue."

"I'm not joking. People don't usually die of CFS, they recover or live with it, hard as that is. You know from translating mysteries that one thing leads to another, and past secrets usually come out and complicate the plot. There usually have to be two or three corpses to make a satisfying thriller." Nicky got up and wandered toward the kitchen, pinching a few candles as she went. There was sweat on her brow from the temperature in the living room. "Just make sure you're not one of them."

Nicky was right about my curiosity, but wrong as well, I thought, as I lay in bed later, with a copy of the first of Stella's mysteries, *Woven into Murder,* propped on my lap. Most of the investigations I'd been involved in were accidental or undertaken to help someone I knew. In one or two unfortunate homicidal events, I'd been under suspicion myself. When you travel a lot, you sometimes have to take matters into your own hands, because the police are inefficient, corrupt, or have no experience with the complexities of queer culture. There was an incident, many years ago in Venice, when Nicky herself had been accused of theft and worse, and it was only my efforts to solve that case that had kept her out of jail. That was hardly curiosity.

What bothered me most about Vonn's death was it didn't seem to matter to the police. She was old, she was a dyke, of course she would kill herself. As I'd often found, it wasn't always virulent homophobia that hindered criminal investigations of the LGBTQ community, it was indifference to the deaths of queers in general. It was the tendency to slot the death of people like me into only a few categories: We died from suicide, usually drug overdoses, and our motives were shame and self-hatred, fear of being exposed and losing our reputations and jobs. If we were murdered, it was through consorting in back alleys with other degenerates, or through love triangles gone wrong, or by people with secrets who feared being exposed and having their reputations smeared.

Law enforcement might be far superior on the forensic front to anything I could do on my own, but when it came to the lesbian community, my understanding of motives surpassed theirs. In my experience, they were less likely to consider claims of inheritance, sibling rivalry, financial skullduggery, professional jealousy, or accidental/on purpose deaths caused by one person acting like an idiot or encouraged to do so ("I think you'll look great standing at the edge of the waterfall," or "No, don't move. I'm sure this water buffalo would like to be in the photo too."). They didn't always see that LGBTQ murders were usually committed for quotidian reasons. Focusing on the LGBT details, the police didn't always get to the Q of the matter.

Where I saw something fishy about Vonn's death, the overworked Met only saw a seventy-three-year-old woman, a breast cancer survivor who might be ill or depressed, who took the opportunity to die on her own terms in a public pond one dark rainy evening. She left no partner, no close family, and not many friends who cared deeply for her, people who had influence and money or might question the circumstances and demand more answers. The police had no way of knowing that Vonn, in addition to once being everyone's least favorite public nuisance, had also once been a sexy charmer with an unflinching attachment to lesbian community.

Vonn hadn't been too much more awful than a few others I recalled from in-person events and letters to the editor in the past. Yet even if she had been the worst of them (and she probably wasn't because I also believed she was sincere and upright in some distorted way), didn't awful lesbians deserve justice?

Maybe awful lesbians especially.

If I were to think about going further in my investigation, it wouldn't be out of mere curiosity. It would be to find some justice for Vonn. If she'd been fifty years younger, a young woman, perhaps slightly tipsy, wandering around the Heath on her own, yes, I could imagine that a random stranger had killed her. But that wasn't Vonn's fate, I was sure.

If she'd been murdered, and I wasn't saying she was, someone who knew her must have done it, and there was some reason for it.

What did I have to go on aside from a feeling that something was amiss here? Very little. An unpublished, partial manuscript that Avery declined to represent. Described unflatteringly as a memoir about the sordid side of feminist publishing in the eighties, a memoir full of resentments, which may have purveyed gossip about any number of people, including Fiona Craig and Stella Terwicker. A table of contents for the Triple L that showed Stella and Vonn may have known each other, confirmed by the inscription in *Schola for Murder*.

I didn't have the police resources to work out the how of her death, but I might be able to work out a why that would shed light on the how.

I could work it out as I'd sometimes done before, using the resources I'd employed before. Persistence, connections, and an understanding of lesbian relationships. My freelance work as a translator guaranteed some level of inconspicuousness. In the literary world we were generally regarded as respectable and innocuous. To be a translator was to be a shadow, and if you were lucky, no one noticed you until your work was done, if at all.

In that, the translator's work was like that of the detective: You stayed one step behind the one who did it, the original author, gathering clues and collecting meanings, until you had the written body of evidence. Then you wove the words into a testimony of other words that created a new and watertight narrative.

I put down the copy of *Woven into Murder* and resolved to see Avery as soon as possible and, through her, find my way to Fiona, and through Fiona to the story of Vonn and Stella. I was certain there *was* a story. Maybe Nicky was right: a good thriller always had more than one corpse and often a murderer killed twice.

Once for love or profit, and the second time to conceal her tracks.

PART TWO

11.

Avery Armstrong had for a long time only been accessible on her own terms, but this was ridiculous. She told me that mid-April was the first lunch date she had available. In an email, she tried to placate me by saying that she'd sent the excerpt from *Verónica* on to SNP: "If they take Lola's book(s), which I believe they will, we'll all celebrate! And if they don't, you and I will still have lunch and plot a new strategy."

This wasn't on. It was only the second week of March and, especially after my conversation with Nicky a few nights ago, I had a lot of questions. They ranged from the basic to the truly pointed: Was there any reason to think that Vonn's death was murder? And if so, could her death be linked to Stella Terwicker's demise ten years ago?

I hoped to get Avery to at least admit that Vonn and Stella knew each other way back when. But what I was really after was the story of Vonn's manuscript and what had happened to it. Only then would I be able to understand if there were other people besides Fiona who might have been threatened by her revelations. Including Avery herself.

Avery was not as warm as usual once I'd barged my way into the ground floor offices of the terraced house on a residential street in Camden Town, but she didn't turn me away.

I'd been surprised to see a young woman I didn't know sitting at a desk in the reception area. She was working at a desktop computer and surrounded by piles of books, manuscripts, and folders, some of them on the floor and others in chairs or on top of cabinets.

"What happened to Samantha?" I asked Avery when I was inside her office and the door was closed. Here the piles were tamed, and her desk was relatively clean, except for two monitors, an iPad, and a smart phone. She had on a beautiful silk scarf, hot pink, and a cream-colored wool jacket; all the same there was a haggard look about her eyes, as if she hadn't been sleeping well. Her blonde coif depended on intricate care; some bits were now too long and flopped over one ear.

"Sam left a few weeks ago," Avery said, gesturing me to a chair. "She got an offer she couldn't refuse, and they required her to start immediately. An Arts Council management job in South Yorkshire, doing something with literary programs. The girl out front is from a temp agency. I thought about offering her the job but really, I need someone more orderly than she seems to be." She offered me a coffee from a pot on a sideboard. I poured a cup, sipped, and put it down again.

"I have a call with Frankfurt in twenty minutes, just so you know. What's on your mind, Cassandra?"

"Vonn Henley," I said briskly. "I'm still confused about what really happened at Fiona's lecture. Why you wanted me along. Where you disappeared off with Vonn."

"Why should it matter?" she said, meeting my eyes. "I wanted some company. I thought you might come in handy as an escort. As I told you in the email I sent later that evening, I was planning to gently reject Vonn's memoir. I didn't want Fiona getting in the way of that, so I needed you to keep her occupied."

"But you've never really explained *why* Vonn might be threatening Fiona."

She paused and smiled a little tensely. "I don't think I ever said that Vonn *was* threatening Fiona. I said Fiona *felt* threatened. That was probably my fault. I'd mentioned to Fiona that someone had submitted a book proposal to me, a personal memoir that spoke of women writers who left their feminist publishers behind to 'chase fame' with the bigger houses, i.e. to make a decent living as a writer. I wanted to alert Fiona that one of Vonn's examples was Stella. Fiona was upset, especially when I told her that Vonn and I had agreed to meet at the lecture. She didn't want her post-lecture Q and A destroyed by Vonn being critical of Stella. I then tried to get Vonn not to attend, but that only piqued her interest. I honestly hoped she *wouldn't* turn up, but as it happened, she was fine. Still, I was glad you agreed to come and distract Fiona."

"You're saying Vonn wrote in the manuscript about Stella leaving Aphra Press, and going mainstream, and that's it?"

"That's the sum of it. In Vonn's fevered mind everyone should have stayed with the tiny separatist presses. Even Aphra was too large for Vonn."

"So, Vonn and Stella knew each other?"

"I doubt it, but perhaps. Vonn mainly was using Stella as an example.

She mentioned others. Jeanette Winterson and Val McDermid were first published by feminist presses or imprints, then their careers took a leap. This was not *selling out,* this was a smart move for them."

"Did Vonn write about you as Stella's agent? Did she blame you for Stella moving to the mainstream?"

"Well, obviously she wasn't going to blame me directly if she wanted me to sell her bloody book for her, was she?" Avery glanced irately at her watch. "Just like any other writer Vonn wanted a decent publisher and a good deal, and remember, she came to me with her proposal. I didn't go looking for her."

"I'm curious," I said, backing down a little. "How did you meet Stella and become her agent? In Fiona's biography it says that Stella worked as an editorial assistant at a publishing house when she first came to London. Did you meet her there?"

"Yes," said Avery. She ran a hand through her already tumbled hair. "She was an assistant to an assistant, and I was on my way out. But I remembered her, and her name, since it was unusual. A couple of years later I saw she'd published a mystery with a medieval theme, and it had a few good reviews. It was a first effort, but a couple of years later there was another one. I went to her reading at Silver Moon Bookshop. She was delightful with the crowd, and they loved her. I chatted with her afterwards, read the book and liked Beatrys and the whole idea. I thought she could easily find a bigger publisher and arranged lunch with her. She made up her own mind and told her editor Lucy at Aphra. They were disappointed, of course, but wished her well. Lucy later went on to work as an editor elsewhere. This kind of thing happens in publishing all the time, something that Vonn refused to see."

"Back to Fiona's lecture then, how did Vonn take the news you didn't want to represent her book?"

"As you know, I didn't really reject her that evening. I simply prepared the way to let her down a bit more gradually. We had a drink, talked about her book. I didn't tell her that evening there was no way I could possibly sell a project like that. I talked in general about the publishing scene, how different it was from thirty years ago. I think she got that, but she still seemed to think that her book had value, if only as feminist history."

"Well, isn't that true?"

"No. Mind you, I only saw a detailed table of contents and one long chapter. I don't think she'd written any more than that, but that was enough to get the picture. A proposed book full of Vonn's righteous indignation and gossip about women nobody remembers and events that nobody cares about. Leave feminist publishing of the eighties and nineties to professionally trained scholars of women's history."

"Libelous?"

"Moral finger-pointing. So-called secrets revealed."

"So you read the whole thing, the one chapter anyway? Did it have a title?"

"'Gadfly,' what else? And no, I didn't read the entire chapter Vonn submitted. It was forty pages about the demise of Brize and the unfair way the other collective members acted toward her. Dreadful."

"What about the other chapters?"

"I'm sure they were just as bad. Fortunately, she didn't include them, and they may not have even been written." She looked at her phone and then at me. "Three minutes, Cassandra."

"Why did she come to you then?"

"I've assumed it was because of Fiona's biography of Stella, which did, after all, have some elements of women's publishing history. You know how authors are always claiming that their manuscript is *just like* some recent book, only a bit different. That was Vonn's line: Fiona was writing about women's publishing history and so was Vonn."

"So you rejected it. And then Vonn died." I watched her closely, but she seemed detached now.

"Vonn had problems, clearly she did, problems I know nothing about. I don't know anything about why she was at the Heath that evening and whether she was on drugs or drunk or whatever. It's a tragedy. But before that happened, I'd already passed on the project, with the usual friendly but firm note. Much as I admired her passion for the subject, I didn't feel we were the best representatives for her work and wished her the best of luck elsewhere."

"When did you write her? Did you return the actual manuscript?"

"Well, I don't know. Sam would have done it. Obviously, it was before Vonn died."

"Was it returned by post?"

"No idea. When we receive submissions electronically, we'll often print them out. Usually they get tossed if we pass." Avery put a hand up to her forehead, where a chunk of gelled hair was worrying her brows.

"It *could* have come by post. I really don't remember. Why this interest in the proposal?"

"I've been helping her friend Gayle Winslow get Vonn's flat cleared out and her papers boxed up and sent off to a feminist archive in Bristol. Gayle thought there could be something in the manuscript that might explain Vonn's death. But we didn't find a copy in any of her filing cabinets. No manuscript, no proposal, or correspondence about it. And her laptop is gone too. I knew that you'd looked at the proposal and rejected it. I thought you might still have a copy of the submission package. Or the email attachment. For the archives."

Something in what I'd said made Avery' eyelids flicker, but before she could say anything, her phone buzzed and she picked it up, "Ingrid! So happy to hear from you. Yes, it's been ages and we have lots to talk about."

Avery blew me a kiss that turned into a hand wave. My twenty minutes was over. In fact I'd had twenty-two minutes of her time.

I left Avery's inner office and closed the door. In the main office the secretary temporarily replacing Sam was valiantly moving packages from chair to desk and sorting through a few at a time. She looked young and not wildly competent. I wondered if she'd just left college and moved to London with a degree in English, some basic typing skills and not much else, to start on the first rung of a career in publishing.

She seemed grateful that I smiled at her, asked her name—Julia— and in general treated her like someone of consequence. After a few minutes of chatting, I asked casually if she might be able to pull up the phone and street address of one of the agency's authors: Fiona Craig. By chance Julia was able to find it on her computer. She scribbled it down on a sticky note and passed it over the desk with a sense of achievement.

"Clever old you," I said, and then, even more casually, I mentioned that I'd come to see Avery about a mutual friend, a woman named Vonn Henley, who had unfortunately died. I explained that several of us were involved in getting her papers to one of the archives that specialized in twentieth-century women's history. That immediately interested her— she'd had no idea there were archival records of that distant era.

I wanted to ask if there were emails to and from Vonn and Avery in their system, but that seemed a bit pushy—and made it more likely that Avery would hear about it and be suspicious. Instead I said, handing her my card, that if she ever came across any files, printed or electronic, with anything by Vonn Henley to just send it on to me, and I'd see it got to the archives. Correspondence, manuscripts, whatever.

"I think the agency considered some of her work and declined it, but it's possible that it didn't get mailed back to Vonn." I smiled conspiratorially and gestured to the various piles around her desk. "It sounds like the last assistant left things in a bit of a muddle for you to sort out. I just wanted to make it easier for you, since otherwise the package would be returned to sender. Given that she's not... at her old address any longer."

Julia looked sympathetic but slightly overwhelmed. "Yes, I'll see what I can do. I just have another week here to try to organize things, and then I have something else coming up. I don't think I've done half what Ms. Armstrong expected, but I've done what I could."

"You've done very well, I'm sure," I assured her. "And best of luck!"

I didn't hold out much hope that there actually was a package containing the "Gadfly" proposal in the piles around the office. It was almost a month since Avery would have rejected the memoir. Vonn would have received it while still alive at her flat if it had come in the post. If it had been sent.

After talking with Avery I was even more certain that something was in the memoir that created a problem for someone, most likely Fiona. "Gossip," Avery had said. "So-called secrets revealed." But what secrets could a retired medievalist have been involved in? And could such secrets have led to the need to hide or destroy a manuscript? Could they have led to Avery or Fiona stealing the laptop? Or even drowning Vonn?

I tried to imagine Avery in her hot pink silk scarf and cream-colored wool jacket holding Vonn underwater. And failed. She was a tough customer, but I thought she had been fairly honest just now. At least her answers made some kind of sense. I'd have to check them with other sources. Fiona was next.

"I don't suppose you have an extra copy of the Stella Terwicker biography?" I asked before I left. "I loaned mine to a friend, before I finished reading it. An old advance galley or something would be fine."

The temp was again happy to oblige. "We have some of those galleys left over," she said, rummaging on a bookshelf. "I'm sure Ms. Armstrong wouldn't mind."

I thanked Julia again and went out to the sidewalk, thinking about

Wee Gayle. She was the friend I'd loaned the biography to. I wondered if I'd ever get it back. Gayle had vanished from my life almost as quickly as she'd entered it in February.

It was cool but sunny, and I considered lunch somewhere near Regent's Canal. Then I looked at Fiona's address. The postcode was NW3, so it wasn't far from here. I tapped the street number into my phone and saw that her flat lay in the northern part of Primrose Hill, in an area with pubs and cafés. There I could get something to fortify myself before turning up unannounced to see if I could find out what the connection was among Fiona Craig, Stella Terwicker, and Vonn Henley. I suspected it had to do with the Beatrys mysteries and to whatever help Vonn had given Stella in the early stages of her career.

12.

Stella had chosen Primrose Hill, according to the biography, for its "country-village atmosphere." The neighborhood was popular with those who tilled the more lucrative fields of creativity, the media. I assumed that Fiona had stayed on Primrose Hill because it was familiar and comfortable. Her flat was in a well-appointed Victorian brick building, not one of the posh, pastel-painted terraces but near the corner of Berkley Road and the shopping street of Regent's Park Road. I thought about ringing the outside bell immediately, but realized that I didn't have a story yet, and would be hard-pressed to find an excuse to have come to Fiona's home.

Meanwhile I was hungry, so I decided to order brunch at Greenberry's, a café with some outdoor tables only lightly occupied, since it was chill and cloudy. From my sidewalk table I had a view of Berkely Road, just in case Fiona came or went from the flat. I tried to imagine what reason I could give for being here besides sheer chance, but even after I'd ordered and eaten, I still hadn't come up with much. Instead, I took out the bound galley of the biography and began looking through it. Usually galleys went out without having been proofread and sometimes you could catch mistakes, characters who changed names suddenly, or slips in a timeline. But presumably Fiona, as an academic, was a careful writer. Instead of typos, whatever was missing from the final version of *Stella Terwicker: A Medieval Life* was likely baked into every draft through the published version. For instance, Fiona had chosen to compress Stella's first years in London to a few paragraphs about office work during the day. There was no mention of a social life. According to Fiona's text, Stella spent her evenings and weekends in the British Library, reading up on medieval history in Flanders and the wool trade between Bruges and London.

The fact that Stella contributed a piece to the Triple L on two possibly lesbian saints made me think that her weekends could have been spent in a livelier way during her mid-twenties. No matter, the first mystery was written and accepted by Aphra Press, and she was encouraged by her editor Lucy Aspin to write another, which she did. There was no account of the bookshop reading where she met Avery Armstrong, and what happened after that: the lunch, the offer to represent her, the third book placed with a mainstream press, Albatross. It was only when Stella contacted Fiona, now living in Inverness with Stan, about becoming her "medieval consultant," that the story really got going again. That left a time span of around 1984 to 1991 only vaguely accounted for.

I wondered what else might be missing from the biography. I'd put the book down after getting back from Bruges, before getting to Stella's chronic debility and Fiona's role as a caretaker, together with her husband Stan, Stella's brother. Now, I found the chapter where Fiona described the onset of Stella's illness.

Like many things that in retrospect seem significant, Stella's ill health came on slowly, almost unnoticeably. She always had been a little fragile, prone to overdoing it, and then needing to rest and catch up. In autumn 1993, she had published the third book in the series, *Schola for Murder*, and had done an enormous amount of publicity, not only in Britain but in Germany, Scandinavia, North America, and Japan (the Japanese were always wild for Beatrys), publicity tours that had taken up much of 1994. At the same time she was hard at work on the fourth book, *The Funeral Specialist*. Her literary agent Avery Armstrong had secured an excellent book deal for her and was working on more foreign sales and the possible television series. So there was quite a lot of pressure for Stella to deliver the manuscript on time. The fourth book was scheduled for the spring of 1996.

Stella had by this time, as I mentioned in the previous chapter, brought me on board as a consultant for her third mystery, *Schola for Murder*, which required research on the musical compositions and performances of the beguines. At the time, I was still in Inverness teaching, but I welcomed the opportunity to contribute to her mysteries and make sure the historical details were correct. I became more involved in the fourth book, which hinged on the beguine tradition of healing and sitting with the ill.

After Stella had finished the first hundred pages of *The Funeral Specialist* and sketched out the rest of the novel, she decided to take a good long winter break, away from the city and in a warm place. She considered several ideas but ended up making plans to treat herself to a few weeks on the Algarve coast in Portugal that winter of 1994-5. The trip was delayed after she developed a bad case of what seemed like flu, but she was determined to travel anyway. Finally Avery Armstrong agreed to fly down with her and get her settled. They left mid-December before the holidays. It was Avery who called us to say that Stella had suffered something of a collapse soon after arriving and had been admitted to a hospital in Lisbon. It was the doctor's opinion that Stella had more wrong with her than just overwork and the flu. Avery brought her back as soon as possible to England.

In London she went through a battery of tests, but even the specialists weren't sure of a diagnosis other than Chronic Fatigue Syndrome that might have been triggered by the influenza, combined with the stress of her career. Chronic Fatigue Syndrome is one of those mysterious disorders that defy easy treatment. Physical and mental activity can make it worse, and sleep doesn't help the fatigue. For almost six months Stella was more or less confined to a chair or bed in her flat with headaches and a lack of energy.

Eventually, she was able to continue writing, and I continued to act as her consultant as she completed *The Funeral Specialist*. I cut back on teaching in Inverness and spent more time in London, helping her with various tasks. Some days were harder for her, and she was not always able to carry out the in-person publicity work required of a writer. Yet her indomitable spirit inspired many of her sympathetic readers, some of whom had also struggled with diseases that were non-classifiable. When *The Funeral Specialist* did finally appear, in autumn of 1996, it became a bestseller, launching Stella on a new and highly lucrative phase of her career. Of all her early books, however, I think *Schola* was my favorite, because I love medieval music and it was a chance to introduce her readers to the history of women as composers.

The narrative switched away from Stella at this point to a detailed discussion of the beguines as composers and performers, which I merely skimmed. This was followed by a brief, unsatisfying summary of Stella's career for the next few years, when her books were translated to over twenty languages and their popularity drew the interest of ITV.

The only other reference in this chapter to Stella's illness was this: "Throughout, Avery Armstrong remained a steadfast presence in Stella's life. Stan and I eventually purchased a flat in Stella's building, and by the late nineties, I too was living in Primrose Hill, where I could act as her consultant on the books and television series and help her with health issues."

Stan's feelings about his sister's health were not mentioned, which was in keeping with how Fiona seemed to treat her husband, in the biography at least: with indifference. Avery was also hardly delineated as a character, which was odd, considering how vivid she seemed to me. But I glimpsed through the cracks of the stolid prose, some larger, more dramatic story: Avery and Stella in Portugal, Stella's collapse, hospitalization, and back home to England, where the degree of her illness became apparent. As her agent, Avery must surely have panicked. As Stella's friend—or something more?—Avery must have been worried frantic.

Biographies written by relatives who also played a role as literary executors were a bit complicated, but some authors managed to carry it off—Quentin Bell writing about his aunt Virginia Woolf, and Nigel Nicholson writing about his parents, Vita Sackville-West, and Harold Nicholson in *Portrait of a Marriage*. You had the insider's intimate memories and access to letters and close friends and relatives, as well as some of the blind spots, about feminism, say. Fiona's biography, so bland and informative on the surface, seemed, the more I thought about it, to be like a dress that should have had a low-cut neck and sequins, but had been altered to look like a nun's habit. Maybe that was the effect of Fiona's background as a medievalist. Or maybe it was a deliberate, tone-lowering attempt to create a picture of Stella that would be more acceptable to her readers.

"Isn't it—Cassandra?" asked a voice, and I looked up to find Fiona standing next to me outside on the sidewalk. She had on a long woolly cardigan over a striped shirt and leggings, and clogs with socks. No make-up except a quick stroke or two of dark rose lipstick. Her chestnut hair was loosely pulled back from her pale face. As it turned out, she regularly called in a lunch order to Greenberry's and had done so today.

"Oh, hello, Fiona, what a surprise!" I said, falling back on sheer chance. "What a coincidence. I was just... reading the biography."

"I see," she said, cautious. "Do you live in the area?"

"No, I was just out on a walk. I love to walk. I think I told you I was a translator, and I have an open schedule. So when I'm not—translating—I'm out and about. I was in Camden, meeting up with Avery Armstrong, about some Spanish authors. She's the agent for an author I'm working with. I got a copy of the biography at her office, an extra galley."

Now that she had reconnected me with Avery, she seemed less puzzled. After all, the Camden office was only twenty minutes away by foot, and she'd often walked over there herself, she said.

"Would you like to sit down?" I asked. "I'd love to talk to you about your book."

"Hmm, it's a bit chilly, don't you think?" She paused, then reconsidered. Maybe she was lonely. And praising an author rarely goes amiss. "Why don't you come back with me to my flat for some tea? I'm just up the street a bit."

"I wouldn't want to disturb your work," I said.

"Oh, my work... truth be told, I don't have much of that nowadays. I'm well and truly a pensioner at this point."

I was there longer than I expected, for tea and some shortbread. For Fiona indeed did seem to be lonely. The best part about it was that I picked up a sense of Fiona and her relationship with Stella without having to make up a reason why I was there. The hardest part was that I was inside the flat on false pretenses and had to be careful not to ask questions that might put her off. I would have liked to have asked her, right off the bat, if Stella had known Vonn, and if Fiona really had expressed worry to Avery about Vonn threatening her. I wanted to know if Fiona was aware of Vonn's memoir, and of what the memoir contained, and why, since Stella was long dead, if there was anything in it that could still be a problem.

I wanted to ask whether she was aware of Vonn's death on the Heath, and whether she considered that suspicious in any way. Whether it could be linked to Stella's death years before.

I couldn't think of a way to ask any of these questions. Instead we talked about translation for a bit, and I found out that in addition to Medieval Latin, Fiona knew Flemish and French, in old and modern forms. She said that she had done some translation herself, particularly from Old Dutch, short sections from writers like Beatrys of Nazareth and the thirteenth-century mystic and poet Hadewijch, and from some of the *vitae* or biographies about the beguines. She'd never translated a whole book and seemed impressed that I'd translated over fifty.

What I did learn about Fiona and Stella came indirectly. Fiona and Stan had bought this flat twenty years ago. Stella had owned a larger flat, one floor above. But after Stella's death they'd sold it, and many of Stella's furnishings and things had come to them. They'd kept the house in Inverness. Stan lectured on environmental science there, at the University of the Highlands and Islands, specializing in shoreline ecology, and often doing lab work in Oban. His heart attack on a chartered boat during a marine science expedition around the Hebrides was unexpected. He was only fifty-eight. That was six years ago. The words came in a steady stream as Fiona boiled water and put together a tray in the kitchen. I murmured a few *ohs* and *I sees*, while I glanced around. The kitchen was small and functional with new appliances and not much personality.

"I'm very sorry," I inserted when she got to Stan's death. "First your sister-in-law, then your husband."

"Stan's death was a shock," she nodded and led the way back into the living room to two reading chairs and a coffee table with just one book, a collection of short essays by classicist Mary Beard. "If he hadn't been on the boat, offshore, they might have saved him. Stella's, well, that had been coming for a while. You've read the biography, so you know about her chronic illness. In the end it was pneumonia. Her lungs were not strong."

She poured out tea and offered me milk and sugar. She'd cut her sandwich from Greenberry's, ham and cucumber on white bread, into small triangles, I noticed. The better to eat and talk. For me, she prepared a plate of Reid's shortbread, several sorts.

"Stan didn't ever take to London, but I like it here. I don't have a wide circle of friends, but there are lectures, plays, and bookstores. It's a pleasant walk to Hampstead Heath, I do that often. Inverness is more exciting now, but not so much back then, though the Highlands are spectacular. Do you know the Highlands?"

"I'm more of a city person, I suppose. I prefer London. Though I do like Scottish shortbread," I added, taking a rectangular biscuit from the china plate.

"Stella, too. I mean, she loved London. Later, when she was making a lot of money, she bought a small flat in Bruges, in the Sint-Anna district, near the English Convent, to use as a bolthole. I go there several times a year. But Bruges never feels like a big city. Have you been there recently?"

"Ah, yes, as a matter of fact. It really gives such a feeling of the past, especially off-season. Isn't that a photograph of Stella?" I said, pointing to a framed picture on the mantle, one of several of Stella that looked like a publicity shot. Next to it was a smaller snapshot, also framed. In this one, Stella was in her twenties, wearing jeans and a blue, oversize sweater. Her hair, ash blonde, was cut short, and she was holding a cigarette. There was an élan about her that was missing from most of the photos in the biography and the other framed pictures on the mantle. Here, Stella's smile was jaunty, as if she'd just said something funny and was waiting for a laugh.

Fiona followed my gaze. "Yes, she was a smoker when she was younger. I don't know why I keep that photo around, but I love her smile there. Stan took it. Before she got sick."

"Were she and Stan close?"

"When they were young. Later, I think she found him boring. He was four years older and always rather serious, devoted to science, anxious about the fate of the earth. But he was there for her when she needed him. He was a reliable man, not the most exciting, but understanding. His career was why we moved to Scotland soon after our marriage. I had to give up a few dreams, such as being hired as a lecturer at the University of York. I have a doctorate, you know. In Inverness I did teach the history of the Middle Ages, but often it was introductory courses, with an emphasis on the Norse heritage of Orkney and Shetland."

I nodded sympathetically. "I suppose you met him through Stella."

"It wasn't love at first sight," she said. "But I wanted a home and Stan was kind." The way she said *kind* for some reason made me want to ask if Stella herself was kind. Somehow, I thought not. In fact, the thought flashed through my mind that it was Stella who Fiona had been in love with, but that being unacceptable, she went with Stan. She wouldn't be the first lesbian to marry the brother of the woman she loved. There were no obvious pictures of Stan in the living room, just as there had been none of him as an adult in the biography.

Thinking of the biography brought me back to the present, or rather, the past. "I haven't read all of Stella's books," I said, "but it's clear that you played a significant role in the research. So as it turned out, you did have a chance to use all your scholarly skills. And were you paid for that research?"

Fiona nodded. "Not for the second book, *Illuminated by Death*. I was just one of several who read it and commented on it. My role as consultant was more formalized by the third book, *Schola for Murder*. Avery arranged for payments to me for research on that book and the ones that followed. I would have done it for free, of course. It was more entertaining than some of my teaching responsibilities. I've never been interested in the whole business of publishing, though I love books."

"You've had to manage Stella's literary estate, haven't you?"

"Yes, though I'm not very good at it. To be honest, I usually just toss the royalty statements in a file when they come twice a year and let the accountant deal with everything. Avery is my interface with the publishing world, and she continues to do an excellent job."

I thought of pressing her a little further on Stella and Avery, but worried that she might take offense if I inquired into Stella's last days and the literary estate. Fiona would have had no financial reason to kill her sister-in-law, it appeared. Stella had steadily produced bestselling medieval mysteries, and it wouldn't have benefited Fiona to murder Stella and her golden pen. All the same, I felt that things could have been more complicated between Fiona and Stella, and that there was much Fiona wasn't telling me.

Why should she? I was after all a stranger to her, here only because of my connection to Avery and her trust in Avery.

I decided to get back to Stella's books and see if I could edge Vonn into the conversation. "*Schola for Murder* has a wonderful plot," I said, "I recently watched that episode with a friend of mine, Gayle Winslow." I waited, but she showed no sign of recognizing the name. "She was in the Tudor Roses and had the chance with her group to be in the choir. It was a highlight of her career."

"Oh, yes," Fiona said, now with more animation. "I was on the set when we were filming that segment. It was up in St. Albans, at the marvelous chapel there. I wasn't the musical director, of course, but I had gone over the choice of music very carefully."

I was just about to match her animation by telling her more about Gayle and how Gayle was a friend of Vonn Henley's, and wasn't it too bad about Vonn's death and, I might be wrong, but didn't Vonn and Stella know each other?

But like many academics, Fiona had already seized the opportunity to demonstrate her expertise in the subject. There wasn't much she didn't know about liturgical music composed by medieval women in the thirteenth century. I was reduced to nodding as I waited for an opening to mention Vonn, an opening that was rapidly receding.

After about fifteen minutes, however, Fiona established that perhaps my enthusiasm didn't match her own. "More tea?" she asked, after a pause where I had failed to say, once again, "How fascinating! I had no idea."

Her hands were very well manicured, I noticed as they hovered over the teapot and then returned to her lap. I wondered if her fingertips only indicated she had a lot of free time or if it was a clue to her character. I suspected the offer of another cup might actually be a suggestion that I end my visit. I've spent enough time in England to understand something of their peculiar modes of communication.

But since I'm American, I can also play the card of social ignorance. "Thank you!" I said. "That would be lovely." Seizing again on the Middle Ages as a pretext for staying longer, I asked, "You mentioned in the biography that your dissertation was on medieval women's lives. The *vitae,* I think you called the biographies of women saints and some of the beguines."

"My dissertation was on medieval women writers and composers," she corrected me slightly, as she filled my cup, and poured an inch or two more in her own. "Hence the appeal of the liturgical music in the beguinages. Regarding the literary beguines, I researched and wrote about several, including Beatrice of Nazareth. She studied with the beguines as a young girl but later joined the Cistercians and became an abbess and founder of a convent in Nazareth, in Belgium. Most importantly she was an early writer of prose in Old Dutch. She wrote *The Seven Ways of Divine Love,* a sort of manual of how love is transformed through seven stages of purification."

I nodded as Fiona ran through the seven stages, beginning with "The first way is a fierce longing engendered by Love." She'd mentioned this book in her lecture in February and in her biography of Stella, so I knew that it was important to her. By the time she got to the seventh stage, sublime Love, far beyond reckless passion and desire, I suspected that this text was not just academic to Fiona but had something to do with how she felt about Stella, or how she had trained herself to feel about Stella.

When Fiona paused to sip her tea, I asked if she was Catholic.

"I was raised in the Church of England," she answered. "In adolescence I developed a strong interest in medieval history and thought of converting. Later, my desire diminished. The Vatican's attitude toward abortion, sexual abuse of children—all that is too disturbing, much as I also know the Church has created great beauty. Stella was a believer, on the other hand. I always found that odd, but then, when you're ill you look for comfort wherever you find it. She loved the music, the churches, the saints. Praying gave her great peace at the end."

I nodded. "I was raised Catholic, too, but I have the same diminished interest. Still, the early Church has so many interesting stories of women, don't you think? I find the Catholic saints and martyrs completely fascinating. Have you ever heard of Perpetua and Felicity?"

The cup she had just picked up fell from her hand.

13.

Shortly afterwards, I found myself standing on the sidewalk in Primrose Hill. There had been a flurry around the broken china, and then Fiona said she had a few things she needed to get done. I didn't bring up Perpetua and Felicity again. She couldn't be sure, of course, what I might know about Stella contributing to the Triple L anthology with a piece on the two North African Christian martyrs who died in each other's arms in the Roman coliseum in Carthage. And I couldn't be sure that she understood that I knew about Stella writing that piece for Brize, and what it might imply. All I understood was that Perpetua and Felicity must have had a special meaning for Fiona. All Fiona seemed to understand was that my visit was now firmly over.

In terms of new information about whether Vonn and Stella had known each other, I was still at zero. But I'd pieced together a few more things about Stella's illness and Fiona's role as a researcher and family member. They had been close, very close. Fiona was living in a flat full of Stella's furniture and belongings and still, after all these years, had photographs of her on the mantle and the walls. She managed the literary estate, even if she probably left many decisions to Avery. I wondered if Avery had also contributed to the sanitized version of *Stella Terwicker: A Medieval Life*. Fiona must know far more about Stella than was in her circumspect biography.

Things that Vonn might know or suspect, things that Vonn perhaps believed should have been in the biography. Stella's queerness perhaps? Or more about her illness? Or something revealing about the way that the Beatrys novels were written? I wondered how long it had taken Stella to recover enough from the breakdown in Portugal in the winter of 1994-5 to resume the writing of *The Funeral Specialist*. Had Fiona helped her write that book?

Nicky had suggested I read those Beatrys mysteries, that they might hold clues to what had happened to Stella, and to Vonn. Perhaps I'd take a look later. For now, I wanted to stretch my legs. The day had warmed up since lunchtime, and a thin cloud cover made the sunshine more luminous. Primrose Hill isn't far from Hampstead Heath. I'd been thinking of visiting the pond where Vonn met her end. Why not now?

The larger ponds of the Heath are on the eastern border of the park, somewhere between Parliament Hill and the grand Kenwood House. They form a chain of what were once reservoirs. As always, I found myself wandering on and off paths through dense woodlands and open grasslands, moving more by memory and guesswork than by signage. Gayle had said that Vonn had been found in the shallows of the Bird Sanctuary Pond, a wildlife reserve near the Ladies' Pond. I only knew I'd reached the bird pond by the absence of women with wet hair and towels and by the presence of individuals with binoculars trained on nuthatches and woodpeckers. Since it wasn't quite spring, the trees were bare and there were still winter migrants on the surface of the pond, gadwalls and shovelers mainly (I was no birder, but I'd once had a Swiss-German lover who was very keen).

The pond was muddy at the edges and surrounded by scrubby bushes and willows with only the smallest of buds. The Bird Sanctuary Pond had no fencing around it. Except for the ducks and the birders lurking around, the area was quiet and the water placid. Had she deliberately come here to commit suicide? Or had she met someone on purpose or by accident who wanted to see her dead? Gayle had claimed that Vonn's back seized up at times, which would have made sense if she were actually swimming. It was hard to see how she simply could have slipped and fallen in unless she was very impaired.

The birders who discovered her the next morning had apparently not watched enough cop shows, because instead of immediately calling the police, they had gone into the water to pull Vonn's body out in case she was still alive. In the process, their boots and the dragging marks of the body had completely muddied whatever other footprints there might have been on shore. That was what Gayle had suggested, anyway, when she told me that the birders had found her body near the edge of the pond.

I could guess at the spot where the birders had gone into the water, since the branches of several shrubs were broken, and the ground was particularly muddy. The police must have been around this whole area with their modern-day version of Holmesian magnifying glasses. Had they dragged the pond? Perhaps not, if the postmortem showed no signs of violence.

How had Vonn arrived at the Bird Sanctuary Pond? The last time I'd seen her, at Fiona's lecture, she'd been carrying a bike helmet, and Gayle had mentioned how fit Vonn was, that she worked out and biked everywhere. Yet now that I thought about it, the whole time we'd been at Vonn's flat there had been no mention of her bike, and I'd seen no evidence in the downstairs entryway of a bike rack. There was also no trace in the flat itself of a helmet, panniers, and other biking paraphernalia. The building didn't have a garage, but it may well have had a cellar with storage closets for each tenant. Wouldn't Gayle have also had to empty those storage closets? Wouldn't she have noticed a bike and have added it to the things to be sold or given away?

And what about the laptop? All of us assumed that the laptop was part of what had been stolen from Vonn's flat. But what if Vonn had had her laptop with her that night, perhaps in her daypack? What if the laptop had gone with her into the water or had been stolen by someone?

I backed up from the pond's edge as if sensing some malevolent force nearby, and then sighed. A couple of teenagers hand-in-hand were passing by, completely absorbed in each other. I needed to get out of here and back to the flat in Islington where I could make some calls and do some online research.

The next couple of days should have been dedicated to the bullfighting world of Seville and Rita's investigations into the financial machinations of someone who siphoned off profits from the ring's takings. I'd received a message from Avery saying that SNPs editors were very interested in the synopsis and sample chapters but wanted to see more. Avery offered to pay me to do another twenty pages by next week. Suddenly, and inconveniently, it was a rush job.

I still made time to look for details of Vonn's death, and of Stella's.

There was more on Stella naturally. She was born in 1957 in Lewes, Sussex. Her father was a businessman who also kept a small stable where Stella worked after school. She studied medieval history at the University of York, worked briefly in publishing in London while writing her first mystery, which was published in 1988 by Aphra Press. Two of the obits quoted her editor there, Lucy Aspin. Another editor, now retired, who'd worked with her at Albatross, spoke of her commitment to historical mysteries as a way to engage and teach the public about the lives of women in the Middle Ages. Other quotes came from Avery Armstrong, and from the actor who had played Beatrys in the series. All the articles spoke of her chronic illness and of the "courage," "fortitude," and "bravery" with which she met this obstacle. It was noted that her health had declined further in recent years. The cause of death was pneumonia. Her surviving family members were her brother and sister-in-law Dr. Stanley Terwicker and Dr. Fiona Craig.

All very sad and tidy.

So far, all Vonn rated were two brief mentions in the popular press as an accidental drowning in the bird pond: "Woman Found in Hampstead Heath Pond," and "Woman Identified in Heath Pond Drowning." Vonn was identified only as an elderly freelance writer who had possibly committed suicide. It had happened February 20, a Sunday evening, around seven or eight. Because of the rain there weren't many people around. No one had heard or seen anything. A spokesperson for the park reminded the public not to swim alone, in the dark, and especially not in any non-designated pond without a lifeguard.

There was nothing in the *Guardian,* but there was an article in the local independent *Camden News*, which had a photograph of Vonn and a short article about her life. She was identified as Yvonne Henley, 73, a freelance editor and resident of Camden, a regular swimmer at the Ladies' Pond. There was a quote from the lifeguard at the Ladies' Pond, who had helped identify her for the police. She said that Vonn had a few medical problems but was a strong swimmer. She added that "Vonn was well known to us as something of a rule-breaker." Out of context the quote suggested that Vonn, by swimming in the Bird Sanctuary Pond, had invited her own death. "Of course it's a terrible accident," the lifeguard concluded. "A real tragedy."

The photograph was not a good one, probably for a passport. I wondered who had given it to the *Camden News*. Gayle, perhaps? There was a byline on this article, but no information that mentioned a police report here or in any of the papers. Was Gayle mistaken that someone from the *Guardian* had had access to the postmortem?

I decided it was time to call Gayle and ask her about that, as well as about the missing bike.

She picked up on the first ring and seemed glad to hear from me at first. She asked about Nicky and again apologized for our little spat. "I shouldn't have been so quick to leave," she admitted. "My friends in Clapham have a dog and in return for staying here I feel as though I have to volunteer to take the beast on walks twice a day. It's only temporary, but I'm feeling a bit homeless."

My heart went out to her, but I reeled it back. "I'm sure something will turn up," I said briskly, and then mentioned the bike. "Do you know how Vonn got to the Heath that evening? It was raining quite a lot. Do you think she biked over? That reminds me, what happened to her bike?"

Gayle's voice shook a little. "I imagine she walked over to the Heath. She often walked in the evening when she couldn't sleep. It never made her nervous to be out late. As for the bike, well, I think it's possible Kristi took it, to give to her daughter or Neville. I know it was in the foyer when I came there the first time to talk to the police, but the second time I went to the flat with Kristi, the bike was no longer there. Kristi's never said anything about it, but she probably also took the helmet and whatever else there was for the bike."

"Would she have taken the laptop? I mean, that's different than the bike. It could be material evidence, about Vonn's death."

"Is that why you called me, just to talk about Vonn again?"

"No, no, I wanted to find out how you are. It's just that," I rushed on, "Could you tell me the name of the journalist you mentioned, from the Ladies' Pond? The one who works at the *Guardian*. The one who knows about the postmortem?"

"Alice maybe, Alex, something like that." Her voice was uncertain. "I didn't actually talk to her myself, you know. I shouldn't have passed on the rumors to Nicky about the cause of death, the possible drugs in her system, what people were saying around the Ladies' Pond about Vonn being drunk or incapacitated. I don't want to believe it was intentional, so I cling to the idea it was an accident. The fact is, we'll probably never know why she was there at the pond and what happened. I wish I'd listened to Vida about getting involved. I never wanted to break up with Vida and turn into a bloody dog-walker!"

The conversation came to an awkward end shortly after that, with promises to keep in touch. Once again, I felt more than a little hostility toward Vida for her overbearing, controlling ways. Poor Wee Gayle. It would probably never occur to her to suspect Vida of murdering Vonn, but I had to keep that in mind as a possibility.

★

I called the offices of the *Guardian,* and they unfortunately had on staff
only one female Alice and two male Alex's. The Alice was up in Aberdeen
on a story about offshore drilling. I pictured her in a yellow rain slicker
clinging to a derrick. If it was stormy in London, just imagine what it
was like in the North Sea.

I left Alice an overly detailed message on her voicemail. I could
have called Gayle back to ask who among her friends might know Alice
personally, since she seemed to be a swimmer, but thought I'd wait a few
days and then attempt to meet up with Gayle in person, and to see if she
felt more inclined to dish on her Spanish ex-girlfriend.

Aside from Vida murdering Vonn out of jealousy, my best guess
was that Vonn's death had something to do either with Brize or with the
Beatrys mysteries. I looked back at one of Stella's obits with the quote
from Lucy Aspin, Stella's first editor at Aphra Press. "I knew from the
beginning that although Stella hadn't yet matured into the popular and
successful writer she would later become, she showed great professional
pride in her work and a strong work ethic. For many years I've watched
her career develop. Her death is not a surprise, but it is a great loss for all
of us who knew her."

The quote didn't sound like they were close friends, but Lucy
would be likely to remember the younger Stella and her circle, as well
as the fateful meeting with Avery and Stella's subsequent move to the
mainstream and her success there. I easily found her work number
online. She was in educational publishing at Macmillan.

Lucy didn't have time to talk on the phone but agreed to see me.
Her only free time was this coming Saturday. We arranged to meet for
a late lunch at a pub in Hammersmith, where she lived. I'd introduced
myself as a translator and journalist, and said I was writing about Vonn
and Brize and wanted a little background on feminist publishing back
then. She sounded genuinely grieved to hear about Vonn. Somehow,
she'd missed the news of her death a month ago.

"Was it some kind of accident or...?"

"I believe the police think it was intentional. Not everyone agrees."

Lucy drew in a breath and said again how sorry she was.

I was relieved when I made contact with Corinne Wheelwright in
Bristol via the email Amina had left with Gayle. I couldn't think of how

to phrase my query that I was looking into the circumstances of Vonn's death, so I said something vague about writing an article about Brize and Vonn's role there. I mentioned Amina's name, and that seemed to be enough for Corinne to invite me to her home. The boxes were there. She'd just started on them, but she was happy to talk with me. We settled that I'd come to Bristol for the day on Thursday.

14.

A few days later I was on the train for Bristol to learn more about lesser-known lesbians, specifically Vonn.

I was glad to get away from home for a day. I'd quickly translated more of *Verónica* for Avery to pass on to SNP. I'd sent the same pages to Lola Fuentes, asking for help with some accounting terminology. I was plagued by the phrase *lavado de dinero*. I know the correct translation is money laundering, but whenever I see the word *lavado* I think more of bathtubs, car washes, and rinse cycles. This is the strange thing about language, that is, translated languages. For me, in English, money laundering only evokes corruption, but when I read *lavado de dinero,* I see a wad of euros mistakenly left in someone's pants pocket and thrown into the washing machine. Was it even money laundering we were talking about in *Verónica*? It seemed to be more a case of falsifying the *cuentas* or accounts. I didn't think twice in English when I said, "cooking the books." But when I saw *cocinando los libros,* the image wouldn't leave my mind of Hemingway's *The Sun Also Rises* bubbling gently in a pot on the stove.

The drive to discover more about Vonn's death had ebbed a little, perhaps due to the gray skies and steady London rain, one front coming in after the next. I didn't have time to do much more, detection-wise. Alice was still on the oil platform if she was even the journalist I wanted. I'd gone twice to Vonn's old flat and rung Kristi's buzzer outside the building, but she wasn't home, and never responded to the note I left sticking to the door. Well, who would, if you thought you might be fingered for stealing a nice bicycle?

So far, I had only a few theories, presuming that Vonn had died not by her own hand but someone else's. One: Vida had murdered her out of jealousy. Two: Vonn's death had something to do with Brize and some of the women who worked there who found out about 'Gadfly.' Three: Vonn's death was connected with Avery, Stella, and/or Fiona. All these theories were severely hampered by the fact that someone would have had to have arranged to have met Vonn at the bird pond or followed her there. But how could her murderer have imagined Vonn wouldn't cry out or fight back, or that there wouldn't be witnesses?

I was nowhere, so far, in understanding either the how or the why. But when it came to theory number three, I wondered if, in lieu of the missing memoir, I could do as Nicky suggested and read the Beatrys mysteries in order and see if they shed light on the relationships among Fiona, Avery, and Stella.

I read the first two in London and finished the third on the train to Bristol.

Having recently watched two *Beatrys* episodes with Gayle, I was familiar with the plots of *Woven into Murder* and *Illuminated by Death,* though the feminist tone of the books had been muted for TV. *Woven into Murder* had some of the faults of the beginning writer, but Beatrys's voice was engaging and strong, even feisty, from the first sentence: "No man tells me what to do. Even if he is my oldest brother and thinks he can sell me to the highest bidder."

This was the memory of the sixteen-year-old Beatrys Hartog preparing to escape from home on the morning of her wedding to a rich widower thirty years older, a marriage arranged by her brother Benedict. With the help of her maid, Beatrys let herself down from the second-floor window to the back garden of the family house in a Flanders town. Dressed in her servant's clothes and carrying nothing but her dead mother's pearl earrings, a purse of coins, and food sufficient for several days, she set off at a run for Bruges and the beguinage there. On the way she had to fight off a would-be rapist and rescue a lost child and restore her to her family. When she arrived at the beguinage after almost a week, fainting with hunger, she was taken in and nursed. The Magistra at the time questioned her thoroughly about her background and reasons for leaving home.

"The abbess of a nunnery might have turned me away," Stella wrote, "on the grounds that I wasn't entering the convent with the consent of my family and appeared to have no spiritual vocation. But the Magistra understood that my reason for leaving home was more than to avoid marriage. It was to establish a sense of independence. To be free of domination, in the one place in our male world where women could gather and live together in peace and harmony. The beguinage of Bruges."

As it would turn out, of course, a women's space could mean refuge from the patriarchal medieval world, but, since *Woven into Murder* was a mystery, it didn't necessarily mean peace and harmony. In the first book the murderer was the father of Marie, the servant girl who'd been seduced by the Englishman Robert, who was hiding in the wool bales. But by the second book, *Illuminated by Death,* the murder suspects were all women, those who worked as illuminators in Bruges and in a sister beguinage in Kortrijk, about two days ride away. The story began with the arrival in Bruges of a beguine named Dorte from Kortrijk who came to teach the illuminators in Bruges a new technique to do with gold leaf. Dorte was given a room with two beguines, long-standing friends who lived together in a home of their own in the beguinage, and there the troubles began. The newcomer was attractive and witty, and she seemed to have her eye on one of the beguines. Their relationship as lovers was never spelled out, but Stella clearly meant it to be there, as an undercurrent to the professional rivalry. When the visiting teacher, Dorte, was poisoned by the red ink in one of her little bottles, Beatrys had to step in and solve the murder.

Although Beatrys's own sexuality was ambiguous, she was curious and attracted to the idea of women forming a partnership. She was able to prove, a bit clumsily, that Dorte had been poisoned by mistake, when one of the beguines got the bottles of ink mixed up. She had intended to kill the friend who spurned her love.

Having seen the episode based on this book, I knew that all traces of a lesbian connection had been erased on screen. That wasn't surprising, because clearly those involved in the series wanted to stay away from the misperception that the beguinages were hotbeds of lesbian intrigue in order to appeal to a broad audience. The television series was made almost twenty years ago, after all. I wondered what the deliberate erasure meant to Stella and what it said about her own sexuality. Was she persuaded into de-gaying the episode, or was it a choice she didn't feel she could refuse on the grounds that the series might not be made otherwise? Or was the choice to edit out any lesbian content from the series made before the scripts were even written, when Avery sold Stella's third and fourth books to Albatross?

The third book, *Schola for Murder,* was different. The descriptions were more vivid, and Beatrys's character and those of some of the other beguines were more artfully delineated. But the biggest change was the more sophisticated presentation of the historical information. In the first two books, the background on the history of the beguine movement, on Flemish history, on the work the beguines did in the wool trade, and as scribes of the illuminated manuscripts, was inserted in the dialogue, as in "Please, Agathe, tell me more about your work here with the manuscripts."

By book three, Stella also seemed to have figured out more subtle ways of telling her story. I noted it in the descriptions of the beguine choir, or *schola* and the kind of music they sang. The ethereal sound of the chants and the ways in which the meaning of the Latin phrases played a role in the solution to the murder. The murderer appeared to be another beguine, but in fact was a young man seeking revenge on his mother, who had abandoned the family to become a member of the beguinage. He had donned a habit and veil and slipped into the choir and stabbed his mother.

The mystery had layers of complexity among the characters as well. A new Magistra, Anna van Hoogstraaten, came to the beguinage after the previous spiritual director departed under a small cloud. This created challenges; Anna was an outsider, from a different part of Flanders. She and Beatrys were at odds from their first meeting (Beatrys never liked being bossed around by anyone). The tension between them grew stronger after the murder occurred, when several women suggested that Beatrys might build on her earlier successes as a sleuth to discover what happened. The Magistra felt this was a job for the local sheriff, the good-looking but stubborn Abel.

The book thus had two points of conflict-attraction. Beatrys and Abel, after some initial friction, worked together well to solve the case, though he took most of the credit. They exchanged a kiss or two, and Beatrys was clearly tempted, especially since things at the beguinage were not as harmonious as they had been because of the new Magistra. The ending of the book was deliberately open, probably to build some suspense for what was to come in the next mystery in the series.

According to what she'd written in her biography of Stella and had told me in our conversation, this was the book where Fiona took on a consulting role, especially around the musical traditions of the beguines. Perhaps she acted as a writing coach as well; perhaps Avery had offered advice. More likely Stella had been given an experienced editor at Albatross. The contributions made by an editor to a less-than-polished manuscript were generally underrated. An editor's suggestions could make the difference between a flat prose style and one with more vigor and poise. But an editor could also influence the content, asking questions, planting seeds of doubt, suggesting additions and changes to better fit the market.

The train arrived at Bristol's Temple Mead station shortly after I finished the last pages. After three books, I had a sense of Stella's voice on the page, but in *Schola* I had a fleeting glimpse of other hands at work, of Avery perhaps guiding the plot to make it sound more exciting in a book proposal, or Fiona making sure all the historical information came across with more confidence. Someone along the line, the publisher, editor, or sales department might have made it clear that Beatrys needed a heterosexual romantic interest.

But what did any of this tell me about the possibility that Stella was or had once been lesbian, that she'd written a piece for the Triple L, that she may have known Vonn well enough to thank her for something on the title page of Gayle's copy of *Schola for Murder*? What did any of this tell me about the possibility that Stella and Fiona seemed to have been estranged for a few years, during which time Fiona married Stan and moved to Inverness, only to return to Stella to help her with her books and to nurse her through her chronic illnesses, to inherit her estate, and end by writing a biography of her? A biography that left out a lot of things, including all mention of Vonn.

Corinne had given me directions by bus to her house across the Avon River, in the Southville district. I didn't know Bristol well at all and was glad that the heavy rains of earlier in the week had let up so that I could find my way more easily. The address was on a hilly street, a Victorian brick now stuccoed, with some sort of palm tree in front, but otherwise indistinguishable from the other terraced houses on the block.

I rang the bell and a hazel-eyed Black woman my own age, but more nicely dressed, answered with a big smile. I'd soon learn that the hazel eyes came from Irish great-grandparents who arrived in Canada in the nineteenth century, and the house itself was bigger than it looked from the outside, with a south-facing garden in the back.

15.

"I can't tell you," said Corinne, over bowls of cumin-flavored carrot soup, "how fascinating it was to go through the boxes that Amina sent up from London. Fascinating," she repeated. "And ridiculous, infuriating, and nostalgic all at once. I've got to sit down at some point and read those meeting notes and all the correspondence. Because I truly would like to understand the crazy groupthink and arguments going on at some of those meetings. As it is, some historian in the future will have to reconstruct what all the sound and fury were about. And she'll be shaking her head, muttering *What the hell? These women called themselves feminists?*"

But she said it good-naturedly, because Corinne turned out to be one of the most good-natured women I'd run into in a long time. We were in the dining room of her house, which overlooked the back garden. The first crocuses of spring were a carpet of purple and white under bare-branched apple trees. In summer, the garden must be a delight, there were so many fruit trees and shrubs.

As it turned out, we'd been born in cities just across the border from each other, Corinne in Windsor, Ontario, and me in Detroit, Michigan. My dad had survived the war to find work at a Ford factory, until an accident cost him a finger. When I was just six months old, our family moved to Kalamazoo, where my mother had grown up and had relatives to help us. My dad drove a school bus until his heart attack. Corinne's father was a bus conductor, who'd come to Windsor right after the war, from Jamaica, when Canada passed a national act to attract labor from the British colonies. Her mother was from a small town in Ontario.

How Corinne had gotten to England, to London, to Bristol, how she'd become a nurse and then a healthcare administrator specializing in the LBGTQ community, were longer stories I wanted to hear, almost more than I wanted to hear the story of Brize and Vonn. I liked the look of Corinne, tall and robust in a long, yellow cardigan over a green turtleneck and slacks. She had a yellow-striped scarf around her head, and long, dark, silvered hair spilling out the back. The hazel eyes were intelligent, the cheekbones high, the mouth toothsome.

"But first things first," she said as we finished lunch. "We'll have some tea and biscuits later before you go. I know your priority in coming here is to look at Vonn's papers. I've only done a bit of basic organizing so far."

We headed to a back room on the ground floor, where the boxes I'd last seen in Vonn's flat off the Caledonian Road were arranged along one wall, with file folders neatly stacked on a polished oak table. Some of the piles were high. There was a straight-backed chair with a cushion.

"You said in your email that you were interested in learning more about Vonn and Brize in general and in the Triple L project in particular. Is that right? Because of the article you're writing."

"Yes," I said, a bit uncomfortable. "Vonn's friend Gayle thought there should be an article about Vonn's life. She was fairly sure Vonn was working on a memoir that we could use as a basis for the article. When I was over at the flat and Amina was there going through the files, there was a lot about the lesser-known lesbians. I thought that could be a through-line in the article. If you think about it, Vonn herself was a lesser-known lesbian."

"Aren't we all?" said Corinne. "Mostly *unknown,* I'd say. You should also mention in your article that 'Lives of Lesser-Known Lesbians' was only the working subtitle. We always thought that at some point there would be a proper title. Like 'Anonymous was a Lesbian,' or variations of 'Name that Dyke.'" She looked down at the file folders. "I didn't find anything resembling a memoir manuscript in here."

"Well, Gayle said there were at least some chapters," I stumbled a little, and asked her if she knew Gayle Winslow.

"I don't think we ever met. Amina mentioned her as the one who was clearing out Vonn's flat. Was she in the collective at some point? A lot of women passed through our semi-open doors."

"Gayle and Vonn were lovers, after Brize was disbanded. They stayed friends and Gayle took on the responsibility of Vonn's flat and all her things. Gayle insists Vonn's death could have been accidental, though I gather the police believe it was suicide. Vonn died by drowning, but there's been some mention of pain medications. For back pain. Antidepressants too."

Corinne didn't say anything at first. This line of questioning must be a little more than she'd bargained for. She touched the folders on the table with a polished beige fingernail. "I knew Vonn in the old days. *That* woman would never have drowned herself by accident, much less intentionally. But after her mastectomies and cancer treatments, she wasn't the same old fighter. That's why it's so fascinating and a bit weird to read some of the correspondence and meeting notes in the files. I *remember* that old Vonn. But I knew a different person in the last couple of years. I don't see her as someone who would abuse drugs. Her brother died of a heroin overdose. And when she stayed with me, she didn't overuse her medication. I would have noticed."

The penny dropped. Gayle had said Vonn moved out of London for several months after her surgery. To Bristol.

"So you took her in?" I said. "Even after everything that happened at Brize, the way she attacked you? I mean, that's what Amina said, that Vonn criticized you for being bisexual and that you ended up having to leave."

Corinne looked surprised I knew all this, then gave a big laugh. "So I guess I'm not all that lesser known, am I? My fame as a double agent lives on. Anyway, yes, I did, I offered space for healing to Vonn. What happened at Brize was painful at the time, but it's years and years ago. Vonn knew I'd worked as a nurse in Bristol. Of course I was retired when she contacted me, but I'm connected with the LGBTQ healthcare community. She just wanted some advice about post-surgical chemo, but it ended with me inviting her to come to Bristol to recuperate. As you can see, I have a lot of room here. My grandniece stays here sometimes. She's at the university. Vonn needed a friend and someone who could steer her through the NHS. So she sublet her place in London and came up here. Slept a lot, read, sat in the garden. I made her healthy food and looked after her meds. She was easy to have around."

"You said she'd changed?"

"Well, yes. She'd relaxed. She had her opinions, but she didn't lash out like in the old days."

"Was she depressed?"

"Wouldn't anyone be? Chemo's not an easy thing to go through. But she came back from it. I didn't hear from her as much after she went back to London, but we kept in touch. I knew she was working on some kind of writing project along with her editing work. She interviewed me one day about my memories of the collective. I was frank: what I went through should never have happened. She heard me. She apologized. I mean, really apologized. I was under the impression the memoir was meant to document Brize, not stir up old battles."

That was pretty much the opposite from what Gayle had said, and Avery, who seemed actually to have read some of the chapter on Brize. But I had the sense, perhaps, that Corinne was the sort of person who inspired others to think they could be a better and more forgiving person.

We turned to the table, where ample evidence of the old battles lay to hand in the file folders. Over the course of Brize's short history, from 1982 to 1986, around twenty-five women seemed to have been part of the collective; sometimes it got up to eight at a time, sometimes it was down to three. The only person there at the beginning and throughout was Vonn, whose idea the publishing collective was, but even she was not able to survive in the end, when four others on the collective banded together to force her out.

"From what I heard," said Corinne, "she didn't go without a struggle. A lot of the original legal documents were in her name. She claimed she didn't want to bring Brize crashing to a halt, but that's what effectively happened. The printers weren't paid, the bookstores were fed up, the other women quit one by one. Vonn told me that all she'd planned to do was make them see how much they needed her, but she never managed to pull things together again. The debts were too great, and nobody wanted to work there. It's a shame, really, because Brize was trying to do something important, to articulate a vision of class and multiracial solidarity. They failed, bigtime, but you can see in their failures that they made an effort."

She picked up some typed, stapled-together sheets of paper that articulated the political position of Brize, as written by "the Brize Collective." The pages were dog-eared, the title was "Where We Stand."

"This was essentially Vonn's analysis of what Brize stood for," Corinne said. "Vonn had been influenced by the Leeds Revolutionary Feminist Group and their position paper, 'Love Your Enemy?' about political lesbianism versus heterosexual feminism. Vonn wanted to put ideas about political lesbianism into practice through a publishing collective. She did have a degree in English, you know. I think she probably imagined publishing her own books through the collective, but she never seemed to find the time to write with all the work there was to do at the press."

"How did you get involved in Brize? Were you a political lesbian?"

"Far from it. I'd done my nursing training in London and had a job there as well. I shared a flat with other nurses, and one of them was lesbian. I started to go to the clubs and discos and had a fine old time." Corinne smiled at the memory. "I was together with a woman named Glo for a bit. She was part of the Brize collective and said they were looking for more Black women to join. We were a very mixed lot. Only Vonn had experience in publishing. You wouldn't think it, but there was laughing as well as fighting. Vonn had a wild side. We went out after work sometimes and stayed late, dancing. She was a swing dancer, among the best."

Corinne shook her head, so her long hair bounced, then went on, "In addition to me and Glo, there was Amina and three white women: Susie, a Brit, and Petra from Germany. And Vonn. And what Vonn called the 'consulting team.' Outside readers, some of whom had been on the collective before, or women from fringy political groups. They were always 'weighing in,' taking manuscripts off to read and never returning them, appearing at the office with articles they wanted us to publish as pamphlets, relaying gossip about various women writers. I never completely understood the power that group had, since they didn't do any of the actual work. They used to call me the Canadian peacekeeper because that was sometimes my role. Later I realized we Black women were mostly tokens. The consulting team was largely white."

Corinne was no longer smiling. "I was only part of the collective about four or five months. I had my nursing work, and it was just too much. And I'd started a new relationship with a man, a Black doctor at the hospital where I worked. Vonn was horrible about it and tried to make me choose. Was I with them or not? I left the meeting in tears, and Glo went with me. For a while I felt guilty at letting the collective down. But I was in love and happy. Eventually my man and I got married and moved to this house in Bristol. We split up after a few years, because I fell for a woman again... and why I'm telling you all this, I don't know!" she added with a wry laugh. "Good thing you're not taking notes! Maybe it's just seeing all these papers. It's brought back projects I worked on, what I hoped for when I joined the collective. I know I should be more critical. But it meant a lot to me somehow. That's why I jumped when Amina asked if I'd like to go through everything before turning it all over to the archive here in Bristol."

Corinne walked toward the door, giving me a chance to admire her curves. "So, I'll leave you to this for as long as you like. I'm going out to do some shopping and then maybe around three you can take a break. We'll have tea and a bite to eat. Do you have to get back to London for anybody?"

I assured her I had nobody waiting.

Then I plunged in.

It might well be that there were no chapters of the memoir here, but there were some transcripts of Vonn's interviews with women who'd been on the collective. Corinne had thoughtfully pulled out these transcripts, along with voluminous correspondence about the Triple L project that began in 1984. There were also the meeting notes, and a fat manila folder marked "Rejections!" The exclamation mark spoke of a certain glee in responding to query letters and manuscripts.

I read through some of the Triple L material first, then switched to the typed and hand-written meeting notes, making notes on some of the names of the collective members. Very few of their names rang a bell. Corinne left for her shopping and returned. I heard her in the kitchen and began to long for teatime. To go through all this material would be the work of days. Perhaps I could make copies of some of papers, the interviews for instance? There were six, and they all followed more or less the same trajectory: woman joins Brize collective with expectations of learning about publishing, or because she wants to make a difference, or because she's new to London and wants to make like-minded friends. She generally is excited and believes she shares the aims of the group. She does not say exactly why she stopped working with the collective, but often mentions that it was an important part of her life.

The interviews seemed to have been edited not just for length, but likely for content, since the tone was consistently positive and political. No one complained that Vonn was overly bossy or that the advisory group was a pain to deal with. Most of them came from the first year or two of the Brize effort. They were only named with their initials in the transcripts. RG, BW, LH.

I wondered who these women were and how I could find out. I turned to the file marked "Rejections!"

To my surprise, none of the copies of the rejection letters that I skimmed, and there were several hundred, were signed by a person, only by "the Brize collective." But it became clear that many of them were written by one person with a distinctive style, who sometimes was briefly dismissive on the grounds of inappropriate content—"We do not publish how-to books. Please see enclosed guidelines for submission"—but more often took the opportunity, sometimes at great length, to point out writing flaws, from large issues to small, even down to overuse of commas and misspellings. Who would take the time to do all this for books that would never be published? The answer could only be an obsessive copyeditor type, and perhaps a frustrated writer herself. Probably Vonn Henley.

There was a certain fascination in discovering a few well-known names among the many rejections addressed to women not only in England and Scotland but in India, Australia, New Zealand, Canada, and South Africa. I hoped that perhaps I'd see Fiona's name or Stella's, because otherwise I was probably going to return to London without being any the wiser about Vonn's death. If any one of these authors nursed a grudge against Brize and Vonn, enough of a grudge to drown her, I was probably not going to find out.

Then, a name jumped out at me, one I wasn't expecting. Vida Carrasco. Compared to some of the other letters, it was short.

Dear Vida,

Thank you for sending us your poetry manuscript. We're afraid after some discussion among our readers and collective members, we have decided against publishing it. Although you have some good lines in several poems, they are just that, individual good lines. They never add up to anything that could be called powerful. Instead, they are like a single chili pepper in a bowl of thin soup. You mention in your letter that you are from Spain, and we remember you from your contribution to the biography project. There, although several in the collective liked the idea of the Lieutenant Nun, you'll recall we rejected it on the grounds of her not actually being an out lesbian, but a transvestite. These poems we must reject on other grounds, namely that the language is awkward and bland. We realize that you are not a native speaker, but some of your word choices are stilted and the meaning does not come across. We recommend that you do more reading to improve your ear. It may be that poetry is not something you should attempt.

Like many of the rejection letters, the original query letter was attached, while the manuscript itself had been sent back in a self-addressed envelope. The letter from Vida mentioned getting some encouragement to send in the poetry manuscript to Brize, which must have made the rejection even worse. As far as I knew, Vida had never published a book, but had turned her attention solely to business after that.

I put the letter back in the pile. Corinne might claim that Vonn had changed. But the trouble with changes brought on by time and illness is that they often came too late, sincere apologies notwithstanding. Self-help books often encouraged us to not drag our past mistakes around with us like dead cats. But the fact was, even if we ourselves let go of past mistakes, other people were still apt to remember them.

And perhaps sometimes, take a last, late revenge.

16.

"The Lieutenant Nun?" said Corinne. "I remember her well. We had an all-day editorial meeting about the Triple L., with the plan of seeing what we had, and getting the biographical essays and essay ideas organized into categories. Vonn called the meeting and we started at eight in the morning with plenty of coffee. By noon when we got some takeaway, we had only gone through about five short essays. And the afternoon was worse, because of the nun from Spain who cut off her hair and became a conquistador in Peru." She took a deep swallow from her glass of red wine and leaned toward me on the sofa. "So here I am, it's my second month in the collective. I'm a nurse, right, with an interest in books. An interest in lesbian history. I've read the bios and think all of them are interesting, including the Lieutenant Nun. I don't have a sophisticated understanding of the ins and out of what makes a lesbian a lesbian. All I know is what I'm picking up from hanging around the clubs and from Glo and from some of her gay male friends, and my impression is that anything goes. That it's not called Gay Liberation for nothing."

Corinne and I had had our tea and biscuits in the kitchen, and then she'd brought out some chilled Tio Pepe and olives, bread, and cheese, and we'd moved to the living room. She'd lit some candles and it was long past twilight. She'd mentioned going out to dinner and I had stopped mentioning that I had a train to catch.

"What I don't get at that meeting is that in spite of the idea that we're a collective, and Vonn's references to wanting to hear everybody's opinion, she doesn't really want those opinions to be different than hers, and she certainly doesn't want our opinions to have the same weight as hers. But most of us don't really understand that, not at first. We think if the majority of us like the piece, then the piece should be included in the anthology. Vonn is smart enough to know that she has to, in theory, accept that. But she doesn't accept it completely. Instead she says, "Well, since there's no consensus on this, let's put it in the 'undecided pile.' And in the interests of moving on, most of us are willing to do that. But one of the white women, Petra from Germany, has been there longer and she's wise to Vonn's delaying tactics. After all, the anthology has been in process for months by now, with some submissions already accepted by members of the collective when it was composed of different women.

"Petra contradicts Vonn and questions the process and provokes Vonn into raising her voice. And sometime in the afternoon Petra walks out and we never see her again. Meanwhile, the debate is raging about the criteria, and the Lieutenant Nun is held up as an example of a woman who's not woman-identified *at all*. She wears male clothes and passes as a man and does all kinds of male things with her sword and even though she appears to flirt with women and desire them, she does that in her guise as a male. Plus, she's part of the horrible Spanish colonization of South America, which the author, Vida Carrasco, has criticized, but not *sufficiently*.

"Although several of us make a point that lesbians in the past could not possibly live openly as lesbians like we can today, and if we exclude women like the Lieutenant Nun, then we'll be left only with Radclyffe Hall and Natalie Barney. Vonn disputes this, pointing to the pile of essays, with a few biographies of women that go back to antiquity. She's willing to include Sappho, and some of the saints. But the Lieutenant Nun, no."

"And you couldn't overrule her?"

"Vonn was cannier than we were. After putting up a good fight, she allowed the Nun to go into the 'yes' pile. But by the next editorial meeting, two weeks later, she'd sent out a rejection letter, 'by mistake.' It should have been obvious what Vonn's idea of an open collective was. I should have quit then. But by then I was seeing my man and keeping it secret and soon enough Vonn got wind of it, and I left anyway. There was no "B" in LGBTQ then, never mind the many other letters." She looked at me questioningly. "That bother you? That I'm bi?"

"I've never paid much attention to identities," I said. "Maybe it's from traveling so much."

"I really tried to be what some women thought I should be," said Corinne. "I loved the idea of women's space, of lesbian space. It seemed so freeing—at first. Then, when I realized I couldn't do that, be the perfect lesbian separatist, didn't want to do that, I was upset and angry. Just because I was sexually attracted to men, to some men, didn't mean

I wasn't a feminist. In fact, for me it's been more liberating to be bi, to express all parts of myself. But some of my friends, then as now, see me as just confused. It was always, 'So what are you today, Corinne? Gay or straight? They'd look at my current partner and that was how they'd think they knew.'"

"Do you think that these days, anybody really cares?" I asked.

"My grandniece, who's nineteen and reads gender studies at uni here in Bristol, thinks the whole idea of calling yourself anything so simple as a lesbian is terribly quaint. *Why would you limit yourselves*? she asked me once." Corinne sighed, "Of course, now that I'm in my early seventies, there's an automatic assumption I have no sexual life at all."

"And do you?"

Corinne laughed and changed the subject. Too bad. For a moment I thought there had been an invitation in her hazel eyes with their curly lashes. But it was hard to believe that such an attractive woman wouldn't have a lover or two.

I stayed two nights in Bristol, sleeping in the guestroom, and would gladly have stayed longer if it weren't for needing to get back to London by Saturday at two for my pub lunch with Lucy Aspin. We didn't talk about Corinne's sexual life or mine, but I was sure that she was interested in me, just as I was interested in her, mind and body. Some might wonder how I could go from desiring Wee Gayle to admiring Corinne's big, beautiful curves, but I've always kept an open mind about the ways of desire. It might also be because Gayle was in London and still hung up on Vida. Corinne was in Bristol, two and a half hours from London, the kind of distance I preferred. I liked her independence. It's always better when a woman has a life of her own.

On Friday, around noon, after I'd spent a few hours looking at Vonn's Brize files without finding anything that resembled a memoir or that indicated why and how she might have died, Corinne and I went on a walk that took us along the river and into the city center for lunch. I hadn't been to Bristol for many years and in any case Corinne's Bristol was a different city than I'd known when I passed through years ago. In the center of the city was a bronze statue of Bristol benefactor Edward Coleson, increasingly an object of scorn and disgust. The city had refused to remove the statue, giving rise to various art interventions over the years: a slogan painted on the plinth that said *Slave-Trader*, and an unauthorized plaque attached to the plinth that described Bristol as the "Capital of the Atlantic Slave Trade 1730–1745." Later came a ball and chain attached to the statue. Another installation had appeared more recently in the form of a hundred figures arranged as though they were on a slave ship.

Corinne had been here a long time. I learned that her older sister had left Ontario just to get away from home. Corinne followed her to study. They stayed at first with a cousin of their father's and his wife, both from Jamaica. Her sister returned to Canada and married. Corinne went to London for a few years and then she and her husband found jobs in Bristol. She eventually came to specialize in issues related to LGBTQ health. Besides her marriage, she'd had a few partners, one for as long as three or four years, but considered herself more of a single person. She'd never wanted children. She'd never wanted to go back to Canada, even though she knew it was far different than when she'd grown up in the fifties and sixties in Windsor. "My mum was white, you see. She loved us all, Dad, me, and my sister, but she didn't really understand racism. Her big thing was, 'We're all the same under the skin.' Yeah, Mum, tell it to the Mounties. But the main thing was, the reason I stayed in England, was that I could be queer here more easily. Mum didn't understand that. And Dad was adamantly anti-gay."

Still, she'd kept her Canadian accent.

We didn't return to the boxes until later in the afternoon and, after our long perambulations through the city, I was too tired to read through many more files.

Lack of thoroughness had often been my Achilles heel in my amateur career as an investigator. I was easily derailed by women, and I was having trouble keeping my mind on Vonn when it wanted to think about Corinne.

Still, over dinner at a neighborhood restaurant, I found myself talking more frankly to Corinne about the problem of Vonn's death. I didn't give away everything I knew, certainly not about Fiona and Avery, but I talked about why some things about Vonn's death seemed unusual. I circled back to Gayle and the experience of cleaning the flat. The missing laptop, the missing bike. No sign of the memoir in her papers, and no correspondence with the agent she'd contacted about the project. Having been through a basic search of Vonn's files, I was struck by the absence of anything that would link her to Avery or Fiona, and particularly by the absence of notes or drafts on the memoir, nothing besides the interviews with former Brize collective members.

Corinne agreed that was odd. "Another thing I noticed, is that her interview with me, the one she did when she was staying here, isn't in the files. That was early on in her memoir project. Maybe she never typed it up. There could be more material from her memoir project that isn't here. Other interviews, other notes. I didn't think about that."

"I *have* wondered," I said carefully, "if there could have been anything incriminating in the files. I mean, maybe it was possible that someone from her past had a key to her flat. Maybe someone from Brize who knew she had the files and that she was writing a memoir."

"That sounds very cloak-and-dagger."

"Did Vonn stay in touch with friends from the early days? The Brize members or maybe others from the feminist movement?"

"Some," Corinne said. "But she'd fought with so many people and, frankly, many never forgave her. She was a solitary creature really, and she regretted that when she got sick. She'd burned so many bridges. She could get a kind of bewildered feeling, she told me, about what she'd believed and thought was possible during the utopian years of lesbian separatism—and how things had turned out. She admitted she felt at sea with the new generation of queer kids. They were messed up, like she'd been messed up, conflicted and angry about how they were treated. But their solutions were different. She was honestly really interested in how I'd navigated all the changes in gay culture. I said it was my work that kept me up to date, as much as I could be. I worked with all kinds of young and old people, AIDS survivors, teens, people of different ages exploring gender reassignment."

Corinne paused, remembering, "She was pretty interested in transfolk, actually. Once she said to me, 'I don't know, maybe if I was sixteen now, that's the way I would have wanted to go. At the time, I thought being butch was me, combining all I liked about being boyish and tough, but maybe if I had the chance now, I'd go for it. Become a man. Even though I dislike most men.'

"'Well, you've already had top surgery,' I told her. I was afraid she'd be angry at my levity, and started to apologize, but she laughed. 'Yeah, that's one way to think about it. I don't really miss them all that much. Small as they were.'

"Like I said, she'd mellowed. Age had humbled her. She'd struggled a lot in the past ten or fifteen years. Some regular editing work that she'd relied on dried up in the mid-2000s. Feminist publishing was over, and she had to take jobs where she could find them. Copyediting newsletters, for instance. But that got harder too, as people turned to software editing programs. By the time she and I were back in touch, I got the impression she was just getting by."

Corinne, on the other hand, seemed very well set up. She didn't have a car, but she had a lovely house, and she mentioned various trips to the Caribbean. I wondered if Vonn had been tempted to stay on.

"You and Vonn?" I asked.

"No way," Corinne said. "Though I would have been happy for her to visit a bit longer. But she had to get back to London and resume some of her freelance jobs. The subletter hadn't been able to pay much."

Something occurred to me. "Did she ever mention who was subletting?"

Corinne thought for a minute. "I don't remember. It's over two years ago. I think she said an old girlfriend, no surprise there."

"Do you remember who some of Vonn's old girlfriends were? Did she sleep with other women in the collective?"

"Always. That was part of how she operated and how she got her way. Glo knew more about it than I did. She told me stories! Sometimes women left the collective in a huff not because of political differences, but because Vonn had lost interest in them or started up with someone else."

"What was the secret of her success with women?"

"I only know from hearsay," said Corinne, shrugging. "I didn't find her sexually appealing, too ratty in that leather jacket and torn jeans. Though she did have a winning smile. But some women just couldn't keep their eyes off her. There was the swing dancing, the motorcycle, weightlifting for a while. Athletic in all ways apparently."

Was it possible that one of these old girlfriends from Brize realized that Vonn was writing a tell-all and didn't like the idea of being included in such a book? Had one of them been subletting the flat and happened to have kept her key? She could have later used that key to let herself in and steal the manuscript in progress as well as the laptop it was written on.

I asked her, "Is there a chance you could write down the names of most of the women who were part of the collective, going from the meeting notes?"

"I could try," said Corinne. "But why? What is it you're after, Cassandra?"

This was not the place to tell her that I had an intermittent history of poking my nose into other people's business. I just said that there seemed to be some confusing things about Vonn's death and a few different opinions. I didn't say the word murder, but Corinne seemed to pick up on my hesitation.

"I suppose that it's important to know how Vonn died," she said. "It's one thing if it was an accident, another if it was intentional. Another if... there was anyone involved in her death. It changes the story of what we say about her now she's gone and about what her life meant."

"It seems worthwhile asking a few questions," I said lightly. "After all, she was a memorable figure in British lesbian-feminist history, wasn't she?"

"I'd say more that she was a lesser-known lesbian, who deserves to have her contributions recognized. I'm glad you're writing your article, Cassandra. Let me know if you need more from me."

"I may want to come up to Bristol again and look through the files," I said.

"Soon, I hope," she said.

Saturday morning I lingered as long as I could, but finally tore myself away from the breakfast table and took a bus back across Bristol, to board a train for Paddington Station. I regretted I'd made a lunch date with Lucy Aspin, but Corinne had a busy day ahead of her, so it was just as well. She might live alone but she was enmeshed in her community here. I was just someone passing through. That was usually just how I liked it.

But I found myself wondering, as I sat on the train rumbling south, what it would be like to, just once, stay longer and keep staying.

17.

From Paddington I went straight to Hammersmith and to the pub that Lucy Aspin had suggested down near the Thames. It was posher than I expected, one of those historic places with a fire within and a garden in back. I was glad to find her inside, even though the weather was warming up to a lovely feeling of spring. I recognized her from her LinkedIn photograph: no-nonsense gray bob with heavy bangs, a thin face, keen blue eyes.

But the photo didn't capture the smile she gave me as she waved. She had a space between her front teeth that was endearing and made her eyes crinkle. And she wasn't wearing a white blouse and suit jacket as she had been online, but a velvety burgundy coat with a loose silk scarf. There was something of the dyke about her, perhaps the utter lack of make-up or the glance she gave me, head to shoes, but she was altogether more prosperous looking than me and some of my friends. I felt self-conscious that I had on the same clothes I'd worn when I set out Thursday morning for Bristol on a day trip, though I'd washed out my underwear and socks at Corinne's. As usual, my curly hair was disheveled with travel and the weather. But Lucy didn't hesitate. She got up and gave me a warm handshake and asked what I'd have.

In a moment she was back with two pints of lager and a menu. "The food here is excellent. And you must be starving from being on the train."

I glanced at the menu. It seemed like I'd eaten a lot at breakfast, but after my two days with Corinne, I felt in need of bulking up. She'd mentioned at one point that I was too skinny. So I opted for some pasta in a cream sauce, while Lucy ordered chicken pie with leek and onion.

"So you've just come from Bristol," she said encouragingly as we waited. I tried to remember just what I'd told her to get her to meet me. Something about Vonn Henley and her papers going to Bristol and being asked by a friend of Vonn's to write about her work with Brize based on those papers.

"Yes," I said, sipping my pint. I had imagined that Lucy would be hard to pry information out of somehow, maybe because she was, according to her profile, some bigwig at Macmillan, but she seemed friendly enough and curious as to what I needed from her.

She said, "You know that I wasn't part of the Brize Collective? I worked at Aphra Press for about eight years, starting in 1987."

"Right," I said. "The heyday of feminist publishing. Amazing to think back on those times and all that was published. Aphra was always at the forefront. Where are the archives for Aphra, by the way?"

"At the Women's Library at LSE, with some of the other presses. I'm surprised that the Brize papers aren't going there. Did Vonn have them all this time? Was there a special connection with Bristol?"

"Yes, I believe so," I said. "The collections at Bristol go back over fifty years, to the beginnings of the women's liberation movement and feminist history in the UK. Posters, pamphlets, newspapers, ephemera, books, clothing, and pins, along with meeting notes and position papers. They wanted the Brize archives. I suppose Brize wasn't so much a publisher, in a way, as it was a manifestation of feminist activism."

I must have sounded authoritative because Lucy nodded. "Of course. Compared to most of the presses, Brize didn't publish much. At one time I was much more involved in feminist publishing, but Brize had dissolved before I was hired at Aphra. My work over the past years has been in educational publishing, mostly digital these days. I'll be leaving at the end of the year, retiring. I'm thinking of moving out of London to be closer to my daughter."

We chatted briefly on the merits of staying or leaving London until our food arrived, and then I began circling around Aphra and Brize again, asking first how Lucy got into publishing. She seemed happy to tell me, in between bites of her chicken pie, which had arrived with a glorious puff-pie crown. I imagined it could have been a while since anyone had asked about that part of her life.

"I got the job as an editor at Aphra by chance. I'd been doing some freelance copyediting for them, and they were expanding around then. An infusion of money from an investor. I edged out some more experienced applicants, mainly because they were familiar with my work and knew I was dying to become an acquiring editor. Vonn had applied as well, I later found out. She didn't get the job at Aphra, but I ended up hiring her for freelance copyediting for a few years. I was the only staff editor who used her."

"She wasn't a good copyeditor?"

"She was a very good editor," Lucy said with her gap-toothed smile. "But she was known as an angry separatist, and she hadn't made a good impression during her job interview by slagging off women's presses with corporate investors. Which was the case at Aphra, of course. For most of our existence we were part of another publishing company. Still, she wasn't too pure to take copyediting jobs from us and to try once in a while to get us interested in editorial projects."

"Such as?"

"Oh, at the beginning she wanted to do a sort of encyclopedia of lesbian biographies and told me that she had most of the short essays in hand. But in fact, this had been a Brize project and was in shambles. There were no contracts with authors, and we would have had to start from scratch. Aphra's director said absolutely not. I did read most of the essays though and discovered a few interesting writers. Aphra reprinted some early lesbian novelists whose work had been forgotten, and a couple of women from the anthology approached us separately about their own projects."

"Was one of them Stella Terwicker?"

Lucy looked surprised. "Why, yes. She was a friend of Vonn's. Vonn told me that Stella had a manuscript about a medieval woman detective and my ears pricked up. You might remember there was a boom in feminist thrillers around then. Some of the first authors were from the States, and we had British authors writing them as well. You wouldn't have had a clue that she'd be so successful based on that first one."

"Was that *Woven into Murder*?" I asked casually, trying not to show how chuffed I was that the conversation was so easily going in the direction I'd hoped for without me having to lie too much.

"Yes. It was just a draft then, not an entirely successful draft, but promising. The basics of the series were all there though: thirteenth-century Flanders, the women of the beguinage, the wool trade and so on. Stella had done her research. The language was sometimes awkwardly archaic, with tons of explanation, and quite clumsily plotted, the murder didn't happen until about two-thirds of the way through. And Beatrys was about forty, so there was a lot of backstory to get through. So I suggested Stella go back to the drawing board and make Beatrys younger, give her some family problems, and create a real villain or two. She changed it quite a bit and Beatrys became a young apprentice weaver. I think she got some help from Vonn as well."

"In what way, help?" I was finished with my pasta, gooey but delicious, and said no to dessert, just tea. But Lucy ordered gooseberry tart with cream, and an Irish coffee. She seemed to be enjoying remembering the old times when she had acquired books and worked with authors, because she went on, now in a more gossipy tone.

"Frankly, I don't think that Stella would have had half the success if Vonn hadn't worked so hard on those first books. People imagine that a copyeditor just removes or inserts a few commas, but there's so much more that happens, from tightening sentences to moving paragraphs around. Just from *Woven into Murder* to *Illuminated by Death* there was a significant difference. Stella was no fool, she was very clever really, about her abilities and her career. She knew what she had in Vonn." Lucy savored her coffee. "Of course, maybe it's general knowledge, but they were involved for a while."

"Oh, I didn't know," I said neutrally. "I don't know much about Vonn's personal life, or anything, really, about Stella except what I read in the new biography. The one by her sister-in-law."

"Fiona Craig," nodded Lucy. "I skimmed it. I couldn't believe she didn't write about Stella as a lesbian. I don't know what happened later in Stella's life, romantically anyway. Fiona never suggests any love interests *at all*. I suppose because of Stella's chronic illness she didn't have relationships later on, but when I knew her, she always had someone in her life. Vonn for a bit, but others too. Broke a few hearts. Not mine, though I was tempted. I had a steady boyfriend then. It took a few years for me to come out, and by then Stella and I weren't even speaking."

"Oh?"

"Well. I'm exaggerating." Lucy polished off the rest of her gooseberry tart. "I was a bit naïve in my early years in publishing. I thought of our main competitor as Harridan. They had more money and a different profile. Aphra was meant to be scrappier and to do more political writers and edgier topics. Sometimes our authors moved to Harridan, and I thought that might happen with Stella, but in fact, she went mainstream. We'd done a lot of marketing for Stella's second mystery, arranged all kinds of readings and interviews, got her on *Women's Hour*, and sold rights to her books in Germany and Scandinavia. When she left us, I was really upset. Honestly, I felt betrayed."

"What happened?" I asked, remembering how Avery had told the story, of going to one of Stella's readings and talking to her afterwards.

"Stella was brilliant in public. Very lively, quick on her feet. Of course she'd attracted notice, but she also often said in her interviews how important the women's presses were. Until Avery Armstrong swept her off her feet and stole her from us. Or that's what it felt like at the time." Lucy sat back in her chair, smiling a bit ruefully. "In those days, it seemed a very non-feminist thing to do. But later, of course, I understood authors wanting to make more money, and the role that agents played in their careers. Later on, while I was still at Aphra, I bought a few books from Avery and found her very professional. She really cares about her authors and tries to keep them happy."

"Are you still in touch with Avery? I've worked with her myself," I said. "With some foreign authors."

"Oh, that's right," she nodded. "You said you were a Spanish translator. You must know Vida Carrasco then. I take my computer problems to her."

I gave a noncommittal nod.

Lucy said, "I wouldn't call us friends—I mean Avery. I haven't seen her for years since she doesn't bring her authors to Macmillan's educational unit. She did a lot for Stella of course, with the television series."

"And what about Vonn? Were you in touch with her at all?"

"Not much after Stella left. I remember she was really furious with Stella for going with a big press. But they were no longer an item, and I don't know if they remained friends. I really lost touch with what Vonn was doing. I left Aphra in the mid-nineties for Macmillan and have been with them ever since. I needed a better salary and benefits after I had a child. My then-partner, a woman, was willing to stay home with our daughter, so I needed to be the breadwinner. We're not together any longer," she added.

She looked a bit wistful but said firmly, "I'm actually rather glad I got out of feminist publishing when I did. No, you must let me get the check, Cassandra. I don't know how helpful I've been, but I felt—well, it was terribly sad to hear about Vonn's death. So I'm glad to hear that you've involved yourself in her archives and writing something about Brize. Vonn was quite a difficult person, I know, but I also rather enjoyed her bluntness. And she had a wickedly attractive smile."

"Yes," I said, feeling guilty at my own deviousness. "I only knew her over the years in passing, but I'm friendly with others who knew her, so I wanted to do my bit to make sure she's remembered."

We parted, and I returned to the Hammersmith tube station. I wasn't sure what I should do next. Without a plan, I stepped into a car on the Piccadilly line bound for King's Cross.

I felt that my ideas about Vonn had undergone a shift in the past two or three days. First of all, Corinne didn't think she was such a bad person and now Lucy seemed to remember her with some affection and respect. I had confirmation that Stella and Vonn had been an item sometime in the late eighties when Stella was publishing her first two novels, and that Vonn worked on the Beatrys mysteries as a freelance copyeditor. Had Vonn worked on other mysteries besides the first two? That would bring Vonn closer to Avery than Avery had indicated. It might bring Vonn closer to Fiona as well, for Fiona was the biographer and had never mentioned Stella's lesbian lovers, including Vonn. Had Avery and Stella then been lovers as well? It wasn't impossible.

But what did that have to do with Vonn's death? Once again it was gossip and speculation rather than hard facts. I thought again about the bike and the bike gear, and what Gayle had said about Kristi probably taking the bike. I remembered that I'd not yet been able to contact Kristi. But today was Saturday and Vonn's neighbor might be at home.

I'd asked Corinne about Vonn's past girlfriends and was particularly interested in whether one of them had sublet her flat while she'd gone to Bristol to recuperate from the mastectomy. Surely Kristi would remember the name of that girlfriend if she'd been there for two months or more.

Could the old girlfriend, by any chance, have even been Gayle Winslow?

Instead of getting off at King's Cross, I stayed on the train to the next station, Caledonian Road.

This time, Kristi answered the buzzer with a cautious "Yeah, who is it?"

"Cassandra Reilly. I met you briefly a couple of weeks ago when Gayle was cleaning out Vonn's apartment."

"Don't remember," she said. She sounded as if she'd had a beer or two.

"Can I come up? I wanted to buy Vonn's bike, if you still have it? I'd pay well for it."

There was a pause. She didn't deny it. "Not a good time. My granddaughter's here."

"Okay, I'll try you again at a better time. Can you just answer one question now?" I said quickly, before she could hang up the phone. "When the police came initially to Vonn's flat, why was it Gayle you called?"

"Had her number on my phone, didn't I? Figured somebody from Vonn's crowd should be told."

"Oh, of course," I said. "And you had Gayle's number because... because she once sublet Vonn's flat a couple of years ago?"

"Too much singing," Kristi mumbled. "But yeah. Gayle."

She was gone. I stood in front of the intercom and then slowly turned away.

My Tudor Rose? She'd never mentioned anything about subletting Vonn's flat for two months. So, she was a liar, Wee Gayle.

And she'd had a key to Vonn's flat.

18.

I stood at the edge of the Ladies' Pond, shivering in a bathing suit I'd last worn six months ago, on a sunny beach in Uruguay. It was some time since I'd swum here in the Heath, and when I had, it was during the hot days of summer. Today the air temperature was in the fifties and the water was even cooler. Nevertheless, I decided to go in. I'd been waiting for half an hour for Gayle to show, and I needed to move. I'd paddle around just enough to get my blood moving, then jump out and take a warm shower in the bathhouse where I'd left my towel and clothes.

It was Gayle who'd suggested we meet at the Pond today at two p.m. She said she was planning to come here anyway, since it was Sunday, and the forecast was for partly cloudy but not too cold. I'd said there was something I wanted to discuss, but I hadn't said what, only that I'd been up to Bristol to look at the boxes now they were at Corinne's.

"Did you find something?" Gayle asked. I thought her voice sounded a bit vulnerable, so I tried to be reassuring.

"Nothing earth-shaking. But it would be nice to see you again. I've been wondering how you are. You're still in London, I take it?"

"For now," she said, without elaborating. Or without saying she'd wondered how I was as well. But she did agree to meet me.

I hadn't wanted to confront her on the phone about why she'd never mentioned subletting from Vonn. After all, maybe it wasn't really a lie, but a simple chronological screw-up. Maybe she'd run into Vonn here at the Ladies' Pond, after surgery but before she'd gone to Bristol for chemo and recovery. Something told me that was unlikely. No one has a double mastectomy and immediately pops into an outdoor pond still wearing bandages.

The water was as murky as I remembered it, with a sludgy feel around my torso and legs, and a brighter sensation where the pale sun had warmed the inch-deep top layer. With my head sticking up, I breast-stroked a little and kicked my legs. There was a rowboat with the lifeguard off to one side and only a few women, one with neoprene gloves and a tight latex swim cap, swimming industriously here and there, like beavers in a pond. No, Gayle had decided against coming today. Maybe she was afraid of me and what I might have found out. It wasn't so much the fib about when she'd reencountered Vonn after some years absence I minded. It was the underlying falsehood of claiming that her closeness to Vonn was all in the distant past.

A degree of closeness that resulted in Gayle subletting the flat and probably either keeping the key or having one made. It made complete sense now that Kristi called Gayle for help. It also brought up the possibility that Gayle could have gone into the flat after Vonn died and removed certain things, including the laptop, to make it look like a burglary. But what would Gayle want with the laptop? I knew she wasn't well-off, but I couldn't imagine her fencing it.

I remembered how she had worked so hard to organize and clean the flat. That was the labor of a friend, even if the landlord was paying her something.

I swam out farther from the dock and ladder, toward some trees whose bare branches overhung the water's edge. As my limbs gradually chilled to sticks of ice, I turned and started back. There was a story here with Vonn and Gayle, but I was damned if I knew what it was. Often, I found swimming a good time to think, but in the numbing waters of the Ladies' Pond, thought was freezing up, not expanding

Suddenly I felt something catch at my foot, like a hand grabbing my ankle. I couldn't see anyone below or how they'd approached. Too surprised to shriek, I flailed around, only to find I'd been captured. My head went under, face first, as someone behind me grabbed my shoulders and then put a strong bare arm around my neck. I struggled and kicked and took in water through my open mouth. Just as I thought I was losing consciousness, my head bobbed back up to the surface and I gasped and choked. I heard my tormentor say, "I've got her, she's okay. I think she just got too cold, she's not used to the water temperature."

The lifeguard was leaning out of the rowboat to help raise me up, but I was coughing so hard I couldn't hold on to the side with my numbed hands. They had to pull and push me into the boat. It was only then that I saw the face of the woman who had pushed my head under.

She had long black hair like a witch, and bony cheeks and a hooked nose.

Vida.

As soon as I could speak, I let out a string of invective, in Spanish.

Once I was dry and dressed again, I had to consider if what Vida had claimed was true. That she had seen me thrashing and had swum over to try to pull my chin above water, but I broke away and went under, so she had to grab my shoulders and put her arm around my neck. Although I said I'd felt something tug at my foot, I knew the lifeguard thought it was just a branch, and that I'd panicked. She knew Vida and took her word for it that Vida knew me, and that it was only because of Vida's experience that I hadn't had to be resuscitated. For the lifeguard had seen her struggling with me, trying to keep me afloat, and had already started rowing over.

It's the kind of thing that makes you doubt your experience. I thought I'd felt a hand or something *like* a hand on my foot. But had I?

I certainly hadn't been expecting to see Vida here today, much less to be "saved" by her.

"Where's Gayle?" I asked when we were in her car near the Heath, since the lifeguard had recommended "my friend" get me home as soon as possible and that I have a hot bath and cup of scorching tea or two. I was in my dry clothes again, and squishy sneakers, with the wet towel wrapped around my head most unbecomingly.

"Gayle couldn't come," said Vida, pulling off Hampstead Hill Road into Swain's Lane to cut through some of the side streets. She was glowing with exertion, in a tracksuit, her long, wet hair bundled under a thick wool watch cap. Her face was more chiseled, but otherwise she seemed to have aged very little since I'd first encountered her years ago. Her accent was still there, but fainter. "She was busy. So she sent me."

"I didn't know the two of you were back together."

"We're not. Not exactly. But I still care about her. And this thing with Vonn. It's no good for her. It makes her nervous all this thinking about Vonn drowning. Nightmares, crying. I'm just glad that she didn't see you in the water today."

"Why?" I asked bluntly. "Would it bring back memories?"

"What?" she put on the brakes at a stop sign, so that I jerked forward. "What are you talking about? Memories of what?"

"I mean, just that Vonn died." I said, "Not that she *saw* Vonn drown of course." I pushed a little more, since I saw Vida was shaken.

"I understand why Gayle would be upset. Evidently, she was closer to Vonn than she wanted me to believe. She probably knows more than she's telling."

Vida made a rude sign to the person honking behind us, a gesture that probably included me. She started driving again in the direction of Tufnell Park. The red BMW wasn't new, but it was well-maintained and had heated leather seats. Her steering wheel was leather as well. I tried not to stare at her long, branch-like fingers on the wheel.

I felt like I was going about this the wrong way. If I wanted to learn more, I should reveal less. Instead I'd flung some cards on the table, face up.

"Look, I can understand why Gayle is upset," I repeated, in a less confrontational voice. "She was close to Vonn. Naturally, she didn't have anything to do with her death, but I did want to ask her some questions today. *She* was the one who suggested meeting at the Pond, not me. And she didn't say anything about you coming. I'm not sure what it means that she was too busy. Are you here in place of her and why is that?"

"Why are you so interested in Vonn?" Vida had assumed a calmer tone as well, but she didn't answer my question. "I didn't think you knew her."

"Well, I didn't, really. But for various reasons that I don't need to go into, I *have* gotten interested. And one thing I'm interested in is why you're protecting Gayle."

Vida drove without saying anything for a few minutes, then seemed to make a decision. Without turning her head from the road, she said, "I knew Vonn in a different way. Before Gayle met her. I knew her as a cruel person, who liked to be smarter than other people, and who used her tiny quotient of power to insult and hurt. I was not aware until Gayle and I got together that she had been with Vonn for a short while as a lover, though it was a long time ago. She said that Vonn had also hurt her feelings when they broke up, but that Vonn had later apologized. She said she'd forgiven Vonn. But then, Vonn died, and I saw Gayle was very shocked and disturbed. I made her tell me why, and she said they had become friends again in the last two years, after Vonn got sick. She tried to tell me Vonn had become a different person and didn't want to be Gayle's lover, just her friend. Since Gayle knew I didn't like Vonn, during the last year she had only had coffee with Vonn a few times and had not told me. But she couldn't hide her feelings about Vonn's death.

When the lady who was Vonn's neighbor called her, Gayle felt it was her duty to help out. I was angry."

We were passing the Tufnell Park station now and heading south through Hilldrop Estate; the traffic was light on this cloudy Sunday afternoon. What Vida was saying was plausible. But it still didn't answer the question of why, if the two of them had broken up, Vida knew that Gayle and I were supposed to have met today, nor the question of why Vida had come instead. Was she here to threaten me to stop calling Gayle and trying to talk with her? Again, I found myself staring at Vida's fingers on the steering wheel.

I said, "I understand why you didn't like Vonn. She was abrasive and mean. I'll never forget a rejection letter I got from her one time. I'd contributed a short essay for an anthology that Brize was doing, about lesbian biography. I wanted to write something about the American actor, Charlotte Cushman, and her many lovers," I added (making it up from an article I'd read recently in one of the many magazines Nicky subscribed to). "Charlotte lived in Rome in the nineteenth century, in a sort of lesbian artists colony. There was so much about it—passion, jealousy, triangles, break-ups—that echoed life in London in our time, that I felt sure the Brize collective would say yes. But instead I got a very stiff letter back, claiming that I couldn't write worth beans."

If I was expecting Vida to say, "Oh, they rejected me too, those *putas!*" I was disappointed. Instead she asked what street I lived on in Islington, and when I told her, she adjusted her route and turned left off York Way. We passed through the neighborhoods around Caledonian Road, and I thought of how, earlier in the day, I'd imagined I'd take a swim with Gayle, ask her about the sublet and key, and find out what she knew about the laptop, and then head to the Caledonian flat block to confirm that Kristi had taken Vonn's bike and was willing to sell it.

Not much chance of that now.

"Gayle and I are not living together now," Vida said, after a long pause. "I know she was staying with you and Nicky, and then she went to friends in Clapham. But now she has gone to Torquay, to visit with her sister for a while. It was a quick decision. She took the train this morning. We spoke on the phone before she left. I'll drive down there in a week or two and then we'll see. She asked me to call you and explain, but I decided to come to the Ladies' Pond instead. I admit, I wanted to meet you in person. Then I saw you struggling in the water. Maybe I wanted to see you because people are always saying to me, Oh you must know Cassandra Reilly. Because of the Spanish translation."

"Yes, people always say the same to me about you."

"It seems strange that we don't know each other."

Personally, I didn't think it was that strange, considering how she'd acted the first and only time we'd met. I wondered if she was going to apologize, belatedly, for lumping me with all the bad *norteamericanos*. But no, Vida had her pride. That was probably the reason she didn't want to admit that Vonn had rejected not just her essay about the Lieutenant Nun, but also her book of poems.

Our last five minutes in the car were mainly quiet. She asked me what I was translating these days, and I said I'd just finished a new mystery by Rosa Cardenes, and that I was hoping to find a publisher for another thriller set in the bullfighting world of Seville. Vida said that she didn't care for crime novels. They were too unrealistic. The detective always solved the crime, and you were supposed to believe the most ridiculous things about long-lost cousins and mysterious poisonings. "I thought you translated literature," she added, reprovingly.

By the time she dropped me off in front of Nicky's building, it was clear that we didn't have a lot in common. Aside from the fact that Vida had either tried to drown me or to save me.

In retrospect I now thought that probably my bare foot had caught on a branch, and I'd panicked. Really, why would Vida want me dead and even if she did, why would she try to push me below the surface of the Pond with the lifeguard nearby?

Still, I didn't trust her, and while I offered a grudging thanks for the ride as I opened the car door to leave, I didn't suggest that we now were at the beginning of a beautiful new friendship.

"Get into the hot shower immediately," she advised. "You look like a soaked rat. And by the way," she added as I got out of the car. "You swear very convincingly in Spanish. I haven't heard some of those words in years."

19.

I spent Sunday evening quietly, glad that Nicky was gone for a long weekend in Scotland, visiting some of her relatives. I didn't want to have to explain my damp appearance as I came in the door, or how I ended up being publicly rescued by Vida and the lifeguard, ignominiously hauled into a rowboat, and then bundled into the bathhouse. The more I thought about it, the more appalling the whole incident seemed. I really hoped that no bystanders or byswimmers had recognized me or had taken videos of me with my goose-bumpy blue skin that would appear on someone's Facebook page.

After some chicken soup heated up from a tin, I lay on the sofa under a blanket and started the fourth mystery Stella had published, *The Funeral Specialist*. The premise was that the beguines were paid by the wealthier citizens of Flemish cities and towns to sit with the dying and to help guide them into death, and then to prepare their bodies for the grave. Sometimes they worked singly and sometimes in companionship with other women of the house in which the death took place. Other times, two or more beguines assisted as nurses and so-called funeral specialists.

I laid it aside after the first few chapters, too tired from the day's activities to go on, and drifted off to sleep on the sofa under my soft merino blanket. But my dreams weren't at all cozy. Long fingers like twigs grasped at my ankles and pulled me down into the world of water ghosts. Then I was in an open coffin, still damp from my recent drowning, and a kerosene lamp burned next to me on a small table. Someone was sitting in a chair, reading a book. It was a wake. I wasn't dead, though they thought I was. I tried to peer over for a better glimpse of who the funeral specialist was. But she was wearing a wimple with wings, and I couldn't see her face. Only her long fingers, slowing turning the pages.

When I woke up in the morning in my own bed, I savored the fact that I was alive. I took another hot shower, drank some coffee, and sat down at my desk in a business-like, non-dallying way to finish a short translation job that I could invoice and be paid for like a proper adult.

I resolved to give up on this ridiculous investigation, at least on the part of it that involved Gayle. Yes, she'd probably been fonder of Vonn than she'd let on. The poor wee thing hadn't wanted her overbearing girlfriend Vida to know that she still saw Vonn from time to time. Okay, maybe Gayle had kept a key. Was that a crime? Nothing I'd seen when we'd been at the flat doing the organizing should lead me to believe anything, but that Gayle cared about Vonn, wanted to make sure her archives were saved and her life remembered. She probably also picked up a bit of cash from the landlord for cleaning out the flat.

But if Gayle were hiding something more sinister, why would she have asked me and Amina to come over and help? I was definitely not going to pursue Gayle down to Torquay. Nor did I hope to see Vida ever again.

Then, around ten o'clock, I got a phone call that made me think again about my wee friend.

It was from the *Guardian* journalist, Alice, who said that she wasn't sure what I'd been talking about in the message I'd left on her office voicemail. She didn't know anything about Vonn Henley's death, didn't know anyone at the coroner's office, and had never been to the Ladies' Pond. She was not a swimmer. She sounded more bemused than annoyed, and I apologized. "My friend must have remembered the name wrongly. So sorry."

But when I hung up, I thought that, once again, Gayle had fibbed. She had definitely said, on two occasions, that a *Guardian* journalist was the source of some of the things known about Vonn's death. She had mentioned an Alice or an Alex.

Like the lie about only running into Vonn at the Ladies' Pond two years ago, it may have been a harmless mistake.

But if it wasn't? If Gayle had deliberately been trying to sow some confusion? Or bolster the so-called claim that there were traces of drugs in Vonn's system but no signs of foul play.

The other thing that disturbed my concentration Monday morning was an email from Avery. It was good news. SNP had expressed a strong interest in the translation of Verónica. They wanted to meet me and suggested lunch this coming Friday. But they also wanted to see more of the translation if possible. The second twenty pages I'd done still wasn't quite enough for them. Could I do one more chapter, with more action in the bullring, so they could see how the writer dealt with the handling of the bulls?

> I know this is loads more work, Cassandra, but I think we have a chance here. SNP are willing to overlook some animal cruelty if it's not "gratuitous." Strange that they publish so many grisly novels where women are murdered and dismembered by serial killers, and then they're bothered about a bull getting stabbed "gratuitously." But here we are. Do you think you could do the chapter this week? Again, I'd pay you for this. Let me know. I'm a bit swamped because the temp left Friday and a new one came this morning and is hopeless.

I emailed back, "Yes. I'll try to do it today. And Friday is fine for lunch." Naturally, I was pleased, but I was less happy to hear that the temp I'd spoken with, Julia, seemed to have departed without finding any documents or correspondence between Avery and Vonn. And now Avery had hired another temp. Why wasn't she replacing her past assistant Samantha properly?

Thinking about Sam, I wondered where exactly she'd moved. South Yorkshire, Avery had said. Rather abruptly, Avery had also said. Was it worth tracking Sam down in the hopes she'd know something about Vonn?

For the moment, I pushed the thought out of my mind. If I were wrong and Sam knew nothing or there was nothing to know, I would expose myself needlessly. For Sam might have remained in touch with Avery and might tell her I'd called.

I finished my short academic translation and sent it off with an invoice, then turned to *Verónica* to find a suitable chapter or two with some actual bullfighting. Compared to the first two mysteries by Lola Fuentes, *Verónica* was a bit shy on bull gore. Aside from all the financial shenanigans, Lola was spending more time on Rita's love life. In this book, the hunk was Pedro, a waiter at an upscale restaurant who had overheard a whispered conversation among two men at lunch, concerning a woman named Gloria and the lesson she would receive. For some reason Pedro, who had himself been involved in bullfighting, was suspicious. That led him to save the cloth napkins used by the two men during their meal. When a woman named Gloria, the wife of a famous bullfighter, was killed, Pedro wanted to go to the police, but was afraid of the consequences.

So he came to Rita instead, with the two soiled cloth napkins, and asked for her help. The cloth napkins would eventually act as evidence when the same DNA as was on the napkins was found on a pillow used to murder Gloria, to send her husband a message that he wouldn't get out of paying his debts.

I finally found a scene in the bullring in a late chapter, where Gloria's husband the matador was prancing around in the ring, executing some of his most famous moves, including a sweeping *verónica*, where he gracefully irritated the bull with his cape. Rita, who was attending the corrida in the shady part of the audience, had a revelation of sorts. The veil of Veronica! An imprint of Jesus's features on the cloth made when St. Veronica wiped his face of sweat on the road to Golgotha. Rita made the connection to the cloth napkins in the restaurant and the pillowcase in the bedroom.

I became so absorbed that I worked through lunch, and then took a walk. When I returned, I found, among all the advertising dreck and bills in the postbox, a thin envelope from Avery's office, not from her, but from the temp, Julia, who'd posted it on her last day, last Friday. Inside was a brief typed note explaining that she'd looked through all the correspondence files in the last year and hadn't found any emails with Yvonne Henley, though her name did appear in a logbook of queries and manuscripts received.

Enclosed were several sheets of paper. One of them was a page copied from the agency's logbook. As Avery had indicated, Vonn had contacted her early this year, in January, with a query letter and a partial manuscript of "Gadfly: My Years in Women's Publishing." Under the rubric in the table "Action Taken," there was only a date, Feb 14, and the word "no." Unlike some of the entries, there was nothing written in the "Comments."

February 14 was a few days after Fiona Craig's lecture. So far, that squared with what I knew. Avery let down Vonn gently that evening, and soon followed up with the rejection. But it seemed odd that Julia had found no correspondence. I would have thought Avery would keep Vonn's cover letter as evidence if she were so concerned that Vonn was in some way a threat to Fiona's well-being.

I looked at the other enclosure, copies of two typed sheets stapled together, a contract. Julia had written in her note: "I came across this contract with Vonn from the nineties when I was refiling some material in the Stella Terwicker folders."

The contract was the first real proof I had that Vonn and Avery had known each other, professionally at least, for many years. The contract was dated March 23, 1995, and it spelled out an agreement between the Avery Armstrong Agency and Yvonne Henley for editorial services related to an untitled Work-in-Progress, a mystery by Stella Terwicker.

I imagined from the date that it was Stella's fourth mystery, *The Funeral Specialist,* which she'd been working on before she went off to Portugal that winter of 1994-5 and returned so ill that she couldn't get out of bed, much less write. The way Fiona had told it in the biography was that the book's publication had been postponed from the spring to the autumn of 1996. With the help of rest and medical care, Stella had gradually recovered her strength and begun writing again. While Fiona had suggested that she and Stan played a role in caretaking Stella that year, and that Fiona herself had continued to do research for Stella on medieval women and the beguinages, there had never been a suggestion anyone else was involved.

The agreement with Vonn didn't spell out what Vonn was doing on the manuscript or how many words Stella had completed before her health became compromised. Vonn's task was described mainly to deliver a fully edited manuscript by January 1, 1996, acceptable for publication. She wasn't considered to be a creator or co-creator, that is, someone who shared in the copyright and thus the royalties. Her work was "for hire" and the fee was spelled out. Interestingly the fee wasn't paid by the publisher, but by the Avery Armstrong Agency, and it was rather high. Higher than I would have thought, even in 1995, for a simple freelance editing job. The other interesting aspect of the contract was the sentence "Editor agrees to consult with a historian on details of the Work and to allow the historian to vet the manuscript and to make appropriate changes before the Work is submitted to the publisher."

This historian must certainly be Fiona.

So now I had some written evidence that not only had Vonn and Avery known each other professionally many years ago, but that Vonn may very well have worked with Fiona, who vetted her editorial work on the mystery.

If both Fiona and Vonn had collaborated with Stella on all the mysteries, from *The Funeral Specialist* onward, why hadn't Avery mentioned that? It wasn't a crime for an author to have assistance on her books. Even as a translator, I had done all sorts of small things to make a book better. Writing sometimes involved major interventions from editors and agents, and publishing was generally a team effort. But when it came to Stella's books, according to the biography it was only Fiona who played a role.

I flipped through my copy of the galley proof of *Stella Terwicker: A Medieval Life*. To my surprise, in this early, uncorrected proof Lucy was mentioned several times, and Vonn once, in connection with Stella's first two mysteries with Aphra. "Stella was introduced to Lucy Aspin at Aphra Press by an acquaintance, Yvonne Henley." I was positive that sentence hadn't appeared in the published print version. I would have noticed. Therefore Fiona had deliberately removed any mention of Vonn, even such an innocuous reference, during the proofing.

I thought back to Fiona's lecture in early February. I'd not seen any overt sign of recognition between Vonn and Fiona, even though Fiona's eyes flicked often to the door. But there definitely had been in Vonn and Avery's body language, now that I thought about it, many indications that they knew each other well. It wasn't the posture of two professionals, one of whom (Avery) was more powerful than the other. It was the tense posture of two people negotiating on equal terms.

Now I was curious.

Why would Vonn have accepted her erasure? Or did she not have a choice? From everything I knew about Vonn she believed in women getting credit for their labor. I looked again at the agreement with Avery for editing services from 1995. The fee was awfully large. Maybe that was the reason for Vonn's silence. Perhaps she did more than edit, perhaps she'd become a kind of ghostwriter.

I remembered Corinne had said Vonn had made a decent income until around ten or fifteen years ago. I'd assumed that Vonn had only faced the same problems as many freelancers—changes in technology, outsourcing of editorial work to newer editors who charged less, the gradual disappearance of a network of commissioning editors—but perhaps her reduced income coincided with the end of the collaboration with Fiona and Stella.

Fiona herself wouldn't have suffered. She and Stan had inherited

Stella's estate, including all the royalties and other income from the translations and television rights. Although Stella was dead, her books were still in print and popular in England as well as other markets. Avery still worked on their behalf, and she also represented Fiona's biography of Stella.

The biography had come out last autumn. The same time that Vonn was said to have fallen into something of a depression and around the time she seemed to have begun writing "Gadfly." I'd assumed that Vonn was angry that the biography didn't mention Stella was or had once been a lesbian, or that she was irritated that Fiona focused so much on Stella's later success and the television series, skipping over Stella's early years in London and involvement with feminist presses. But what if Vonn was most upset about her own role, as an editor and possibly even a ghostwriter of Stella's Beatrys mysteries, being erased? It was worth considering. Had Vonn really threatened Fiona with exposure? Or had she used her purported memoir as a bargaining chip with Avery, to squeeze out money to keep silent? Was it Avery who Vonn had been threatening, not Fiona?

I was getting ahead of myself here, by leaps and bounds. I didn't have any evidence to suggest that Vonn worked on all the mysteries or just the early ones for Aphra. There was no way I could ask Vonn because she was dead. And since all evidence of Vonn's work as an editor seemed to be missing from both Vonn's file cabinets and Avery's office, there was no corroborating proof unless I could locate those files. Just like a translator, an editor doesn't always leave a trace.

If I wanted to continue this investigation and bring it to a conclusion, I'd have to find that trace, that veil of Veronica that left an imprint on cloth or, in this case, paper.

20.

"So you met a beautiful woman in Bristol but didn't act on it and instead returned to London to be almost drowned in the Ladies' Pond," said Nicky. "All during the few days I was away visiting my mingy auld auntie in her cottage, which still doesn't have indoor plumbing, may I add?"

Nicky paused in her consumption of a small fruit scone with clotted cream, her second, washed down with cups of Russian Caravan tea. Getting to and from the Isle of Arran twice a year was a major effort, given the trains, buses, and ferries, but Nicky was fond of her mingy auld auntie, now about the same age as Queen Elizabeth and still living as if it were the nineteenth century, according to Nicky anyway. I happened to know that her aunt had a radio, though no wi-fi.

Nicky had texted me earlier from Glasgow to say she'd be coming into Euston and perhaps I'd like to meet her at the Wellcome Museum on Euston Road for tea. She'd stash her bag at the station, and we could have a wee snack and then a keek around the museum. She wanted to catch the latest exhibition, "Hypochondria." The Wellcome was a free health and science library and museum, and Nicky rarely missed an opportunity to stop by its café and reading library when she was in the vicinity.

I was glad of the break as well. I'd stayed up until two in the morning finishing a draft of the chapter in *Verónica* with an actual bullfight, and this morning had been up earlier than I liked to polish it and send it off to Avery. A pot of tea and Nicky's company revived me. Just her colorful clothes were a bright spot in the gray day.

"I wouldn't have almost drowned," I told her, "if Vida hadn't grabbed me so that I had to struggle with her. I'm sure I took in a good pint of pond water."

"Well, obviously Vida is our murderer then," Nicky said. "If she had the nerve to try and drown you in daylight, in plain sight of the lifeguard, then what would have stopped her from drowning Vonn in the dark at the bird pond?"

"It's not that simple," I said. "I don't get the sense that Vida came to the Pond with the intention of doing me harm. But I did get the distinct feeling she thought I'd been hounding Gayle."

"*Have* you been hounding Gayle? I haven't heard a peep from her myself since I got back from Denmark."

"No, of course not. I just had a few questions for her. That's why I called her and asked to meet. *She* was the one who suggested taking a swim at the Ladies' Pond. I would never on my own have suggested getting into a swimsuit in March and submerging myself in icy water. Then she didn't come, and Vida popped up—literally—out of the water behind me."

"Do you think Vida persuaded Gayle not to come?"

"No clue. Vida *said* she'd taken Gayle to Paddington that morning. Gayle was off to Torquay to stay with her sister for a bit."

"So it's come to this. Torquay." Nicky reached for her third scone, which was on my plate. "Do you mind? It was five hours on the train and the buffet car was out of service." Through crumbs, Nicky went on, "But why did you call Gayle anyway? What did you want to find out?"

"Do you remember, that evening I came back from the lecture, and you were eating curry, that Gayle told us she hadn't seen Vonn for some years. Then Vonn had a mastectomy and chemo and moved out of London for a while."

"I remember," said Nicky. "But?"

"As it turns out, it was Bristol. Vonn went to Bristol for two months, to stay with Corinne. Corinne is… "

"Yes, yes, the delightful new woman in your life. I want to hear all about it, and we'll get back to her. But how does Bristol involve Gayle?"

"Corinne mentioned that Vonn sublet her flat for two months while she was in Bristol."

Nicky shook her head. "I'm not following."

"Don't you see? The chronology is wrong. Gayle said she ran into Vonn by chance at the Ladies' Pond sometime after she'd returned from Bristol. But in fact, according to Kristi, Vonn sublet her flat to Gayle while she was away. Something Gayle never mentioned."

"Kristi? Who's Kristi?"

"Vonn's neighbor in the building. I went by the block of flats Saturday afternoon, after I'd had lunch with an editor from Aphra in Hammersmith to learn more about Stella Terwicker and the Beatrys books. I'd wanted to ask Kristi about Vonn's bike, but in the course of our brief talk she confirmed that Gayle had lived in the building two years ago. That *she* had sublet from Vonn. Which means that Gayle probably still had a key to Vonn's flat."

"My God, hen, you *have* been busy. So you think Gayle could have been fibbing to us? Why?"

"I'd already suspected that Gayle had an ongoing relationship of some sort with Vonn for years after they broke up. I mean, she basically told me that. She didn't say it was sexual, more that they'd just get together occasionally when things were tough with Susan or Joan, but I was given the impression they got together fairly frequently. Until Vida came along. Gayle also told me she'd hardly seen Vonn since last autumn, when she moved in with Vida. I don't know if that's true. If Gayle *had* continued seeing Vonn, maybe that explains why she and Vida broke up. But the key is what I wanted to ask Gayle about, and now she's left London. Don't you find that suspicious?"

"Possibly. On the other hand, it's not like she's gone to the Arctic. And she already told us she was considering moving in with her sister if she couldn't find a place in London." Nicky sighed. "Poor Wee Gayle. I don't say this very often, being the ardent lesbian that I am, but it's very possible Gayle might have been happier as a straight woman. A nice husband and kids, and none of this ramfoozle with women who break your hearts. The lassie doesn't have our stamina."

A waiter came by and asked if we'd like anything more. With an effort Nicky said no, nothing except a slice of that delicious apple cake the café served, and two forks. And a refill of her tea pot and more milk, and don't forget the vanilla custard for the apple cake.

"There will be an explanation for all this," said Nicky. "And the explanation will have something to do with Vida, mark my words. But now I want to hear all about Corinne, and not just the bits where you discuss feminist publishing and why it ran into such difficulties!"

Half an hour later, our teapot refreshed and the delicious apple cake with custard shared, mostly by Nicky, we put aside the idea of visiting the exhibition on "Hypochondria." We left the museum, crossed the street, and retrieved her rolling suitcase at Euston, then began walking down the sidewalk in the direction of King's Cross underground, intending to take a bus back to Islington. I didn't know about Nicky, but I was thinking of a nap before dinner.

We were still talking about Corinne and whether I planned to go up to Bristol again anytime soon. I realized that Nicky probably felt the same stirrings of unease as I did when any of her attractions looked more serious. In our earlier days we simply shrugged off each other's long and short relationships as having nothing to do with our friendship. These days we both seemed more apt to worry that our years-long bond could be altered by a third person.

As to what Corinne would think about my living with Nicky, I hadn't yet given it much thought. I'd answered her question about whether anyone was waiting for me in London with a casual no. But I was aware I'd deliberately not mentioned that I shared a flat with someone in London and that, if I were to get involved with Corinne, we would probably meet more often in Bristol. It had seemed too presumptuous to discuss details like that, especially when I didn't know Corinne's situation either.

Deep in our conversation, I was hardly paying attention to the crowds surging around us as we drew closer to the intensely trafficked area between St. Pancras and King's Cross. A black cab had stopped by St. Pancras and a woman emerged, pulling her wheeled suitcase with her. Chestnut hair, pale face, scarf, and suit jacket over trousers. It was Fiona Craig. With that, all the pleasant thoughts about Corinne vanished.

I suddenly remembered that since talking to Lucy on Saturday about Vonn's editorial help with the first two Beatrys mysteries, I had some questions about how much Fiona had known about Stella's affair with Vonn back in the eighties. There was also the contract between Avery and Vonn for editorial work on what became *The Funeral Specialist,* and the way that Vonn Henley had not merited even a mention in the biography. Wee Gayle may have fibbed about staying at Vonn's place and having a key, but Fiona had intentionally obscured much more about Vonn and Stella. And then complained to Avery that Vonn had threatened her.

Fiona headed into the entrance of St. Pancras, and I dragged Nicky along by the arm, a safe distance behind. "That's Fiona Craig," I whispered. "Where's she off to?"

Nicky, knowing me, did not attempt to break away. "By the look of it, probably Brussels or Paris," she said in a normal voice. "She's headed to the Eurostar departures."

"She must be going to Bruges," I said excitedly. "Nicky, do you have your passport?"

"Woman, I just got off the train from Glasgow. I need to go home and enjoy a bath and a wee snooze. I'm not going off to bloody Belgium."

"But you don't have anything planned for tonight or tomorrow, do you?"

"No."

"Well, then, come on. I need to talk to her. The train is perfect. We can get off in Brussels, turn around and come back tonight. Or have dinner and stay the night. You like steamed mussels, don't you?"

"I do like steamed mussels, but that's not the issue here. What's so important that it can't wait until Fiona returns from her trip?"

"But I don't know when she's returning. She has a small flat in Bruges and goes there often. What if she's staying for days or weeks? What if she's fleeing the country?"

"You think she killed Vonn?"

"Well, it's possible."

Nicky looked thoughtful. "I do have my passport. It's still in my purse from the trip to Denmark. What about you?"

"I always have my passport."

"Oh, all right, if it's just there and back. And dinner."

We had paused once or twice to talk and had lost sight of Fiona. No, there she was, already going through passport control. There were few passengers, which might mean that the train was departing soon. There was no time to waste. I rushed to the ticket machine and hastily bought two tickets. Somehow, we managed to get to the platform and to board at the last minute. Nicky was speedier than she looked, the result of traveling so much for concerts, often with a giant bassoon in tow.

We settled into our seats, laughing, and then Nicky closed her eyes and was out like a light. I decided to wait half an hour before going to find Fiona. Then I too, closed my eyes, for just a minute. I woke briefly when the conductor came through and took both our tickets from my hand, only to fall asleep again.

The next thing I knew was Nicky pulling at my arm and we were alone in the carriage. "It was the scones," Nicky said. "All those carbs. And then the excitement of following a suspect. Now here we are in Brussels, with no Fiona in sight."

We got off the Eurostar and came into the main concourse of Brussels Midi. No sign of Fiona. I scanned the overhead board. "There are loads of trains to Bruges, and it's just an hour away," I said.

"And you're sure she was going to Bruges?" Nicky said, now grumpily.

"Oh, of course!"

I bought tickets and we found our train, which I hoped was Fiona's train too. Diligently I went through all the carriages but didn't see any signs of her. Well, this complicates things a bit. We would have to stay overnight. But at least I knew the general district where she had her bolthole: Sint-Anna. We'd simply find a charming little hotel and wait until the morning.

It was raining now, and the Belgian twilight was very melancholy. I could see from Nicky's mulish expression that she was not pleased about how this adventure was turning out. In the old, pre-internet days, it might have been worse. We would have arrived in Bruges in the pouring rain and then had to trudge around the city asking about rooms. Now I could simply search for *small hotels in Bruges, Sint-Anna district. Near the English Convent* on my phone. Within ten minutes I'd found a couple of bed and breakfasts, showed pictures of the rooms to Nicky, and called to make a booking at one of them. I even chatted with the innkeeper about where to find a good meal in the neighborhood. I spoke in an intentionally cheerful voice, repeating his words about Flemish stew and bouillabaisse and a lovely wine list.

All the same I knew it would actually take a glass of wine or two before Nicky stopped wishing she'd ever listened to me.

21.

I rarely travel with Nicky, and the next morning in Bruges I recalled why. She's a leisurely breakfaster and likes nothing better than to have a long natter with fellow guests, waiters, and innkeepers. Our B&B was shy on guests this March weekday. A businessman sat at a table over by a window in the corner of the small dining room, reading a newspaper, but left quickly when we entered. The breakfast spread was the usual: rolls, soft cheeses, and thin slices of ham, along with boiled eggs, and lots of coffee. But the innkeeper, Piet, also made us his version of spiced French toast from stale brioche, and served with a large chunk of butter, powdered sugar, and berries. He was a chatty fellow in his forties, with a round face and rounder tummy under his crisp white apron, and he and Nicky were soon fast friends.

He soon winkled out of her that she was a musician and yet had rarely been in Bruges and had never visited the Concertgebouw Brugge, built in 2002, and with "the world's most perfect acoustics." If we were free this evening, he would recommend going to a concert. He also ran through all the other possibilities of the day, visits to the museums to see work by the Flemish masters, a tour of the historic center, and the *Begijnhof Ten Wijngaerde*. Even here, in the quiet corner of Sint-Anna, there was much to be seen. For instance, the English Convent just a street or two over, on Carmerstraat, established in the sixteenth century after Henry VIII dissolved the Catholic Church in England. There was a popular working windmill very close, by the canal and park.

"We also have two guilds here, established for centuries, for the archers of the town." Putting down some plates, he struck a pose, with the left arm outstretched, and the right pulled back to the shoulder to explain what he meant. "And also the *kruisboog,*" he added, "I don't know the English."

"The crossbow?" Nicky said, rapturously, through her French toast. "My dad had a crossbow and he taught me to shoot when I was just a wee girl. I helped set up an archery club at my school and won a regional prize."

I thought to myself, in admiration, that when people thought about lesbians and what lesbians did, they likely never thought about lesbians who played the bassoon and could shoot a crossbow.

"Yes, the *kruisboog*," said our host with almost equal enthusiasm, "it is the crossbow, and the shooting of it is still practiced in their big garden of the guild, just steps away, down the street. Saint George's Guild. You can visit it later today when they are open. You are staying two nights, I think?" Nicky didn't wait for my response. "Oh, definitely two nights. And a concert this evening sounds divine. I'll find out what's on and get tickets. My friend here has some other business today."

While Nicky set off for the historic center, the Burg and the Markt and the Memling Museum, I resigned myself to lurking around the Sint-Anna quarter in hopes of sighting Fiona. Because of the rapidity of the decision to follow her to Belgium without having sufficient information to actually track her down, I now found myself unable to enjoy being a tourist. Instead, I'd have to hope that if I wandered around the neighborhood long enough, I'd run into her in a shop or café.

But the streets in this area seemed to be mostly residential, two and three-story terraces, row upon row, as in England. Many were whitewashed stone or brick; a few were more colorful. They didn't have front gardens, only window boxes. The big painted doors directly opened on the smooth cobbled sidewalks and the sidewalks were only slightly raised from the narrow, cobbled streets, so that cars could park or in some cases pass each other by driving up over the curb. Some of the doors had plaques with a name, or a small sign under the doorbell to the side. It would take hours to read each plaque, and not all doors had them.

I headed to Carmersstraat and the English Convent, the only landmark that Fiona had mentioned. You couldn't miss the church, but where there had once been a door onto the street, there was only a bricked-up arch. I walked back and forth on the street wondering how the public was able to enter, then gave up. If I couldn't get in, neither could Fiona. I kept walking. My footsteps echoed on the stone sidewalk, so much so that I occasionally looked behind me.

Unlike the center of Bruges, awash in bistros, bars, tea rooms, and food carts specializing in *frites*, these streets were dead quiet, though I did notice a bar with some outside seating at the end of Carmersstraat: *De Windmolen*. The windmill. And sure enough, a giant, boxy, wooden thing on stilts, with lattice-like arms that turned slowly in the breeze, loomed on a small hill in a park across the street.

Soon I was up inside the windmill, where an attendant was only too happy to explain that this windmill was erected in the 1770s, one of many along the eastern ramparts of Bruges, and the only mill still grinding grain (in the summer, weekends only). He pointed out the landmarks: the ramparts, the towers, the canals. I nodded and looked out in the direction of the dome of the English Convent, willing Fiona to walk by. The sky was light blue, with fast-moving white and gray clouds that occasionally obscured the sun. That same strong breeze turned the arms of the windmill with a heavy, wooden creaking sound. The air smelled damply of grass and fertilizer, and in the near distance were polders and small woodlands, with canals running through them.

The windmill overlooked a large canal that seemed to ring the city's core, edged by this long, green park. The attendant confirmed I could walk all the way to the train station from here. It would take about half an hour. He pointed out that the train station was quite near the beguinage. Why should I assume Fiona would confine herself to Sint-Anna? It was the beguinage of Bruges she was attached to. In fact, wouldn't that be the most likely place she'd visit?

Forty minutes later, my legs well-stretched from the walk, I walked over the bridge and through the main stone entrance of the beguinage. This time I noticed the motto carved into the arch, just the way it was in the opening credits of the TV series: *Sauvegarde*. Safeguard. I knew the word from present-day French, though in a different context. *Copie de sauvegarde* meant *backup copy,* while *fichier de sauvegarde* was a *backup file.* But here in Bruges, *sauvegarde* meant under the protection of the Duchy of Burgundy. It meant, "Don't mess with these women."

Stella had used the word *sauvegarde* repeatedly in her Beatrys mysteries. The beguinage was a place of safety where women were protected. A refuge from male aggression and violence, a retreat from worldly pressure to conform to traditional women's roles, an oasis of calm, run entirely by women, a place where women came first. That was the great appeal of Stella's mysteries for many women readers and viewers, I suspected. Once the beguines closed the doors of the beguinage, no one could abuse or threaten them. But the price of the closed outer door, the cloistered female-centered life, was that you were hostages to security. Danger was outside, safety within. And was it so safe inside? Some of the murders took place inside the beguinage, and rivalries and conflicts persisted even within women's communities.

Fiona had emphasized in her biography the attraction of these medieval women's communities to both herself and Stella as places of refuge and religion, but also as centers of learning and artisanship. Fiona had written about the fact that, throughout most of Western history, women were purposefully kept undereducated. In the Middle Ages, for instance, young women were illiterate unless they were part of the nobility or schooled in convents, which were also for the daughters of the well-to-do. Yet the lay beguines, from all classes, placed an emphasis on teaching each other to read and write. They ran schools for children, particularly girls, where they taught life skills, Latin, music, and theology. They taught girls not just how to manage accounts as merchants, or dispense herbs and remedies as nurses, but how to think. How to understand their existential situation as women in a man's world. And how to conceptualize religion so that women took a central or at least equal role in Christianity.

Yet, although Fiona was less emphatic on this point, I could also imagine that Stella, having lived as a lesbian in London in the eighties, saw the downsides of women's communities. How could she have avoided encountering the strife abounding among feminists of that era? Especially since Stella had clearly known Vonn, a frequent instigator of some of that strife. Unlike Fiona, who was a scholar, Stella was a writer of mysteries, a genre that depends almost entirely on conflict, on secrecy, and on violence. The four books of hers that I'd read had plenty of emotional engagement between women. It was part of what made them so readable.

There were daffodils. Not hundreds, for it was only mid-March, but all it would take was a few days of warmer weather and the meadow within the walls would indeed be carpeted in nodding whites and yellows. Perhaps this was why Fiona chose to visit Bruges at this time of year, in memory of those spring days she and Stella had first enjoyed here.

Certainly, if I waited long enough, Fiona would appear? But even as I nurtured that hope, I thought it depended far too much on chance. The unwelcome thought crossed my mind that I didn't even have any proof

Fiona was in Bruges. We'd botched our chance to run into her on the Eurostar and lost her in Brussels Midi. What if she had stayed in Brussels, or was going to another Belgian city for unknown reasons?

I'd had my phone off to conserve the battery, but now, seated on a cold stone bench inside the beguinage walls, I turned it on, idly, as one does, to check messages, of which there were none of note.

I was an idiot.

Why didn't I just find Fiona's phone number and call or text her? Surely, she was in a UK data base, like 192.com.

Somehow, perhaps because this adventure had started out with the coincidence of seeing Fiona alight from a black cab at St. Pancras, I'd woken up this morning firm in my conviction that I would need another coincidence to find her somewhere around the English Convent in Sint-Anna. Even Nicky had never suggested that I just use my smart phone in the normal, modern way as a people-finder and communication device. Nicky at least had an excuse, given that she'd immediately entered into conversation with Piet about Flemish archery guilds of the Middle Ages and *kruisboogs*. She was in a medieval, pre-tech state of mind even more than I was.

I had no luck quickly finding a number for Fiona in London, though I did see how old she was (61) and how much her flat was worth (a lot). Of course I could pay for a background check, and almost did, but then recalled that when Avery's temp, Julia, wrote down the address in Primrose Hill, she'd added Fiona Craig's phone number. I'd been so focused that day on what had happened to Vonn's manuscript and engineering a chance encounter with Fiona, that I hadn't remembered the scrap of sticky paper.

I dug into my wallet and, yes, there it was, folded in two.

There was still the problem of what I'd say to Fiona on the phone. I decided to tap in a text message and read it several times before sending. I'd come to Bruges with a friend of mine after reading her biography of Stella and a few of the mysteries. We were just here briefly but I wondered if Fiona had any suggestions for places we should visit connected with the books, aside from the beguinage. I mentioned that my friend was visiting the archery guildhalls, and I had wandered down to the beguinage. So beautiful with the daffodils.

I didn't give any indication I knew she was in Bruges, or that Nicky and I had actually been on the same Eurostar train. If I were lucky, Fiona wouldn't be suspicious, she'd answer me soon, and be delighted that I was here and even more delighted to show me around.

To my great happiness, Fiona did answer soon, not in a text, but by calling me. But she didn't sound that delighted. And maybe she even sounded a little suspicious. Nevertheless she said that she herself was here in Bruges for a week, by chance, and that she could give me suggestions. She'd been planning herself to come down to the beguinage today. She could be there in half an hour if I wanted to wait.

Fiona was wearing a beige sweater under a tweed jacket, with brown slacks and walking shoes. She could have been Flemish in her solid build as she strode toward my stone bench. She carried a purse and on her chestnut hair was a felt hat of nearly the same color, pulled down against the strong breeze. I was briefly aware that I was wearing the same clothes as yesterday in London, and that included the same far-from-fresh shirt and underwear. My hair was probably tangled by that same breeze. But I never let things like that bother me unduly. It had happened too often in my life that I found myself in different circumstances in the morning from where I had been the night before.

We shook hands. "Something of a fluke, isn't it?" she asked. "That this is the second time we've met by chance. Or is it chance you're in Bruges?"

I felt it best not to lie, but I didn't want to start asking questions immediately. "I didn't know much about Stella before Avery asked me to go to the lecture," I said. "But I admit you really awakened my interest about the beguines. It turned out my flatmate Nicky had the DVD series of the books and is an enthusiastic fan. And then I started reading the mysteries. I'm up to the fourth one now. After you were kind enough to give me tea and tell me more about Stella, I talked Nicky into a quick visit to Bruges. Kind of a spur of the moment thing, but then, we're mostly retired, so it was easy. But I would love to know more, now that I'm actually here, about the beguinage in its heyday."

She seemed to relax a little, and we started walking around the edge of the meadow. Like many professors, Fiona had a weakness for explanation; questions on her subject triggered an almost Pavlovian response. She knew so much, so very much about the beguines, and here was someone asking. All I had to do was put in an encouraging question now and again.

Having regained her trust, the problem was only going to be how to keep it if I tried to shift the subject to Stella, Vonn, and Avery. But almost an hour later, I was no further along. And I was getting cold out here. We had trudged around the circumference of the meadow a half a dozen times, with Fiona occasionally stopping to point out buildings where there might have been an infirmary or a school, or a dormitory for the poorer women. Finally, I suggested that we might have lunch if she knew somewhere near.

I added that I was in no hurry as Nicky would be busy all afternoon with the archery guilds

"Is he an archer?" she asked.

"Actually, Nicky's a she, but yes, she is very big on bows and arrows. Her father taught her to shoot. In Glasgow."

"Sorry," Fiona said. "When you said Nicky was your flatmate, I thought you meant he was your partner. But maybe Nicky is your female partner?"

"No, Nicky—Nicola—and I have been close friends for decades. Because I travel a lot for my translation work, I never had a place of my own in London. So I'd bunk with her, first in Hampstead, now in Islington. It's platonic." I meant to clarify that we were only uninterested in sex with each other, not with other women, but the expression on Fiona's face, eagerly sympathetic and curious, made me pause.

"Maybe like you and Stella?" I suggested. "Just close friends?"

"Women have *always* had intimate friendships," said Fiona fiercely. "But people don't understand any longer that not everything is about repressed sexuality!"

"I understand," I said. "People often imagine Nicky and I are a couple, and we have to explain that we're just... well, family. Of course in your case, Stella really was family."

We had reached the door of a bistro, with a sandwich board outside promising endive soup and *waterzooi,* a creamy chicken stew. Fiona held the door for me. "Yes," she said. "But even before Stan, she was like a sister. We had a period of estrangement, but then she came back to me. I was with her all through her illness and at the end."

Felicity and Perpetua, I thought. But I didn't say anything.

We went in and ordered, and she told me more than I'd expected, though still less than I needed to understand about why Vonn had died.

22.

"Fiona asked me, Why does everything always have to be about sex? She wondered why she couldn't be a feminist without being gay. She had no interest in physical sex with women, or men for that matter. In the Middle Ages women were often celibate, she said."

Nicky and I were in our guestroom at the B&B, lying on our separate beds and talking about crossbows, beguines, and Fiona. Soon we'd have to get up and find our way to a restaurant and the concert hall. Nicky had picked up a velvet tunic to wear while she was in the center. As usual, I'd forgotten all about fashion, but Piet had loaned me a clean sweater, which I planned to wear with my black jeans.

"So Fiona never had sex with her husband?"

"That, I don't know. But she did say that Stan was always very preoccupied with his research and classes, so maybe the topic never came up. And I think in the latter part of their marriage, Fiona spent most of her time in London, helping Stella with one thing or another."

"And by then, Stella was her sister-in-law and sex with Fiona would have been out of the question, even if Stella's health permitted it, I suppose? Goodness," Nicky said. "How did this conversation get started?"

"Because of *you*. First, she thought my companion was a man named Nicky, obviously, because who else would spend the entire afternoon at not just one archery guild, but two? Then she was reassured to hear that our friendship was platonic. That prompted her to tell me more than I wanted to know, though it may have some bearing on the case I guess."

"What else did she say?

"I got the story of the close friendship between Fiona and Stella when they were at university. I gather they had kissed from time to time, cuddled a little, and Stella had made noises about wanting more, wondering if they might be lesbians. Fiona squashed all that, she told me. So Stella moved to London and got a job and a flat she shared with some other women in North London. Fiona came for a visit and was shocked to realize that all the women seemed to be gay. Stella had cut her long hair off and gotten a tattoo on her wrist and was wearing 'shapeless' clothes. Fiona fled back to York in horror. She started working on her doctorate and wrote her dissertation on medieval women's literary and musical culture in the beguinages of the Low Countries. Stan, whom she'd known for years as Stella's brother, came into the picture around then. They dated for a year or more, Fiona said, though she wasn't all that keen on him at first. But after she finished her doctorate and was having some trouble finding steady teaching, he proposed. He'd been hired by University of the Highlands and Islands in Inverness, and they offered Fiona a part-time lectureship. So she said yes."

"Romantic."

"Not very," I agreed. "I'm sure she was still in love with Stella. The wedding was in Sussex at the family home. Stella came with a woman. They were definitely a couple though the parents seemed not to be fully aware of it. Older than Stella, well-dressed, handsome in her way. Fiona couldn't stand her. No, it wasn't Vonn, or she would have said. Anyway, Vonn would never have come to a heterosexual wedding, or any wedding for that matter. Fiona still seems upset that Stella brought this woman to the family house, to Fiona's big day. They didn't meet for a few years. The next time was Mr. Terwicker's funeral. Stella was working at a publishing house. She told Fiona she'd written a medieval historical mystery, set in a beguinage in the late thirteenth century, and it was going to be published by Aphra Press."

"Was that the first one, *Woven into Murder*?"

"Yes. Fiona read it when it was published. She wrote to Stella and pointed out a few errors, but mainly was positive, about the feminist aspects. Fiona offered to help with a follow-up mystery, should she need any help with historical details. She sent Stella her dissertation, Stella responded, and they were back on good terms. There was just a lot they didn't talk about. But Stella apparently was inspired by the dissertation. In the next mystery, *Illuminated by Death,* she used bits and pieces from Fiona's research about the beguine poets. That's the one mystery with an overt lesbian theme. Fiona said she thinks it's Stella's poorest novel. The next Beatrys mystery required a lot of research, especially about the choral schools and liturgical music. I gather Fiona was very key in that. And then of course, Stella got sick, and Fiona became a crucial part of the team helping Stella. Fiona was cagey about all that. She preferred to talk a lot more about celibacy and friendship in the Middle Ages. She wanted it to be clear that there were different kinds of love and that her love for Stella had been pure. She said Stella understood that after she became ill. According to Fiona, Stella's gayness was just experimental and not serious. I honestly had the sense Fiona was relieved when Stella's fragile health pulled the plug on further relationships with women. Fiona told me that the years that she and Stella worked on the Beatrys books were happy ones, especially after she and Stan bought the flat in the same building as Stella in Primrose Hill. It was kind of perfect for Fiona, with Stan up in Inverness most of the time. She had the chance to immerse herself in research for the new mysteries and consult on the television series. She did everything for Stella, from borrowing books from the library to taking her to medical appointments."

"What about Vonn? Did she talk about Vonn? I mean, that's the reason we're in Bruges, isn't it?"

"We didn't get that far," I had to admit. "The soup came during the discussion of celibate love, and then suddenly lunch was over, and Fiona insisted on paying and we were out the door. I had to be content with all I learned about her long relationship with Stella and about Fiona's role in the research. You can't always push these things. In detective novels the investigator is always putting suspicious characters on the spot and forcing them to admit guilt, but in real life you're sitting in a cozy little bistro with someone who is sipping endive soup and looks the soul of respectability. You just don't say, 'So tell me about how you killed Vonn. And did you murder your beloved sister-in-law as well by any chance?' It would be absurd."

"I suppose so," said Nicky. "Still."

"I *did* mention Vonn, as we left the bistro. I asked if she knew Vonn had died. She said yes, that a couple of weeks ago Avery had told her that Vonn had a swimming accident caused by undetected health problems. So, nothing about a possible suicide. I asked how well she'd known Vonn and she said at first, *Not really*, and then, rather grudgingly, that Vonn was a freelance fact-checker hired by Avery on a few of the books. Then, she shook my hand—she's very formal—and said she hoped that you and I enjoyed the rest of our stay. By that time, I'm sure, she'd twigged that I wasn't just here by chance and that I had some sort of agenda to do with Vonn. She wasn't having any of it."

"So, basically, you didn't learn much. Remind me again why you think Fiona might have something to do with Vonn's death?" Nicky yawned and drifted off without waiting for an answer.

Why indeed? There was the information from Lucy Aspin that Vonn had been a key part of Stella's editorial team at Aphra Press. There was the editing contract between Vonn and the Avery Amstrong Agency for the fourth book in the series. There was the continuing mystery of why Avery had asked me to come to the lecture and keep Fiona busy while she talked with Vonn, and the bit about Vonn threatening Fiona. Was this true and if so, why? What had Vonn known about Fiona, which presumably had to do with Stella and her books? And then, there was the question of why Fiona had come to Bruges—was she fleeing London or just traveling?

In sum, what I had to go on was very slim evidence indeed, with many more questions than facts. And although I had managed, twice now, to engineer meetings with Fiona, in Primrose Hill and here in Bruges, I hadn't honestly learned very much, except that Fiona had been deeply in love with Stella.

I had to admit I'd been interested in Fiona's discussion of the seven ways of love, though she thought of it as a divine pathway to God, and I rarely thought of love at all. Certainly, in the course of a long life, especially in my youth, I'd fancied myself in love, with a teacher, with a traveling partner, with a total stranger glimpsed in a Spanish bar. But these passions were usually fleeting. Unlike so many of my friends, I've never looked for permanent relationships and avoided commitment at all costs, usually by booking a ticket elsewhere. I could excuse that by explaining that I wanted to see so much of the world and that by traveling alone I kept myself open to chance and experience. But I also didn't feel myself capable of the sort of intimacy that lesbian coupledom seemed to require. When I watched my friends and acquaintances fall madly in love, make promises they couldn't keep, struggle with monogamy and domestic life and in-laws, I didn't envy them one bit. When I saw them suffer horribly from jealousy and prolonged break-ups, I only felt pity and relief that I was well out of that sort of thing.

Fiona was apparently celibate, which was fine, but that didn't mean she wasn't capable of love in all its sweetness and serenity. In some odd way, in fact, I thought, when I looked over at Nicky drifting into sleep on her single bed next to mine, a pile of velvet and silk and tawny curls and Danish socks, I thought that I understood Fiona's chaste love for Stella better than most people. I'd never entertained a single lustful thought for my old bassoon-playing friend and landlady, but that just made our friendship stronger and, in some ways, more pure. Yes, pure. I closed my eyes and drifted blissfully away.

Because of the napping, Nicky and I barely got to the concert in time, having missed the chance for dinner. It was a selection of early music pieces, performed to a full house by a string quartet. I am one of those concertgoers who tends to think of other things than the music much of the time. In lieu of dinner I gnawed on the circumstances of Vonn's death at the bird pond. I knew now, from my recent immersion in the Ladies' Pond, how cold that water was in March, and it must have been colder in February. There were also things like branches in the pond, branches that might not pull you down but could cause panic. If Vonn were in any way impaired, she might have panicked, but she didn't have to have ingested anything to get a shock from the water and to rapidly develop hypothermia and drown. A verdict of misadventure was more palatable than one of suicide, but neither explanation seemed satisfying. I could believe that Vonn had gone for an evening walk on the Heath and ended up at the bird pond. I could believe that she was prone to depression or that she took a painkiller from time to time. But there were other factors at play here, factors that suggested a more violent, unexpected death.

The problem was, the police didn't seem to have asked any of the questions that interested me. They put the absent laptop down to a burglary. They didn't care what was on the laptop, or what was missing from Vonn's filing cabinet. They didn't give a toss what happened to the manuscript of "Gadfly." The police had clearly never spoken to Fiona and didn't see a link between a respectable scholar and homeowner in Primrose Hill and a scruffy old dyke floating at the edge of the bird pond.

I should have grilled Fiona more when I had the chance today. Instead I'd wasted so much time on making her comfortable with me that I hadn't gotten to the point of questioning her as I should have. Nicky and I had come all this way for nothing and now we'd be going back to London tomorrow morning, more or less empty-handed except for Nicky's velvet tunic and several boxes of seashell-shaped pralines.

Nicky was also quite happy about her encounters with the Flemish chaps at the archery guildhalls of St. Stephens (longbow) and St. George's (crossbow). In a short time, she'd become chums with a man called Bernt at the crossbow guild, had gotten him to show her their collection of bows, and had learned a lot about the important role the archery guilds played in Bruges, not just for defending the city, but for parading around and contributing to the welfare of the poor. Bernt was a retired policeman. He'd demonstrated one of the ancient bows and, when he heard that her father in Glasgow had actually built a replica medieval crossbow and taught the art to Nicky as a young girl, he'd even allowed Nicky to have a go. They had exchanged addresses and he had made noises about wanting to show her more of Belgium when she could spend longer in the country. He and his wife had a small farm and Nicky would be welcome there. Once again, I was astonished by the easy rapport Nicky seemed to have with the most masculine of men and their hobbies. My own dad had been more of a sports-on-television man, a fascination I'd never shared.

I was glad Nicky didn't regret coming to Bruges. But I didn't feel the same sense of achievement. I didn't even know where Fiona lived in Sint-Anna, and I was fairly sure a follow-up text to her about Vonn wouldn't result in anything.

Our train was scheduled to depart at ten the next morning, leaving time for Nicky to have a leisurely breakfast and another chat with Piet about the *kruisboog*, while I went back up to the room and used my phone to retrieve email. To my surprise there was a message from Gayle. She said she was sorry to hear that I'd almost drowned in the Ladies' Pond, and she apologized for skipping out on me on Sunday. She went on:

I know I've been acting a bit strangely, Cassandra. Vonn's death really threw me into a state of unexpected grief. I wasn't completely honest with you about my friendship with her. We broke up, as I told you, a long time ago, but we didn't really lose touch. It was more than just having coffee and talking. I cared about her as a human being. She had a softer side most people didn't even glimpse. Vida saw my grief, but she didn't understand it. I'm telling you this because I didn't like how you and I parted and just wanted to set things straight. I still love Vida and want to be with her, but I'm in Torquay now, at least for a few weeks. My sister has plenty of space. So, if you ever want to come down to Devon, you'd be very welcome.

Love, Gayle

I reread the text. I didn't buy the bit about only caring about Vonn as "a human being." She'd clearly been sleeping with Vonn on and off all these years and keeping it secret. Even after Vonn died, poor Wee Gayle couldn't acknowledge the long-time affair, not to me and Nicky, certainly not to Vida. No wonder she hadn't mentioned that she'd sublet the flat for two months. No wonder she'd felt the need to go through Vonn's flat and organize it, and no wonder Vida had been jealous of something she didn't understand: Why should Gayle be so upset about Vonn's death if their relationship had ended thirty years ago?

All the same, none of this really solved the problem of what happened to the laptop and "Gadfly." Had Vonn written in her memoir about Gayle? Was it as simple as Gayle removing the laptop and destroying the manuscript just because Vonn mentioned Gayle as a lover? Surely, she could have just deleted those sections or tossed the pages?

Vida, on the other hand? I felt again the sensation of fingers around my ankle.

Gayle said Vida had been angry and jealous after Vonn's death. But what if Vida had been angry and jealous *before* Vonn died? What if she had taken the laptop and had read "Gadfly" and found incriminating evidence of Gayle and Vonn's affair?

Perhaps that was the direction I should be looking in.

All the same, it bothered me that I had missed my chance to question Fiona thoroughly, and I made a sudden decision. I didn't want to spend the day with Nicky visiting the market square and art museum in Brussels before the Eurostar left at 16:00. I wanted to find Fiona and have another conversation.

This one wouldn't be about divine love, but about the possibility of profane death.

Nicky was a bit disappointed but understood. She set off alone for the station, and we agreed to meet in Brussels at the Eurostar terminal at three o'clock. Piet was helpful, once he knew what I wanted, although whitepages.be didn't show a Fiona Craig in Bruges. It was only when I suggested we look under Stella Terwicker that an address showed up. Just off Carmersstraat, on Speelmansstraat, across from the large property still belonging to the English Convent.

The house was like many in the district, identifiable only by a number, with no name plaque. Across the narrow street was a long, low building wall, whitewashed and tiled, with bare tree branches visible inside, part of the English Convent's garden. Fiona's house was whitewashed as well, the door set into the wall under an arch. There was no outdoor speaker plate, just a knocker, so I knocked. From inside I heard medieval music, a choir of women's high, fluting voices holding note after note.

When she opened the door, she did not look surprised. "I know you're following me, but I don't know why," she said. "You'd better come in."

23.

"Hildegard von Bingen?" I asked, throwing out a name I knew.

"No. It's sacred music composed for the beguinages, from a Flemish plainchant group called Psallentes. I know the director because their music was used in the television series." She stood there calmly, but with an apprehensive look on her pale face. She was wearing the same beige sweater as yesterday, but with jeans, and indoor slippers. Reading glasses were pushed up on her head.

"Beautiful," I said, edging a bit farther into the room. She was clearly not going to be offering me tea and shortbread.

The flat was an appropriate setting for the women's soprano voices. A modest bookcase with history and religious titles. No sofa, just two modern sling-back chairs in white leather and a coffee table. A few books on an end table and a reading lamp. A dining table with a laptop and some neat piles of periodicals. Pine floors and throw rugs. Everything restrained, except for a few rich touches on the white walls from framed reproductions of illuminated pages and artworks by Flemish masters. In a corner of the room by a door leading to a kitchen was an altar of sorts, an end table with a vase of fresh flowers and above it on the wall a reproduction of the Annunciation, probably by Rogier von der Weyden.

Fiona interrupted my silent and intrusive gaze around her flat. "Why exactly are you here, Cassandra?"

"Why do you think?" I parried with an ambiguous smile.

"I'm guessing," she said, seating herself on one of the white leather chairs, and gesturing to me to do the same, "that you're a journalist, a literary critic perhaps, and that you've found me out. You know about Beatrys. Not through Avery, I hope."

I sank into the opposite chair and answered cautiously, "Well, I suppose I did have some questions about your role in the creation of the Beatrys books. I can't be the only person who has asked whether Stella had some writing help. You've told me you did research for her. Was it more than that? It wasn't Avery who made me curious, it was your biography and what you've told me about Stella's illness."

"And so you tracked me down," she said, nodding. "I suppose I'm not surprised. I've been expecting it for a while."

"I don't want to put you in an awkward spot," I said. "If you helped Stella, it was out of affection or necessity, I'm sure. Do you want to tell me about it?"

I sensed she did want to tell me about it. As much she feared being exposed, she also probably longed to tell a story that would explain and exonerate whatever her secret was. I remembered the lure of the confessional booth. To wipe the slate clean and start over, forgiven for our sins. The liturgical music soared and then drifted off at the last notes, echoing in the bare white room, before resuming with a new hymn.

"It was just research in the beginning," she said. "As I told you yesterday after lunch, I could see in the first book how weak Stella was on the details of the wool trade between England and Flanders, and how she got some crucial things wrong about the making and trading of cloth. England had the sheep, but it was in Flanders that the art of weaving had been perfected. Stella, as long as I'd known her, could tell a story, but she skated over details. Oh, she knew what a warp and weft were, certainly, and how a loom worked—in general—but all the rest, she couldn't be bothered to learn everything about how wool was spun into thread, dyed, woven, fulled in vats of urine, spread on the grass with tenterhooks, made into clothing."

Fiona sighed, taking her reading glasses off her head, and placing them distractedly on the side table. "I wrote to her after the first book, gently suggesting that if there were a second edition, she might correct or add a few facts. She didn't answer directly, but when she started plotting the second novel, she asked me a few questions about the illuminated work that the beguines did, the composition of the inks, the pens. I sent her my dissertation. Later, when she was writing *Illuminated by Death*, she asked for some ideas about creating a female character who was a poet. She asked about a line from one of Hadewijch's poems that she wanted to use in her mystery: life as a river of darkness, where tiny lights were lit by every act of love."

Fiona's brown eyes suddenly grew damp, and she stopped speaking. I encouraged her gently, "So it wasn't just research you did? You helped her with ideas? I've noticed that in *Schola for Murder* the scholarship is woven into the storyline more easily."

"Yes, by *Schola for Murder* I was very involved in research about the liturgical music and choirs. And to the extent that Stella was confident in the scholarship behind the story, the storyline improved and made more sense."

Her mouth smiled a little, while her eyes stayed sad. "I wasn't a mystery fan, not at the beginning. When we were students, I remember Stella was always reading Agatha Christie and Ngaio Marsh and historical mysteries, to relax and get to sleep at night. I found them rather trivial. But later I began to see that historical mysteries had educational value. As time went on, I made more suggestions about the plot and characters. And I pushed back a little over the years, on some things that her agent Avery and her publishing house thought were important but absolutely weren't."

"Like what?"

"Their insistence that the relationship between Sheriff Abel and Beatrys was crucial to the story. In my opinion, and I think Stella agreed, a silly flirtation with its tiffs and reconciliations wasn't needed. The real conflict and love were between Beatrys and the Magistra, Anna van Hoogstraaten. I thought Abel's role was mainly to show off Beatrys's detective skills. He rarely figured anything out, or he went after the wrong suspects. But he was considered important, not just to arrest somebody at the end, but to provide romance and create character conflict. I didn't manage in any of the books to get Stella to kill him off, but he did have a child eventually with his mistress, who died in one of the plagues. If you've read *A Plague of Orphans,* you know that Abel placed that child in the care of the beguines as an infant, and then he disappeared to the Crusades, leaving it open whether he would return or not."

I hadn't gotten that far in the series yet, but I'd skimmed descriptions of all the books. "Sometimes, if I'm remembering correctly, the murderer was not a man," I said. "Did Stella let the women murderers off a little easier? I don't recall Abel sending the female poisoner in *Illuminated by Death* to the gallows."

"Of course Stella made different choices when the murderer was a woman. She tried to understand the motives behind a woman taking another woman's life. Generally the female suspect who... does that, who ends up doing that has a reason. Or it's an accident."

Immediately alert, I held my breath. Was Fiona actually about to make a confession?

As I leaned forward, she drew back.

"Who did you say you were writing for again?"

"So far," I said, unwilling to commit to a full-on lie. "I'm not sure. Maybe no one. I'm not really sure there's even a story here. I did speak to Lucy Aspin, at Aphra, about Stella. And I had lunch with Avery before your lecture. Not that she said anything about you helping Stella with her books, of course. Avery's very discreet."

Fiona nodded, neither agreeing nor disagreeing.

"Avery was the one who brought you onto the various projects, wasn't she? Not just as a researcher on the books, but the television series? Basically, to help Stella continue her career."

"Avery presented it as my moral duty," Fiona said. "The illness came on at such a bad time, for Stella obviously, but also for Avery. Stella was writing *The Funeral Specialist,* but except for the first hundred pages, it was still very rough. Some chapters were just summaries. She planned to work hard on it in Portugal for two or three months after a brief holiday. I had helped her some already, with all the details of how the beguines created hospitals and cared for the sick. I've sometimes wondered whether the writing itself, about illness and death, caused Stella to get sick. She was already down with what seemed to be the flu when she went off to Lisbon mid-December. She shrugged it off when she called Stan and me to say good-bye. Nothing a bit of sunshine wouldn't help.

"Since you've read the biography, you know what happened, how Avery flew with her to Lisbon and helped her settle into a rented flat. Within two days, Stella was in hospital, and no one knew what was wrong. Avery didn't let me and Stan know for almost a week. She waited until Stella had stabilized enough to get back to England. Stan and I came down to London and were with Stella over the Christmas holidays, and when Stan went back to Inverness, I was able to spend another two weeks in London. Then I had to return to teaching as well. Stella was on bedrest. The tests were inconclusive. She just slept all the time. She literally couldn't hold a pen. This went on for two months. Finally there was a diagnosis, CFS.

"Avery was frantic. The manuscript due date was September first. She arranged for the publication to be postponed one season, hoping that Stella would improve. But Avery also asked if I could give the manuscript a close read and write up a report of what needed to be changed or added to or corrected, especially in the second half. I did, of course. I wrote pages and pages of notes. Anything to help Stella.

"Avery said it was important we not suggest that Stella was incapable of writing now. The television series deal was in the works. It was important for Stella financially. I understood. I said I'd be glad to do whatever it took. Avery mentioned that there was a freelance editor she knew, who had helped Stella on one or two of her projects before. That all together we'd get a final manuscript of *The Funeral Specialist* to the publisher. By the time it came out, Stella was bound to be better, and could do the publicity. Stella liked doing readings and interviews and was very good at them. If we could spare her the challenging work of researching and writing, her health would improve more quickly."

Fiona looked at her watch, and I thought I'd better move this along before she turned me out of this bare white room in Bruges the way she'd turned me out of the flat in Primrose Hill.

"But Stella didn't get better quickly, did she?" I prompted. "And she never returned to the full strength that would have enabled her to write a book every two or three years, the way the market demanded. She couldn't have done that *and* also promoted her books and the television series."

"No," said Fiona. "She *wanted* to, and she still came up with all the ideas. We discussed them and she outlined the plot and ideas and wrote some scenes. She could still write, just not a whole book. The ideas were mostly hers," Fiona said miserably. "So now you know. It's a relief to get this off my chest. You can understand I didn't want to write about this in detail in the biography, to protect Stella's reputation. But as a scholar, I'm ashamed of obscuring the truth."

"I can see it's complicated. Was there ever discussion about putting your name on the cover as a co-author?"

"No," said Fiona. "And I wouldn't have asked for that. Not just because I wanted Stella to get the credit, but because by the time the books came out, they weren't really mine anymore, either. Avery weighed in and suggested changes here and there to the plot to create more conflict and tension. The freelance editor did all kinds of things, from changing people's names to inventing dialogue to moving scenes around. It often changed the meaning. There were some struggles. Stella would be the arbiter, when she could, but sometimes I wrote to Avery and the freelance editor and put my foot down."

"So it was sort of a team effort?" I noted that she hadn't yet been able to say Vonn's name. "You must have known the freelance editor pretty well," I said. "This was Vonn Henley, I'm assuming."

She gave a brusque nod and her mouth twisted. "Yes, no, I didn't know her well. At first, not at all. In the beginning I didn't ask Avery much. I understood she'd arranged for an outside editor to pull my notes and Stella's rough draft together into a final book before delivering the manuscript to the editor at the publishing house, Albatross. I then dealt with the editor and copyeditor *there*—usually through Avery."

"So the editors at Albatross weren't aware that Stella wasn't fully engaged in writing the books?"

"I don't know what Avery told them. What Avery told me is that most authors who were successful had research assistants and close readers, so we weren't doing anything out of the ordinary." Fiona stroked her hands, one against the other, as if her circulation needed help. "You must understand. I was preoccupied all around that time with Stella's health. By the summer of 1996, I'd given up my lectureship in Inverness and was in London full-time. *The Funeral Specialist* came out and was a success. I went with Stella to her readings or book signings, and then I took care of her afterwards. She would shine brightly during the event and then collapse. She was far from her old self. It was at one of the bookstore readings that I met Vonn. She had the nerve to come up to Stella and give her a big kiss on the mouth, in full view of everyone waiting in line to have their book signed. Outrageous.

"When we got back to her flat, Stella admitted they'd been involved once, some years ago, and that Vonn had actually helped her get the first novel published with Aphra and was the paid copyeditor on the first two mysteries. She'd also commented on and made suggestions for the third novel, *Schola for Murder*. Stella had never once mentioned that to me. Stella confessed that Vonn had worked on *The Funeral Specialist* too. I confronted Avery, and she tried to talk me out of being so upset. Avery said that Vonn really appreciated and understood Stella's mysteries, that Vonn was a good copyeditor, and that I didn't have to have anything to do with her. Avery was the go-between. She was so reasonable that I felt ridiculous. Anyway, we were all committed to books five and six, because of the publishing contract. So I gritted my teeth. That's when I started pushing back though. I refused to meet with Vonn, though we did sometimes spar over email."

"Do you still have those emails?" I asked. "I mean, if you wanted to prove anything about how the team effort worked?"

"I don't want to prove anything," said Fiona. "I'm ashamed of those emails. Vonn was always professional, just assertive. But I was often sarcastic, and the worst thing is, I sometimes pretended to be Stella in the emails. I wanted to break up whatever friendly feelings still existed between them, and I did. Stella didn't want Vonn to work on the seventh book, *The Mystery Play Murders*. She didn't think she needed anyone but me."

"That was published right before her death, wasn't it?"

"Yes, in the autumn of 2007. She had worked far too hard on the book for months and then insisted on doing a publicity tour in England, and went to Stockholm and Oslo as well, in November. She picked up a cold and it turned to pneumonia. By January she was on a ventilator, and then she was dead."

Fiona clasped her hands together and twisted them. "And there's more. There was an eighth book, as you know, *The Confessor's Tale*. It was published posthumously, but it shouldn't have been published at all under Stella's name. She barely had anything written, just the ideas and basic plot. It didn't get great reviews. Critics mean to be kind, but the tone was patronizing. They excused it because it apparently was written by a woman on her deathbed." Fiona pinched her lips sardonically. "Actually the writer was not on her deathbed, the writer was sitting in Stella's flat, the writer was Stella's literary executor, someone who wrongly imagined she could write a novel as good as one of Stella's because she'd half-written them before."

"I'm sorry," I said, and I was. "And Vonn wasn't involved with that book?"

"No," said Fiona. "Afterwards Avery was firm with me. No more mysteries. A few years later, she suggested that I write a biography of Stella instead and got me a reasonable advance. She didn't want me to mention the team effort though or say anything about *The Confessor's Tale,* and I agreed. So know that if you publish an article about that, I'll lose my scholarly reputation completely."

"I'm not here to expose you," I said. "It's Vonn's death I'm looking into."

There was a long silence, and for the first time I noticed that the soprano voices were gone. They had probably stopped singing a while ago. Fiona seemed paralyzed in her chair. Then a fierce, defensive look, like a shield, seemed to drop over her face.

"What do you mean? Avery said it was a swimming accident. That Vonn had some heath problems."

"It may well have been an accident. Possibly suicide. But there are some unresolved aspects to the case. Vonn wasn't swimming. She was dressed. And it happened in the evening. Some of her papers and her laptop went missing from her flat afterwards, including all the material connected with the memoir she'd been writing about feminist publishing. I had been hoping you might be able to shed some light on this."

I was watching her closely yet didn't see outrage. Her eyes were brown doors, closed. Her voice was frosty and dismissive. "But surely, you don't think I had anything to do with this. I don't know anything about the memoir."

"No, no," I said, but I left a bit of uncertainty in my tone. "But Avery told me that Vonn had threatened you in some way. It's even possible Vonn might have written about Stella in her memoir. Perhaps she wrote about your contributions to the Beatrys mysteries. Didn't Avery alert you that Vonn might bring some of these things up at the lecture?"

"Avery did say something about Vonn being a bit obnoxious about my biography. And I did see a woman I thought might be Vonn, at the end of the lecture, but I couldn't put her together with the woman who'd kissed Stella after the bookshop reading twenty-five years ago."

"So you never read Vonn's memoir manuscript?"

"I would remember if I had!" Fiona was flushing back to life now, the redness in her cheeks traveling down to her neck. "As for Avery, I haven't seen her much since my book was published last autumn. She appeared at the launch with flowers. I was surprised she said she was coming to the lecture in February in fact. As a rule we don't meet often. The royalties are deposited directly to my bank account. Occasionally there are contracts to sign on behalf of the estate, for new editions or translations. I sign and return them."

She stood up, as if testing her strength after these confessions and revelations. "Was Vonn trying to blackmail Avery, is that what you're saying? About the Beatrys books? Surely Avery wouldn't kill her over that. Don't be ridiculous. It might be a little embarrassing for Avery, but she could easily put Vonn in her place. As Avery always liked to tell me, collaborations happen all the time in publishing. The books were Stella's and the way Stella talked about them in her interviews made it clear that the ideas came from her. We were just her 'good angels,' as Stella liked to say."

I noticed that she'd made the story about Avery being blackmailed, and Avery being accused of killing Vonn.

"You didn't mention Vonn in your biography," I said stubbornly. "Neither as Stella's past lover or as her editor and/or collaborator."

"I didn't want the biography to be one of those tell-all books that are so popular," said Fiona coldly. "Yes, Stella experimented with the gay thing in London, but when she got ill, all that was over. I would never call her an actual lesbian. In spite of whatever brief flirtation she'd had with Vonn."

I had to ask. "And Avery? Were Stella and Avery ever involved?"

"That's a terrible accusation to make," Fiona snapped. "Stella was much younger than Avery and thought of her as a mother figure."

Avery, a mother figure? I didn't say anything, but I thought that Fiona, if anyone, would know if Stella and Avery had been in love, the way Fiona had monitored Stella's life.

"I know I should have mentioned Vonn, for scholarship's sake," Fiona said in a calmer voice. "Vonn did play a role in polishing some of the Beatrys books. Like other editors and scriptwriters and so on. But you pick and choose when you tell a life story. A biography can never be fully comprehensive. I didn't write much about Stan either, or their parents. I was trying to capture her spirit, her sincere interest in the Middle Ages. It's really more of scholarly book about the beguines, written in the form of a biography. I hope you'll take that into consideration when you write something about the Beatrys books. If you do, which you may choose not to, of course."

Fiona was out of her chair and standing, and I realized that once again, I'd misread her signal that I should go.

I wasn't sure, but I thought I'd gotten what I'd come for. More of the details and motivations. How the collaboration had worked. Avery's role as mediator. And perhaps, a tentative feeling that Fiona, for all the years of hiding her role and Vonn's role in Stella's life and work, had not gone so far as to murder Vonn. Why would she? Even if it came out that Fiona or Vonn had helped with the book, no one could prove anything, and Avery would certainly shrug it off as business as usual in the publishing world.

I was barely out the door when I heard the music of the beguines start up again inside the flat. I wondered how many times Fiona had listened to their consoling voices.

PART THREE

24.

William Short was tall and thin, with black-frame glasses, floppy hair, and an expensively thrown-together look that included a gray, single-breasted blazer over a white tee-shirt and slim black trousers that ended well above his ankle boots and intentionally showed two inches of purple sock. He was the publisher of SNP books, while Adrian Pryce, shorter, balding, pink-faced, in an open-necked, blue-striped Oxford shirt and jeans, was the senior editor. They were even younger than I expected. Short had sharp blue-gray eyes and spoke in crisp sentences, using numbers and percentages, while Pryce was given to long-winded commentaries on publishing and the list they were building. They'd done well with thrillers, true crime, noir, and hard-boiled, but were looking to expand their offerings, since (a fact surprising only to themselves) SNP's crime series seemed to lack women writers. This had recently been pointed out in an article somewhere by an unpleasant feminist sort of reviewer.

Publishing a thriller series about a female ex-bullfighter turned private eye would take care of that problem. Pryce confessed himself enthralled by the character of Rita: how tough she was, how smart and aggressive, how appealingly wounded, physically and psychologically. Short was more interested in Lola Fuente's sales figures in Spain and whether I thought there would be a strong market in North America. They were asking the Spanish publishers for all English language rights, of course.

Only Adrian Pryce had read my translated samples and summary of *Verónica*. He found the story intriguing and clever. "Sheer genius plotting to link the verónica pass in bullfighting with the whole veil of Veronica thing." He thought it especially ingenious to have the murderer smother the victim with a pillow, so the pillowcase then had the DNA imprint of not just the victim's face, but the DNA traces of the man who killed her. William Short mentioned bullfighting several times; he had been to Spain as a student and had run (I suspected not far) with the bulls in Pamplona.

We were lunching in an upmarket Japanese restaurant not far from their Soho office on Old Compton Street. While Avery and I had ordered sushi, served on hand-built, rough gray plates, the boys went for the beef teriyaki bento box. Perhaps to show that, unlike some publishers, they were not wimpy vegetarians and could handle the public slaughter of bulls as well as any cold-blooded killers Rita might encounter in Seville.

Avery and I had arrived almost simultaneously at the restaurant, before Short and Pryce came along to join us, and I immediately thought of all the questions I had for her about the team efforts that had gone into Stella's books and about why she told me that Fiona was being threatened by Vonn. I couldn't start off with that, however, given that we were meeting the publishers and had business to discuss, so I contented myself by mentioning, as if casually, that I was a bit bleary-eyed today as I'd just gotten back last night from a spontaneous trip that I'd taken with Nicky.

"Oh?" Her indifferent tone suggested that, since I was always traveling, where was the news?

She herself looked a bit bleary-eyed behind her reading glasses, though she'd had a hair cut since I'd last seen her and her clothes were crisp and fresh. Yet I noted her hands shook slightly as she held the menu, and she didn't regard the offerings with her usual attentiveness. I suspected a hangover, because she said a firm no when the server asked if she'd like a drink. Not for the first time I wondered if Avery struggled with alcohol.

"Bruges!" I said. "Nicky wanted to hear a particular early music group, and their concert hall has fabulous acoustics. So we zipped off on the Eurostar for two nights there. Found a great little B&B and went to the concert and back home the next day. Oh," I added casually, "I ran into Fiona Craig, of all people. Apparently, she has a flat there. Did you know that?"

"I... well, yes." She kept her eyes on the menu and her voice even. "That is, I mean, Stella had a small flat there, and of course Fiona inherited everything. I suppose I've not thought much about it. I don't see much of Fiona anymore," she added, as if unaware that only four or five weeks ago she'd requested my attendance at Fiona's lecture. "Oh, here they are!" She brightened up. *Sotto voce*, she added, "Let's see what we can wring out of them for your translator's fee. You know they want to do all Lola's books, the first three and the next when it's published, so that could be a tidy sum in the next few years."

"Will, Adrian!" she gave an animated wave. "Darling boys, how well you look!" she added as the darlings seated themselves at the small table. "And congratulations on snagging the rights to that true crime superstar from Florida. A great investment."

SNP and Avery had already agreed on a deal to present to Lola's publishers in Madrid, which included beginning with *Verónica* late this fall. Avery's role in all this had now become that of broker, working on commission for Lola and her Spanish publishers, but also making sure that I had a good contract and that I could deliver.

I had to promise to finish the translation by July 1. That gave me three and a half months. "Don't disappoint me, Cassandra," she'd said when I'd told her I'd meet the deadline easily.

Now, in between bites of sushi, she hinted to Short and Pryce that I was hugely in demand, and asked me several times, solicitously, if I could squeeze in the work in between those bestsellers by Rosa Cardenes. She started from the premise that I was doing SNP some kind of extraordinary favor by bringing Lola Fuentes to their attention, and that the translation would be a triumph. As she spoke, she convinced herself, and the fond, conspiratorial glance she threw my way seemed real, not put on.

I had to hand it to Avery. She was a superb negotiator. She knew how to flatter, and she knew how to bargain, and she knew how to hold her ground. No wonder she was financially so much better off than I was. It wasn't that I undervalued myself as a translator. I knew my value. Yet as a businessperson, I was an amateur. The only kind of calculations I seemed capable of were those that had to do with productivity. I knew I could translate quickly when under a deadline, particularly mysteries that had a lot of dialogue. Ten pages a day was relatively easy when whole pages were composed of lines like:

"And what did you see in the alleyway?"
"I saw nothing."
"You're lying."
"No."
"I'll prove it to you."
"No need for a gun. I'll talk."
Ten pages a day multiplied by thirty days is three hundred pages, in

just a month. Assuming you never took off a weekend. And that was just the first draft. The harder part with Lola Fuentes was not only all the arcane language of the bullring, but some of the terms to do with the financial skullduggery in the book. Money laundering, false accounts, pay-offs, and offshore holding companies. I hardly knew what some of these terms were in English, much less the precise meaning in Spanish. I wasn't completely sure that Lola Fuentes knew either.

Of course, even as I was deep in admiration at Avery's agenting techniques, I was also thinking how I could corner her after lunch and get some answers. There was the problem of the so-called threat to Fiona from Vonn, which may or may not have been true. More pressing was to understand if Avery had deliberately destroyed correspondence with Vonn and if so, why? Was it because she was afraid it would come out that Vonn and Fiona had played such key roles in the Beatrys mysteries as editors and perhaps even co-writers? Did Avery imagine that would hurt sales or damage her agency in some way? I wanted to reassure Avery that such a subterfuge meant little to me. It all happened years ago. Fiona may have initially worked for free out of her love for Stella, but now she had royalties and other fees coming to her through the agency on a regular basis. Vonn too had presumably been paid, either by Stella directly or by the publisher. Research assistance, intensive editing, and ghostwriting were things that happened daily in the world of publishing.

I was more interested in identifying anything else Vonn might have known or might have written that could have led to her death. Something to do with others in the women's movement or in feminist publishing of the time. Avery had told me she'd skimmed the manuscript and found only "spleen and scandal." If only she could trust me with any suspicions she had—together we could perhaps puzzle out the mystery of whether anyone had killed Vonn, and why.

I allowed Avery to run the conversation with SNP, while I finished off my sushi and drank my tea. I answered Avery's leading questions to me with becoming modesty and tried to present Lola in the best light possible, as the grandniece of one of the great matadors of the mid-twentieth century, not as well known as Manolete and El Ciclón ("the cyclone") but a skilled man in the ring, who had also appeared in one or two movies. Lola's whole family had once been involved in the bullfighting business. She was an expert and had inherited posters and newspaper clippings, as well as some of their decorative fighting costumes, the beautiful *trajes de luces*, some still stained with dried blood.

Short and Pryce loved this, and I was so caught up in some of the stories myself, that I hardly noticed that Avery excused herself for the ladies. Though I eventually noticed she didn't return. William's phone buzzed, followed by my own, with a text: *Sorry, sorry. Had to run and didn't want to interrupt. I'll get your translation contract to you soon. A.*

I headed back to the Islington flat after a little more friendly back and forth. The imagined pleasure of a nice check from SNP to deposit in my bank account began to fade as I thought of how much work awaited me. I emailed Lola to tell her the good news, and then opened my laptop and searched for the folder with all the *Verónica* files. In addition to the Spanish print copy of the book, I had Lola's final manuscript in Word to work from. My copy of the final had ended up acting as backup for Lola. Like most of us at one time or other, she'd made the mistake of deleting what she thought were older files, only to find she'd sent the final to the wastebasket. At that time she didn't have an external drive to automatically make *copias de seguridad.*

I wondered if Vonn had backups of her work, and if so, where were they? So far, I only knew about the two diskettes I'd found in the shoebox in Vonn's closet. I pulled them out of my desk drawer again. Vonn made her living as an editor, so the diskettes could have held anything. But I knew now, from Fiona, that those were probably the years Vonn was working on two of Stella's books, *A Plague of Orphans,* published in 1999, and *Death Comes to the Magistra,* published in 2003. They were the years that Fiona and Vonn were forced to work together, separated by Avery, and they were probably the books that Vonn contributed most to. When the so-called burglar took the laptop, did they take an external drive or some flash drives as well? Gayle had said Vonn had bought a new laptop in December.

My eyes went from the new model HP laptop I was working on to the old HP laptop I'd used until last year. I'd transferred most of the files myself, and deleted many more, but had left old drafts and notes, and a lot of miscellaneous junk on the old one, intending to give it a proper look one of these days before I recycled it. Meanwhile it acted as a backup, a safeguard, a *sauvegarde,* in case I needed it.

For the first time I wondered what Vonn had done with her old laptop. Had she transferred the files herself to the new one or had she, like many people, taken both laptops to a shop to have the files from the old transferred to the new?

Was it at all possible that Vonn went to Vida Carrasco's shop in Stoke Newington to have her files transferred? The idea seemed preposterous, given that Gayle was in a relationship with Vida. On the other hand, as far as I could tell, almost every dyke in North London besides me took their computer business to Vida. Perhaps Vonn reasoned that Vida had forgiven and forgotten her rejection from the Triple L project. Perhaps Vonn wanted to get to know Vida again and make nice with Gayle's new girlfriend.

Corinne had said that Vonn had put aside her old ways, her old grudges and spitefulness, and had turned over a new leaf after the mastectomy. I wasn't so sure. Whether or not Vonn and Gayle had remained lovers all these years later I didn't know, but they clearly were closer than Gayle had first led me to believe. Who did Kristi call but Gayle to help dismantle the flat? And why else would Vida and Gayle part ways unless Vida was jealous of Vonn, even after her death? Gayle had told me that herself.

I doubted that Gayle would have suggested that Vonn take her laptop to Carrasco's Computer Sales and Repair, but what if Vonn, in her role as gadfly, had done it just to tweak Vida's nose, to make Vida jealous? And if that were the case, what had happened to the old laptop? Was it possible Vida still had it? And had looked at it?

I stared at my old laptop on the shelf. It was a bit battered looking, but it still worked and should do the trick. I wondered if I could trust Vida with Vonn's diskettes and, after some hesitation, put them in my pocket.

I went out to the Essex Road and caught the 73 bus northbound to Church Street in Stoke Newington.

I've been in computer repair shops often since I bought my first laptop. Before that, I'd been an electronic holdout, hanging on to my portable Hermes typewriter in its sturdy, aqua-colored case. I've had decent laptops as well as those that disappoint sooner rather than later. Often they fail me when I least can afford repairs or when I'm in some part of the world where some parts aren't available.

Many of the computer shops I've frequented while traveling were either in someone's cellar or back shed, or on a side street difficult to find. They were modern Old Curiosity Shoppes, with shelves of monitors big as microwaves, scavenged motherboards, and early-version modems, boxes of tangled cords, earphones, and adapters. Some stores also sold radios, secondhand stereo speakers, and Walkmans. There were even personal fans and toasters in a few places, but most of it was electronic stuff, encased in dirty beige or dusty black plastic. The disarray wasn't a reflection on the skills of the repairmen, most of whom were highly ingenious and curious people, who saved my ass countless times.

Vida Carrasco's shop wasn't like that. There was most certainly a back room or workshop where she or her assistants actually fixed software glitches or repaired electronic failures, but the shopfront on Stoke Newington's high street was clean and brightly lit, with a long, polished wooden counter, and a few art prints on the walls.

When the door buzzed, Vida came from the back in a white coat, like a doctor. Her dark hair was pulled back in a low knot. Now that it was dry, I saw she had white threads throughout. But the professional smile on her lips changed to puzzlement when she saw me and my battered laptop.

"I never thought I'd see you here," she said, with her usual forthrightness that so easily could be mistaken for rudeness.

"I have a couple of issues with my laptop," I said. "It's slow, and I should probably get a new one soon, but I wanted to at least see if I could get everything I want to save onto a new external drive. Right now I don't have one of those, just some flash drives. And I use Dropbox for some important work files. I know that that there are lots of other cloud-saving services. Is that the right term? But I've heard that they have a terrible environmental impact, with all the electricity they consume and the e-waste and chemical coolants and so forth."

For a moment I thought I'd overdone it. Had I shown too much ignorance? That could hardly be possible. She must deal with people who brought in electronics still running software from ten or more years ago.

But Vida only nodded professionally and asked me to turn the laptop on. Slowly the HP came to life. While it woke up, she went into the back and brought out a couple of models of external drives. She then looked at the control panel and systems and confirmed that maybe the computer needed some apps and files removed to run faster.

"Do you want to leave it and have us look at it more closely?" she asked. "We can remove some of the apps that may be slowing things down. Unless you play some of these video games?"

"Oh, no," I said, thinking about some old personal correspondence as well as tax information for the Inland Revenue. "Tell me what apps to remove and I can do that."

She listed a few on a slip of paper, and then explained the merits of the two small external hard drives she'd brought out to show me. I picked one of them up and examined it, adding, "I probably really should upgrade to a new model laptop if I want to keep up with the times. I mean, I got this laptop ages ago." I paused to watch her plug the external drive's USB cord into the laptop, and said, "I was talking to Gayle about upgrading when she stayed with me and Nicky. She sang your praises. How is Gayle, by the way? Enjoying Torquay?"

"Fine, she's fine," said Vida. "Of course there's the sister to deal with, but Gayle's fine. I'll see her this weekend," she continued, and then stopped to explain how the drive worked.

I nodded vigorously, "Oh, that looks easy enough. Are you taking the train?"

"No, I'll drive tomorrow morning. I plan to swim in a few spots. There's a whole group of people who get out to Dartmoor for wild swimming. And in the Channel too, some great locations near Torquay." She smiled. "Care to join me? Or did you get enough water in your lungs last Sunday?"

I laughed and hoped that it didn't sound too fake. "Something caught my foot. Normally I'm a very good swimmer. Not so much in England, I suppose. But I always swim when I'm in Uruguay or Argentina. And I have a friend I stay with on the Costa Brava. We go swimming there a lot, her place is near some lovely beaches."

We chatted a little about Spain, and I chose the cheaper of the two external drives. She put it in the box again and ran my credit card through.

I fingered the diskettes in my pocket, and said, "Speaking of backups, I have a couple of old floppy disks from probably fifteen or so years ago. Any chance you could put them on a flash drive for me?"

"If they're not malfunctioning or corrupted, yes."

I brought them out and she looked at them.

"I don't know their state really," I said, "since I haven't been able to put them in the laptop. Even this old one doesn't have a floppy disk port anymore. It's getting more and more complicated to transfer files from machine to machine."

"In some ways," she said. "But we're experienced with all kinds of computer systems now and the software makes it easier. In the old days people stuck with their computers for ages, but now it's more common to upgrade every couple of years."

"I know, I should really buy a new one," I agreed. "That reminds me, Gayle mentioned to me that Vonn bought a new laptop recently, you know, the one that was stolen after she died. I gather Vonn brought it to you and you transferred all the files from the old one to the new one? I wonder if and when I buy a new laptop, probably within six months, if you could do the same thing, transfer the files, for me too?" I saw her stiffen and her black eyes narrowed. I saw then that my guess was probably right. She knew something about Vonn's laptop and had worked on it.

Vida put the box with my new external drive in a bag and said coldly, "I'd be happy to help you transfer your files if and when you buy a new laptop. I could even advise you on what to buy and get it for you. I do that with some of my less confident computer customers."

Now it was my turn to stiffen. I had to hold my tongue so as not to defend myself. First, she thought I couldn't swim, now she classed me with people who didn't understand computers. She always had to have the upper hand, didn't she?

"That would be great," I forced myself to say. I didn't follow up with questions about what kinds of documents she might have seen on Vonn's old laptop, whether she'd read the manuscript of "Gadfly" for instance, whether she'd made a copy of the files, or had even kept the old laptop under the pretext of recycling it. For, surely, Vida would deny any allegations, and without a search warrant I could hardly force my way into her workshop area and look for an old laptop.

I'd get nothing further from her at the moment, I knew. I 'd have to go directly to Gayle, and that meant going directly to Devon.

25.

Beatrys and the Magistra were at loggerheads. Again.

On the train from Bruges Thursday night I'd read most of *The Funeral Specialist* and finished it in London. Now I was on the 18:04 train from London to Torquay, deeply into *A Plague of Orphans*. After leaving Stoke Newington, I'd gone back to Islington, packed a bag with a swimsuit and dashed off a note to Nicky. I reserved a hotel in Torquay for a night and let Gayle know I was coming. I should have been using the three-and-a-half-hour trip to work on my translation of *Verónica*. From now on, every day I didn't work on it was a day lost.

But the train was crowded this Friday evening; a few passengers were loud and had been drinking. So the best I could do, at least until Reading when a number of people would detrain or change for other points west or north, was put in ear plugs and bury myself in thirteenth-century Flanders.

At the end of *The Funeral Specialist*—in view of how Beatrys solved the mystery of the beguine Griet, who was accused of poisoning and robbing the wealthy merchant at whose deathbed she sat—the Magistra had promoted Beatrys to assistant head of the infirmary, in addition to her weaving work. Now Anna van Hoogstraaten was sorry.

Once again, Beatrys was spending far too much time away from the beguinage, and far too much time in the company of Abel, the handsome sheriff. At the end of *The Funeral Specialist* he had more or less proposed marriage to Beatrys, but she had asked for more time to decide, given her new duties in the infirmary. Now it turned out, as plague took hold in the city of Bruges, that Abel had a double life. His married mistress of several years, Flora, was expecting a child, and not by her husband.

Abel had wanted to end the relationship, but Flora refused to give up without a fight. She accused Beatrys of stealing her lover, an accusation heard by one or two other beguines. Then Flora came down with the plague, shortly after having given birth, and died. Or was it the plague?

Perhaps it was the deadly monkshood concoction she'd been given. Both Beatrys and Abel were accused of murder, and the Magistra was on the point of expelling Beatrys when Abel was able to prove it was Flora's husband who had killed her.

I'd noted that number four, *The Funeral Specialist,* improved on number three, *Schola for Murder. A Plague of Orphans* was superior still, with its vivid scenes of conflict between the Magistra and Beatrys and many detailed descriptions of the infirmary's dormitory beds and adjacent room full of dried herbs, stoneware bottles, mortars and pestles and pots simmering. There was a great deal about herbal potions in this book, and I imagined that Fiona could well have contributed her knowledge of medieval herbal lore to that. It's likely Fiona's hand was visible in other ways, primarily in the conflict between Beatrys and the Magistra. For Beatrys took too much upon herself to investigate the death of Flora by setting a trap for both Abel and Flora's husband. In solving this complicated murder, Beatrys went farther than she ever had in stepping out of the women's world the beguines had created. She had to be brought to heel, to *accept* that the rules were there for her own good.

Just like Stella had to learn to accept that there would be much she could no longer do, that she would need Fiona and Stan and Avery to do for her. Everything from accounting to housekeeping to writing itself. In the biography, Fiona had made it clear that life for Stella changed after 1994 and that for the next fourteen years Stella had to be careful not to wear herself out. Fiona had written about how Stella rebelled from time to time, only to find herself in bed for a month after a book reading. She could no longer stay up late or go out pubbing; she couldn't travel on her own or drive around town in case she fainted. Her publishers provided a driver occasionally; more often Fiona took her where she needed to go. "Managing a successful career and a chronic illness were constant challenges," Fiona had written.

Between the two challenges it was no wonder Stella had trouble finding the energy to write. I could see in *A Plague of Orphans* how the Magistra/Fiona struggled to explain to Beatrys the importance of structure and how, by the end, Beatrys made the decision to conform to the reasonable rules of the beguinage in order to experience freedom within the walls. I skipped ahead to the ending, to see how Stella would resolve this, and discovered that, after hanging the murdering husband

and consigning the orphaned baby to the care of the beguines, Abel punished himself by saddling up for a pilgrimage to Rome, intending afterwards to fight for Jerusalem in the Crusades.

I thought about *Stella Terwicker* and about how Fiona could have written a different sort of book, a memoir about her personal relationship with Stella, not a biography that skirted all the interesting social and sexual aspects of Stella's life. A biography could be many things. In a manner of speaking, the whole Beatrys series formed a biographic body of work where, if you knew the story of Fiona and Stella, you could trace the conflicts, loyalty, and love of their friendship.

But there must be another story of Stella's life, not the one recounted by Fiona in her hagiographic *vita*, and not the one told obliquely by the Beatrys novels. People had shared bits and pieces. Lucy Aspin, Gayle, and Avery all had something to say about Stella. But Stella's own voice was missing. Why hadn't I tracked down some interviews with her?

My carriage had emptied its cargo of drinkers at Reading, and I was able to remove my earplugs. I was looking for older interviews and articles of substance and found a lengthy Q & A that touched on both her fiction and her life, in a women's journal. It was from the autumn of 1990, to coincide with the second Beatrys mystery, *Illuminated by Death*. The questions were ordinary, but the vigor of Stella's replies and the answers themselves surprised me. Somehow, from the various adjectives attached to Stella by others—*fragile, ethereal, otherworldly*—I'd had the impression that Stella was too incompetent to manage her life on her own, even before her illness; only the efforts of multiple people editing, promoting, and essentially writing her books had enabled her to sustain a significant career. Not only her chronic illness, but her underlying personality seemed badly suited to the rough and tumble of the publishing world. Instead, this interview showed someone eager to engage with life, with writing, and with the literary world.

In 1990, of course, she wasn't yet sick. She told the interviewer that she'd had an active childhood, the second of two children raised in Sussex. She'd had a pony, and she still liked to ride, as well as to dance, and to walk miles in the countryside and to travel, especially to Southern Europe. Just as interesting as the image of her as more athletic than I'd imagined was her self-presentation. While not overly intellectual like her sister-in-law, Stella was clear about what had attracted her to the Middle Ages and to the characters in her books. She emphasized that women in medieval times played a far greater role in society than they did in so-called more progressive times, like the Renaissance and Enlightenment.

There was hardly any other time before the twentieth century, the late twentieth century, when women had so many positions of authority and economic power as rulers, as abbesses, as merchants and artisans. Not coincidentally, it was also a time when they created and supported communities of women. I know it was in the context of patriarchal Christianity, but in spite of that, they managed to maintain their own space and financially support themselves outside the male-dominated society. The beguinages, in particular, were such an attractive idea to many women! They offered not just a refuge from forced marriages, but a vision of how independence, friendship, and cooperation could exist. There's surprisingly little written about the beguinages as early feminist societies, so one of my aims has been to introduce this idea to a larger public. I think of my audience as mainly women, but it may spur some male readers to assess the Middle Ages differently as well.

In 1990, published by the women's press Aphra, with women's journals and bookstores proliferating around the world and gay rights definitely on the agenda, Stella could also speak openly about the lesbian element of her second book, the love and sometimes jealousy that arose among the beguines. You could glimpse how the series might have developed differently if Stella had felt able to write from a queer perspective. Later books, as far as I could judge from *Schola for Murder* and *The Funeral Specialist,* continued to be feminist, but all traces of lesbian love were scrubbed. Instead, with Abel on the scene, working together with Beatrys and tempting her occasionally with thoughts of marriage and family, the books signaled that woman lived together in their female community because they wanted to be safe, not because they wanted to explore. After Abel was gone at the end of *A Plague of Orphans,* did Beatrys still think of him? Was the plan to bring him back again, or to give Beatrys another love interest eventually?

Was Avery to blame, or the book's editor at Albatross, or the marketing department that wrote the catalogue copy, or the sales reps and publicists, or the media that reviewed and promoted the books in ways that signaled and reinforced the idea that feminism wasn't threatening, that the beguinages were only places of temporary refuge, not serious alternatives to patriarchal culture.

Stella's illness may have played a role too, in her backing away from a more overt lesbian vibe. It was quite possible that she had never had a woman lover or any lover after she developed chronic fatigue. Perhaps she ceased to identify as queer, or just didn't have the strength to manage a public identity as an out lesbian. Her later interviews often focused on the mini-series. In every interview or article I found online from around 2000, when the TV series first showed, the questions were usually about the cast of *Beatrys* and about all the research that went into the settings and costumes. Stella invariably mentioned Fiona, "my scholarly sister-in-law" with the advanced degree from York, whenever the topic of historical accuracy came up.

In these later interviews, Stella was described as fragile looking with delicate features, wearing dresses and shawls. She was often asked, with smarmy sympathy, about her chronic illness. "Yes, I do get tired," was all she'd say (tired of your bloody questions, I thought to myself). And she admitted that she used a cane and occasionally a wheelchair. Yet she came across as just as direct as in her early encounters with the media. "Feminism is not a dirty word," she told a male journalist. "The beguines were definitely on to something in their vision of a women's community seven hundred years ago. They didn't call it women's liberation, but we can recognize what they managed to achieve, especially considering the obstacles. Women standing together is a scary thought for many men, but it's the only way forward. It's not old-fashioned, and neither were the beguines."

Another journalist, in an interview in 2003 on her just published book, *Death Comes for the Magistra,* pressed into her private life. "Do you feel your illness impacts how you write about Beatrys? In the later books, starting with *The Funeral Specialist,* there's more emphasis, it seems, on the infirmary. In your newest novel, Beatrys herself contracts the plague and so does the Magistra. Since the death of the Magistra is mentioned in the title, I don't think I'm spoiling the plot to say that between Beatrys and the Magistra, only Beatrys survives. Do you see yourself as Beatrys? What made you kill off the Magistra, one of your most memorable characters?"

"It was time for her to go," Stella answered. "And for Beatrys to assume a greater leadership role in the beguinage. Plague and illness were a large part of life in medieval times, and since one of the core functions of the beguines was to heal and to sit with the diseased and the dying, it's natural that Beatrys finds herself in the infirmary or out in the city tending to people. As someone familiar with medicine from my own experiences, it has been a fascinating challenge to write about the ways people thought about illness in the Middle Ages."

The journalist didn't want to head off in the direction of medieval medicine. She persisted, rather unpleasantly, I thought. "Some mystery authors get tired of their characters and fantasize killing them off. Is that what happened to the Magistra? Would you consider killing off Beatrys at any point? Or is that too personal a question? After all, most authors have something of their characters within them. Do you?"

Stella answered, "Are you asking me if I'd ever commit suicide? No, I thought not! I hope not. It's something I would never do. I want to enjoy my life as long as possible. For me, the imagination offers a kind of freedom from illness. I've always thought that the writer is blessed among humans because she can live multiple lives. Just in the most basic sense, with my particular condition, chronic fatigue, I can't be as active as I was as a young woman. But through my characters, especially Beatrys, I have a double life. She lives for me. Or you could say, I get to live twice."

"So we can expect many more books about Beatrys and the beguinage in Bruges?"

"Yes, I hope so. I love imagining and shaping these books and I am still very interested in Beatrys. I hope to continue with this character for a long time to come. But it's true, just as a writer lives a double life with her character, I might experience a double death. First the character and then myself. Or maybe the other way around. Perhaps I'll die before Beatrys does. Yes, that's probably likely, isn't it?"

By 2007, the television series was in the past, and there was a certain asperity in Stella's tone that year when she was interviewed on the occasion of a new book. She said she was disappointed but unsurprised by the decision not to continue with the *Beatrys* series.

"It was expensive to produce," she was quoted in an article in the *Guardian*. "They also felt worried that *Beatrys* would be competing with too many dramas about women. Too many as in *one or two*. The scripts in the second series were written to bring in more male characters, but even that wasn't enough. Something about the idea of women in large groups is very off-putting to most men, I discovered. And even to women sometimes. You think of the audience for *Cadfael*. No one thought it strange that ninety percent of the actors were men. But *Beatrys* seemed to make viewers uneasy, in spite of all the efforts with Abel and the other decent blokes in the series. It suggests that women might do well, even do better without men, and that's quite an intolerable thought."

The Mystery Play Murders had just been published, and Stella's interviewer gave it a mixed review, noting that it had been four years since the previous book, when the Magistra had died of the plague. In that mystery, the spiritual leader of the beguinage had been replaced by a well-meaning elderly beguine. In *The Mystery Play Murders* Beatrys, now in her late thirties, was in line to take over as Magistra, though other factions preferred their own choices. Into this "stewpot of feminine intrigue" as the reviewer called it, came a traveling puppeteer and mystic, who brought her "sacred pantomime" to Bruges.

The reviewer noted that according to Stella Terwicker's acknowledgments, the puppeteer was based on the life of Elisabeth de Spalbeek, from Liege. Elisabeth didn't live in a beguinage but at home with her mother and sisters, and she traveled around, like certain other women at the time, using dance and song and puppets to tell the stories of God and to celebrate him. "The book's theme is manipulation," said the reviewer. "How the truth can be manipulated for evil, even by religious people."

Fiona had said Vonn didn't work on *The Mystery Play Murders*. Was that part of the manipulation that Stella was referring to as well? That Fiona had separated Stella from Vonn's editorial help? The reviewer seemed to think that the story was somewhat far-fetched, and the writing less engaging than previous books. Was it Vonn then who had so improved the earlier books? Even ghostwritten parts of them, adopting Stella's style and voice?

Once again, I wondered how the plot and characters in a Beatrys book might be related to Stella's life. First, she had killed off the Magistra, who bore a strong resemblance to Fiona Craig. Now in the last book published before her death in 2008 Stella seemed to be exploring some sort of manipulation. Was it too far-fetched to wonder if she felt Fiona and Avery, were too much in control of her life and career? Did she bridle at Fiona having dismissed Vonn as one of the collaborators or was she glad that Vonn was out of the picture?

I saved some of the interviews and links and shut down my laptop. Was I taking all this too far? Was reading and *reading into* most of Stella's Beatrys series helping me in any way? Or was it simply directing me away from the real mystery of Vonn's death, which might have had absolutely nothing to do with Stella and Fiona, and everything to do with a triangle among Gayle, Vida, and Vonn, with answers that could be found on Vonn's laptop or in Vonn's correspondence sent to Bristol.

It was about eight and dim in the carriage. I picked up the phone and found Corinne's number. We'd had an exchange of texts immediately after I arrived in London a week ago, where I thanked her for her hospitality, and she thanked me for the company. Perhaps I should have followed up, but events took over. How could I have explained in a brief text my soaking at the Ladies' Pond or the impulsive trip with Nicky to Bruges?

"Cassandra, how nice to hear from you! Where are you? It sounds like—are you on the tube, or a train? Not on the way to Bristol, I'm assuming." I couldn't tell from her voice whether that thought made her happy. It sounded more like it slightly panicked her.

"No worries. I wouldn't break in on you unannounced. As a matter of fact, I'm approaching Taunton. I'm going to spend a day or two on the Devon coast."

"Oh, too bad," she said lightly. "I'd love to see you. Not tonight. I'm... over at a friend's for dinner. But soon."

Hah, I thought. I knew there was someone in her life.

I felt a sudden, surprising pang, but ignored it.

"I'm on my way to visit Vonn's old girlfriend, Gayle," I said, though she hadn't asked. "I have a theory that Gayle knows something about the missing files from the archives that went to Bristol. *She* was the subletter, as it turns out, and she must have had a key to Vonn's flat."

"Interesting," she said. "Let me know if you find more boxes. There's definitely a gap. Clearly Vonn went to all the trouble to save reams of stuff from the Brize collective, all that correspondence and notes from five years of collective meetings. It makes sense that she'd preserve correspondence and notes and drafts from her memoir. It's a bit weird there's so little on that, or on her editorial projects, books she worked on."

"It *is* weird," I agreed, and I mentioned the whole problem with the laptops, old and new, and my visit to Vida's shop. How I had had the sense that Vida was hiding something.

"But that's only the electronic files," said Corinne. "Vonn was still very much a paper person, whether that was age or inclination. I know most of her editing work was done electronically, but she still believed that paper was important and potentially longer lasting. I've wondered, is it possible that Vonn could have had a storage locker in the building or even off-site somewhere?"

"Maybe she did have a storage closet or unit," I said. "But it wasn't in the block of flats. Gayle looked in the cellar. There were just some old weights and a yoga mat, things like that."

Corinne's voice grew fainter, and I couldn't hear her for a few seconds. Was it the phone or was she talking to someone with her hand over the microphone? Her voice returned, "Sorry, Cassandra. That's all I have to report for now. Must get back to the table. He's made Brazilian fish stew for us."

He? I wanted to say. *Us?* Maybe it was really *she,* and *us* included other people at a dinner party. And it was none of my business, anyway.

"Corinne?" I said, as her voice faded, and the last thing I heard before the phone cut out was a choppy, "let you know if I find some..."

The train went into a tunnel. I didn't need to ask myself why I was suddenly so grumpy.

26.

I'd expected to find Gayle in one of the contemporary mansions on the hillsides above Torquay or in a Victorian villa along the coast itself. I'd played with the notion that she was from a wealthy family or that her sister had married into wealth—after all, Gayle had a posh accent and had attended an Oxford college to study useless subjects like Renaissance music and Anglo-Saxon literature. But as it turned out, Gayle's sister lived in a semi-detached, red-brick house with some Swiss-cottage ornamentation on a pleasantly ordinary street above the harbor, in a neighborhood that abounded in hedges and mature trees. A large, solid sort of English house, with no view of the sea, behind a low red-brick wall, its garden brightened only by bunches of flashy daffodils and early yellow and pink tulips among the well-pruned shrubs.

The woman who came to the white-painted door after my ring resembled Gayle or Gayle as she would have looked with lipstick and mascara. White curly hair, tight as a poodle's, peach-soft skin, sagging at the throat, and the same narrow, tilted brown eyes. A simple skirt and pastel blouse, with a knit cardigan. A wedding ring, earrings, necklace, gold watch.

"Cassandra?" she said, with an encouraging smile. "I'm Judy. Gayle's sister. Do come in."

I'd called Gayle late last night and had gotten the address. Gayle was surprised to hear from me but seemed pleased enough when I said something about a spontaneous mini break. "I needed a change. And the hotel has a spa and indoor pool. I packed my swimsuit." I put a smile into my voice. "I also thought maybe you could use some company."

I could hear her smile back. "Oh, you didn't come for the wild swimming in Devon, then?"

"I wouldn't mind a swim," I said. "Either a swim or a walk tomorrow? Just to spend some time together, hear how you are. Of course, you probably have things to do today. Or maybe other visitors?"

I was thinking of Vida of course, how she said she was driving down to Devon today.

"I may have a visitor tomorrow evening," said Gayle. "I can't count on it, but Vida said she'd come. But the day is free. I'd be glad to show you around a bit. We could go into Dartmoor. My sister's got a car I could use. Bring your swimsuit, in case we find a river or pond to take a dip in."

She offered to pick me up at the hotel at nine, but I said I'd booked an hour massage after breakfast, and that it would be good afterwards to stretch my legs. I could walk to her sister's house and be there around ten. There had been no scheduled massage. I'd simply wanted to get my bearings in Torquay and knew no better way than through walking.

My choice of the Grand Hotel, in a last-minute, online-discount deal, was largely because it was near the train station. It had turned out to be one of those vast, Victorian-era establishments, a white wedding cake with a hundred and thirty rooms, which had refashioned themselves as spas, keeping the ballrooms and swimming pools, and yet not updating the interior decoration too much, since the primary clientele was likely, as it had always been for this holiday resort town, retirees, and other genteel holidaymakers. The amount I knew about Torquay you could put on the back of a postcard, but I did know that Agatha Christie had been born here, and that the seacoast had been dubbed the English Riviera, for its mild climate and beaches.

My discounted room naturally had no sea view, but the hotel itself was on the bay, and I took a walk after breakfast along the seafront boulevard. The nineteenth-century charm of the resort town had faded somewhat, and the many bars along the seafront and a few men sleeping it off on park benches suggested that Torquay might also struggle with ubiquitous British binge-drinking culture. But the breeze was fresh from the west and the sailboats rocked happily along the docks. The bay itself was the color of green glass in the morning sun. It was going to be a good day, weatherwise. Maybe it would actually be possible to swim.

I walked a mile to the marina and back again, before heading up the hillside behind the hotel to her sister's address. Traveler that I am, it only flummoxed me a little to have been in Bristol, Bruges, and now Torquay within the space of a week.

★

Gayle didn't embrace me as she would have in London, and although Judy offered tea and some fresh scones, Gayle didn't seem to want to linger, though she did accept the offer of sandwiches we could take with us. "Thanks for the car, Judy, I'll be careful. Back later this afternoon, cheers."

"Maybe Cassandra, would like to have dinner with us today? Or we could all go out, there are tons of lovely places in Torquay."

I couldn't hear a trace of homophobia or sarcasm in Judy's voice. Instead she looked friendly, even eager to get to know me.

"I may be otherwise engaged this evening. We'll see," said Gayle, before hustling me out the door and over to a late model British sedan.

Gayle was in walking shoes and jeans, with a windbreaker and a knit beret on her feathery white curls. In the driver's seat, she scooched up close to the wheel, just as small and vulnerable looking as I recalled.

Yet I was positive Gayle had misled me, even outright lied, even if some lies might only have been omissions that she later rectified. She'd had plenty of opportunities when I was at Vonn's flat with her, organizing, to tell me that she'd sublet the flat and probably retained a key. She wasn't initially truthful about the fact her relationship with Vonn had been closer and had lasted longer than first suggested. She hadn't been candid about there being two laptops, an old and a new. Was she fibbing about there having been a burglary? And what about all the files going missing for "Gadfly"? Surely Gayle misled me there as well. The question was whether Gayle's caginess and misdirection meant anything more than self-protection.

Or was she protecting someone else?

"She seems nice, your sister," I said, as Gayle drove out of her sister's neighborhood. Red brick gave way to villas set back from the street, and then suddenly, surprisingly, we were at the outskirts of Torquay, with thatched cottages, woods, and farms, on the Totnes Road. The sky was light blue with drifting clouds. I rolled down my window a bit. The countryside smelled of sun on damp leaf mold, grass, and a whiff of manure. There were sheep here and there and a white horse in a field.

"Yes, Judy is nice," Gayle agreed, with a slightly grim smile. "Almost a caricature of nice. It's fine for a couple of days, then it begins to grate. She's my older sister, not by much, but enough. We lost our mum when I was sixteen and she was almost eighteen. Dad was heartbroken, useless really. It was Judy who took my life in hand. Made sure I kept up with my lessons, did well with my A levels, got into Oxford. She herself trained as a nurse, something practical, but she encouraged me with my musical studies. She's always encouraged me."

"That's not the worst thing."

"Yes, when you're a teenager, a little encouragement is fine. But I'm sixty-five," Gayle said. "I've lived in London for decades. I don't need her arranging my life. I came to sort myself out, not to settle down here. I'd hardly arrived in Torquay when she wanted me to join her church choir. There are some other 'gays' in the choir, as she called them, so she thought that would be a good starting point, a way for me to meet local people *like me*. She doesn't know about Vida, not really, but she knows I left someone and am hurting. She's always striven mightily to *understand* this part of my life. To make sure I know that it's perfectly *fine* to be a lesbian. She's pointed out in the last week that I don't have to be in London to have a gay community. I can have that right here in Devon! 'But only if that's what you *want*, Gayle.'"

I laughed a little at her description, but I was thinking, well, at least you had a place to go. Someone to take you in, with a big house in Devon. There are worse places. Perhaps Gayle just needed reminding how lovely this part of the country was. I said, "I'm always so struck, when I get out of London, how varied the English landscape is, how much of it is protected from sprawl. One minute you're by the sea, and the next you're in the countryside."

Gayle was driving more quickly now, through farmland tidily enclosed by hedgerows and some stone walls. We crossed the A380, into the village of Maldon and out again. "Yes, it's lovely to get out of the city so quickly," she admitted. "I thought we'd go into Dartmoor by a lesser traveled road, through Totnes and Buckfastleigh." She sighed and then continued, "It was worse when Judy was married. They couldn't have kids so there was always pressure to join them for Christmas, birthdays, weddings, etc. They lived closer to London then, in Reading, where Bill owned a medical supplies firm. He had three brothers and a sister, and the gatherings were large and boisterous with kids. I felt horribly guilty when I said no, can't make it, and very much worse if I came. I always came alone because I couldn't imagine bringing anyone. Susan, for instance, who tended to lecture people about politics. Or Joan, who couldn't be trusted around the drinks table. Or Vonn. Can you imagine *Vonn* in a suburban house on a circle drive in *Reading*? And yet Judy would have welcomed any and all of them—as part of the family, *their* family. Straight people don't see our lesbian families. We're always sort of orphans to them."

"I know," I said, "that's why I moved from Michigan as soon as I could and disappeared into Spain and South America. You always have an excuse not to go to a wedding if you're permanently out of the country. Most of the time they didn't know where I was. Then they sort of forgot about me."

"I wouldn't want my sister to forget about me. I love her, really, I do. It's just that, oh, I wish I'd traveled more," Gayle said, wistfully. "I mean, I went to the usual places during uni and afterwards, sometimes with the Tudor Roses. We gave some concerts in Holland and in Germany and once we all flew to Stockholm for a gathering of early music ensembles. But I never traveled by myself or did any of those adventurous things you're meant to do in your twenties and thirties. That *you* did. I was absorbed in music, singing, arranging, researching, I didn't look into the future, didn't save, didn't have a plan other than a life with Susan. Her house was my house. Until it wasn't. Susan had always said, 'Don't worry about earning money, Gayle. Just keep doing what you love.'"

Gayle grimaced. "Bad advice, as it turned out. I should have gotten a proper job with a private pension. I *could* have, with my degree, I could have taken an academic route. But I didn't and couldn't really make up for lost time. I felt into the same trap of false security with Joan. She adored me, she said. I'll take care of you, she said. Seven years I gave her, and at the end: No house, no savings, nothing, once again, just me alone, older and with fewer prospects."

Her voice wobbled, and I was caught between sympathy, and a new emotion, which was irritation. I had to remind myself I was here to find out more about Gayle and Vonn, Gayle and Vida, and possibly Vida and Vonn. Not to pass judgment on Gayle for her tendency to make bad choices.

I had made some ill-conceived decisions in my life too, though I didn't have Gayle's needy streak. I'd never expected anyone to support me. I could support myself, thank you very much. All the same, I knew I was dependent on Nicky not only for companionship but a reasonably inexpensive place to live in North London. Our housing arrangements had been settled long ago, but from time to time I had wondered, not without a slight sense of panic, what would happen if Nicky were ever to leave London for Scotland, as she threatened occasionally when she was irate about Brexit.

I might not then be so smug about Gayle's tendency to seek out women who had property.

We approached the town of Totnes, built on the banks of the River Dart but also climbing up a steepish hill to an old fort or castle, one of many built by the Norman conquerors. In other circumstances, I would have liked to stop for a gander at the motte castle and a cream tea on the high street. But we were already passing the train station and soon were past the town: more farmlands, the river, and a two-lane road with high hedges on either side and no shoulder should you meet a lorry.

I kept my voice level, interested. "All those years, when you were with Susan, and Joan, you were still friendly with Vonn?"

"I told you I was friendly with Vonn, didn't I? I mean, in my email a few days ago. That I cared about her."

"Yes, as a human being."

She glanced at me sideways, the brown eyes scrunched up in a way that was familiar but that suddenly made me nervous as a passenger. Was there some chance her squint was really because she needed glasses? Still, I persisted: it was time to begin confronting her on her falsehoods.

I continued, "I went to Bristol a week ago to meet with Corinne Wheelwright, to see if she'd found anything of interest in the boxes of Vonn's papers. She told me that Vonn had stayed with her for some months right after the mastectomy. Someone had sublet Vonn's flat in London. It was you. I don't think you ever really let go of Vonn, did you? You were more than friends, I suspect. For many years."

Gayle kept her eyes on road. "And if we were, if I did see Vonn from time to time, what business is it of yours?"

"Your romantic life is not my business," I said evenly. "But if it's true that you sublet from Vonn, then it's clear you had a key to the flat."

She hadn't been expecting me to make that connection, not so quickly, and had nothing to say at first. Then she laughed a little. "I'd half forgotten you have a sleuthing streak, Cassandra. You've found me out. Yes, I did continue a sexual relationship of sorts with Vonn, for many years, while I was with Susan, while I was with Joan, when I was single or in other shorter relationships, and even when I was with Vida. I didn't say anything about it to you because I thought you might tell Vida. And I don't think Vida and I are finished. I still have hopes."

So she was hoping to brazen it out. I said nothing, and she continued:

"Neither Vonn nor I wanted to get back together, but we had a connection, we always had. I could be myself around her, whinge as much as I wanted. She was a great person to complain to because she too had a whole litany of grumbles and grievances. We'd have some drinks, get things off our chests, and sometimes end with a romp in bed. We were always good together like that. But she didn't ever want a permanent relationship, never wanted to live with anyone, and never even wanted to see me all that much. It was just a casual thing for her. And for me too. Because afterwards I'd feel guilty, not just for the sex, but for gossiping about my partners."

"You had a key to her flat," I repeated. "From the sublet or before."

"I may have, once. I'm sure I gave it back." Her eyes were still on the road. I tried not to look at the delivery van that seemed to be heading straight for us. We were now crossing the River Dart, the first of several times.

"Was there really a burglary?" I said. "Or did you go in after you heard about Vonn's death and remove the new laptop and pretend that it had been stolen? Did you take the old one as well?"

"Cassandra, you're going too far with this," she said. "Why would I take her laptops? Why, if I had done that, would I ask you and Amina to come and help me with the flat and take the trouble to go through Vonn's files and organize them for the archives? You're acting as if I'm hiding something and I'm absolutely not."

Here I felt myself in a quandary. I didn't want to reveal quite yet that I'd been to see Vida and had heard that Vonn had brought in her old laptop so the files could be transferred to the new one. That there was a good chance Vida had looked at Vonn's files and seen Gayle's name.

"It just seems suspicious that Vonn's memoir manuscript has gone missing and so has the laptop, which probably had the full manuscript of her tell-all memoir."

"There was no full manuscript," said Gayle, now in control of her voice and her face. We were coming into the village of Buckfastleigh at the edge of Dartmoor. "And Vonn was never going to finish one. Oh, there were drafts of chapters, some notes, and transcripts of some interviews. But I don't believe there was a book in Vonn. She wasn't a writer, not really. She was too critical to be a writer. She was an editor."

We set off across Dartmoor just as a light fog was drifting in.

27.

The wispy, low-lying clouds didn't seem too worrisome at first; the mists simply amplified the drama of the green and brown farmlands and woods near Buckfastleigh. But by the time we were on the main highway into Dartmoor, a thicker white blanket obscured even the road ahead. There wasn't much traffic fortunately, and when we arrived at the Dartmeet car park, there was only one other vehicle and no one in sight.

Gayle persisted for a while in her optimism, telling me that Dartmoor's fog could lift as quickly as it descended, and that it wouldn't hurt to take a short walk down to the river. We could bring our swimsuits and sandwiches, along with the thermos of tea Judy had provided. Dartmeet was where two branches of the River Dart came together and became one, eventually making its way to the sea at Dartmouth. In the summer, Gayle assured me, the car park was full of families. Wild swimmers preferred to arrive in the evening or early morning; they came year round, some wearing wetsuits or at least neoprene booties, caps, and gloves.

"Vida is tough," said Gayle. "Doesn't bother with too much gear except her cap and shorty wetsuit. She looks great in a wetsuit." She sighed significantly as we made our way along the path to the river, skirting a grassy field. "We came here for a week back when we were first getting together last autumn. It was September, the water was still warm, the air had that autumn tang, the leaves were gold. It was really magical. I felt we had something special. I know she can be brusque, that's just her way. But I've always been drawn to women who are strong and speak their minds."

"Like Vonn," I prompted. "I guess there was a lot of speaking her mind in the memoir?"

"I told you, there was no memoir, not a proper memoir," said Gayle. "Just fragments, things she remembered, chapters she'd start and abandon, with a note that she planned to interview so-and-so. I barely know anything about what she thought might be the final shape of it."

"How do you know even this much? Did you read some of the chapters or fragments?"

We'd come to a gate with a sign for the Nature Reserve. "It's about a kilometer to the river, maybe less," said Gayle. "But there's a good path, we won't get lost or anything. And the fog could lift. I'd like to see the river again. I haven't been here for ages." She walked faster, as if to put my questions behind her.

I asked again, "Did you read some of Vonn's memoir?"

"Yes," she finally said. "I did. Last year I read a chapter-thing, a rant mostly, about the disintegration of Brize that began when Vonn was voted off the collective. There was nothing new there—I'd heard about it for years. She never really got very much distance from Brize or could see why the supposedly open collective was so dysfunctional. I know she was aiming for some sort of objectivity, but it was hopeless. She did some interviews, with women in the community who'd supported her and some collective members, but not with the actual women who'd voted her off the collective. I suggested she contact them and see what they had to say, and to my surprise she did make some effort. But one of them had died, and another had moved back to Mumbai. A third didn't want to speak to Vonn—she slammed the phone down. And there was one she couldn't even track down, a German or Dane. I don't think she tried very hard."

I could hear the river rushing somewhere out of sight but getting closer. I could see Gayle in front of me, of course, but not well, and her voice had a slightly muffled sound. The thermos clanked in her daypack against something metallic. A cup? A spoon? A knife for the sandwiches?

"Did she ask you to read anything else? About Brize or other women's presses? Maybe about Stella?" I threw that out, imagining Gayle would evade the question, but she answered yes.

"I believed I'd accepted that's who Vonn was. I told her she was a bit of a rake, and she loved hearing that. Somehow it also elevated me in my own estimation to have been chosen by a woman like that. She made me feel sexy and feminine in a whole new way. It was different when she took up with Stella Terwicker, even though that was six months after Vonn broke up with me. I ran into them once, and it was clear Vonn was completely besotted. I'd never seen her like that."

"So that would have been in the late eighties?"

"Yes, somewhere around then. They'd first met when Stella dropped off a piece for the Triple L anthology a couple of years before they got involved. Stella was apparently quite nervous when she came to the Brize office. But she got over it. Vonn pursued and courted her and eventually Stella succumbed—that was Vonn's story anyway. Stella was working on her first Beatrys book. Vonn helped her as an editor, and Aphra Press published it. It was Stella who ended things with Vonn, though Vonn ended up being involved in most of her books as an editor."

"So Vonn did write about that, in a chapter for 'Gadfly'?"

"Yes," said Gayle and then sounded confused. "I suppose it was for 'Gadfly' anyway. Maybe not. What I remember was how resentful she was of being pushed away from Stella by Fiona. She called Fiona a repressed old closet case, who'd been in love with Stella for years and took over her life completely after Stella became ill. I didn't realize that Fiona and Vonn worked together so closely on a few of the Beatrys books. But it was only Fiona who got the credit. I only began to understand why Vonn was so angry when I started to read the biography you lent me. Fiona doesn't even mention Vonn."

"Do you think it was meant to be a secret that Vonn contributed to the mysteries? Did she talk about that to you over the years?"

"She never came right out and said she had ghostwritten the Beatrys mysteries. But she strongly implied she did much more than just edit. It may have become unclear to her, what she actually did. When I saw her at the holidays in December, she'd read Fiona's biography and said it was outrageously dishonest. Fiona had put herself front and center. I asked her if she was going to include her experience with Stella in the memoir and she said no, well, not exactly. She wanted to talk in general about how the mainstream had stolen lesbian writers from the small presses and made them more acceptable to the public. Stella would be only one example."

"But you knew earlier than December that Vonn had worked on the Beatrys books? If you'd been seeing Vonn off and on for years?"

"Well, I knew there was an ongoing connection, since Vonn had already edited the first two mysteries for Aphra, but I didn't know details. Vonn was always professional about her freelance editorial work. Keeping quiet must have been part of the deal, don't you think? Oh, she'd criticize the books as they came out and she didn't like the TV series, though she was excited that the Tudor Roses were filmed for one episode. She wanted to know all about the launch party I went to, what Stella said and how she looked and whether she seemed ill."

I weighed all this. Most of what Gayle said about "Gadfly" corresponded to what Avery had told me in her office a week or so ago about Vonn's proposal that included the long, ranting chapter about Brize. But it seemed like Gayle had read more than Avery had admitted to skimming. Had there been a chapter with more about Stella? Was that the source of Avery's worry in February that Vonn was threatening Fiona in some way? Clearly Vonn had been upset by the biography and had been trying to find a way to tell her side of the story. Maybe the fragments from "Gadfly" about Stella and Fiona had gone missing from Vonn's file cabinets.

Gayle must have read my thoughts. "I don't know why most of the material on 'Gadfly' disappeared. I've had a suspicion that Vonn herself might have put the files and even the laptop itself somewhere for safekeeping."

Safekeeping from what? I was uncertain whether to turn the conversation back to Fiona and Avery and Vonn's arrangement or to question Gayle about Vida and whether there was a chance Vida had also read some of "Gadfly" during the process of transferring it from one laptop to the next. Was it possible Vonn had written something about Vida in one of her fragments on Brize? Was it possible that Vonn had written something about Gayle and their ongoing affair and Vida had read *that*?

I hadn't rejected the suspicion that Vida knew more than she was saying about Vonn and that she could have had something to do with Vonn's death by drowning. Could Gayle have been a reluctant accessory to murder? It seemed preposterous, and yet something wasn't right. Each time Gayle told me the story of her relationship with Vonn, it grew more complicated, with truth apparently replacing fib and falsehood, until that truth proved partial or false as well. I'd asked a simple question—"Did you have a key to Vonn's flat?"—and still hadn't gotten an answer that satisfied me.

Meanwhile, we'd come to the banks of the River Dart, darkly rushing and burbling over unseen rocks in the dense white fog. Somewhere on the river were pools of water where wild swimmers dunked themselves in mini-waterfalls and experienced life at its most bracing and revitalizing. I hung back. Gayle remained in front, fiddling with her daypack, which clanked metallically. Ominously.

Why had she brought me here? Why hadn't I resisted this suggestion that we walk down to the river? Had Gayle called Vida to tell her I was coming to Devon and had the two of them cooked up a way to shut me up? Was that why Gayle had been so chatty and confiding? Because soon I wouldn't be a threat any longer?

I never feel more superstitiously Irish than when confronted by a gurgling body of water, expecting at any moment that a wraith will spin out of the current and grab me by the forearm. Genetic memory, I'd venture, passed on by the few lucky sods who escaped the bog wraith.

The idea of even dipping a toe in the freezing water of the river, much less putting on a swimsuit to submerge myself, was impossible. I took a step backward, and then another and another.

Gayle followed me back along the path. "I know," she said. "It's eerie, isn't it? I don't know why I thought we could have our lunch here. Back to the car, shall we? We can have our tea and then head back to Torquay."

My heart, which had been racing, slowed down. As if Wee Gayle would push me into the Dart and leave me here. She was not that unhinged by love for Vida.

But I saw another side of Gayle once we were back at the car. We'd just finished our cheese and cucumber sandwiches and had had our cups of milky tea, when another car pulled into the car park some distance away. The fog hadn't lifted; in fact it seemed to have settled on the moorland more heavily, so it was difficult to see the features of the three people who emerged from the car. One of them was tall and wore a watch cap.

Gayle suddenly stiffened. "She came here without me," she said in agitation. "She came here with other people. She was supposed to come to Torquay!"

"Are you sure?" I said.

"It's her, it's her. The tall one. I recognize her. Oh, my God. Now it really *is* over. She lied. She doesn't want to see me." Her voice went up and she clung to the steering wheel. "I've got to say something."

Gayle had her hand on the car door. "I've got to get out. Say something," she repeated. "That I know it's her, that she was supposed to come to Torquay, we were going to talk. I was going to apologize, make her see how much I want to stay together." Tears began to run down her face. "I can't lose her. I just can't."

The group began walking in our direction, and one of them gave us a quick, curious glance, as if we too might be wild swimmers, friends of theirs. Then they passed behind the car. The tall one wasn't Vida, but a much younger woman, with her two friends.

Gayle reached for her phone and quickly texted something.

I thought how, earlier in our drive today, when she told me about Susan and Joan, she'd used the language of loss, not just of a loved partner, but of economic well-being. Because they'd made no financial agreements, Gayle had lost the middle-class life she'd been accustomed to. Now the same thing was happening with Vida. I thought how women's liberation and the welfare state should have done away with such calculations, which seemed to belong to centuries past when women had to marry or face poverty.

Gayle's phone buzzed with a text, and a sense of relief suffused her face. "Vida had some things to finish up in London, so she's made a late start," she reported. "But she's well on her way. Barring traffic, she should be in Torquay in a couple of hours."

The tears were still wet on her cheeks, but she looked delighted as she texted back. What did I know? Maybe she really loved Vida.

But if so, why had she still been fooling around with Vonn during her relationship with Vida and putting her meal ticket in peril?

As we got closer to Torquay, the fog dissipated and the sky was blue again, the sun cheerfully shining on the fields and woods. It was three by the time we arrived back at the Grand Hotel.

"I feel bad that we didn't swim outdoors," said Gayle as we sat in the drive by the front entrance. "I know you're going back to London tomorrow, and I'll be busy this evening. But, well, what would you think of a quick dip in the sea? We have our suits, and there are some sea caves nearby that are lovely. Depending on the tides, you can climb inside them or swim a short distance to them. I went with Vida once, on our trip here last September. The water was the most beautiful aquamarine. What do you say? That may make up for not having swum in the Dart."

I thought she might be trying to call up some bravery to brag to Vida about.

"Okay," I said. This wasn't the Ladies' Pond with its creepy underwater branches. It was Torbay, the sea, and I had swum hundreds of times in salt water.

28.

I stood on the smooth shingle of a tiny beach, my skin goose-bumping even though I wasn't yet in the water. The sun came and went behind clouds, but when it was shining the sea sparkled green and blue. A strong breeze came steadily from the southwest, with a few gusts from the north as well. The waves and wavelets themselves seemed confused as to what was directing their movement, the current or the wind. Yet while the sea was a bit choppy, it didn't look dangerous, but inviting.

Although I'd grown up in the Midwest, with lakes and ponds, I was a sea-swimmer at heart. First the Mediterranean when I was twenty, then the beaches of Argentina, Chile, and Australia. I had a strong breaststroke, a stronger crawl, and a good kick. Now, having made a fool of myself at the tame Ladies' Pond, thanks to Vida, I felt the necessity of proving myself to Gayle. I wanted to show her that I too could plunge into the waves without shrieking.

For she'd already dived in and turned to wave and call, "Follow me!"

In her swimsuit she was tiny, but well-made, and more muscled than she looked in street clothes. She knew these waters, too. I presumed she did anyway. She'd left her bag in her car, as had I, and just brought down towels to the beach. She'd also pulled on a yellow cap, so I could track her in the swells offshore.

"We won't stay in long," Gayle had said. "The sea cave is just around the point. We'll pop inside and out again. It's very pretty when the sun is shining in. When the tide is low you can stand up and see some pools left behind, all the shells and little creatures. The tide's a bit higher now, but we'll still see the bottom, I imagine."

I couldn't help it. A gasp escaped my lips when I ran into the freezing water and a wave broke over my head. My eyes burned with salt. But I valiantly followed the yellow cap, which was making for the rocky point, not far away, or at least from the shore it hadn't looked far away.

The sea looks so different when you're in it. You feel a massive, shuddering power. It's not just the current, but some surging, living energy.

Still, I had my crawl. And I was determined Gayle would not say to Vida that poor old Cassandra couldn't make it around the point and into a dinky cave for two minutes. I was chilled, but there was freedom being away from land, the kind of freedom you only feel in deep water, when you pit your body against the push and pull of that briny power all around you.

Gayle's yellow cap had cleared the small headland and I swam out well past it too, so that I wouldn't be swept onto the rocks, which looked sharp and barnacled closer up. The sun was still out, and the wind was stronger, and for a moment all I felt was joyful to have taken this risk that made me feel so much more alive.

Not far off I saw Gayle's head bobbing in a slight cove, in front of a narrow cleft in the rock. She shouted something, but I couldn't hear her. Then, she vanished.

I could only assume this was the entrance to the cave. It was not low tide, but you could definitely swim in with room to spare above the sea's surface. At least we could scramble up on the stones inside and have a quick rest and look around before heading back around the point and into shore.

The current made it easier than I thought to be slurped into the cave mouth. It was a little smaller than I thought it would be, the water a bit closer to the ceiling than I expected, but it was as pretty as Gayle had said. The sun streaked in, and the walls were smooth and almost pink. I joined her on a slab of stone, glad to get out for a moment. I realized I was panting just a little, and that my arms shook slightly.

As she'd said, you could see the bottom, and the water was almost aquamarine at the edges. You could see several shelves where shells lay, and frondy things waved.

Our voices reverberated. "Whew," she said. "That was a bit tougher swim than I expected. I'm glad you were up to it, and you got a chance to see this amazing place. Vida calls this cave a *matriz*. That's Spanish for womb, but you know that. I like *matriz* better, it's like matrix, isn't it? A place of origin where something develops."

"Oh, it wasn't too bad a swim," I said, trying to sound offhand. It *was* something like a womb in here, a little claustrophobic unless you were an actual baby, or if you were a baby that wanted to get out. As my mother often told me. "Of all of you kids, you were the most eager to be born. I could hardly get to the hospital in time, they rushed me to the table, and you shot out alive and well. I thought, this girl is no trouble. How wrong I was!"

Gayle was admiring the light through the water, but she wasn't reluctant to leave. The tide was definitely coming in, in smaller and larger surges.

"I'll go first," she said, slipping into the water. She timed it so she arrived at the narrow entrance just as the surge receded and she was sucked through. Her small, compact body was an advantage I didn't have. I was at least six inches taller, and my limbs were more gangly. My arm hit the side of the cave and spun me around; I missed the outward pull, and a strong wave threw me back deep inside the cave, almost up on the slab, with only a mouthful of salt water to show for the attempt. I coughed and dogpaddled, trying to get my bearings in the swirling waters. Another wave gushed in. The slab was covered with an inch of water.

The sun disappeared and the water turned from aquamarine to greenish pewter.

In the space of a few minutes the sea cave was no longer pretty, but a death trap.

I attempted to escape twice more, then a third time under the water, all with the same result. Temporarily exhausted, I retreated to the safety of the slab. There was still plenty of space between my head and the ceiling of the cave.

For now.

I thought that I'd see Gayle's yellow cap any minute. Surely, she would notice that I hadn't emerged, surely she'd return to check on me and show me how she'd gotten through so easily. It was only timing, but there must be a trick.

How high would the tide go, that was the question. Was there another way out? Did the sea cave connect to other caves, or was it self-enclosed, a true womb? Had Gayle brought me here on purpose to let me drown?

I remembered earlier today when we were walking in the fog by the River Dart, how I'd instinctively jumped when I heard the metallic clatter of a cup or a spoon in Gayle's daypack and had thought the word *knife*. Was my intuition correct? Not about a knife, but about some danger in Gayle's company. Perhaps it had been her original plan to suggest wild swimming in a dangerous spot on the river, where I'd be swept up in a waterfall. When the fog had turned us back to the car park, she may have had to come up with another idea.

But why? Was what I knew about Vonn or about Gayle and Vonn sufficiently incriminating that she'd want to off me? It was ridiculous. No, she hadn't satisfied me with her answer about the key to the flat, or the laptop, but there must be something else, something else I wasn't seeing and that I might never figure out if I didn't get out of this cave.

The ceiling was definitely getting closer. I'd have to try again. Swim under the surface, straight as an arrow, kicking like hell while making sure to keep my arms at my sides.

But before I could get off my slab of safety, a dark figure appeared in the entrance. Not Gayle, but someone in a short-armed wetsuit with a cap covering her hair.

Vida. Looking angry.

So this is how it was going to end. She'd hover at the entrance to prevent me from leaving. Of course it was Vida who had murdered Vonn, out of jealousy. Gayle had helped her, or at least protected her. They were working together. First Vonn and now me.

"*Puta madre,*" she said, along with some other curses I didn't understand.

My scream filled the cave.

Then she was inside and making for me.

There was more Spanish, but now I got the words. "Don't panic. *Que no cundo el pánico.* The one thing you must not do is panic. It will be okay. *Estara bien.* You just have to do as I say. I am going to help you. So listen. *Entonces escucha.* You go first. Arms at sides, hold your breath. Wait for the pull and let the sea take you through the opening, it will take you. And then start swimming, fast as you can. You must not stop until we round the point. I'll be right behind you, and then at your side. Okay, you understand. *¿Comprendes?*"

"*Comprendo.*" The sound of her Spanish was calming itself. I remembered swimming offshore in Valparaiso, Chile, in waves much bigger than I could handle. But I managed to surf through them on to the beach. I'd survived. I would again.

"*¿Lista?*"

"Ready."

I'm still not sure how I managed it, except she was behind me and gave me a push at exactly the right moment. The tide was just as strong out as in, and I took a deep breath, filling my lungs, and went with it. The word for being born in Spanish is *nacer*. But the word for giving birth is *dar a luz*. To give light. That's what it was like, to shoot through the slit and into a brighter world.

As soon as I was out, I started swimming as hard as I could, not thinking about being cold, or tired, but just swimming in my strong crawl with my strong legs. I was so relieved, so suddenly alive, I felt almost happy. I rounded the point with Vida right behind me. I heard her even though I didn't clearly see her. And then the current and the tide brought us into shore.

I only flailed around when we got to the little shingle beach, and I couldn't quite stand up. My legs were shaking. But Vida grabbed me, gently, before I could fall, and led me out of the water.

Gayle was there, with two towels, crying uselessly.

"I thought I'd never see either of you again! Cassandra, I'm so sorry. I thought you were right behind me, it was only when I got round the point that I realized you weren't there, but the waves were strong by then and I couldn't get back around. Then I saw Vida on the beach. I'd texted her we were coming here. She realized what was happening, and came right in."

Vida grabbed the two towels and put them around me. She wasn't interested in Gayle's excuses. "That was very foolish of you, Gayle, to do such a thing. Didn't you look at the tide table?"

Gayle continued to cry. "No, and I'm really sorry. I want to make it up to you, Cassandra. I'll take you back to the hotel right now. Then we can see you later, for dinner, after you get warmed up."

"No," said Vida. "I'm taking Cassandra back to her hotel. Don't argue. I'll see you at your sister's. We have some things to talk about."

"Cassandra, I'm so sorry!" said Gayle again.

"It's fine," I said.

I was so over Gayle.

29.

This was the second Sunday in a row I'd found myself in the heated passenger seat of Vida's red BMW, this time on the motorway back to London. Unlike last week, I wasn't soaking wet, but, wrapped up in a wool blanket from Vida's trunk, I was sniffling with the beginnings of a cold. My head felt twice its size inside the wool cap that Vida had also given me.

"I don't think you were really in any danger," Vida had tried to tell me yesterday, but I knew that I had been. I just wasn't sure if it was Gayle's inexperience or her intention that had almost killed me yesterday in the sea cave. The end result would have been the same. As much as Gayle had tried to apologize yesterday when I stood on the beach like a drowned rat, I didn't fully forgive her.

I still nursed a suspicion that she might have wanted me out of the way for some reason.

Vida drove expertly, if a bit too fast at times. I don't know much about cars and, as a frequent traveler, I've never in fact owned one, but that doesn't mean I don't enjoy driving and watching other women drive well. Her fingers on the steering wheel no longer reminded me of underwater branches, pulling me down into the Ladies' Pond.

"I'm lucky you came along," I said, still grateful. I'd spent the evening under the bedclothes and had ordered room service: a double portion of soup, piping hot. When a text came at eight this morning from Vida, saying she was driving back to London and did I want a lift, I eagerly accepted. I asked if there was time for coffee and some toast, and she said, yes, that she wasn't in Torquay, but had spent the night with a friend in Totnes. She'd be with me in half an hour.

"It was probably the right decision," she said now, "for Gayle not to try to swim back to you, but to get to the shore and let me know. I'm glad she'd told me to meet you two there." She shrugged it off, as she'd shrugged it off yesterday. What she really wanted to know was why I had, in fact, taken the train to Devon and what Gayle and I had done yesterday, what we'd talked about.

Vida's black hair was again in a ponytail, and she wore a turtleneck up to her chin. Her dark eyes gave off a glint both curious and a little hostile. When she was suspicious, I'd noticed, Vida had the instinctive habit of "throwing an evil eye," *echando mal ojo,* as the Spanish has it. In English we often call it giving someone the stink eye. I thought at first that Vida's questions came from jealousy. But I couldn't figure it out. If she were still involved with Gayle, why hadn't she spent the night in Torquay and why had she driven to Devon only to leave early this morning?

"I wanted some answers," I told her, looking straight ahead at the road, to avoid that eye throw. "About her relationship with Vonn. What she really knew about Vonn's death. She wasn't fully honest about a few things." I paused, "I'm not sure you've been honest, either. Though I'm sure you have your reasons."

I thought she was going to parry once again, and demand to know who I thought I was, messing about in affairs that had nothing to do with me. But instead she sighed, and said, "You're right. There's been a lack of frankness. Gayle never told me that she'd asked you for help sorting out Vonn's things or that Nicky had gone to Copenhagen. I knew you lived with Nicky, but I supposed you and Nicky were in a relationship. Then Gayle asked me to meet you at the Ladies' Pond and say she'd gone to Devon. She said you were showing signs of interest in her. I went because I admit that I was curious about you. I didn't realize that you were poking around Vonn's death until you turned up at the shop Friday."

"*She* was the one who flirted with me, trying to make me feel sorry for her," I said. I wouldn't dare mention I'd been mildly attracted to Gayle. Once but never again.

"Yes, I know that dodge," said Vida. "*Pobrecita.* A taller woman could never get away with it. Anyway, I could see that you didn't have anything she would want."

I sputtered through my sniffles, but it was just Vida being her usual brusque Galician self. The truth is, Gayle had practically told me that herself.

"I believe she was trying to make me jealous," Vida went on. "But I could never be jealous of you. Still, I've wondered why you really came to my shop, why you followed Gayle to Devon. If we are talking honesty, I've had nothing but make-believe from you so far."

Again, a slight turn of the head and the *mal ojo*.

"It's a complicated story," I said. I told her pieces of it. How I'd been asked to go to a lecture by Fiona Craig in early February, because Vonn was supposedly threatening Fiona. How I'd left London for Barcelona and heard first that Vonn died on the Heath, probably a suicide, possibly accidentally. How Gayle had turned to Nicky for a bed because she and Vida had separated, and how Gayle had asked me to help her organize the boxes at Vonn's flat so they could be sent to Bristol to a feminist archive. How there seemed to be no sign in the flat of an old or new laptop or files connected with a memoir that Vonn was supposed to be writing about Brize and other aspects of feminist publishing. How I had followed up with Fiona and gone to Bristol to see if the papers were there. How I had gradually noticed that Gayle might not have been telling the truth about what had happened to Vonn, about the laptops, about the missing files.

Vida drove and listened for a long while without interrupting or asking questions. It was only when I admitted that I had developed suspicions of Vida herself having something to do with Vonn's death that she spoke up.

"As if I would kill a woman!"

"I didn't say I was accusing you of that," I said hastily. "Otherwise, I suppose you would have let me drown."

"Worse and worse," she said, and stepped on the pedal to pass a lorry. I didn't like the way she glared at me as she did.

Somehow, I had gotten carried away with my tale. I apologized. After all, hadn't she saved me, wasn't she driving me back to London? I had nothing on her, nothing at all.

We were silent for a bit, as she digested what I'd told her. Finally she seemed to decide that I was still only the clueless *norteamericana* Cassandra she'd met years ago at the bookfair.

"*Bueno,*" she said. "I'll tell you what I know about Gayle and Vonn. But first I will say, I am not a particularly jealous person. Just because I am a Spaniard. Okay?"

I nodded, and said, "Okay, of course."

"First, my meeting with Gayle, how we got together. It will tell you something right there." She glanced over at me, making sure I was paying attention. "It's like this. A friend told me she knew of a woman who needed a temporary place to stay. Gayle was 'between apartments,' as they say. I had several bedrooms in my house, and I'd put up friends or acquaintances before. I didn't rent out rooms, you understand, it was just hospitality. That was late last summer. Gayle seemed very sweet, very vulnerable, her head in the clouds with her choral music. If you've heard her sing, you know this angelic side of her. She told me that she'd not been lucky in some of her relationships, but that she still believed in love. She's so tiny, it didn't feel like she was taking up much space and suddenly I realized she was there, and I liked her, and she said she was falling in love with me. So she stayed. She was like a cat who you feed a little bit and decides it wants to move in."

"Yes, I can see this about her," I started to say, but Vida waved a hand. I'd had my turn to speak, at length. Now she wanted hers.

"I said to Gayle, back in the autumn when we got together, that I wasn't good with open relationships and especially triangles. I had not been involved for a while. I am not like many, one after the next."

Again she threw me the evil eye, but I said nothing. Okay, so *I* was like that, but women are different, aren't they?

"Gayle answered me that she was free too. She didn't say Vonn's name, but she mentioned a friend who'd had a double mastectomy who had needed help. Eventually she told me it was Vonn and that they had remained very distant friends. I had bad memories of Vonn, but they were long ago. I believed Gayle when she said Vonn belonged to her youth, years ago.

"I did not keep tabs on Gayle or ask her questions about where she went and what she did. She had various occupations within her musical world, and Christmas was an especially busy time with choral performances. She was out a lot, sometimes late. Then in January Vonn comes to my shop. She wants me to transfer her files from the old laptop to the new. She's never come to the shop or hired me before, but I don't say no, of course. I'm curious how she mentions Gayle a couple of times. She wants me to understand that they have seen each other in December. She leaves the two laptops for the transfer. I feel like she's daring me to look at the files. But of course I never do that. I just make the transfers and two days later she picks up the laptops. Once again, I feel like she's suggesting she and Gayle are more than distant friends. I don't say anything to Gayle. I have already noticed that she tells little lies sometimes, things you wouldn't think anyone would lie about. She always says she loves me, and I see that she tries to make me happy. But there's something wrong. She needs a lot from me, and when she doesn't get it, she feels very insecure.

"Then, in February, comes a phone call from this woman Kristi, who has the police at her building saying Vonn has drowned. Gayle is hysterical, she runs out of the house, and over to Vonn's flat. She doesn't want me to come. I don't see her for hours, and when she comes back later that afternoon, she's changed.

"I know she can't have had anything to do with the actual death. If it happened sometime that evening or night, she wasn't at the Heath. We were at home the whole evening, having dinner, watching telly, sleeping in bed, like usual. But she's acting very strange about the news, crying and crying, like she is guilty. She says it's because they are calling it a suicide and maybe Vonn took an overdose, but she won't believe that. It must be an accident. Gayle says she must have taken a walk and slipped at the edge of the pond. Because of her back. She had a bad back." Vida shook her head, so the black ponytail quivered. "What rubbish. You don't fall over into a pond at night by mistake. I think Vonn was an unhappy person, because of how she lived and who she was. She was cruel. And so she killed herself. But Gayle won't see that. She feels like she failed Vonn. So I begin to understand that it is not me she loves, it is Vonn. She has always loved Vonn."

She looked at me again, but now with eyes that held more disappointment than reproof. "And I don't believe I am wrong to say this about Gayle. Or about Vonn. Whatever they had, it was a form of love. I told Gayle, we must separate, for a while at least, while you are doing all these things at Vonn's flat and thinking about her all the time. She agreed and called Nicky. I didn't ask for my keys back to the house yet, and she still has some things in the cellar, but I've told her we are over. I'm glad in fact she has moved to Devon."

I was trying to put it all together, but my brain was fuzzy. I felt feverish and as if I wanted to sleep, not puzzle out the latest conundrum. One thing was probably for certain, Vida hadn't killed Vonn in a jealous rage. I was embarrassed for even having thought that.

"So you came to Devon to make an end to the relationship?" I asked. "She told me she thought you were getting back together. She was hopeful yesterday. You know, she just saw me as a friend, of sorts, someone she could confide in." I stopped, recalling the content of some of those confidences. It was true what Vida intuited; Gayle had never stopped wanting to be with Vonn. She thought she could have both, a home with Vida and a bit on the side with her old lover.

"Yes, I had decided to come to Torquay, to speak frankly to her, and tell her good-bye in a calm way. But then, you know, the sea cave. So that happened, and you needed to get to the hotel. Gayle was so upset, you shouldn't believe she wanted to harm you. She's not like that."

I would reserve judgment on that. But I only nodded and said, "So then you went to her sister's house after dropping me off?"

"Yes, it was difficult. Awkward in that British way of polite staring at the hands, not the face, and offering tea. I was still in my wetsuit, with a towel wrapped around me and my hat. Judy wanted to ask me questions, I knew, and also probably wondered what happened to you, but she also didn't want to interfere. Gayle had already been in the shower and took me upstairs to the bathroom and brought me my bag. She could see I was angry. We went into her room, and I said what I needed to. She started crying of course, threw herself on the bed. I just wanted to leave. I called my friend in Totnes, a swimming chum. Judy had made herself scarce."

Vida's voice tightened, with aversion. "Gayle followed me out to the car and there was a scene. In the quiet British street. She accused me of abandoning her, of getting a new girlfriend. That's not true, my friend in Totnes is a wild swimmer too. A normal person, a shop owner in Totnes, who loves the rivers in Devon. I was trying to explain this, but in the end, I just had to drive away before Gayle humiliated herself even more." She almost closed her eyes with the memory, but I was glad she didn't, at the speed we were traveling. "She was clinging to my waist at one point, crying that she had no home, that she loved me, that Vonn meant nothing."

"But Vonn didn't mean nothing to her," I said.

"No," said Vida, "I think she meant everything."

We were both silent for a bit and then Vida gestured to her glove compartment. "I've brought you a flash drive I made from the two diskettes you brought on Friday. You'll find the files are legible."

I took out the small bag and opened it. "Thank you, Vida. You didn't, by any chance, open the files?"

"Only to see that they were readable." she said. "I think Vonn described them correctly on the labels of diskettes. One is editorial files, mostly long documents, manuscripts she worked on. And the other diskette had more miscellaneous things, like correspondence. Perhaps they will be of help to you in your search for the truth. But personally I still think that Vonn committed suicide. She was not a happy person."

"You knew her, I've heard, back in the eighties." I said, shivering a bit, in spite of the heated seats. "I did find a few things in her file cabinets that related to you, including the Triple L anthology. I know you probably hardly remember that project, it was so long ago, but two people I talked to, Amina and Corinne, remember the story of the Lieutenant Nun. They fought to include it."

"Did they?" said Vida with retained bitterness. "They must not have fought very hard. I heard Brize was interested at one point, but then the collective altered itself. The new members now said she was too male-identified, Catalina de Erauso. I think it was more likely because they were so ignorant about women from outside England and Europe. The anthology was filled with writers who did nothing interesting except write. Catalina was not only a writer, she was a brave traveler and soldier."

"I suppose it all comes down to definitions. What a woman is has changed over the years. Nowadays, the very fact that Catalina was gender fluid makes her fascinating. You wouldn't have a problem getting something published about her now."

She nodded. "Yes, but now I'm not interested in writing. Vonn and the others killed something in me. I was already insecure about writing in English, and their mockery of me pushed me away from trying anymore. Those so-called feminist presses have a lot to answer for," she added, and then her mood changed. "It is possible, of course, that I just really wasn't so strong a poet. Because if I really had been, I wouldn't have stopped after the first rejection."

"If it makes you feel better," I said. "I used to write poetry too." I didn't explain that it had been when I was thirteen.

"Maybe it's a stage," she said. "After all, I have a good life now, many interests. When you're a writer or like you, a translator, you have to sit a lot, don't you?"

"Too right," I said.

"I'm more physical. I've always needed to run, to swim, to ride my bicycle. Also horses. I had a horse some years ago, in a stable in Kent."

Our conversation became less about Vonn and Gayle, and more

about women who dared have a physical life out in the world and who were only called "male-identified" because they assumed they could do men's work and take male pleasures without apologizing or considering that they were crossing boundaries. From there we began talking about bullfighting. I told her more about *Verónica*, and she acknowledged that, while she'd never heard of the mystery writer Lola Fuentes, she had been to a number of corridas, and she did follow the fortunes of some of the women matadors and toreros in Spain and Mexico, especially Hilda Tenorio, one of the greatest female matadors, who had distinguished herself in 2016 in Mexico by becoming the first and only woman to perform an *encerrona*.

She looked at me inquiringly and, when I told her I knew that an *encerrona* meant the matador was alone in the ring for the entire corrida with six bulls, she gave me a rare grin of approval.

People had always assumed I knew Vida Carrasco because we had so much in common. Now, for the first time, I felt that might be true.

30.

Nicky hadn't seen me walk in the door after my dunking in the Ladies' Pond last Sunday, but this time she was home, lolling in her favorite armchair in the living room, reading the Sunday papers, and I couldn't minimize what had happened in the sea caves off Torquay. I wasn't soaking wet when Vida dropped me off at the Islington flat, but I was feverish and snuffling.

I gave Nicky the briefest summary I could: Gayle suggested a swim, the current was stronger than I expected, I got caught in a sea cave, Gayle swam away, Vida saved me and brought me back to London.

I had to respond to a few follow-up questions, along the lines of "You were almost swept into the Channel?" and "Was Gayle trying to get you drowned?" But eventually, I crept into my bed and slept for about ten hours straight, waking up in the middle of the night only to pee and drink a large carton of orange juice and then return to bed. I didn't wake up again until around noon Monday. The flat was silent, but Nicky had left a note. She'd gone off for two days to Canterbury, where she was working with a contrabassoonist on an upcoming performance. "I've laid in some boxed soups and things. You lie here on the sofa and watch telly and drink a lot of fluids. Call me if you get worse and I'll come right home."

On the kitchen counter, next to a variety of herbal teas and soups, she'd placed a box of Boots Chesty Cough & Congestion Relief, along with a bottle of aspirin. I took two aspirin and a gulp of the Boots mix, even though I didn't (yet) have a chesty cough. After a hot cup of black tea and a slice of toast, I felt my head shrinking to near-normal size and my nose ungluing. I didn't get dressed but went back to bed with a second cup of tea, my laptop, and the flash drive that Vida had given me of Vonn's files, transferred from the two diskettes.

From the diskette labeled "Editorial Work 1997-2002" were two folders connected with mysteries five and six in the series: *A Plague of*

Orphans and *Death Comes to the Magistra*. Each folder had three versions of the book in question. An initial draft from Stella; Vonn's edited version with extensive notes, deletions, and insertions in the text and lengthy comments in the margin; and a final, clean version. It was clear at a glance that Vonn really had done a wide-ranging job on the text, far beyond copyediting or even fact-checking.

The other folders and files that Vida had transferred onto the flash drive were correspondence and unsigned contracts, mostly to do with *A Plague of Orphans* and *Death Comes to the Magistra*. There was also a contract and a few letters regarding the seventh mystery, *The Mystery Play Murders.*

I got up and searched in a pile on my desk for the envelope that Julia, the temp from Avery's agency, had sent me last week, with the editing agreement for number four, *The Funeral Specialist,* which Stella had not finished when she became ill. This agreement, like the ones for the other books, was between the Avery Amstrong Agency and Yvonne Henley. The last three agreements, for mysteries five, six, and seven, were similar to one for *The Funeral Specialist,* but more restrictive. That first contract had only discussed the terms of the editorial work and the payment schedule. Nothing was spelled out about credit, confidentiality, and termination, all of which were part of the next three contracts.

These three later editing agreements made clear what was expected from Vonn, starting with a description of how the editing on the manuscript would proceed: "Editor will make suggestions on plot, scene structure, characterization, and language, to be incorporated by the Author as desired in the final work. The Author will own the Work, including all copyrights." The agreements spelled out when the manuscript was due and how the Editor would be paid. There were also clauses about Vonn not being entitled to royalties or any published credit on the title page or cover. Vonn also had to agree that "Editor will have access to privileged information during the course of this project. Editor agrees to keep all information confidential during and after the course of this project. Editor will further not disclose her role in any Work she has done for Author."

Vonn would likely have printed out two copies of these electronically sent contracts, signed both and returned them by post. After which the agency would have returned one signed copy for Vonn's files and retained the other. I did this sort of thing all the time for my translation contracts. The problem was that all these signed contracts should have been in the agency's files, and they should have been in Vonn's business files. They apparently were in neither.

The contracts explained both Avery's silence on having worked with Vonn, and Fiona's insistence that Vonn had just been a sort of fact-checker. They were in their rights, since the agreements specified confidentiality, to expect discretion. Also of interest was how the standard termination clause had been invoked on *The Mystery Play Murders,* in a formal letter from Avery, emailed as an attachment and dated March 10, 2006, saying she was writing on behalf of the Author. Vonn's services were no longer required, and she would be paid only half the editorial fee, as specified in the contract. The termination letter also specified that Vonn still was required to respect the confidentiality clause.

Fiona had told me she'd managed to drive a wedge between Stella and Vonn, and that Vonn had not worked on *The Mystery Play Murders*. Now it appeared that Vonn may have been terminated midway through her editing work. The date, 2006, made sense. It was around then, Corinne had said, that Vonn had begun to experience a significant dip in her income. According to the contracts, she'd been earlier paid quite well for the work she did on Stella's books, and she had every expectation that Stella had more books in her, more books for Vonn to edit.

Surely, given the confidentiality clause, Vonn wouldn't write the truth about her contributions to Stella's novels and then ask Avery to represent the memoir. All I could think is that Vonn was trying to use her knowledge as a bargaining chip, in effect saying she wouldn't publish this story if Avery agreed to take her on as a client.

Yet that didn't really make sense. Avery's solicitor could have made short work of this threat by writing a letter to Vonn advising her to cease and desist or suffer the consequences. There was no reason the solicitor couldn't taken action against Vonn for threatening to break her confidentiality agreement.

I got up and went into the bathroom to take a shower and wash my hair, which still smelled faintly like seaweed to me. While I was dressing afterwards, I thought again about the simpler language of the first agreement Vonn had signed back in 1995 for *The Funeral Specialist*. There was no confidentiality clause. Did that mean Vonn was free to talk about her role in that book? It was lucky Julia had found it and sent it to me. Where the hell were the other files in the agency office?

As I dried my hair, sneezing occasionally, I suddenly thought of Samantha, Avery's assistant, who had left for a new job in South Yorkshire. Was there a chance that Sam knew something, and that her departure had anything to do with that?

There was no need to ask Avery for Sam's contact information. Within a few minutes of searching online, her name and photo came up: thin face, soft shoulder-length dark hair, parted in the middle, a schoolgirl look about her, though she was now in her early thirties. Avery had often complained that Sam was easily distracted, but I imagined she liked Sam's background (upper-class and very well educated) for the cachet. Sam was now at the Arts Council in Sheffield. I didn't know if she'd remember me as a lunch friend of Avery's who occasionally tried to interest the agency in one of my translation projects. I decided I'd play the role of volunteer archivist again and ask about Vonn's manuscripts, both "Gadfly," and the edited versions of Stella's books.

Sam did remember me, though she was surprised to get my call. I was cautious in my approach. I told her that friends of Vonn Henley's were working to catalogue her papers for an archive in Bristol. It would be mainly about her work with the feminist press, Brize, back in the eighties.

"Oh, I see," said Sam, though she clearly wondered what this had to do with her. She had worked with Avery perhaps five years, I thought I remembered, so she would have had no personal memory of Stella Terwicker or known much about how the Beatrys books were produced. But she would know Vonn in regard to the "Gadfly" proposal, which must have come in sometime in January, when she was still working at the agency.

"When I stopped by to see Avery recently," I said, "I asked about Vonn's manuscript. I also asked the temp who was there. There was a record of it in the logbook being submitted apparently, but not rejected."

"I suppose Avery must still be considering it," said Sam, "Or at least she was considering the proposal when I left."

I was confused. How could Avery still be considering it? Then I realized that somehow Sam had missed the news that Vonn had drowned.

Indeed, she had missed it, and was obviously shocked. "Oh, oh gosh. I'm awfully sorry. When did this happen?" she asked.

"The evening of February 20," I said.

"But February 18 was my last day in the office," said Sam. "So it must have been, in the flurry of leaving and coming up here that I didn't hear about it. I wasn't reading the newspapers that week."

The day I'd had lunch with Avery was February 10. I'd left for Barcelona two days later. We hadn't met at her office before going to the lecture. Avery had said nothing then about Sam leaving.

"You must have left London quickly," I said.

"Yes, I got a job offer February 11. It was something I'd been thinking of, changing careers and getting out of London. My family comes from near Sheffield. Avery and I had discussed it a couple of times in December and January, and she'd said how much she'd miss me if I left. But when the job offer came, she was quite happy for me. She didn't even mind that they wanted me to start immediately."

"She didn't put in a good word or pull connections?"

"No, it's a job I applied for," said Sam, putting paid to my suspicions on that score. "I wanted to be nearer my mum, as she's not well." She continued, "I took a week to wind things up at the agency. Avery said she'd get a temporary secretary, and she'd be in contact if the girl had any questions. I haven't heard from her, so I assumed everything was fine. It seems like she would have told me about Vonn. But then, I guess, Vonn wasn't really a client. So you're saying that Vonn Henley's proposal seems to have disappeared from the office?"

"Yes, and there would have been other files. Files from years ago. Vonn did some freelance editing on three or four of the Beatrys mysteries. It would be interesting to have copies of the correspondence and editorial work around those projects for the archives."

"I can't tell you anything more about the 'Gadfly' proposal," said Sam. "But I can guess where the other files are. Maybe two years ago, Stella's sister-in-law and literary executor, Fiona Craig, who's also a client of the agency, asked if she could borrow some of the files from the Beatrys books. She wanted to take a look at the manuscripts and correspondence for the biography she was writing about Stella. Avery wasn't around that week, she was in America at a book conference, but I didn't think she'd mind. Fiona came in and we packed up a lot of files and put them in a cab. She didn't keep them too long. She made copies of some correspondence she wanted to quote from and then she brought back the files. There were two boxes. I thought I refiled everything, but it's possible I just left them in the boxes. We have a back storeroom in the office. I may even have decided that they didn't need to go back in the main filing cabinets in the front office, because they were more than ten years old."

She sounded relieved. "I'm sure that's what happened. If you ask Avery, I'm sure she can find them for you there. Maybe, somehow, the 'Gadfly' proposal is still around the office. Otherwise I don't know. Avery had said she would handle Vonn's submission herself. She sometimes does that with people she knows or who she thinks will be tricky."

I thanked Sam for her time and wished her well.

Avery might not have arranged for Sam's new job, but one thing was for sure, she'd definitely told me that Sam would have been the one to send Vonn the rejection letter, while she'd told Sam she'd handle it herself.

Avery had lied to me, that was the inescapable conclusion here. But so had Fiona. She'd mentioned nothing about having had access to those office files. Perhaps she'd even destroyed some of the folders. The biography was proof that Fiona didn't want Vonn to get any credit at all for contributing to the Beatrys mysteries.

Either Avery or Fiona could have figured out a way to spirit Vonn's files out of her flat, I supposed. Avery was clever enough to have done it, but Fiona had the more likely motive.

Last Thursday after leaving Belgium, I'd convinced myself that Fiona couldn't possibly have murdered Vonn. She just didn't seem like the murdering type, with all her talk of medieval spirituality and beguine love.

I had, instead, concentrated my energies on a triangle where Gayle couldn't give up Vonn, and Vida killed Vonn out of jealous rage. Now, that scenario seemed ludicrous. Vida didn't care enough for Gayle to kill her past lover. And Gayle, I was convinced, would have never killed Vonn on purpose.

The effects of the hot tea and aspirin were wearing off and the Chesty Cough & Congestion Relief syrup was doing its job only too well. I was both dry-mouthed and sleepy. Still, I had to make at least one phone call. To Avery.

I would do that. I would definitely do that, after I'd had a brief nap.

31.

I didn't wake up until close to four in the afternoon and was almost too groggy and clogged up to remember what day it was and what I'd been thinking before I took my nap.

As soon as I did, I called Avery's office, and reached her new temp, Susanna, who informed me that Avery had left last Friday for a weekend in Paris. She was then on to Frankfurt for meetings. She'd be back in the office Thursday morning.

Yet again, I employed the volunteer archivist ruse and said I was looking for some files on Vonn Henley, a freelance editor who had recently died. She'd worked on the Beatrys mysteries by an agency author named Stella Terwicker. I'd heard that there were a couple of boxes of old files on Stella Terwicker in the back storeroom and wondered if I could come over and look through them.

"Now?" she said. "I was hoping to close the office a bit early."

"I can be there in fifteen minutes," I said. "It will hardly take any time at all to check whether the boxes have what we're looking for. I'm a friend of Avery's," I added. "We go way back, and we're working on a deal with a publisher right now."

Half an hour or so later I was there, buzzed in by a young woman who couldn't very well show her resentment openly, given that she was being employed to work a full eight hours and by rights had to stay until five thirty. But she hadn't lifted a finger to check whether the boxes I wanted were actually in the storeroom. She simply pointed to the door and then went back to her phone.

The storeroom was fortunately small, and unfortunately packed almost to the ceiling with banker's boxes. I had thrown on a coat and muffled myself with scarves and a hat because of the head cold. I began sneezing as soon as I took off the coat. It took a while, but at last I located a box labeled "Beatrys Rights." With anticipation I took it down and started pawing through the folders.

Disappointingly, there was nothing in the box that seemed to have a connection with Vonn. Instead, there were lots of exchanges with subagents in Europe and other parts of the world regarding foreign rights, and correspondence about the TV series, including scripts for some of the episodes. I worked as fast as I was able. I could always ask to come back tomorrow, now I knew that the material was here, but I feared that the temp might think twice about letting me in again to rummage around and might call Avery to confirm I was who I said I was. Leading to questions on Avery's part about what the hell I thought I was doing.

My watch said it was now ten to five. I scanned the labels on other boxes and pushed and pulled at the stacks, hoping they wouldn't topple on me. I was sweating like a pig by now from exertion and fever. But I didn't give up and was rewarded by the sight of a second box labeled "Beatrys/Stella Terwicker" behind several others.

This one didn't have as much in it, but what it had was of interest: a manuscript of *The Mystery Play Murders,* this one marked up by both Fiona and Avery with queries about historical facts and suggestions for changes. There was also some correspondence between Avery and Fiona, as well as a folder of what seemed to be royalty statements from the Beatrys mysteries.

I thought I should look at everything more closely, but it was too cold and dusty in here for me. I started sneezing and couldn't stop and had to use the end of one of the scarves to blow my nose. Disgusting. Especially since the scarf was Nicky's.

All I could do was shove the folders with correspondence and royalty statements into my capacious bag and stagger out of there. At the last minute I took the manuscript of *The Mystery Play Murders* with me. Maybe Fiona and Avery's queries and comments would shed some further light on how the books were written and edited.

I thought the temp might at least ask me if I'd found what I was looking for, but she hardly raised her eyes from her phone as I said good-bye. I went out the door and leaned against the railing. Fortunately, it wasn't hard to get a black cab in Camden High Street and soon I was home again, albeit with a throbbing headache and sore throat.

I made myself some soup and more tea. The royalty statements, assuming they could yield any information, would need to wait until I had a clearer head. I looked at my current inbox and found a message from Lola Fuentes, asking about when she might possibly get her contract and her advance, and answering a few translation questions about some expressions in *Verónica* regarding *contabilidad creativa,* "creative accounting," which Lola explained were things like keeping costs hidden or disguised as other expenditures. This too would have to wait until I could think straight.

I turned to the correspondence between Fiona and Avery about *The Mystery Play Murders.* There wasn't much, three printed letters without envelopes from Fiona and copies of responses from Avery, on the agency's letterhead. They were all dated early spring of 2006 and concerned the editing of Stella's current mystery and Fiona's increasing frustration with Vonn. According to Fiona, Stella didn't need Vonn's "meddling" any longer. She was feeling much stronger these days and found it burdensome to have to deal with layers of editing, specifically that coming from Vonn. Stella had quite a decent editor at her publishing house, and they hired excellent copyeditors. "Of course, I'll continue on with my research assistance, which is always very welcome to Stella. What she's tired of is Vonn rewriting so many of her sentences and inserting her own lesbian-feminist ideology into the books."

Avery's initial response was cautious. They did, after all, have an editing agreement with Vonn for *The Mystery Play Murders.* She knew that Vonn had already sent Stella her editorial comments on the first half of the manuscript, and that Vonn expected to finish by the deadline of May 1. She agreed that Vonn occasionally had a heavy hand but reminded Fiona that Vonn always came up with excellent questions about the plot and characters. Her suggestions often had led to great improvements. Was it possible that this discussion could wait until after Vonn turned in the fully edited version? She added that she'd heard no complaints from Stella herself about Vonn over the years.

Fiona was having none of this. She claimed that Stella had been overwhelmed and irritated after seeing the first half of the manuscript and simply couldn't bear to go on. She said that if Avery wanted to talk with Stella, that would be fine. "Obviously, Stella feels some loyalty and concern for Vonn," she wrote. "But she must also think of her own interests. It has simply become too onerous to respond to all Vonn's hundreds of comments. Stella doesn't want to deprive Vonn of income, so we suggest paying the full fee, plus a bonus."

It seemed that Avery did indeed talk with Stella and that Stella must have confirmed what Fiona said, for in Avery's next letter to Fiona, a very business-like one, she said that "At Stella's request, I've written to Vonn to terminate the editing process, and to send her the full fee and a bonus of a thousand pounds with Stella's thanks."

The last letter from Fiona was also business-like, but she could not repress a hint of glee when she ended. "I am so glad this chapter is ending with Vonn. Thanks for your support on this, Avery."

This gave me pause, somehow, this mention of the full fee, and a bonus. In Vonn's editorial files saved on a diskette and transferred to a flash drive, I'd seen Avery's formal letter canceling Vonn's work on *The Mystery Play Murders*. There, Avery had told Vonn that the agency would only pay her half the fee, as per the termination clause in the editing agreement. Nothing was said about a bonus. Apparently, Avery had decided not to honor Stella's wish to reward Vonn. The question was, had the agency charged Stella's account for the full fee and bonus?

For now it was bed again, after some soup and more decongestive syrup and aspirin. The next time I woke it was after eight in the evening, and I felt somewhat better. I made hot tea and sat on the sofa wrapped in a blanket, trying to recall the dream I'd had. Something to do with a windmill. A rather ominous Dutch windmill, as in a Hitchcock film, turning and creaking in a polder, by a canal.

After a while, I opened one of the folders I'd taken from Avery's office. The royalty statements were the originals of what Stella's estate had received from the Avery Armstrong Agency since her death. There was nothing too unusual about them. As was typical, like most statements that involved multiple titles, markets, discounts, and rights, the numbers were a little hard to parse. It did seem that the income from book sales had diminished over the years. Not surprisingly since Stella had stopped publishing new titles. At the same time, subsidiary rights continued to be sold in other countries, which partly made up for the slowing sales in the UK.

These statements usually had fees attached, for postage and copying, as well as for "administrative services" that went unspecified. This was in addition to the 25% that the agency took off the top of all royalties. The percentage was higher than customary, and I assumed it was because Avery had extra work managing the literary estate. Still, I wondered about the extra fees tacked on to every statement. Once, perhaps, there had been extra expenses connected with the Beatrys books, for Fiona's research and for Vonn's editing, maybe for some lunches and taxis, but how could the fees still be so large given that Stella had died in 2008?

Was it possible that Avery had systematically been overcharging Stella's literary estate? Most authors or their literary executors, if they suspected fraud, had the right, according to contract, to request an audit. Had Fiona ever done that? I doubted it. She'd told me she paid no attention to sales. She'd suggested that she was so disinterested in that end of things that she simply tossed the agency statements. Yet Fiona had taken away the contents of the two boxes for a short while and must have looked at everything. That was a couple of years ago. Had she known what she was looking at?

These files didn't include the original royalty statements from Albatross, so I couldn't compare what their accounting department sent the agency, and what Avery sent on to Fiona. It was a risky business to defraud an author or author's estate. Avery would be, if not convicted of a crime in the courts, removed from the British Association of Authors' Agents for violating their clear code of honor between agents and authors. I could hardly believe that Avery would gamble with her livelihood and reputation. I'd always thought of her as one of the cleverest women I knew and had admired her astuteness in choosing authors who were successful. She wasn't wealthy, but I assumed she did have a decent income. Did she want more than a decent income? Had she found it too tempting to swindle Stella's estate, reasoning perhaps that Fiona had plenty of money, along with Stella's property and everything that came to Fiona as Stan's widow, pensions and investments, their house, and life insurance?

I was fairly sure that Fiona could not be aware of the possible extent of the fraud, assuming there was fraud. She probably trusted Avery too much. But then again, Fiona had her own secret she'd confessed to me. She'd been the invisible author of the last Stella Terwicker mystery, published posthumously, something she now regretted. Maybe she and Avery had mutual secrets that they quietly agreed to keep for each other.

What was my interest here, and what was my responsibility? I'd gotten involved in this case because I wanted to know what happened to Vonn. Her death was odd, it was untimely; it came too close on the heels of Avery's supposed rejection of the "Gadfly" proposal and the disappearance of the manuscript. Strangest of all, it seemed connected, in some way I couldn't yet fathom, with Avery asking me to come to the lecture because Vonn was apparently threatening Fiona, and the unspooling of the story of Vonn, Avery, and Fiona, all of whom had something to do with Stella and Beatrys.

I wished I could talk about this with someone who knew something about fraud. Was it possible that Amina, with her work in finance, might be able to shed light on Avery's creative accounting? I picked up my phone and hoped it wasn't too late to call Corinne.

Our initial exchange was awkward. "Amina?" she said. "It's nine thirty in the evening and you want Amina's phone number?"

"I only wanted to ask her a small bookkeeping question about fraud. She's in finance, right?"

"Yes, she is," said Corinne. "She works for the World Bank, in the women's economic empowerment sector. I doubt she knows anything about fraud on a small scale. If you still want her number, though, I'll give it to you. You could just ask for it without explaining, you know."

"But I *do* want help with a money problem, to do with Vonn's finances," I said, and the words tumbled out, "I'm trying to figure out some contracts that Vonn had with the literary agent Avery Armstrong for the editorial work she did on the Stella Terwicker books. I found some correspondence in Avery's office—she's away so I sort of smuggled myself in—and it's making me suspicious. Royalty statements, maybe fudged, fees mounting up, fees for what? Vonn not paid properly, why shouldn't Vonn be angry, and I'm upset too, thinking about Avery stiffing Vonn. As a freelancer, I mean, that can happen, but it's so unprofessional. Really, it's criminal. And maybe it led to something that really was criminal."

"Are you entirely well, Cassandra?" Her voice was suddenly concerned. "You sound very congested. What happened in Devon? Are you back in London?"

I tried to give the briefest explanation I could muster, without mentioning the mists of Dartmoor, the sea cave, death and rebirth, Vida's red car, or too much about Gayle's perfidy in the matter of Vonn. "There was a bit of outdoor swimming," I admitted. "I regret that now. But I did rule out Gayle as a villain. A liar maybe, but not a murderer. Now I'm back to thinking Vonn could have been tangling with either Fiona or Avery, threatening them, but maybe being threatened herself. I'm still so much in the dark. About Beatrys, the Magistra, about Stella herself."

I was clearly confusing Corinne even more. "I really wonder if you might have a fever," she told me. "Why not rest and call me tomorrow? Is there someone there to take care of you?"

"No," I said, once again making the spontaneous decision not to mention Nicky. "I'm on my own, but I'm fine. Well, I'm not quite fine, actually I'm really wondering why I'm pursuing this. I mean, I didn't even know Vonn. And I guess the reason I'm calling you is actually that you *did* know Vonn. You seem to be one of the few who liked Vonn, who had a good relationship with her, and who could tell me why it's important that somehow I find out what happened to her."

"It *is* important," Corinne said. "I had my differences with Vonn. But I cared about her. She had a lot of life left in her, and she wanted to do better. She really did think her life might be turning around. I don't know Gayle, or Fiona, or Stella, except as the author of the mysteries. But I do know that Vonn deserved more than to be found in a pond, drowned and forgotten. If you can shed any light on what happened to her, then you should. You should do whatever you need to do. But you still need a good night's sleep. This is your nurse speaking and my prescription is rest and more rest."

"About our conversation on the train," I said, then broke off. It had been in my mind to ask if she was seeing the person who made the Brazilian fish stew on Friday night, if they were lovers or just friends. It had been in my mind to explain that I was open to getting to know her better, and that I quite liked her. But I realized she was right. My forehead was hot, and my thoughts were somewhat disordered.

"Prescription noted, "I said instead. "Good night, Nurse."

She laughed. "Call me if you don't feel better soon. We'll get you sorted out. Do you still want Amina's number?"

"Sorry, no."

"He was just an old friend," she said softly and hung up.

32.

I dozed off surrounded by folders, then awakened on the sofa with a jolt around eight a.m. I felt well enough to go into the kitchen and make a hearty breakfast of scrambled eggs with cheese and tomatoes, though I didn't feel well enough to eat all of it. I took a shower and changed my clothes and then, with another cup of tea, returned to the sofa to look again at what I'd taken from Avery's office. I would have liked evidence that Vonn had known of Avery's possible fraud in the form of a threatening letter to the agency saying she'd talk if Avery didn't publish "Gadfly," but I supposed that Avery wouldn't just keep a letter like that in her file cabinet. Besides, how would Vonn ever know about the extra fees and likely discrepancies? She didn't get statements from the agency; her own work had been paid in two or three installments per project, years and years ago.

Instead I found myself flipping through the edited manuscript of *The Mystery Play Murders*. It did seem rough and unfinished, with spaces left by Stella for "description," and "more historical detail here." I wondered if this is how all the books since Stella's illness were conceived, as basic drafts that she depended on her team to help fill in, add to, and otherwise massage. These comments here, on the margins, and in the text itself, were only by Avery and Fiona, mostly the latter.

From what I'd read about the book, I knew that this one had a more spiritual tone than some of the earlier mysteries. One of the main characters was a female mystic who performed religious plays for the members of the beguinage and the public. Fiona advocated writing more about this character, Clotilde, perhaps even inserting sections or chapters in Clotilde's own voice. Some of Fiona's margin notes were so long they carried over for several pages. They were full of encouragement to Stella to risk more. She wrote, "Now that the TV series is over and you don't have to pander to the public, you can really explore what is in your heart."

Avery had a different opinion. "While I think the character of Clotilde is a terrific addition, you might consider toning down the descriptions of stigmata, flagellation, and the crown of thorns," she wrote in one section. "I know you want to suggest that Clotilde is possibly unhinged, but you may drive away certain readers."

Fiona had fenced back, "This description of religious hysteria is quite accurate for the time."

I found myself wondering what Vonn's comments would have been. There were none from her in this manuscript. Nor were there any from Stella. I wondered what Stella's collaboration with Vonn had looked like in the early days, when it was just the two of them revising and polishing the first two books. Stella seemed to have trusted Vonn and worked well with her, according to Lucy Aspin, her editor at Aphra.

Could Lucy be taken into my confidence about Avery? I'd only had the one lunch with her, and she seemed quite decent, but I hesitated to set something into motion regarding Avery's possible swindles. I needed the original royalty statements from Stella's publisher to compare with what Avery sent Fiona. And if I couldn't get those, I needed some other kind of evidence. I did have a copy of the termination letter Vonn received from Avery about *The Mystery Play Murders,* with its firm offer of half the fee. And I now had proof, from the files I'd taken from the office, that in fact Stella and Fiona had wanted Vonn to be paid the full fee plus a bonus.

There must be more proof, in the missing papers from Vonn's flat. If Avery or Fiona had taken them, I was out of luck.

But what if they hadn't?

A chance remark from Vida during our drive back to London came back to me suddenly. Vida had said Gayle still had a key to her house, and that she'd left boxes in Vida's cellar until she got settled elsewhere. Was there any possibility that among those boxes were some of Vonn's files relating to the Beatrys books, even to Stella and to "Gadfly"?

Had Gayle even suggested to me that Vonn might have put the files "somewhere for safekeeping"?

I called Vida at work and asked if I might be able to look at Gayle's boxes in her cellar today to see if there was anything connected with Vonn. Right now, in fact.

"You don't sound very good, Cassandra, your voice is very nasal. You should be resting. Why must you do this today? Can't we do it on the weekend?"

"I'm fine. And I just have feeling that we need to move quickly on this. Call it an intuition. There may be nothing in Gayle's boxes about Vonn, and if not, then I'll need to look elsewhere."

"I am uncomfortable," she said. "They're Gayle's property. You haven't checked with her if this is all right, have you?"

"We won't paw through her things," I promised. "Just open the boxes up and take a quick look. After all, if we find what I'm hoping we'll find, it won't be Gayle's property. It will belong to Vonn." I didn't add that if I were to call Gayle and if she were to tell me I couldn't look, then I'd have a different problem.

"I suppose you're right," said Vida. We agreed to meet at her house as soon as I could get there, and she gave me the address in Clissold Crescent in Stoke Newington.

From a real estate perspective, I could see why Gayle had latched on to Vida and been so reluctant to part. The exterior of the two-story house on a quiet street not far from Clissold Park, white-painted brick with a large door of terracotta-rose, wasn't flashy, but Vida had done up the rooms in stunning fashion. The ceilings were high and fireplaces abounded, along with period details in the molding and window frames.

Vida shrugged with offhand pride when I gaped at the modern kitchen with glazed glass doors that led to a landscaped garden. "It was a shambles, a shell when I bought this thirty years ago. I still have things I want to do."

She led me to a door that led to the cellar. "This was a coal cellar in Victorian times, with a chute. It's dry not damp, but if I had the time I would get it dug out more, and convert it to a nice space with a sauna. Maybe in a few years when I retire."

Right now the cellar was partly an exercise room, with a treadmill, exercycle, and weights, and partly a storage area, with boxes and trunks on a platform above the floor.

"These are her boxes and things," Vida said. Along with four boxes of neatly packed books were two banker's boxes, an old-fashioned leather suitcase, a duffle, and a variety of Marks & Spencer shopping bags, the plastic, single-use kind as well as the new recyclable tote bags that proclaimed their virtue in a printed slogan.

I started with the banker's boxes, but they mainly held scrapbooks of the Tudor Roses, packets of letters, musical scores, and programs.

There was one photo album. I wanted to open it and see if there were photographs of Gayle and Vonn in their youth, but I feared Vida would find that intrusive. I was supposed to be looking for one thing only: Vonn's papers from her flat. Unfortunately there didn't seem to be any such material in the banker's boxes, and Vida seemed impatient. She looked at her watch, climbed onto her exercycle and started peddling hard. She was wearing narrow black slacks and a white shirt under a red jumper. Her black ponytail bounced.

I moved to the suitcase but found only clothes that suggested performance wear: a Tudor gown and cap, a black crepe dress. Vida looked a little regretfully at the dress from her bike seat and pumped her legs faster. The duffle held only sheets and towels. The tote bags were next, and I wasn't hopeful. Inside most of them were only kitchenware and some toiletries. But when I came to the plastic M&S bags I was surprised. Underneath a jumper in one and a towel in the other were folders, loose papers, and large manila envelopes. They were from Vonn's office, from her filing cabinets. I had handled many papers of hers in the last weeks, and I recognized her handwriting.

One bag contained folders and large manila envelopes connected with the Beatrys projects Vonn had worked on, and the other bag held some folders that seemed to have something to do with "Gadfly," including a copy of her book proposal to Avery, a detailed table of contents, and what could be a sample chapter, a long one, titled "The Collective Disbands." I caught sight of the words "Lives of Lesser-Known Lesbians."

Bingo. The missing manuscript, or at least some of it. The other folders in the M&S bag looked stuffed with notes on other feminist or lesbian presses, clippings, and some interviews.

"I think I may have found what I'm looking for," I said. "Do you mind if I take these two bags with me?"

Vida got off her exercycle and came over to where I stood. "So she did steal Vonn's papers and she hid them here. And then she lied to everyone that she didn't know where they went. Are Vonn's laptops in other boxes or bags?"

"I didn't see anything." I went back to the tote bags with the kitchenware and found a handheld mixer and a blender. "Nope."

"It's possible she hid them somewhere else in the house," Vida said. "*La pequeña mentirosa.* The little liar."

"I'm sure she had her reasons," I said. "But I don't think Gayle would have wanted Vonn to die. Anyway, you're her alibi. She was here at the house all night."

"Yes, that I know." She stared at the suitcase that held the black crepe dress. "So you still don't believe Vonn's death was suicide, or an accident?"

"I believe that someone, not Gayle, but perhaps Fiona or Avery, had a reason for meeting Vonn that evening at the Heath. They may not have meant to kill her, so maybe it actually was an accident. But I believe one of them could have wanted her out of the way. And it probably has something to do with whatever is in these bags."

"Then take them," she said. "If Gayle gets in touch with me about her possessions, I'll tell her you have these files. But I don't think she will contact me, at least not right away. It was too awful between us on the weekend." She looked at her watch again and apologized that she couldn't drive me back to Islington. She had an appointment in ten minutes with someone about their computer back at the shop. She insisted on calling me a local minicab. "I don't think you're well, Cassandra. Your cheeks are flushed."

"Just with excitement," I said. But the truth was, I wasn't all that well. I was both nervy and tired. I knew I should be staying home, drinking fluids, keeping warm, and working on *Verónica* to meet the deadline. But I wanted the answer to questions about Vonn that had plagued me for over a month.

Already, in the back seat of the minicab, I was reading through the folder with the proposal material for Avery. This must be what she submitted back in January and what Avery had rejected. I flipped eagerly through the pages, searching for compromising material on Fiona or Stella, but was disappointed. I'd thought that Avery and Gayle might have been dissembling when they'd said Vonn hadn't really written much of the book. When I'd gone to Avery's office some weeks ago, she'd said the proposal was sketchy and there was only one chapter about Brize that she could barely read, it was so boring and vituperative. At the same time there *had* been something that worried Avery about the proposal, something to do with Stella. Was it the table of contents? Or was it a cover letter that Vonn had sent with the manuscript that I didn't see here? Or was it just a fear that Avery had that Vonn was ready to make a claim for her work with Stella if Avery didn't agree to represent "Gadfly"?

The table of contents looked innocuous enough: an introduction that covered the history of British women's presses in the eighties and nineties, and six chapters, two on Brize, three on the other women's presses of the era, and a last chapter on mainstream presses that created various imprints in order to co-opt feminist themes and authors. Maybe Stella was in this chapter. Maybe this was where Vonn planned to assert that she had ghostwritten parts of the Beatrys mysteries.

None of these chapters were written except the one about Brize's demise. I looked at the folders of clippings, notes, and a few transcriptions of interviews. Gayle had said, when we were on Dartmoor, that the book was in fragments, that Vonn talked more than wrote. Gayle had apparently read a version of the long chapter included in the proposal, "The Collective Disbands," and had been just as dismissive of it as Avery had been.

But I was mystified. Gayle had gone into some detail about Vonn's account of her relationship with Stella and mention of their work together on Beatrys. Was that a chapter in "Gadfly" or something else? It didn't seem to have been submitted to Avery as part of the proposal and didn't correspond to anything in the table of contents.

When I got back to the Islington flat, I took out all the folders, envelopes, and papers from both bags and separated everything into small piles on the kitchen table. The bag with the Beatrys material yielded a trove of copies of Vonn's emails and letters with Avery, Fiona, and Stella, along with copies of signed contracts and invoices for the work she'd done. The letters to Avery were the most business-like. Only in regard to the letter of termination in 2006 did Vonn allow herself to vent. Interestingly, she didn't haggle about the fee but accepted that she was getting only half. The money wasn't, at least at the time, what bothered her so much. Instead she blamed Fiona and Avery for planting ideas in Stella's head. There was real anguish in this letter, blame, and undisguised contempt for Fiona.

The folder of editorial correspondence with Fiona was usually polite enough on Vonn's side; Fiona wrote with more irritation, as she'd said herself. The letters involved the three books that Vonn had worked on with Fiona: *The Funeral Specialist, A Plague of Orphans,* and *Death Comes for the Magistra.* Only once or twice did Vonn attempt a stronger defense of the lesbian subtext of some of Stella's writing. "It's no good you trying to squash that part of Stella's life, Fiona. She had a life in the dyke community in London in the eighties, and a few people remember that. I'm not the only one. You needn't be afraid anyone will put that tainting word on her *now*. All the same you should respect Stella's interest in women's intimate relationships, even though you may not share that interest. Or at least *admit* to an interest."

I would have been curious about Fiona's response, but there was none.

I eagerly opened up the folder titled "Stella" to find just a few editorial letters Vonn had written to both Fiona and Stella. While Fiona sometimes wrote detailed answers in return, Stella never answered Vonn's letters with a proper letter of her own. Instead there were only a dozen postcards, sent from various towns and cities around England and Europe, that said, "Thanks for your comments, Vonn!" or "Hope you like the latest version, Vonn!" They were as bland as rice pudding, but they all were signed "Love, Stella."

Stella's folder had no reference to Vonn's dismissal as an editor from her work on *The Mystery Play Murders*. Had Stella instigated the termination? I couldn't see a letter of explanation anywhere.

But there were some indications in a second folder of material on Fiona that Vonn was well aware of the biography's publication last year. Along with some reviews of the book and an interview with Fiona was an angry letter from Vonn to Fiona, dated last October. In six pages Vonn laid out point by point all Fiona's falsehoods and omissions about Stella's life, everything from erasing Stella's sexual preference for women, to ignoring the contributions Vonn made to Stella's books, to actually writing *The Confessor's Tale* herself. "Oh, yes," said Vonn in the letter. "It's obvious to anyone like me who actually had something to do with Stella's books that you wrote that piece of shit."

At the top of the letter was scrawled in Vonn's handwriting, in red pen: "Not sent!"

It seemed that Vonn had written this as a means of blowing off steam, not because she planned to set the record straight. But I didn't know that for sure. Maybe Vonn did ultimately send some version of this letter then, or later. Something like this could have definitely been perceived by Fiona, and by Avery, as a threat.

I still didn't know why Gayle had taken all these documents and stuffed them in some bags and stored them in Vida's cellar. She hadn't gone to very much trouble to hide them.

I turned to the last large manila envelope, bulging with newspaper clippings and other papers. There was nothing written on the outside, but when I opened it to dump out the contents, it seemed that everything inside had to do with Stella Terwicker.

33.

Along with a pile of reviews of the Beatrys books and interviews with Stella were half a dozen obits from January 2008. A paperclip held them together with two reviews of Stella's last book, *The Confessor's Tale,* published posthumously in 2009. The *Times* was polite, and merely alluded to "a waning of Terwicker's powers in this, her last mystery, finished shortly before her death and edited by her sister-in-law Fiona Craig," while the *Guardian*'s reviewer took a ruder approach, and lambasted the publishing house for trying to make money off an inferior work.

On a sticky note attached to that review, in her recognizable handwriting, Vonn had written, "That's because Fiona obviously wrote the whole thing, you twit."

As I sorted through the reviews, I found no other post-its that might hint at Vonn's feelings. But buried at the bottom of the large envelope were ten sheets of paper, single-spaced and typed, folded in thirds, and addressed to "My darling Stella." The date was January 15, 2008, a week after Stella's death.

The pages were seemingly composed in a rush of emotion after Vonn had returned from a memorial service, to which she'd apparently not been invited. She'd gone anyway, by herself, and had sat at the back of Corpus Christi Catholic Church in Maiden Lane, near Convent Garden. Being Vonn, she had to put in a critical paragraph about the patriarchal, homophobic Catholic Church, but most of it was a love letter to Stella, tracing their meeting at the Brize office and how Vonn had fallen in love with her at first sight, how she had pursued Stella for two years before experiencing the joy of making love with her the first time.

The letter was never meant to be read by the likes of me, and so I refrained from my usual automatic shudder at sentiment. I was touched in spite of myself at how very much Vonn had longed for Stella to return her feelings. "You never really did. I will always maintain that you were a lesbian, that you were queer to your fingertips, in your love for women and disinterest in men. I know, after me, you went on to date several women, but I doubt they had any better luck than I did in arousing your desire. You may not have been fully able to respond to me, but in other ways, I always considered you mine. I never really loved anyone else but you. Oh, I know it seemed like I always had girls on the string, and some of them I remain fond of, like Gayle, but as for love, no. I couldn't be faithful, so I know that's why you left me, but the others didn't mean anything.

"I've never loved anyone but you, Stella, and now you're gone without my telling you that properly."

There was much more. Her sorrow that Stella was never really healthy after the trip to Portugal. Her anger at Fiona for keeping Vonn away from Stella. "I never should have signed those agreements with their confidentiality conditions. I thought that editing your work would keep us close, that I could make sure Fiona wouldn't distort and hide your love for women. But by signing away my rights to have my name even mentioned in connection with the books, I participated in my own erasure. In the church today I wanted to stand up and shout, 'I loved Stella. I was Stella's lover. I helped draft her books. I would have died for Stella.' But the British don't do those kinds of things and even I, radical dyke that am I, am still a grocer's daughter, raised in Kidderminster."

For some reason, it was that sentence that struck me most. I wasn't raised in Kidderminster but being the daughter of a bus driver in Kalamazoo, Michigan was probably similar. It takes some courage to break away from family and pursue a life of queer revolt, loving freely and in spite of all obstacles. Whatever else you might say about Vonn, she was courageous and unfaltering in her desire for women and for women's liberation.

As I tucked the letter back inside its envelope, I realized this must be the document that Gayle had read. It wasn't a chapter from "Gadfly," and it certainly wasn't anything that Vonn would have given Gayle to read. Gayle had read it either in Vonn's files at the flat or after she'd taken the bags to Vida's cellar.

It must have been painful to learn that Vonn considered Gayle only one of several women she'd been fond of but had never really loved. That these women "didn't mean anything" was something I doubted; Vonn was clearly overwrought when she wrote this letter to Stella's memory. But Gayle still would have felt its sting.

I made myself yet another cup of tea and swigged the last of the Boots concoction, thinking of Nicky. If she were here, she'd probably be getting out the *hygge* paraphernalia, the warm socks, the candles, and some suitably Danish food like cabbage soup with meatballs. I didn't feel particularly well after waking so early and spending half an hour in a chilly cellar. But I didn't want to just lie on the sofa all day under a duvet. I was wired and restless. Was I getting any closer to finding out how Vonn had died, and why?

Gayle answered her phone immediately. It was a while before I could get her to stop apologizing for the fiasco at the sea cave, especially when she could hear the nasal hoarseness in my voice and realized I'd taken ill.

I was forced to say I forgave her in order to stop her from going on about how sorry she was, and about how she'd realized that she and Vida were never meant to be, and maybe her sister Judy was right, and it was better to just accept that she would be in Torquay for the foreseeable future.

I finally managed to interrupt her with the information that I'd just been over to Vida's house, to the cellar, and I'd found the missing files from Vonn's file cabinets, in two M&S plastic bags.

She was abruptly silent.

I went on, "To be honest, I'm a bit mystified why you would take these folders from Vonn's file cabinets and then make such a fuss about packing up all the rest of her papers and sending them to Corinne for the archives. *These* are the important papers, with the written histories and notes for 'Gadfly,' and her editing correspondence about the Beatrys books. You've let me go around like an idiot asking questions about what happened to Vonn's memoir and papers when all the time these folders were in Vida's cellar."

"Well, I didn't *know* you were going to start asking so many questions, did I?" Gayle said defensively. "I mean, I told you about some of my personal history with Vonn and about not thinking she would have committed suicide, but I wasn't expecting that you'd be launching your own little investigation. I specifically *asked* you about having solved a couple of suspicious cases in the past, like that one in Venice, but you just laughed and said that was a long time ago. I wouldn't have asked you to help me with Vonn's things at the flat if I'd thought you were going to start seriously snooping and stealing. Those were not your files to take, they were with *my* things in Vida's cellar. And what gives you the right to ask all these questions?"

I ignored that. Basically, I had no right, only the sense that no one else in this bloody case was going to find out the truth, especially when so many of the key people were lying.

I coughed loudly, if only to remind her that she'd practically left me to die in a sea cave, and then enquired in a calm and reasonable voice, "So why *did* you take Vonn's papers, Gayle? I'm assuming you also probably took her old and new laptops as well?"

"I'll tell you," she said, a bit sullenly, "On the condition you don't mention any of this to Vida. I don't want her to think worse of me than she probably already does."

"She doesn't think badly of you," I said, ignoring the fact that Vida had called her a liar, and that in Vida's mind, Gayle would remain *La mentirosa* forever.

"I got together with Vonn, in February, a week or so before she died," Gayle said. "I hadn't seen her for a while, not since the Christmas holidays. We... made love in her flat. She told me that she'd missed me and asked if I was happy with Vida. I said yes, but I still had feelings for her, for Vonn. She laughed and said that she'd taken her new laptop in January to Vida's shop so the contents could be transferred from the old laptop. She said that she wouldn't be surprised if Vida had looked at the contents of the old laptop. If so, she might have read some of our emails with each other.

"I was furious. I was panicked too, thinking that Vida hadn't told me about Vonn coming to the shop. I knew Vonn had done this to wreck what I had with Vida. First Vonn defended herself, then she told me that she was lonely. That after I'd moved in with Vida, she'd missed me. She'd been taking antidepressants because she felt so down. I didn't believe her. I'd *always* been the one who loved her more. I thought she was just being her usual wicked, infuriating self, pretending to feel things she didn't and stirring up trouble.

"I was so angry that the next day, when I knew for sure she'd be at her clinic for a check-up, I let myself into the flat with a key, and I took both her laptops and left. I was just getting back at her. But I also was terrified it was true, that there was something on the old laptop that Vida might have seen, some compromising emails. Vonn knew it was me who'd taken the laptops, of course. We talked later on the phone, and she swore she had erased our emails and was certain anyway that Vida hadn't looked at anything, Vida was too upstanding. She wanted her laptops back, and I said I would return them on the condition she was telling the truth about erasing our emails."

I could hear that Gayle had started crying. "Then just two days later, I get a call from Kristi, saying that the police are in the building, and that Vonn has been found on the Heath, drowned. I was frantic, absolutely beside myself. I went over to the flat and answered questions. A day or two later, there *did* seem to be a break-in, and I expect Kristi could have had something to do that. It was convenient to tell everyone that a laptop had been taken then.

"Cassandra, I felt so guilty. When I saw the police in her bathroom, dusting and packaging up her bottles of painkillers and antidepressants, I knew Vonn must have been telling me the truth, that she *had* been lonely, that she *had* missed me. I didn't believe she could have killed herself, but I did think, yes, I believe, she could have been muddled in some way and died by accident." She dissolved in sobbing.

I waited for her to get control of herself. "What about the files?" I asked.

"I stuffed a bunch of things in bags and took them away before you and Amina came. I'd looked through the filing cabinets and had seen folders and envelopes for 'Gadfly' and stuff to do with Stella. I wasn't going to destroy them. I just wanted to look through everything myself, on my own, to try to understand Vonn better. Then, all of sudden, Vida and I were arguing badly about why I was still so attached to Vonn, and I thought she must know about the affair, how Vonn and I continued to see each other. I was ashamed but couldn't apologize in case she *didn't* know. I said in a fit of anger that maybe it was better we separated for a bit until we calmed down, and she didn't say no, she said that would be best. I packed up my stuff and put it in the cellar with the two bags of Vonn's papers. I was intending to go back to Vida's, you know."

"What about the laptops?"

"In one of the boxes, underneath a lot of books about the Middle Ages."

If I hadn't been so annoyed, I might have laughed at how close Vonn's electronic files had been all this time, over in Stoke Newington.

I changed the subject. "Did Vonn ever talk about threatening Fiona or Avery? Asking them for money, for instance?"

"Vonn mentioned, the last time I saw her, that her financial situation might be improving. She said that if I left Vida, maybe she and I could get a place together, a nicer place, somewhere out of London. I didn't take it seriously."

"Why not?"

"I'd heard her say that kind of thing before," said Gayle with a sigh. "I knew for certain that living with Vonn would be difficult. And I didn't really believe that her financial situation would improve significantly. How could it? She wasn't in the best of health and wasn't working, she was over seventy. I assumed she thought somehow, she'd finish her memoir and it would be a bestseller. I'm sure she'd never stoop to outright blackmail. Do you have any evidence of that, Cassandra?"

If Vonn had sent that accusing letter about Stella's biography to Fiona, that might be a form of evidence, except that it didn't include any demands, financial or otherwise. Maybe Vonn didn't send that letter though, but another. If so, would Fiona tell me?

I took refuge in a coughing fit and muttered something about needing to lie down before ending the call with Gayle and searching for Fiona's phone number.

She'd said she was just spending a week in Bruges, so probably she was back in Primrose Hill by now. I'd rest a bit and go over there with the royalty statements. If she were prepared to ask for an outside audit of the royalties sent to the Avery Armstrong Agency from Albatross, she would probably uncover fraud. I could suggest she get a solicitor to advise her. That still didn't explain Vonn's death. All the same, realizing that Avery had cheated Vonn out of her termination fee in the past and suspecting that Avery had been defrauding Stella's estate put me out of charity with her. If Vonn had confronted Avery with anything she knew or suspected about financial skullduggery, or if Vonn had tried to bargain with Avery over "Gadfly," then what?

It was the easiest scenario for me to imagine, that Avery and Vonn had met up that rainy evening on the Heath and that something had happened between them that ended with Avery pushing Vonn into the pond. Perhaps it hadn't been premeditated, but that didn't mean Avery shouldn't be called to account and punished.

Fiona answered on the second ring, but she wasn't in England. She had decided to stay in Bruges a few days after I left. She didn't sound unfriendly, but wary. "What can I help you with?"

"I wanted to talk to you about something." I hesitated. "About some papers I found in Vonn's files. They suggest that perhaps Avery could possibly have been fiddling a bit with the accounts for the Beatrys books, maybe sending you less than you deserved."

"That's very unlikely. I trust Avery. She's always explained everything. And I'm not that interested, anyway, if a few accounts don't add up. As if Avery would do that. Avery was *devoted* to Stella." The disjointed phrases resolved themselves into a vote of confidence, even though her voice was a little tight.

"You don't have any reason to protect Avery, Fiona. You have a right to ask for an audit, to get the full account of what's owing you."

"This is none of your business. But if you insist, I can ask Avery about it tomorrow. We're having lunch."

"You'll be back in London tomorrow?"

"No, Avery's coming here. She's been over in Frankfurt and is driving back to London. The motorway goes right by Bruges, so she said she'd stop and see me before going on to Calais. Now, if you don't mind, I'll ring off. And I'd appreciate it if you'd stop calling me with these kinds of abrupt questions. I know we share the same agent, but I think Avery would be appalled if she thought you were gossiping about her."

She didn't give me a chance to ask about whether she'd gotten a letter from Vonn that accused her of errors and omissions in the biography. In the old days you could hear the anger as someone slammed the phone down. Nowadays it was done with a fingertip.

Snuffling, I boiled the kettle for tea, downcast with the idea that I'd made everything worse. I had wanted to alert Fiona to the likely fraud. Or at least to suggest to her that Avery wasn't on the up and up. Now Avery would hear about my suspicions from Fiona tomorrow. If the suspicions were unfounded, my friendship with Avery was over and so, probably, was the translation deal she was brokering for me. Of course, if Avery was a crook or, God forbid, a murderer, the friendship was already over.

Was it even a friendship? Of course not.

I found myself walking around the flat restlessly until I went into my room and started packing a bag. On top of some warm clothes, I threw the paperback of *The Mystery Play Murders* and folders with the royalty statements and other material. It was around three o'clock now, and I knew there was a train to Brussels at six, getting into Brussels at nine fifteen. I'd stay in a hotel near the station, get a good night's sleep, and take an early train to Bruges.

I had to talk to Fiona before she talked to Avery. I had to convince her that this was more important than some extra fees. Vonn had *died,* for pity's sake. And Avery was probably responsible.

I texted Nicky with my plans to head to Bruges tonight. She must have been still in Kent and in the middle of a bassoon lesson because I didn't hear back. I bought an open-return ticket for Brussels and called an Uber to take me to the station. At St. Pancras I hit Boots pharmacy and bought two bottles of Chesty Cough & Decongestant syrup and some energy bars and water. That should see me through.

34.

I checked into a hotel near Brussels Midi station and conked out immediately. During the night I woke up several times before falling into a light sleep plagued by worries and by the sensation I couldn't breathe. Normally I enjoyed the sound of raindrops pattering against a window. Now the sound only reminded me I was going to have to travel to Bruges in the rain. I had my hooded raincoat with me, but no umbrella, and in my morning dreams I was searching for shelter. The word *sauvegard* echoed through the corridors of my mind.

I roused myself at nine. As I'd apparently slept in my shirt and sweater, I merely had to put on my jeans and shoes, slug some more cough syrup, brush my teeth, and ignore my hair. I wrapped a wool scarf around my neck and put on my raincoat. I didn't feel better, but I didn't feel worse, either. I'd get some coffee at the station and take the first train leaving for Bruges.

It was only when I was in my seat on the commuter train, nursing a tall cup of black coffee, and nibbling on a roll with cheese, that I thought to check my phone. I'd turned it off last night when I fell into bed. Nothing from Fiona, but several texts from Nicky and two missed phone calls, also from Nicky. When I felt sufficiently caffeinated to speak coherently, I called her and discovered she was on the Eurostar, halfway to Brussels.

"When I didn't hear from you, I fretted," she said. "So I got up early this morning and left Canterbury for St. Pancras, then just went from the platform to the Eurostar check-in and caught the 08:55. Are you still in Brussels?"

I admitted I was en route to Bruges and that I hoped to be there to talk to Fiona before Avery turned up for lunch.

"Can't you hold off?" she said. "You sound very stuffed up. Are we staying at Piet's again? Why not go there and lie down until I get there, and then I'll walk over to Fiona's with you. Can't this all wait, or did you find out something new? You think one of them, Fiona or Avery, is involved in what happened to Vonn?"

The rain was sliding down the window of the train carriage and I could see my face reflected: I was a gaunt, gray version of my usual energetic self. I didn't want to admit to Nicky that I had a slight pain in my chest when I breathed and that I would like nothing more than to get into a bed at Piet's B&B under a goose-down duvet and forget all about this quixotic search for justice for Vonn.

I said, "I believe Avery was skimming money from Stella's literary estate through excessive fees, and she was probably misstating the amount of the royalties that the agency paid twice a year to Fiona." I added, "I tried talking to Fiona on the phone, but the connection was bad. That's why I'm going to Bruges. She and Avery are having lunch today, and I don't want Fiona getting me in trouble with Avery. Because of our long-standing professional relationship."

I thought this sounded logical, but Nicky knew me better. "Reilly, I don't think you're telling the me the whole story. I knew I shouldn't have gone off to Kent and left you on your own in London to get up to God knows what in your feverish condition."

I did feel a bit feverish, but it only increased my need to get this all sorted out and soon. "I won't do anything drastic," I promised. "Simply meet for a short while with Fiona and convince her to ask for an audit of the statements once she gets back to London. And beg her not to ask Avery about any fiddling with the accounts. Then I'll go back to Piet's and lie down. I won't try to talk to Avery until I feel better, back in London."

"Maybe that's all right," said Nicky doubtfully. "But I want you to promise to wait until I get there to do anything that would put you in danger. I don't like the sound of that wheeze in your voice."

Was I wheezing? I tried to laugh, but it made my chest hurt. "I'm fine, Nicky. You worry too much. See you this afternoon. Thanks for coming," I added belatedly. "I appreciate it."

After we hung up, I picked up *The Mystery Play Murders,* and read the first chapter. I was confused at first. Instead of Stella's typical opening, a sort of wide-screen depiction of women working in the infirmary, the weaving rooms, or the school at the beguinage, an opening that introduced or re-introduced Beatrys, a year or two older in each book, this seventh novel began with an eerie depiction of Jesus's last days, blood, sweat, and suffering, as enacted by a woman in the grip of her visions. This voice emanated from the mystic and performer, Clotilde, who traveled the Flemish countryside, from town to town, in search of audiences for her pantomimes and puppet shows that reenacted stories from the Gospel and the Passion. She also sang, danced, recited, and revealed her visions.

Clotilde's short chapters, written in image-laden language that hinted at death and the macabre, were interspersed with those of Beatrys, first as an onlooker to Clotilde's performances in Bruges, and then as her investigator, when it turned out that Clotilde may have committed murder in a neighboring village. I thought as I read that this was quite a departure for Stella, whose previous mysteries had often had a lighter tone, with many scenes of singing, weaving, and stirring up medicinal brews. The back cover copy to *The Mystery Play Murders* spoke of puppetry. Puppetry to me always suggested manipulation and the possibility that puppets longed to get unentangled.

I must have drifted off, because before I knew it, we were pulling into the station at Bruges, and the paperback had slipped to the floor of the carriage. I retrieved it and tried to pull myself together. This was the end of the line for this particular train, and I was the last person off. I came out into the wide-open square and took the first taxi I saw to Fiona's flat in Speelmansstraat.

"Not again," said Fiona, when she opened the door. "Please don't tell me you were in the neighborhood."

"I need urgently to speak with you," I said. "It's important we talk before you meet with Avery. Is she coming here?"

"I'm meeting her in less than an hour at the restaurant down the street," she said. She was dressed already for the date, with lipstick and earrings, with a silk scarf patterned in red tulips, a color like blood that was too strong for her pale skin. I could see that she wanted to shut the door in my face, but probably feared that I might make a scene.

"Please may I come in out of the cold?" I asked, with a slight cough.

"Are you ill?"

"Allergies," I said. "Twenty minutes, that's all I ask."

Once inside, I didn't waste time, but held out the folder with the royalty statements. She only glanced at them briefly. "I told you, the money is not important to me," she said. "I have plenty and I'm not going to quibble with Avery about a few extra pounds that she charges the estate."

"It's more than a few pounds," I said. "I would suspect it's hundreds of pounds, even thousands, and that her fraud probably began after your husband died, if not before. Avery knew that you didn't pay attention to the statements and that you'd simply accept that after Stella's death that the sales of the Beatrys books dropped. Perhaps she alluded to the poor reception of *The Confessor's Tale,* and its lack of sales, in a way that made you feel guilty about having pretended Stella wrote it. Even though that had probably been Avery's idea."

A flicker of pain in Fiona's eyes made me realize I'd hit the target. I was sorry to wound her but pressed on: "There was likely fraud earlier, when Stella was still alive, in the form of extra fees subtracted from the semi-annual statements. Travel or meal expenses for Avery perhaps to do business on Stella's behalf or inflated editorial expenses. Most of those can't be proved. But with the royalties you've received, it will be possible to prove there are discrepancies between what Albatross or its parent company sent to the agency and what the agency sent to you. All you have to do is ask the accounting department at Albatross for an audit. Or get a solicitor to do it. And the solicitor can ask the agency for their records and compare them. If there's no discrepancy, then there's no problem. But I think you'll find the statements don't match up."

"*You* think," Fiona seized on this. "*You* think, Cassandra, and you act, and you expect me to possibly destroy a twenty-five-year-old working relationship with Avery, who did *everything* for Stella and who made her life so much more comfortable financially than it could ever have been, just because *you* are suspicious. Do you think I'd have this flat in Bruges without Avery, or have had the chance to work on a television series, or to have participated in Stella's amazing career, or to have been able to care for Stella as I did *without* everything Avery did for us?"

Fiona had been sitting across from me but now she stood up and took a step in my direction. This time there would be no teacup dropping or indirect hinting that I should leave. Her eyes blazed. I'd be surprised if she didn't forcibly kick me in the direction of the door in a minute.

I held my seat and pointed to the other folder I still held, with correspondence. "I found a copy or a draft of a letter that Vonn wrote you last autumn when the biography came out. In it she points out many omissions and errors in the book. Some of them are small, many are more significant. She reminds you that she played a significant role as an editor and even ghostwriter of several of Stella's books. There's a lot of other material in Vonn's files that backs this up, from documents of the novels with her Track Changes, notes and letters between the two of you, and even the agreements that she signed with Avery with confidentiality clauses."

Fiona sank back down. "She wasn't a ghostwriter," she muttered. "She simply edited and that sometimes meant rewriting and suggesting ideas."

"Did you get that letter?"

"I got that letter, or something like it," she said. "I didn't respond."

"You didn't try to meet with Vonn or discuss it with her?"

"No, of course not." Fiona's eyes had gone from angry to wary. "What is there to discuss with someone so crazy as Vonn?"

"You didn't do anything?"

Pulling herself together, Fiona said, "I took it to Avery. I took it to Avery, and Avery said she'd deal with Vonn, in person, or legally."

"When did you get the letter, was it last autumn, when the biography came out?"

"No, not then. Later. More recently. I don't remember. Avery said she'd deal with Vonn."

"Did you think Vonn was trying to blackmail you? Trying to get money from you? Or just trying to get you to admit that Stella was a lesbian, and that Vonn was her lover at one point and always cared for her?"

The anger was back. "Stella was not... what you're saying, and she didn't have a long relationship with Vonn. Or any other women. Oh, she experimented, yes, and she was a feminist. But Stella didn't really respond sexually to women. It just wasn't... in her nature."

All of a sudden, I realized that whatever I'd been thinking about Fiona, whatever I'd believed about her being asexual, just wasn't true. She *had* desired Stella, but Stella hadn't desired her back. Perhaps because Stella had less interest in sex—Vonn had suggested that too—or perhaps because she lost interest in early cuddles with Fiona after she moved to London and met different sorts of women. How painful it must have been for Fiona to see Stella living as a lesbian when Fiona was too conflicted about doing so herself.

"I suppose," I said, thinking aloud, "it made things better after

Stella became ill. The two of you no longer struggled over desire. You took on a larger and larger role in her life as sister-in-law, as co-creator, as caretaker. Only Vonn really knew what was missing from the biography."

"You're wrong if you think I was glad Stella was chronically ill," Fiona said. "It saddened me immeasurably to see her suffering. But it made it clear that the ways I loved her had nothing to do with physical desire. I never thought of myself, in that way. It was only Stella I had feelings for. Those feelings never changed their intensity, only their form."

Fiona cheeks were flushed now, and with the red tulips and red lipstick she looked less chilly than usual. She said, "In Beatrice of Nazareth's book, *The Seven Ways of Divine Love,* she speaks of changing base desire through a gradual purification to love that is allied with holiness. People saw Stella as some sort of beautiful, ethereal being. But being with her in her fragility wasn't easy. It was about taking her to the doctor, making sure she slept well, helping her to the bathroom, giving her sponge baths, shopping and cooking and driving and worrying. I didn't put that in the biography either, all my efforts. I believe in service, and I believe in love. Vonn knew nothing about any of that."

"You were Perpetua, weren't you? She was Felicity."

Fiona gave the faintest of nods. "Our nicknames for each other way back to our first year in York."

We were both silent. Then Fiona said, uneasily, "I've always trusted Avery. I would hate to think she had something to do with Vonn's death. Personally, I find it very easy to believe that Vonn had an accident at the pond. That no one is responsible."

"There are many ways that Vonn could have threatened both of you," I said. "Your reputation as a scholar, for instance, as we discussed the last time I was in Bruges. For Avery it could have been more serious, if it came out that she passed off *The Confessor's Tale* as written by Stella and that she'd fiddled with the royalty statements."

I paused so that Fiona could take this in. Avery, a cheat, and maybe a murderer? Let her think about this. She would come to the same conclusion I had. That only by accusing Avery would Fiona untangle herself from Avery's manipulations and deceit.

Fiona bowed her head and there was worry on her pale face when she lifted it again. "And now I'm going to have lunch with her. How am I going to face her, with this suspicion?"

"I would recommend you say nothing," I said, getting up with my folders. "Wait until you get back to London and call a solicitor. Let the process of the audit begin and talk to the solicitor about what to do about Avery and Vonn. He or she will have ideas and help you go to the police."

"I don't really feel I should thank you, Cassandra," said Fiona, walking me to the door. "But thank you. I hope you feel you can just return to London now, and not worry about this anymore. I'll follow your advice, but please, now that Vonn is dead, can we keep any discussion of Stella's personal life out of this?"

I nodded doubtfully. I hadn't said anything about Vonn's other files now in Bristol, nor the fact that I thought the two M&S bags might end up there too, though possibly they'd be required in a court case against Avery.

Only after I was out on the street again did it occur to me that Fiona had come over to my side a bit too suddenly.

35.

Piet was happy to see me but seemed concerned at my cough and bedraggled appearance. He insisted on carrying my bag up to my room and making me a cup of tea. It was only with great reluctance he let me leave again after an hour. I told him I needed to have a brief meeting with someone at the restaurant down the block, *De Windmolen*, and then I'd be back for a good rest. Nicky should soon be here, and Piet was obviously delighted with the idea of seeing Nicky once again and talking crossbows.

In the brief time since leaving Fiona, I'd grown anxious that she might not be able to refrain from telling Avery what had just transpired and about my role in this. After all, Fiona and Avery had known each other a long time, and although I thought I'd brought Fiona around to reconsidering the trust she'd placed in Avery, I couldn't be sure what would happen when Avery was sitting across from her. Avery was a strong personality, a persuasive, clever woman. If Fiona did bring up fees or royalties, Avery would have an answer.

I'd never known Avery not to have an explanation or to be two steps ahead of me.

Was I concerned for Fiona's safety? Not at first, but when I didn't find them at *De Windmolen*, I backtracked to Fiona's flat on Speelmansstraat. On the sidewalk in front was a Ford with a British license plate.

No one answered the door. Now I was beginning to worry. It was only drizzling now, but the sky had an ominous look. I returned to *De Windmolen*. Perhaps they'd eaten somewhere else. No, said the young woman at the bar, two women speaking English were here, but they didn't stay long. They had a drink and left without ordering a meal.

I asked, "Were they having a fight?"

"No, no. But they did not agree and seemed unhappy. Then they paid and went over to the park. I saw them cross the street to the Sint-Janshuis windmill, two old English ladies."

Avery would not be pleased to hear herself described that way. "How long ago was that?"

"Not long. Half an hour?"

I thanked her and headed across the street. Could Fiona have confronted Avery about the royalties, or were they disagreeing about something else? I prepared myself for Avery's anger. At least we'd have it out in a public place.

A text came in from Nicky. She was now on the train to Bruges. She hoped I was resting safely at Piet's and being careful.

"Great," I texted back. "I'm on the trail of Fiona and Avery. They're at the park near your crossbow guilds. I'll catch up with them at the windmill. See you at Piet's."

I was tempted to turn the phone off so I didn't have to read any more messages about being careful, but I thought that it might come in handy to have the ability to record a confrontation, if it came to that. I checked that I remembered how to record. I had actually only done this a few times on my phone, mostly in Spain or South America when I'd recorded audio from a lecture or panel discussion. Then I put the phone in my raincoat pocket and pulled the hood over my head before my hair got too wet in the gray mist. I was already shivering.

The blades of the windmill turned in the wind with a forlorn creaking and heavy sighing. I contemplated climbing the steep steps to the platform to look for Fiona and Avery or to get a wider perspective on the park, but it turned out the rampart hill looked down on the canal and paved path along the channel with its bare gray trees spaced just so. The drizzle wasn't thick enough to obscure two figures on the path. One was unmistakably Avery in a narrow blue wool coat, tightly belted, and slacks. She wore low heels and a scarf but no hat. Her irregular blond locks trembled in the breeze. The other figure was wrapped in a too-large tan raincoat and wore a familiar brown hat. From the red tulip scarf peeking out and the sensible shoes, it could only be Fiona.

No one else seemed to be about on this wet morning except, in the distance, a man and a tiny dog, though traffic went by on the street I'd just crossed. I supposed this was public enough.

I pulled my hood down, went down to the path, and approached with a brisk step. I could hear snatches of English; they clearly didn't imagine that passersby could understand them, otherwise they would have lowered their voices. But their conversation wasn't about money. I heard the words "Stella" and "Vonn," and something, from Fiona, like "You told me to do it. You said no one would ever know."

Suddenly Avery caught sight of me and said, "Cassandra?" Her years as a poker-faced literary agent stood her in good stead, as she quickly arranged her expression to one of polite disbelief. But not before I'd glimpsed something I'd never seen in Avery's wrinkle-free, bronzed face before: panic.

"Hi there," I said, trying not to cough. "Nice to find you both together here. Fiona knows I've been here in Bruges, but I suppose it's a surprise to you, Avery."

"I am surprised, Cassandra," she said flatly. "Why *are* you here?"

No sense beating around the bush. "You know I've been helping organize Vonn's papers for the feminist archive in Bristol. Some were in her home office, and some have been harder to track down. I recently found some correspondence and other files that show you were right to tell me that Vonn was threatening Fiona. What you didn't say was that Vonn had something on both of you. Vonn may not have realized you were defrauding Fiona, but I suspect she was prepared to claim some of the income from the Beatrys books. She probably was hoping you'd offer to represent 'Gadfly,' but when you turned it down, she might have threatened to get a solicitor. You could have fought her on that due to the nature of the confidentiality clauses in the contracts, but in the process, the solicitor could have requested information from Albatross about sales, and that would have likely led to someone noticing the discrepancy between the royalties paid to Stella's estate and what you paid Fiona."

"Ridiculous," said Avery dismissively. "Fiona knows I've always had her best interests at heart. Stella would never have been as successful as she was without my years of effort on her behalf. And without Stella's success, Fiona would have spent the last twenty-five years up in Inverness."

"It's not just that you swindled Stella's estate out of royalties and added bogus or inflated fees, Avery," I said. "You made money off a mystery that Stella hadn't even written! I told Fiona I knew Vonn had written her a letter outlining all the omissions and outright lies about how the last four Beatrys mysteries were created. Fiona feared that Vonn was planning to out her as the author of *The Confessor's Tale*. You would have been implicated, Avery. The help Stella received from Vonn and

Fiona on the other books could have been explained away as research and editorial assistance, but to knowingly represent *The Confessor's Tale* as written by Stella was a greater scam."

Fiona said nothing to confirm or deny this. She simply stared at me in dislike, but without the panic I'd seen briefly in Avery's eyes.

As I thought, it was Avery who had something to hide, Avery who had lured Vonn to the Heath and somehow pushed her into the water and left her there to drown.

I turned back to Fiona. "Maybe that's the reason, the last time I was here, Fiona, you confessed to me that you were author of that book. You knew it might come out, and you thought I was a journalist. Avery had said she'd take care of Vonn. And you did, Avery. You were never planning to represent Vonn's manuscript, you doubted she even *had* a manuscript, that she was only using that as a pretext to talk to you about getting what she felt she deserved from having helped write Stella's books. Fiona's biography enraged her, and she wanted to tell her side of the story. But she also was willing to talk money. Vonn wanted to be compensated, at the very least, for all the work she'd put into making Stella a successful author."

Avery rolled her eyes. "How much more of this do I have to listen to? Fiona, you can't possibly believe any of this. Yes, Vonn sent me her wretched proposal with a letter that I could have found threatening but was just basically pathetic. I felt sorry for her, and a bit concerned that she was harassing poor Fiona. I did think she might make a scene at the lecture, which is why I asked you to come, Cassandra. But as I've maintained, my only purpose was to talk to her that afternoon and prepare her for a rejection. I may have suggested that I could find her some editing work, just to show her some support. Vonn made no financial demands, there was no talk of extortion. Nothing was said about a solicitor or the nonsensical idea of her getting paid *again* for editorial work she'd already performed. For Godsakes, be reasonable, Cassandra. Vonn did some editorial work on those mysteries years and years ago. She was paid then, paid well, and that's the end of the story."

I didn't feel like being reasonable, at least in the way Avery meant. "You told Vonn to meet you at the Heath so you could talk more about this. Maybe you even suggested you'd give her some cash. Maybe you didn't mean to kill her, but maybe she made you angry because Vonn never could hold her tongue. Maybe she threatened to expose you and pursue you in the courts. You probably didn't think, you lost control, you pushed her into the pond and held her down. Or maybe she stumbled and her back seized up and you didn't help her out. I don't know the details, but I know you killed her!"

"You've lost your mind," said Avery. "Fiona, you're my witness. Cassandra has gone around the bend. Surely you don't believe this."

My nose was running, and I was shivering, but I didn't want to give up. I still had the phone in my hand inside my pocket but couldn't recall if and when I had punched record. Never mind, I'd get the truth out of Avery, and Fiona would be my witness, not Avery's.

I said to Fiona. "And it's not like you're totally innocent! You must have known that it could be no coincidence that Vonn died soon after you told Avery she'd sent you a threatening message. You must have suspected it was no accident, that Avery had something to do with it. You've known for weeks that Avery murdered Vonn. And yet you did nothing. You were probably glad that the Met didn't investigate more fully, that they just chalked Vonn's death up to suicide by an elderly, depressed lesbian. You wanted Vonn to die, because you didn't want anyone to know that Vonn and Stella had been lovers and that Vonn knew all about you from Stella, how you'd pursued her, and she'd rejected you as a partner. In fact, I wouldn't even be surprised if it turned out you'd murdered Vonn."

As soon as I'd said that, I knew it was true.

"Fiona?" said Avery.

"Of course not," she replied, glaring at me. "For reasons I don't know, Cassandra is making up some incredible story. Avery, think about it. First, she accuses you of murdering Vonn, then she accuses me. Are either of these things remotely possible?"

But she could see that Avery was suddenly thinking it *was* possible.

Avery said, "You did say that you wanted to have it out with Vonn, for the last time. And I persuaded you that was unwise. Did you for some reason agree to meet her on the Heath?"

"No!" Fiona raised her voice and the words quivered strangely. "I never expected to see her ever again after she crashed Stella's funeral. And then she came to the lecture. And then she was just there on the Heath, one rainy evening, when I was taking a walk. She tried to talk to me, and we argued, and I walked away. She kept *following* me, *badgering* me, angry I never answered her letter about the biography, on and on about Stella being a gay person and me erasing her. It was nauseating. Finally she left. That's all."

"That's not all," I said a little wildly, fumbling at my pocket and the phone, which was buzzing with a call. Nicky. I took the phone out and held it out in Fiona's direction, pressing talk. "I've been recording this."

"For the record then," said Avery. "I'm not a murderer."

"I'm not a murderer either," said Fiona. "You weren't there, you can't prove anything. There's no proof, no confession, no murder."

And with that, Fiona wrenched the phone out of my hand and threw it in the canal. I ran over to the edge and saw it plunk into the water twenty feet away. And as it plunked, I saw it all:

Vonn, following Fiona that evening at the Heath, browbeating her about Stella. Taking out her phone, maybe telling Fiona that she'd been recording their conversation. Fiona grabbing Vonn's phone and tossing it into the bird pond, Vonn going after it, slipping forward in the mud and water, her back seizing up. By then, Fiona had probably walked away in anger. It was raining, it was dark, no one was around to help Vonn get up.

That would have been the reason there were no footprints besides Vonn's on the muddy pond edge, the reason Fiona didn't know that Vonn had died until days later, the reason she'd persuaded herself it was an accident that had nothing to do with her.

Unlike Vonn, there was no way I was jumping into a Flemish canal to get my phone back. But I didn't have a choice.

A firm push from Fiona, and I was in the icy cold, gray-green water, fully dressed and flailing.

I was obviously not going to drown in a canal in Bruges, but Fiona wasn't making it easy to climb out, even though Avery was holding on to her arm and trying to prevent Fiona from stomping on my hands as I tried to get a purchase on the grassy edge. The drizzle made the grass slippery and there was a current, though not a strong one, that made it hard to paddle in place. I didn't know where the bottom was. The canal was deeper than I'd thought. I couldn't kick my shoes off—they were side-zip short boots—and their weight dragged me down. I struggled out of my raincoat and let it float away. At least my wallet was in my jeans.

I was cold and getting colder and decided that my best bet was actually to swim to the other side of the canal, and to crawl out there, where Fiona couldn't break my fingers with her sensible shoes. But then there was splash and Avery was in and screaming, "Help, I can't swim in my coat!"

I wondered why I'd never screamed like that. Too surprised, I suppose.

I didn't want Avery to drown if I could help it, so I paused in my swim across the canal and returned to her. She was practically immobilized by the belted, tight wool coat. Her multi-layered blonde hair was plastered to her skull and hid her eyes. Now Fiona was bending over to hit at Avery's hands grasping the edge of the canal. In a minute Avery could go under and I'd have an impossible time rescuing her.

Suddenly from the hill above, where the windmill reared up, I saw a strange and unexpected sight: a burly man in a canvas jacket holding a massive crossbow and pointing in the direction of Fiona.

"Halt!" he cried, and when she didn't, an arrow came zinging toward her into a tree five feet away. Nicky had said that crossbowmen were the snipers of the medieval world, but I couldn't figure out where this man came from and whether he was on our side or just an amateur sportsman on the loose in Bruges.

But the shock of the arrow did stop Fiona from trying to pry Avery's hands off the edge of the canal. She looked at the man in complete terror and then started to run down the paved path.

In the near distance were the sounds of police cars and, as it turned out, an ambulance.

36.

Later that evening in my room at the hospital, I woke up to see an anxious Nicky in a chair by my bedside. Her tawny hair was piled on her head, and she wore a bright orange wool caftan and fingerless woolen gloves to match. Her hand grabbed mine when she noticed me open my eyes.

With her was Piet, our good innkeeper, round of tummy, worriedly kind.

"If I had known you'd end up in the canal, I never would have let you out of my sight," he said.

"Never mind that," I said. "Where's Avery?"

"A hotel somewhere," said Nicky. "She's fine. They didn't admit her to the hospital."

"Why am I here then?"

"Because you already had a cold when you were pushed into the canal," Nicky informed me. "You were almost hypothermic by the time they fished you out. They had to wrap you up and get you to the emergency room right away. The doctor won't let the police talk to you until you're stabilized. They're worried you might develop pneumonia." Nicky tightened her grip on my hand. "Bloody hell, Reilly, what *were* you thinking?"

At the moment, I couldn't really say. It seemed very wrong that in the space of only about ten days I'd found myself in cold water, on the verge of drowning and having to be saved, three different times. This last dunking in the canal, of course, must be counted the most serious, even though I'd been far more frightened in the sea cave. I hadn't considered it life-threatening when Fiona first shoved me in. But I certainly didn't feel very good. I had a memory of people in yellow vests hauling me out of the water and bundling me up in blankets. Then I was in the ambulance with a blood pressure cuff, being asked questions in English. It grew vaguer after that. I remembered only some concerned faces, and questions about relatives. I did have some sodden ID in my jeans, including a card for Piet's B&B. They had called him.

My phone, of course, was in the canal. Fortunately, I'd pressed talk when Nicky called, so she'd heard some of the confrontation followed by a glugging sound and silence.

"When that happened, I immediately called Bernt."

"Bernt?"

"The man with the crossbow, who shot the arrow. He's the retired cop I got to know last week, the guy who volunteers at the Guild Hall of St. Sebastian. He'll come and visit you tomorrow. He was thrilled that the medieval crossbow worked as well as it did. He's in a bit of trouble for shooting it in the park though."

"What about Fiona?"

"They caught up with her, but I don't know what happened after that."

"I have a lot of questions."

"I'm sure you do, but they can wait." Nicky still had hold of my hand. "When you get out of here, Piet will take care of you. I'll have to return to London for some performances, but then I'll be back to bring you home."

"Home," I murmured. "*Hygge*."

I spent ten or twelve more days in Bruges. The first couple of days in the hospital, and then a week at Piet's B&B recuperating. I didn't get pneumonia, but I did develop a body-racking, bone-shuddering, eye-watering cough that kept me indoors and up at night. It couldn't have been too pleasant for Piet's other guests to hear a woman hacking miserably in the bedroom next to them, but Piet explained the circumstances to everyone and only one couple asked for their money back.

The police interviewed me in the hospital and then again when I got out. They asked both times if I wanted to press charges against Fiona Craig for assault. I tried to tell them the lengthier story of Fiona's probable role in the death of Vonn Henley in London in February, but they reminded me that this was something out of their jurisdiction and that I should take it up with the Met once I got back to London.

I asked if Avery Armstrong had pressed charges against Fiona and they said no. Avery had explained it was a misunderstanding of some sort about a mutual friend in London. She said that I had gotten too close to the edge of the canal, then had accidentally dropped my phone in the water and had foolishly jumped in to retrieve it. After which, believing me to be drowning, she'd heroically gone in after me. Bernt the crossbowman had sworn that Fiona was trying to pry Avery's fingers from the edge of the canal. Avery claimed that Fiona was only trying to help her up by grasping her hands. She could not explain why neither of them had called for emergency services or why Fiona had dashed off, except that she must have felt frightened by the arrow zinging past her ear into the tree.

Avery had gone back to London without talking to me, and by the time I was released from the hospital Fiona had departed for London as well.

The Belgian police declined to dredge the canal for the phone and without the phone the chance of recovering the audio recording was nil. Assuming that I had pressed record in the first place.

Back in London, I had to get a new phone to replace the old, but that made no difference to Avery or Fiona, neither of whom would take my calls.

In the interviews with Stella published during the height of her success, journalists often commented on the fact that the lay women of the beguinage who Beatrys had tracked down and who were guilty of theft or even murder often got off without apparent punishment. Gayle and Nicky had pointed this out too, how, in the television series, Sheriff Abel often hauled off the male malefactors to prison and death by hanging, while the women criminals, especially the beguines, were treated differently. Fiona had made the point as well, the first time I'd gone to her flat here in Bruges. In words that seemed prescient, she'd claimed that Stella seemed to be more understanding of her women characters who committed murder. I recalled Fiona saying that maybe the woman who took a life had a reason. Or that "maybe she didn't mean it and it just happened."

I'd likely never know what exactly had transpired the evening Fiona and Vonn met by chance at Hampstead Heath. Maybe Vonn really did threaten Fiona with exposure; maybe Vonn asked for money not to write anything in "Gadfly" about Stella's queerness or about Fiona's role writing *The Confessor's Tale*. Maybe Vonn, angry at having her book project turned down by Avery, turned to Fiona with the warning that she wanted a share now of the royalties or a negotiated sum of money for the unrecognized work she'd done on the Beatrys novels. Maybe Vonn held up her phone, claiming she was recording their argument or Fiona's confession. Fiona wouldn't have known that Vonn's old flip phone was probably not even turned on.

I could imagine Fiona grabbing the phone impulsively and throwing it in the middle of the pond, and then without waiting to see what happened, stomping off into the twilight. She might have heard a splash or two, but she wouldn't have imagined Vonn would be so rash as to wade very far into the pond. She knew nothing about Vonn's bad back and how, if Vonn had tripped and fallen forward at the edge of the pond, her body might have seized up and made it impossible for her to get up.

When Avery told her that Fiona had died at Hampstead Heath in an accident, Fiona would have of course realized that someone could have seen her that evening. But when no one knocked at the door to question her, she'd persuaded herself that it was an act of foolhardiness that had nothing to do with her.

Maybe she even told herself that Vonn deserved it.

In Stella's books, women who caused others' deaths never went to jail or the gallows. But that didn't mean they were let off scot-free. They were punished by conscience and by the judgment of their peers. They might be expelled from the safe haven of the beguinage if their crime was murder. A lesser crime of theft might involve making amends through good works. In most cases, unless the woman was a maleficent evildoer, the pangs of life-long remorse were considered sentence enough.

Stella in her interviews defended this choice:

In addition to trying to create a physical and spiritual women-centered world, where women pray, work, care for the sick, and educate the young, I wanted to make an attempt to create an alternative justice system. Consistently throughout the series I've attempted to substitute moral justice for instinctive, violent retribution. No person, male or female, gets off lightly, if they've engaged in misconduct, particularly if they've taken a life, but I have tried to think through the issues of punishment and penance in a medieval world, where misdeeds were harshly corrected, usually by cruel means.

In writing about the beguinages, where the emphasis among the beguines was on love and cooperation, I attempted to show that withdrawing trust from a woman offender was just as effective as corporeal punishment. The Magistra weighs many possibilities when judging a woman who's done wrong. Many are forced to leave the beguinage, others are asked to atone in other ways. Beatrys initially wants women to face severe punishment. Later, she grows more subtle. She finds ways to suggest punishments that fall short of imprisonment, but that have an effect all the same of discipline.

I thought about this idea when I was back in London, after I'd considered going to the Met with an accusation of murder against Fiona Craig. It was clear to me now that Avery would never accuse Fiona of killing Vonn, and that Fiona was unlikely to confess to having been at the Heath, much less to having anything to do with Vonn that evening. They had secrets separately and together that they wished to protect. I imagined that Avery would quietly go back to paying Fiona the full amount of royalties, and that Fiona would never mention the past embezzlements to anyone, just as Avery would never reveal Fiona's role as author of *The Confessor's Tale* or any suspicions she had about Fiona playing a role in Vonn's death.

Did that mean I couldn't still find some sort of justice for Vonn, annoying, abrasive, pain-in-the-neck Vonn? Ghostwriter, bicyclist, editor, swing dancer, and crusader for lesbians? A member of our tribe, a witness to our history?

I rang up Lucy Aspin and arranged another lunch, at the same pub in Hammersmith. She listened attentively to my story of Avery's business dealings with Stella Terwicker's literary estate. After I showed her copies of the royalty statements for the Beatrys books and suggested they might not match up with those sent by Albatross to the agency, Lucy knew immediately how serious that would be.

"I know a couple of editors at Albatross," she said. "They can compare the statements and if it's true that Avery wasn't paying out the correct amount to Stella's estate, they won't be happy. It may be that Avery never admits to fiddling the books, but I suspect her career as an agent is effectively over if they prove she did keep money owing to an author. That's about the worst sin an agent can commit. No one will trust her."

It took a month or two, but by May the Avery Armstrong Agency no longer had premises in Camden Town. The official line was that Avery had been offered a job in Frankfurt with a German publisher, to acquire English language books. Rumor was she had become involved with a German editor, Ingrid Somebody, and that was the real reason for the move.

As for Fiona, I wondered what her punishment might be. Was it enough that she didn't know for certain whether my phone was recovered from the water and the data was somehow intact, including a recording of that conversation by the canal? Enough that she lived in fear I might tell the Met everything I knew about her meeting with Vonn? Enough, even, that she lived with the knowledge that she could have turned back to the pond when she heard splashing and saved a woman from drowning?

Maybe Fiona's punishment would be more complex. After all, the new additions to Vonn's archives—the papers I'd found, the flash drive, and the files on the laptop—would corroborate a long history of Vonn working with Fiona and Avery on several of Stella's books, as an editor who was also at times a ghostwriter. The files would also document how Avery had cheated Vonn out of the full fee and bonus for *The Mystery Play Murders,* and how Fiona had fudged the truth about the whole process of creating the Beatrys books in her biography of Stella Terwicker. It wouldn't bring Vonn back or give her a more financially comfortable life, but Vonn's papers would turn out to be important in establishing that yes, Stella Terwicker had been a lesbian, as well as a feminist, and that Vonn had been her lover, and that Vonn had always loved her. Even though "Gadfly" had hardly existed and would never be published as a book, what was in Vonn's files would exist as a counternarrative and a corrective to Fiona's *Stella Terwicker.*

Fiona, in fact, would find life more difficult once she was identified as an academic researcher who had suppressed the truth and played fast and loose with accuracy. Present-day journalists as well as historians and biographers of the future would revise the stories that Fiona had told and the *vita* she had given her beloved Stella.

I suspected that it might only be a matter of time before Fiona, like Avery, found it convenient to leave the country. Perhaps to take up residence in Bruges and to atone for her past sins by doing good works with the nuns of the English Convent.

★

With Gayle's permission I packed up the contents of the Marks & Spencer bags with Vonn's remaining files, contracts, editorial correspondence with Avery and Fiona, and her memories of Stella. Vida extracted all the data from Vonn's laptop and put it on a backup hard drive. Then she and I drove up to Bristol and deposited everything with Corinne for the archives.

Corinne was expecting us and had made a three-layer chocolate cake decorated with caramel swirls. She was wearing a warm yellow cardigan that reached her knees, and a print bandeau around her head, the silvered black hair spilling out behind. She was every bit as calm, vivid, and gorgeous as I recalled, and she wrapped me in a warm embrace at the door. "Oh, you're skin and bones, you pitiful thing!"

I'd rung her from Piet's to explain about Fiona and Avery and my unexpected plunge into a cold canal. Even though she was unaware I had already been in the drink and in danger twice before, this newest near-drowning in Belgium—"when you were already sick!"—had elicited great sympathy. Once again, she asked me if I had anyone taking care of me in Bruges. I told her about Piet, and then I launched into a muddled account of my long-time friendship with Nicky Gibbons and how I'd begun staying with her in my thirties and now I still called her flat home, and she had come to Bruges, and luckily had a friend with a crossbow who was also a retired policeman.

Corinne interrupted me. "I know all about Nicky," she said cheerfully. "Amina told me when I called her recently. Apparently, you happened to mention your friend-slash-flatmate when the two of you were at Vonn's flat, dealing with the files."

"I meant to tell you," I said. "But really, I can't count the times people have misunderstood."

"I don't misunderstand friendship," she said. "In fact I understand a lot of things, especially when they're shared."

That day in Bristol, Vida and I ate our fill of cake washed down with mugs of hot tea, and the two of them talked about home remodeling and gardening. When Vida said that it would be good to get back on the motorway before afternoon traffic, I looked at Corinne and she looked at me, and she said, "You're welcome to stay and guide me through the material a bit more," and I said, "I can help go through the files at greater length. It's easy to catch a train back to London."

Vida shook her head and said to me, in Spanish. "*Eres una zorra astuta, mujer.*" A sly fox.

We embraced with fond affection, but a different sort than Corinne soon showed me.

The deal brokered with SNP was off. The boys claimed they had reservations about bullfighting and always had, only Avery had rather twisted their arms on Lola Fuentes. I thought that, once again, Lola might be disappointed, but instead, her editors in Madrid found a new English-language publisher for her, not in London, but in New York. They used my sample translations to secure the deal, but the editors in New York decided to go with another translator, someone they had worked with frequently. I wasn't sorry. Lola's books were really not my cup of bull's blood. In fact, I felt a bit off the mystery genre and its conventions.

"I so didn't want this to be a lesbian love triangle," I told Nicky. "I was happy when I realized I'd barked up the wrong tree suspecting Vida and Gayle. Not that I wanted Avery to be the culprit, but at least it would have been about financial skullduggery. Well, I did find evidence of that, not that Fiona was grateful. It *was* all about lesbian love in the end. Fiona and Vonn both had loved Stella and loathed each other. And that's why Vonn died."

"You did the right thing, hen," said Nicky firmly. "And at least you proved that Vonn didn't commit suicide because she was a miserable old dyke."

"No, she was in fact as good as murdered by Fiona, who hated the idea of Vonn and Stella having been together. That's a gay tragedy if ever there was one."

"You should have been more patient and let me help you," Nicky said. "If I'd been there, and the phone hadn't gone into the water, and you hadn't gotten so sick, maybe we could have done more. As it was, we had to rely on Bernt and his crossbow."

"Once again," I said, "just like a Beatrys mystery where Sheriff Abel turns up to save the day. Maybe, if you'd been there, you'd have borrowed his crossbow and shot Fiona?"

"I would have loved to!" said Nicky. "If you were in danger, I mean if she'd been strangling you, I definitely would have. You probably don't think of me as that bloodthirsty. Does that shock you?"

"No," I said. "I find it oddly reassuring."

Epilogue

It was a warm, brilliant Saturday in mid-May when the memorial service was held for Vonn Henley at Hampstead Heath, in the vicinity of the Ladies' Pond, on a grassy rise. I was surprised that so many turned up.

Women recalled Vonn's drive and her energy, her rebellious nature, and her willingness to take on the patriarchy. Several women teared up when they recalled their short relationships with her, and more than a couple of former Brize collective members spoke passionately about the intentions of the collective, the good times, the laughter and dancing, as well as the stapler that was once thrown at Vonn's head. Gayle was the main organizer of the event. She gave a heartful talk, ending with a medieval motet that soared through the bright green leaves above and blended with the blue sky.

Gayle brought a new friend she'd met in Torquay, Sylvia, the director of the women's choir there. Gayle introduced her to me a little shyly and said afterwards, "I'm not moving in with her. I'm staying with my sister and making my life with her. We'll need each other as we get older. But you'd be surprised, there's a nice women's community in Torquay. I'm starting to think I made the right choice."

Amina and Corinne spoke, Amina with brisk humor, Corinne with forgiving love. I'd seen Corinne a few times, always in Bristol, over the last two months. She'd introduced me to some of the women at the archives, including the grad student who would organize and catalogue Vonn's papers. Most of the time we spent walking, eating, or in bed. Without a translation project demanding my immediate attention, I could have been anxious, but instead, I found I was enjoying myself.

Nicky said, "Careful, you might get used to being happily retired."

"As if that's ever going to happen."

I'd looked forward, a little nervously, to introducing Nicky and Corinne to each other this weekend, but Nicky had gone back to Denmark for a musical conference and concert. Although both of them expressed regrets about not meeting, I wondered if it wasn't easier this way. It had been a long time since a woman had stayed with me in London. I'd have to get used to it slowly, the way you get used to the temperature of water sometimes, first one foot, then the legs, then the stomach and the arms, before you slip in, still having to decide whether you want to submerge completely or to keep your head dry.

Corinne and I had both brought our swimsuits; hers was yellow and ruched, mine was an old blue Speedo. Like many at the memorial, afterwards we adjourned to the Pond and swam and splashed around for a good hour. After some lazy laps, Corinne and I found a sunny corner to float in.

"I thought I'd feel sadder," said Corinne. "Especially since we know more now about how Vonn died. So I'm glad we all gathered here today to remember her, and to celebrate the best parts of the past. It's made me happy to see everyone from the old days. Just to be here, like this, in the present moment." She looked at a group of women cavorting like teenagers near the opposite shore. "I need to swim over to Amina and tell her how much it meant that she came and spoke about Vonn so generously."

She made as if to leave, and I ran a tentative hand over her round shoulder.

"But you'll come back soon, won't you?"

For answer, she gave me a watery kiss.

In my quiet corner of the pond, I floated on my back while Corinne breast-stroked away. This was sun-warmed water as I liked it, surrounded by trees and ladies on the grassy green banks. Sometime in the future I might like to return to the rosy sea cave in Devon and try my luck again in the wild surf offshore. But for now, floating gently with other women in a city pond seemed just about perfect to me.

Further Reading

I first became interested in the beguine movement and the beguinages of the Low Countries thirty years ago and visited a number of the remaining beguinages in Belgium and the Netherlands. At the time there wasn't a great deal written about the beguines other than brief mentions in feminist history books. Since then, several in-depth studies have appeared, including *Cities of Ladies: Beguine Communities in the Medieval Low Countries 1200-1565* by Walter Simons, and *The Wisdom of the Beguines: The Forgotten Story of a Medieval Women's Movement* by Laura Swan. Both were helpful to me in my research.

Wild swimming in England has been beautifully described in *Waterlog: A Swimmer's Journey Through Britain* by Roger Deakin. Lynne Roper's book, *Wild Woman Swimming: A Journal of West Country Waters*, is a lovely, inspiring read. *At the Pond: Swimming at the Hampstead Ladies' Pond* is an anthology of writing that captures the special ambiance of this beloved institution.

ABOUT THE AUTHOR

Barbara Wilson is the author of eight previous mysteries, most recently *Not the Real Jupiter*. Her earlier mysteries set in Seattle featured printer Pam Nilsen. In 1990 she introduced translator sleuth Cassandra Reilly in *Gaudí Afternoon*, which won a Lambda Literary Award and the British Crime Writers' award for best thriller set in Europe. It was made into a movie starring Judy Davis, Juliette Lewis, and Marcia Gay Hardin. As Barbara Sjoholm, she is the author of fiction and narrative nonfiction, including *Incognito Street* and *The Pirate Queen*. Her translations from Norwegian and Danish have been awarded prizes and fellowships from the American-Scandinavian Foundation and the National Endowment for the Arts. She was also co-founder of Seal Press, a women's publishing company in Seattle, and founder and director of Women in Translation, a non-profit press specializing in translation. She lives on the Olympic Peninsula in Washington state. Visit her at www.barbarasjoholm.com and www.barbarawilsonmysteries.com.

CPSIA information can be obtained
at www.ICGtesting.com
Printed in the USA
LVHW031843261122
734035LV00002B/239